# ENDGAME

# ENDGAME

Bob Rueff

*Enjoy the chase –*
*Bob Rueff*

NORTH STAR PRESS OF ST. CLOUD, INC.

This is a work of fiction. Any resemblence to persons living or dead (except otherwise noted) is purely coincidental. The Devil's Kettle in Judge C.R. Magney State Park, however, is a very real place worth a trip up Superior's North Shore to visit.

ISBN: 0-87839-201-7

First Edition

Printed in Canada by Friesens

Published by
North Star Press of St. Cloud, Inc.
P.O. Box 451
St. Cloud, Minnesota 56302
nspress@cloudnet.com

1 2 3 4 5 6 7 8 9 10

*To Jim*

*&*

*To Gayle*

*See you later friend, and neighbor.*

Author's Note:

This is a work of fiction. There is no Normandale tower, per se (although the scene from Darcy Austin's office window does exist), and the brand-name products that are instruments of death employed herein are also fictitious. The characters are as well, save one. Thanks for the persona, Brad.

That aside, most of the places and locations named in this book are real. I point this out because the Devil's Kettle on the Minnesota North Shore, with its mysterious dissolve, sounds to be fictitious but is not. Like to see the Devil's Kettle on the Brule River for yourself? Be prepared for a hike, and watch your step at the crest lest you vanish forever. While visiting the area, check in at the Naniboujou Lodge (the house that Ruth and Dempsey built). Then tour Grand Marais and the Lutsen surround. It's a delight, Lake Superior's North Shore. Just don't test the Brule River anywhere near its spill. Okay?

While my family and early readers of this manuscript know of my many years in the advertising business, and my passion for certain philosophies of marketing, they have still questioned the details in the first chapter of this book. I told them, and now you, that it's a personal statement I feel I need to make. Also, for me, it plays into the story and the character of Edson Janes. Please bear with me. It's only four pages before all Hell breaks loose, anyway.

The word used in referring to BMWs, while pronounced *beemer*, usually appears either as "bimmer" or "beamer" in automotive parlance. The most common of these is "bimmer," and that's the way it appears in this book.

I've done my damnedest to spell "damnedest" correctly. So know that it isn't an inadvertent miscue even if it does look funny in print. The word "lubberly" is used to describe Darcy Austin's physical state at one point in the adventure. And while it doesn't call up on my Mac dictionary or thesaurus, according to Webster's it portrays her condition very well. I like the word, so I used it. Call it author's indulgence.

—B.R.

# Acknowledgments

My thanks to all those who helped give birth to *Endgame*.

Lieutenant Bob Vaughn for his primer on the Bloomington Police Department and its procedures. Departures from protocol in these pages are all mine.

Kevin Horrocks was my "go to" guy on matters of ballistics when I got stuck on some point or other.

Brad Hoyt not only contributed his aviation skills and expertise to *Endgame*, he donated his persona to its content.

Son Greg, a police academy graduate, acted as my unannounced technical adviser for *Endgame*, whether or not he realized the role he played or the large contribution he made.

The first draft of *Endgame* was written "with the door closed." My wife, Lou, patiently waited for me to finally "open" that door. She then read the draft, gave it her blessing and, through edits, assessment, and encouragement, helped it, and me, to the next level.

Clark Griffith, attorney at law and mystery novel aficionado, became my first outreach reader of the still-fledgling manuscript. His critique and input were both helpful and heartening. *Endgame* was now on full course.

Corinne Dwyer, of North Star Press, steered the way to *Endgame*'s fruition, three others contributing to the process: Dan Cohen, former business associate and professional writer, whose edits and perspectives helped immeasurably; Harry Durham, friend since army days, came from Clemson, South Carolina, to northernmost Minnesota in order to record the Devil's Kettle panorama, plus yours truly, on camera; and Kelly Gothier, whose tasteful art direction (cover design, chapter headings, typography) graces this book.

Finally, there is Whittaker—always at my side through this, no matter what the hour.

I'm grateful to them all.

# ENDGAME

# Chapter 1

# T E R M I N U S

**EDSON JANES WAS** into one of his all-nighters. When was he going to learn? Never. He was too old. More often than not he went into these sessions planning to finish up somewhere around the witching hour, but it seldom worked out that way. In his younger days, he remembered working through the night and returning home for a shower and change of clothes before boarding an early flight from Minneapolis/St. Paul International Airport to make an all-day strategy session with a client in Detroit reviewing "the plan"—on more than one occasion. He hadn't done that for several years now, but the all-nighters continued as a part of his regimen. Advertising was a business of deadlines, and too much money was riding on things occurring on schedule to tolerate any major postponements. And, of course, it was always the agency's fault when deadlines or budgets weren't met, even when the client's indecision, machinations, or other dithering effected either factor. That aside, the hectic environment of an advertising agency's normal business hours, with all its distractions, were not conducive to developing an in-depth marketing plan.

Thus the all-night sessions . . . cohesive concentration.

He was laboring at what he regarded as the most critical part of any marketing plan: Targeting. It shaped everything. The tone of the advertising, what words were used to relate to the target consumer in copy, what media were chosen to convey the message, which in turn, determined the most proficient budget for the campaign. To Edson Janes, effective targeting meant going beyond demographics, the Holy Grail common to most advertisers. Sure, there was market research that provided specific information about current customers, customer prospects, and rejecters of the product. Along with the demographics of each group. But none of this revealed the target consumer's basic beliefs, motivations or intrinsic values—the "why" of certain behavior, not just the behavior itself. Yet the slavish seeking of eighteen- to thirty-five-year olds remained the reigning import to marketers everywhere, with education and income kicked in. It was as if everyone in an age and income bracket was the same, Edson Janes thought. To him, eighteen to thirty-five wasn't a segment, it was a national convention—practically anyone who can fog a mirror.

Janes' approach was through the VALS psychographic service, providing a much better fix on prime consumers of any particular product, to his mind—*this* particular product. The problem was convincing the client of that. Hell, most agencies needed convincing themselves. It didn't make sense to him, yet demographics remained supreme. But then, the VALS program required an understanding and application of principles and techniques not readily decipherable without some study and trial. Like a fine violin, one had to learn how to play it before it made music. Compounding that, agencies were sometimes more interested in pleasing their clients, or worse, with winning awards—a big deal in the ad game—than they were in pursuing new marketing disciplines that were often resisted by their clients anyway, in his opinion.

No, Edson Janes could not absolve clients in this scenario. Bad advertising often resulted from client intervention and dictates, rather than the doings of their agencies. He'd seen successful advertising results dissed out of corporate-culture assertion, trashing successful campaigns; and, at times, an agency was fired because the client simply didn't like it, or *them*. In doing so, the powers that be would always find some justification for their actions, perhaps out of self-denial. Results be damned. One of his favorite sayings was, "What has success got to do with it?"

He knew that many excellent campaign proposals never saw the light of day because of client rejection out of the box. A dread among agencies is when the CEO takes a campaign presentation home to his wife for her critique. Hang on for that one.

The ad game was not always played in the most forthright manner, from either side, he knew full well—self-interests, egos, and just plain ignorance resulted in potentials lost and successes curtailed.

Edson Janes could just go along with his client's inclinations and make life easier for himself, but his professionalism wouldn't let him. He knew the prime target for Midland, the *psychographic* target, was a narrower portion of the demographic grouping than the client was prone to chase—causing a waste of media monies plus ads that didn't cut to the core of a more defined, more efficient target. "Too generic," he was told, when it came to applying his psychographic approach when, in reality, the opposite was true. Another errant assertion made out of hand.

Demos gave him age, income, education, and 2.3 kids. Psychographics gave him richness beyond that. He was able to determine that Midland's prime target was a very traditional sort, playing out traditional family roles. That they were independent to the extreme and resented government restriction on personal liberties, opposed gun control legislation, and generally mistrusted politicians, news media, and large corporations. That they mostly desired to travel inside the United States—often camping out in preference to staying at hotels or resorts. That home cooking was more appealing to them than dining out. That they drank domestic rather than imported beer, preferred white bread to whole wheat, bought American cars and trucks—mostly trucks—and didn't try to impress their neighbors with their possessions. Keeping up with the Joneses was not important, here. He was also aware of their media preferences, including viewing/listening/reading proclivities. Not just what they tuned into, but why they tuned into it. Too generic? What the hell are demographics if not too generic?

He ran his hand through forelocks a decade past thickness. He'd pull this off if it killed him—achieve a marketing plan honed to a tighter, more pertinent target, while not tipping his hand to Lakeland Recreational as to how he got there. Perhaps he could fake a primary market-research study, gratis, of course, that the agency supposedly conducted on its own for Lakeland. Lakeland was in love with market research and doled out tens of thousands of dollars every other year, to the exclusion of the dynamic marketing tool they could subscribe to for a relative pittance. True, primary market research told them a lot about the likes and dislikes of RV consumers, and Midland's customers in particular, but little about what drove the segment from a psychological standpoint—which can be critical to a marketing strategist worth his salt.

**STILL PONDERING HOW** he'd proceed, Edson Janes came up hungry as well as agitated. Glancing at his watch he saw it was three a.m.—time for a reprieve.

Making his way down the corridor to the agency kitchen, he pulled down a family-size can of Mother Svendsen's Soup from the food cabinet. Using its new pull-tab top—that his agency introduced in an ad campaign he supervised—he opened the container to an accompanying *poof*. He poured the generous contents into an oversized porcelain bowl, added a shot of water, shoved it into the microwave and punched the keys for six minutes at full power. He liked it hot.

Pacing back and forth on the tile floor until four beeps signaled "soup's on," he removed the container from the oven and tested it with a sip from a spoon. Satisfied it didn't need any more rays, he transported his steaming meal to a room-center table, along with a pitcher of water, pulled up a chair, and began slurping its contents while reviewing scribbles on a yellow pad he brought from his office. He put down his spoon, underlined, "Why certain people do what they do," with his pen, and went back to his spoon.

HE WAS NOT alone in the office that night. Someone watched from an unlit hallway leading into the kitchen area. Unnoticed by Edson Janes, that person was now approaching from behind him.

The leather-bound sap struck the adman on the back of the head, splashing his face down into the hot soup he was no longer capable of tasting. The person stepped up alongside the adman, seized the back of his head and plunged his face down into the large bowl to where his lungs sucked up its contents.

As Mother Svendson's Soup advertising proclaimed: "It's a goodly-sized portion. Although you can add a smidgen of water, should you desire even more." And so it was done.

There were the reflexive spasms common to a drowning person—the body's attempt to discharge the liquid invasion of its lungs. But Edson Janes was held secure. His struggling became weaker, and then there was calm.

"*Bon appétit*," the person at his back uttered, toasting with a half-full pitcher of water no longer needed.

*Why certain people do what they do*, was the last conscious thought Edson Janes had in a lifetime career in that pursuit.

*Chapter* **2**

# CRIME SCENE

**THE OFFICES OF** Williams/Bailey on the eleventh floor of Normandale Tower, Bloomington, Minnesota, were sealed off. Employees arriving for work found themselves docketed for later questioning and sent home. A distraught Williams/Bailey receptionist fielded calls from an off-premise station set up by the Bloomington Police. All calls, including direct-line voicemail, were being electronically monitored and recorded for later scrutiny.

As far as Darcy Austin knew, she was the only W/B employee on the premises. On that she was correct—except for the dead one. She sat behind her desk, a police lieutenant in one of the two barrel chairs opposite her. They had been at it for a while.

"Do you normally show up at the office at five in the morning?" Lieutenant Douglas Hankenson asked with a demeanor more FBI than local cop, in Darcy Austin's opinion, along with the arrogance she imagined of a Fed. Perhaps his was a logical line of inquiry, but no matter. It was taken as insinuating and added to what already seemed an accusatory tone to her. And he was poking into some disturbing issues covered earlier in the session. She was resentful, and it showed.

"It happens in the ad business," she answered. "There are demands. Deadlines. We have to get the job done."

A stare, no response.

"Do you only chase after criminals between 9:00 and 5:00, Lieutenant?" she asked, knowing that was a little too smart-ass as soon as it was out of her mouth.

If it bothered the policeman he didn't react. "You found the body when you went to the lunchroom to make coffee around five-fifteen. Right?" Another irritating redundancy.

"Exactly five-twelve—I told you. I checked the time when I called 911." *Take that.*

"So you did. Lot of presence of mind—weren't you a little bit concerned the perpetrator might still be on the premises?"

Panicked was more like it. Darcy Austin was still shaken. Why she struggled so hard to cover it up she didn't understand, herself. She suspected she'd appear more sympathetic to this cop, and he might just back off, if she'd let go a little. But no! Something inside wouldn't let her, lest she display some terrible vulnerability. Maybe it was her job conditioning—not letting the client see her sweat—like in presentations important to the agency in dollars as well as creative investiture—or when things weren't going all that well with the folks paying the bills, or any other reason. Sometimes that reason stemmed from a lack of client backbone when the creative got too edgy for them—or so the agency was prone to believe. In any case, a big part of the account manager's job was to help pull situations like those out of the fire. And one could only hope to do that appearing cool and confident under siege—even when one wasn't. Darcy Austin learned that lesson well. Now she was faced with pulling herself out of the fire.

———————

LIEUTENANT HANKENSON SAT back in the barrel chair, looking much like he could be a prospective new client for the agency in his well-fitted suit. He examined the reactions of Ms. Austin with discernment, knowing that the discoverer of the body was many times the murderer, drawn back to the scene out of nervousness about the situation. And he knew that a nervous murderer might appear as distraught as an innocent intruder on the crime scene. *Is Ms. Austin distraught? Yeah, but also petulant.* That was a twist. He needed to push further, and putting her on the defensive served his purposes.

Unlike Lieutenant Hankenson's formal business attire, Darcy Austin was wearing a casual blouse with worn-before jeans, and her auburn hair was done up in a bun, not with great care. No client presentation scheduled for today.

She brushed some wayward strands from her face "Perpetrator?" she responded to his latest assertion, more shrilly than she intended. "How can you be so sure there was one? Couldn't he . . . Mr. Janes . . . have fainted or something and just happened to fall . . . into the soup that way." It sounded so preposterous as she proposed it—drowning in a bowl of soup, she barely got it all out—might even have snickered if it weren't so damned awful. Her nerves were playing tricks with her.

She had been pretty sure Janes' death was no accident when she discovered him. Too messy—there'd been at least some sort of violent action. A chill passed through her now, as she acknowledged to herself that the murderer could have been lurking about when she found the body, just as the lieutenant had proffered. Maybe even watching her. Another chill.

"Believe me, he had help dying," Lieutenant Hankenson said.

"I know," Darcy Austin said, lowering her voice in concession. Nothing for a time, then offered, "Our soup, too," from under her breath.

"What?"

She raised her eyes to his. "Our client. Mother Svendsen's—you know, the brand. I saw the empty container . . . in the lunchroom."

"Mother Svendsen's 'The soup to die for'?" he asked.

"We created that slogan, here at the agency." She answered, then trailed: "Minnesota wild rice flavor" as though that were somehow significant.

Lieutenant Hankenson jotted in his pad, shaking his head at what he was hearing.

SOUNDS FROM THE lunchroom tumbled down the hall from time to time. The detective seemed to ignore them. Darcy Austin couldn't. It brought images to her of investigators pouring over the fateful scene— all the things she'd seen in movies and TV cop shows so many times before. She wondered how they'd draw the chalk outline around Edson Janes' body hunched over the table with his face in that bowl. Would it include the Mother Svendsen's empty container as well? Ludicrous thoughts again—she couldn't help it.

More questions, more answers, more notes. Some rehashed, some new:

"How close were you to Edson Janes?" Then Lieutenant Hankenson thought he should propitiously add: "At work."

"He was my group supervisor," she answered. "He is . . . was . . . over all of our food accounts, and I handle Gold'n Tender Chicken."

"Did he have enemies, antagonists?"

"None in the agency. I don't know about his private life." Then she thought about it and added: "He clashed with two people who left the firm, though."

"Did you?

"Did I what?

"Get along with him."

"Of course."

"Two people left because of him?"

"In large part, I guess." A wave of her hand.

"Who were they?" Note book poised.

"Roland Bennett, a former partner. He has his own agency now. And Frank Ramstead. Used to be our executive vice president. He went to another agency."

"When did they leave?"

"Less then a year ago. They left close together. H.R. can give you all that."

"And where they can be reached?"

"I think so."

"Who's normally around here late at night?"

"The cleaning crew that the building provides, but not that late. There usually are some hangers-on in the office, but again, not that late. Then there's Terry."

"Terry?"

"A handyman around here. Works crazy hours. Terry Barnhard."

"Ah-huh. Anyone else?"

"Could be anyone of us, working late. Or starting early," she added, reflecting on this very day.

"How many people work at Williams/Bailey?"

"Mmm . . . fifty-seven, I think, not counting Fantasy. Again, you can get that from H.R."

"Fantasy?"

"Fantasy Publications. A subsidiary of W/B down in the warehouse district. Half a dozen people or thereabouts."

"What's Fantasy got to do with Williams/Bailey?"

"Nothing directly, except maybe for some financing," Darcy answered. She'd given up being difficult for the moment, lost in explanation. "Fantasy publishes a couple of comic books. Mr. Williams set it up for Josh, his son. Lets him do his thing. He's creator and illustrator of the comics."

"Didn't want to join the agency?" Lieutenant Hankenson wondered out loud. "He'd have a better thing going right here in the shop, wouldn't he?"

"Josh marches to his own drummer. Free spirit. Different motivations. Besides, it's not that easy to just insert your son into a thriving agency without causing problems."

"Oh?"

"People get nervous—pecking orders, things like that. Anyway, the guy's done pretty well. Magenta is his creation. He's got Sterling and Cobalt, too, but Magenta's the one that's really caught on."

"No kiddin'. I've heard of her. Isn't she supposed to be the Dark Avenger, or something?"

"That's Batman. She's the Night Vigilante. He's found a niche with Magenta.

Hankenson jotted down "Josh Williams—Fantasy publ." He'd check it out.

AFTER SEVERAL MORE desultory questions and cross tabbing, the detective tucked his note pad inside his breast pocket and stood up, signaling that the session was over. He was medium height, Darcy Austin noticed, and his dark suit was accordant to an adman at a new-business presentation—Shelby-knotted wide-rep tie, spread-collar pale-blue dress shirt, and tasseled loafers completing the ensemble. Quality was way up there, too, she could tell—good as any around the agency. And as with most advertising agencies, the threads were exceptional at Williams/Bailey.

He was a few inches taller than her five-foot-eight, she guessed, probably just under six feet. In her heels they'd almost be eye to eye. Almost.

"That's all for now Ms. Austin—or can I call you Darcy?"—friendlier than the staccato interrogation just ended.

"Darcy," she said with some reluctance, while accepting the business card he held out to her. She didn't know just how friendly she wanted to be in return.

"Good. I go by Hank," a smile turning up on one side more than the other as he said it—different, yet kind of engaging. "There's an office number and home number there," he added, gesturing to the card in her hand. "Call anytime if you think of something else—even if it doesn't seem important. You never know."

How many times had she heard that on TV before? "I'm not one of your suspects am I, Lieutenant?" she asked in an acerbic tone, side-stepping his "Hank" offering.

"Just doing my job. Questions first, suspects later," he said with a disarming wave of his hand. "I'd like you to stick around, though. I'll probably need to ask you a few more questions as we move along. Okay?" His one-sided grin again: "Unless a motive turns up . . . no, you're not a suspect, Darcy."

"Nice to know, Lieutenant. I'll be here if you need me."

"Well, not here," he replied. "Not for the rest of the day, anyway. Everyone at Williams/Bailey is on furlough till the crime-scene folk wrap up."

"Will it count against vacation days?" That acerbity again, but she smiled.

"I'm afraid you'll have to ask your management about that," he grinned back. Then more seriously: "I'm going to the lunchroom for a moment. Stay put till I get back. Then I'm escorting you out of this place. There's an officer posted out here in the hall—just so you know." No venturing out on your own Ms. Austin. He closed the door to her office as he left.

DARCY TURNED LIEUTENANT Douglas L. Hankenson's card in her hand as she stared out her office window overlooking Normandale Lake. The leaves would be turning before long, her favorite time of the year in Minnesota. She fixed on the Normandale ski jump looming above the hilly tree-lined backdrop to the lake in the foreground—larger than the storm-damaged one it replaced a few years before. Suddenly it seemed strangely out of place to her, surrounded, as it was, by greenery—the thought hadn't struck her before now. *Well in a few more months it'll be very much in sync with its surroundings,* she reflected. *Stick around—in Minnesota you soon had weather befitting any situation.* But could she ever be in sync with her surroundings, again? She wondered.

A tear rolled down her cheek and splashed on her hand still holding the business card the detective had given her. She glanced at the card, noting, for the first time, the inscription under LIEUTENANT DOUGLAS L. HANKENSON read CRIMES AGAINST PERSONS—not Homicide as she would have expected. Then it occurred to her. How many homicides do they have in clean-cut Bloomington, Minnesota? The prospect only served to point out the rare circumstance into which she had stumbled. Somehow, that was all the more frightening to her.

*Chapter* **3**

# D I S C L O S U R E

**THE NEWSIES WERE** positioned all over West Eighty-fourth Street out-side of Normandale Tower, some of them lounging in front of the build-ing's street-level parking ramp entrance near where Lieutenant Hankenson now escorted Darcy Austin on the way to the slot where her SUV was parked.

With nothing to distinguish the two of them from the mix of civil-ians and uniforms moving about the ramp this morning, they wouldn't have drawn attention, had not one member of the press, familiar with the Bloomington beat, recognized the police lieutenant from a previous incident.

Her reporter's mind kicked on alert. Wasn't Hankenson shepherd-ing the woman he was with a little closely? Could she be the person rumored to have discovered the murder victim? Shaking off her hang-around lethargy, the reporter signaled her cameraman to follow as she moved toward the couple as casually as she could, trying not to alert her competition. Closing in, she called out to her quarry. Hankenson glanced back and spotted the reporter, portable mike in hand, trailed by a waddling accomplice with a video camera riding his shoulder as if it were part of his body. "Get moving," the lieutenant warned Darcy, "unless you want to be the lead on *News at Noon.*"

"No way," Darcy Austin snapped, remote-keying her Toyota 4-Runner as they approached it. She mounted the high step into the truck, slammed the door shut, hit the lock button and cranked the engine. By the time the two newsies arrived, she backed out of the slot and screeched down the passageway. "Atta girl," Hankenson rooted under his breath, watching the SUV diminish down the ramp, heading for the exit he had cleared for her in advance. Frustrated, the reporter poked her mike at Hankenson getting, "No comment," as he strode away.

The reporter was convinced that her first-blush suspicion was correct—she had just seen the woman who had discovered the body. And while she failed to get the complete story she was after, the reporter knew her effort wasn't a total loss. A thumbs-up from her associate told her the intercept attempt was on videotape. *This'll do for starters,* she consoled herself.

*Chapter* **4**

# I N C E P T I O N

**"HOW YA HITTIN'** 'em, Hank?" the attendant at the Highland Driving Range on Ninety-eighth and Normandale asked as he passed by the stall Hank occupied.

"Not bad, Don, considering," he replied. Hank was a frequent visitor at the Highland range and knew its operators—guys retired from lifelong careers, now partaking in part-time employment for something to do and all the free balls they can hit. To Hank, hitting balls at the range was needed therapy.

"Yeah, I heard on the radio," Don said. "Holy crap, that murder's practically next door. You need more down-time, it's on the house."

"Thanks, pal. I may take you up on that before this thing is over," Hank said, turning back to his depleting bucket of balls.

"You might narrow your stance—and slow down a little," the attendant advised.

**HANK CARRIED HIS** bag back to his BMW 530i, punched the trunk open with his remote on the ignition key, and settled the clubs into the trunk nest, complete with a mounted diagram showing how to arrange multiple golf bags in it. Germans have a system for everything.

**DRIVING EAST ON** 102nd Street, Hank jogged right at Penn Avenue, crossed Old Shakopee Road, and entered the Bloomington Municipal Building parking lot. He passed by the west side of the squat brown-brick building, descending down a slope to a walk-out level not visible from the street, where the Bloomington Police Department was housed. It wasn't all that old a building, but it wasn't much of a building either, considering that Bloomington was Minnesota's fourth largest city. Taxpayers had voted down a more ambitious government campus that proponents thought more appropriate for the big Minneapolis suburb. But voter turndown not withstanding, the expansion-minded city council came up with the necessary funds from a set-aside, as if it hadn't emanated from the taxpayers in the first place. A huge government complex was now under construction where he would soon maintain his new province.

He pulled into one of the open spaces marked "Police Vehicles Only," the black 530i looking out of place among the Tauruses, Camrys, and Hondas gathered in neighboring slots. The BMW was one of his indulgences. He liked cars, clothes, and golf and ski equipment—was an "equipment" guy. He wasn't rich, but he could afford more than his police salary permitted, and he wasn't above collecting a few adult toys.

Entering the building, he walked down the hall past the Interrogation/Conference Room to the office marked JAMES B. LOTT, CHIEF OF POLICE. He knocked and entered without waiting for a response.

Jim Lott and Mayor Margaret Magneson looked up from the small conference table they were seated around. "Hi, Hank, join us," the chief said.

The chief was cheerful under the circumstances, Hank felt. Bloomington was a quiet residential community for the most part, even though it was host to thriving hotels, restaurants and bars strung out along its "strip" on I-494, which included the giant Mall of America. Major crimes, not to mention high-profile murders, still rattled its 90,000 inhabitants—and rattled inhabitants usually reverberated in city hall. That's what surprised him about Chief Lott's relatively calm demeanor. Maybe he was enjoying the notoriety.

"Mayor, Chief," Hank responded, peeling off his coat and draping it over the back of the chair he fit himself into.

"Margaret and I were just talking about the situation." Chief Lott didn't have to say what situation. "Find anything?"

"Definitely homicide. We can put accident or natural causes to rest," Hank said, although those possibilities were considered in the initial phase of the investigation. "Blow to the back of the head—some kind of sap, looks like. Definitely held face down while he—well—drowned. Bruises on his upper neck and base of his skull."

With Bloomington's lakes, plus the Minnesota River on its southern border, Hank had seen his share of drowning victims. The puffy face, bulged eyes, and bluish-white complexion told him what forensics would later confirm. Scratch marks on the table and several broken fingernails further debunked the common view that drowning victims drifted off into blissful peace as they passed over. The body's natural struggle for breath and its reflexive attempt to reject the incursive liquid from its lungs can be gripping and violent, as Hank knew.

"Drowned in a bowl of soup? Gawd, I can't believe it," Mayor Margaret Magneson exclaimed, although it was obvious she did.

Hank nodded. "It was Mother Svendsen's Soup—a Williams/Bailey's client."

Chief Lott was incredulous. "You mean '*The Soup to Die For*'?"

"That's the one," Hank answered.

"Now I really can't believe it," Mayor Magneson said.

"Minnesota wild rice," Hank contributed next, almost enjoying himself.

Chief Lott changed course. "Who's doing the lab work?"

"BCA," Hank said. He'd called on the Minnesota Bureau of Criminal Apprehension just once before, and that was two years back. The need didn't come up very often in Bloomington.

"Their facilities are top-rate," the mayor chimed in with more assuredness toward BCA's capabilities than she possessed.

"The task force?" Chief Lott asked.

"Joe Baines is pointman. He's as good as we've got at this sort of thing. Maybe a long shot but we're asking for an assist from Minneapolis Homicide, too. They've got more experience than we can put up. Besides, we've got a ton of questioning to do. Fifty-seven people—well, fifty-six now—at Williams/ Bailey and a half-dozen more at Fantasy, just for starters. We'll need everyone we can muster for that alone."

"Fantasy?" the chief asked.

"Comic Books. Magenta. Williams/Bailey owns 'em," Hank said.

"Oh, Magenta," Margaret Magneson joined in. "My kids read her—the Dark Avenger."

"That's Batman. She's the Night Vigilante," Hank stated with complete authority.

*Chapter* **5**

# B R O T H E R H O O D

**SERGEANT JOSEPH R.** Baines, sitting across from Lieutenant Douglas Hankenson, wore a rumpled suit, cheap haircut, small moustache, and fifteen or twenty pounds of extra body. His shirt, tie, and scuffed shoes, not from Nordstrom's, completed the package. It was a study in contrasts, these two men, but that didn't mean that they weren't a good fit. They were a team, as Bloomington bad guys had discovered.

"Group taking shape?" Hank asked.

"Got Vince, Marge, and Marvin going as of now," Joe Baines answered. "Should have Jeff and Dan freed up by tomorrow."

"Good, we need questioners. Minneapolis come through?"

"Think two homicide guys are gonna help out for a few days— Minneapolis would just as soon have a piece of this one. Look like Good Samerians to their burb brethren in time of need—all that good horse shit."

"'Good Samaritans,'" Hank corrected.

"Yeah, I gotta get to church more often."

"I'd recommend that. Qualified?"

"Top cops in their way. Dex Ames and Sig Nadler. I met Nadler in a bar last winter."

"What's he like?"

"Whiskey, I think."

"Okay, smart ass."

Joe Baines kept going: "Seems like a good guy, but MPD's probably happy to hand him over for a while. Ames is not fair-haired, neither."

"Oh?"

"Nadler's got this reputation—don't take shit from nobody. Shot
and killed two guys once."

"That's twice."

"Whatever."

"Bad guys?"

"Like I said, they're good cops."

"Not them, the ones Nadler shot."

"Real bad. Another time, he beat up a couple macho jerk-offs in a
bar he was doin' off-duty. Claimed they jumped him. He doesn't take
crap from the department either. Been called up a few times, but no sus-
pensions. His chief doesn't like 'im, the mayor hates 'im. Gets along fine
with other cops, though."

"Read about some of his escapades in the *Strib* awhile back. Think
he'll be a problem to us?"

"Who cares? Nadler's got a nose like a Doberman. Don't know
about you, but I don't plan to give him no shit. Ames is good, too.
Worse case, we send 'em back to Minneapolis."

"Right." Pause. "And it's 'bloodhound.'"

"Oh, yeah, them, too."

The lieutenant pushed his chair back from the desk, got up and
headed to the Bunn coffeemaker on his office credenza. He couldn't
tolerate the swill Joe Baines carried with him from the cafeteria in a
Styrofoam cup. And while the Bunn wasn't up to Caribou's in-shop

preparation, it did a passable job with Caribou's carry-out ground coffee beans.

"How'd it go with the girl?" the sergeant asked.

"Girl? You'd be referring to the young woman who discovered the vic?"

"That'd be her," he said, as if he really had to.

"Not the easiest session—kinda feisty. I don't think she likes cops."

"Could be it's you. Ever thinka that?"

Hank spread his arms. "Moi?" Then answered for real: "She's covering up."

"You think she could be the one force-fed Janes the soup? "

"No, but her psyche's involved. Wasn't about to let me know she was shook—like that was important to her." A sip from his porcelain mug. "Wanted me to know she was no fragile female—that kind of cover up."

"Huh."

Hank put the mug down on his desk, resting it on a round pad for that purpose. "I know you'll ask . . ."

The sergeant perked up at the opportunity. "She a babe?"

"For no makeup, hair a little untidy, worn shirt and jeans—yeah, she could qualify."

"Figured you'd notice. Anything else?"

Dropping the Darcy Austin personals, Hank offered: "Williams/Bailey has a subsidiary company, downtown—Fantasy Publications. How's that for police work?"

"Fantasy?"

"Ever hear of Magenta?"

"Oh, yeah—the Street Avenger, ain't she?"

"Close," Hank answered.

Chapter **6**

# M A G E N T A

**MAGENTA COMICS WAS** familiar comic book fare albeit with a niche of its own. It had retro appeal in that there were no super-power denizens within its presentation. Nor were there death rays, finger-shooting lightning bolts, or otherworld creatures threatening to devour the human race or destroy Earth. Just goodies and badies having it out in tight-fitting wraps—in its way, reminiscent of the early comic book series of the late thirties and early forties. Another variance, the clashes were mostly female to female.

Magenta, despite prowling darkened city streets, seeking out and battling villains that legal authorities could never seem to cope with, Magenta seemed more real than most of today's superheroines. Despite some anatomical exaggerations of the artist's pen, she was not in the elongated, over-busted mode common to many computer-generated depictions of current superheroines. Not that the physiques of Magenta and her various combatants lacked fine musculature and alluring pulchritude. Far from it. Just more real—as in S.I. swimsuit real.

So were Fantasy's clashes more realistic, by comic-book standards. Not so much Biff, Zap, Smack, as Grapple, Tumble, Tangle. And while the Night Vigilante always emerged triumphant, the outcome was seldom assured until the very end. Antagonists usually got their licks in, often taking Magenta to the limit before succumbing to her.

There was titillation. The rough and tumble of Magenta's battles sometimes induced scant costumes to lessen their hold or even strip away on occasion. In the latter instances, long-flowing tresses or strategically placed obstructions within the panels avoided disclosure beyond the propriety of the genre.

Magenta's costume was amatory to begin with. Her split bodice made a sensational dive from her shoulders, forming an open V that reached its point at her waistline. It provided only essential coverage in front, nothing in back. Her miniscule skirt was slit up one side, revealing side-cut panties, with its proneness to part. The completed ensemble included mid-calf boots, forearm gloves, and a teardrop mask—all toned in a deep—magenta—red.

Magenta had archrivals. She tangled with the notorious bad girl Reva in three episodes. And although emerging victorious each time, the going was rough. In their second battle (eminent among Magenta aficionados), Reva dominated the vigilante toward the end. But in the bad girl's haste to finish off the heroine, she struck her head in a headlong leap over the downed Vigilante. With that fortuitous happening, Magenta was able to recover from what appeared to be certain defeat and turn things around. "That was close," Magenta said in a concluding panel, adjusting her bodice. "Give us more," readers said.

Sadanna, the supreme fem-fighter among the bad girls, was Magenta's foremost antagonist. On two previous occasions, she and Magenta clashed to no conclusion—their pitched struggles interrupted before a victor was determined. This feud had to be settled—the last of their skirmishes spiking reader interest for another clash of the unde-feated luminaries. In that conflict, both women had their hands full in the figurative sense, as was expected. But, much of the time, Sadanna had her hands full in yet another sense—much to the apparent distress and detriment of the Night Vigilante.

Fantasy publications was pushing the envelope.

What was yet in store, Magenta followers pondered?

*Chapter* **7**

# T I M I N G

**CHANNEL SEVEN DID** its homework that day, tracing the 4-Runner's license plate to its owner. The news anchor's narration, over video, played out on *News at Noon*:

Channel Seven News reporter, Patti Ann Grey, spotted Lieutenant Douglas Hankenson of the Bloomington Police escorting the woman believed to have discovered the body of Edson Janes early this morning, Darcy Austin. Janes was the apparent victim of a homicide in the offices of Williams/Bailey Advertising Agency, in Bloomington, where he and Ms. Austin were both employed.

Neither Lt. Hankenson nor Austin would comment on the situation when approached by Patti Ann Grey.

The victim, a long-time principal of the advertising firm, located in Normandale Tower, was associated with some of Williams/Bailey's most popular and successful campaigns.

Channel Seven will bring you further details on the suspected homicide as they develop.

Channel Seven's *News at Six* carried a similar version of the story but its 10:00 news contained an updated paragraph. Behind a visual that flashed, LATE BREAKING NEWS, the anchor concluded the segment with:

> Channel Seven News has now learned that Ms. Austin may well have been an eyewitness to the murder. We'll keep you informed as more breaks on this story.

Why this was inserted into the script, without corroboration from the Bloomington Police or any other investigative authority as it turned out, would soon be a point of contention. But there it was.

LIEUTENANT DOUGLAS HANKENSON was only half listening to the Channel Seven report while pouring over his notes at home. He had viewed it before, at 6:00. But the new "eyewitness" conclusion to the story caught his attention.

"Holy shit," the policeman exclaimed, looking up to the TV on a shelf at the other side of the small room he called an office. "Where did that come from?"

The news report with its new twist was like a revelation. That Darcy Austin could have been thought to be an eyewitness to the murder was something that should have occurred to him—even from the earlier reports. Now it was right out there for the public—and for the killer—like it was fact.

Chiding himself, he grabbed his portable desk phone and punched in the preprogrammed two-digit speedcaller, getting two rings before pickup. "You see the news on Seven?" Hank asked without identifying himself. And before the party on the other end could reply, continued with: "Channel Seven's now saying Darcy Austin might have been an eyewitness to the murder."

"Holy shit." Sergeant Joe Baines blurted from the other end of the connection. "Where did that come from?"

"That's what I said. Get some surveillance on her pretty quick. Maybe some of your Minneapolis friends. I don't like this."

"I'm on it." And in a lower voice: "We shoulda thought about covering her before, Hank."

"Don't I know. See what you can do. I'll call and alert her to what we're doing—and try not to scare the piss out of her."

"Got her number?"

"Williams/Bailey's roster's right in front of me."

"Okay," Joe Baines said, and clicked off.

Hank pushed the numbers and got Darcy Austin on the first ring. "Ms. Austin . . . Darcy?" Hank asked as if he didn't know who was on the other end of the phone. Stupid. "This is Hank Hankenson."

She was a little surprised to hear from the police at that hour, but then cops even had goofier hours than ad people, she reminded herself. "What is it Lieutenant?" Darcy asked.

"Did you catch the news tonight on Channel Seven, by any chance?"

"No, I was reading. Why?"

Hank cleared his throat. "They speculated—suggested—you might have been an eyewitness to the Janes murder. I don't want to alarm you but I think we need to take some precautions—just in case."

"Precautions? In case of what?" Darcy questioned, concern beginning to show in her voice.

"Well . . . some protective measures," he danced. "Like keeping watch for a while . . . surveillance—you know." He could sense her response coming, and he tried to head it off. "Just for a while," he added. "Till we get it out that you're clearly not an eyewitness—and things calm down a bit. Precautions . . . like I said."

Ms. Austin wasn't placated. "You want cops buzzing around my block?" she replied. "How nice, Lieutenant. The flashing red lights won't keep the neighbors up all night, will they?"

Her sarcasm was getting all too familiar to Hank. "Just ordinary headlights—a squad or two. And maybe a security plant," he added under his breath.

Darcy blanched at his last proposal. "And where might that plant be—in my backyard bushes? Mr. Nussebaum behind me will just love that."

Hank's tone got more personal: "I don't want anything happening to you, Darcy."

That gave her pause—the way he said it. "All right," she relented. "Do what you have to."

"Thanks, Darcy, we'll keep it low key," he assured her, before hanging up.


IT WAS A long day and the next one promised to be its equal, if not longer. So Hank decided to pack it in for the night. Entering his bedroom while opening his shirt, he wondered if he shouldn't have covered some other matters with Darcy Austin—like making sure her doors were locked and keeping her blinds closed—maybe inquire about how secure her place was, generally. He debated whether he should call her again. Did he really need to, or did he just want to? And then, how would she react to another bothersome call from him?

Shutting down his internal dispute, but still feeling foolish about the decision he came to, he went back to his portable phone station, drew the handset and used the digits now stored in its memory. A click, then nothing. He pressed off and tried again. Same click, same nothing. He would try a third time, but something was telling him his day wasn't over yet.

**"ME AGAIN, JOE."** Hank said, on his hands-free car phone.

"Where are you?" the police sergeant asked, hearing the suppressed road noise behind Hank's voice.

"Right now, College View Road," he answered. "Listen, dispatch a squad over to the Austin house, fast. Her phone line is dead, and I don't like the timing. Notify Edina, too—they're closer, and time could be critical here. Got the address?"

"5117 Winetta Lane. You headed there?"

"Right. Got her place on GPS.

"Maybe a false alarm," the veteran cop cautioned. "Could look pretty foolish."

"Yeah, gotta take the risk."

"Copy that." And Joe was gone.

**HANK TOOK A** right turn onto Normandale Road when he punched off the carphone, heading north. He crossed under I-494 where Normandale became Highway 100, doing eighty-five, and wove around the few cars staggered out ahead of him, then hunkered the BMW into the straightway, his red and blue grill strobes flashing. The speedometer soared above the highway's identifying numbers, reaching 120 on the orange-lighted dial before he touched the brakes for the Vernon exit where the GPS was telling him to peel off.

Heading east where Vernon blended into Fiftieth Street he was forced to drive more cautiously, but not much. Swerving around a startled driver without disturbing the paint on either car, he did a hard right, screeching onto the quiet residential street of Winetta, three blocks west of the Tony shopping area at Fiftieth and France. He had covered the 7.4 miles to this point in less than five minutes.

**DARCY AUSTIN THOUGHT** she heard an unfamiliar sound from her kitchen area. She lowered the book she was reading and listened. Nothing. After a while she wondered if she actually had heard anything, or if it had just been her imagination? That damned Hankenson had her edgy. She decided to investigate her quaint little dollhouse, now turned spooky.

Nothing seemed out of order in the kitchen when she got there. Still inquisitive, she turned into the darkened dining room located behind the front-facing kitchen, and at the rear of the house. Then she saw it—felt it. A pane of glass was missing from the French doors leading to the backyard, a breeze wafting through the opening it created.

Alarmed, Darcy whirled on her heels, retreating back toward the kitchen—too late. Footfalls closed behind her. A blow to the back of her head spilled her to her knees. Bright lights flashed before her. She pitched forward, tried to crawl, only to collapse face down on the hardwood floor, loosing consciousness all together.

**"TAKE IT EASY**, DARCY," a voice was saying with calming assurance. "You're safe now."

Darcy's eyes fluttered as she attempted to bring the image bending over her into focus. A groan escaped lips that couldn't yet form words.

"You're gonna be okay," the voice assured her once more.

"Nize'ta know," she slurred, before leaving again.

*Chapter* **8**

# C O N N E C T I O N

**DARCY AUSTIN SAT** propped up in hospital bed at Southdale Fairview, if you can call that sitting, where she had been admitted to Emergency the night before. She had a slight headache, and the back of her head was sore as hell to the touch. Otherwise she was well off given her harrowing experience. Release from the hospital was scheduled for after lunch if all went well. No concussion, but under watch till then in case she threw a clot or something, she guessed. She was informed that there was a uniform stationed in the hall outside her room so she should feel safe. And, at that very moment, she was host to two visitors seated at her bedside with guns under their jackets. She could see one of the "peacemakers" from where she was perched. *All this protection, how wonderful.* Her normal acerbity returning with her recovery.

The men with guns had already informed her that she would be under police protection for a time after her release from the hospital. At least until it could be established through the news media that Darcy Austin was not witness to the Williams/Bailey murder. Even then they would take precautions. Of course, that she was not an eyewitness was now only part of a bigger story with the newsies: the attempt on her life and her dramatic rescue.

A nurse's aide cleared the empty breakfast tray at the side of her bed. With all that had happened to her, she still had an appetite, even for hospital food. *Rats*, Darcy lamented. *You'd think something good would have come out of this.*

Something good occurred as far as Hank was concerned. With quick action, and luck, he may have prevented a homicide from taking place. No small thing, although he was still feeling somewhat derelict in not anticipating the threat posed to Darcy Austin by the earlier TV reports calling attention to her. It shouldn't have taken the last version of the story to alert him to that danger. Nonetheless he was being treated like a hero by the media, and Bloomington/Edina police were being hyped as great examples of inter-city teamwork.

"When you get home, you might wonder about those tire tracks in your front yard," Hank smiled, attempting to lighten the formal tone of the conversation up to then. Besides, he had just informed Darcy that they wanted a Bloomington policewoman to move in with her for a time, and she was still chewing on that. Some levity was called for, and tire tracks from his car in her front yard was as good as he could come up with.

"It's not the tracks so much as the skid grooves that'll matter," Sergeant Joe Baines said, picking up on the mood switch. "A load of black dirt, a sack of seed—you won't notice, a couple more years."

Darcy had been introduced to the police sergeant only minutes before and, despite the circumstances of their meeting, she liked him. He was a little crude, but there was something warm about him, like he cared about people. "Oh great." Darcy smiled, though it hurt when she did. "Are the Bloomington Police going to come out and regrade my yard for me?"

Hank was relieved to see her joining in with them. "We'll see if we can round up some green thumb off-duties," he said.

"The black skid marks in your driveway are Edina's responsibility," Joe Baines added. "Their cops did that, and nearly took out your garage door. Mario Andretti here was the one almost crashed through your front window."

Joe Baines' last remark stirred something in Darcy. She looked at Hank. "That bright light I saw. Could that have been you?" she asked, recalling her final moments of consciousness.

"Was the light blue?" Joe Baines asked?

"Well, yes . . . sort of," Darcy answered. "How did you know?"

Hank started to reply, but Joe Baines stayed on. "They'd be from Mario all right. Xena, Zeenon, or whatever they call them headlights us ordinary cops can't afford."

"Xenon," Hank inserted.

Joe Baines ignored the correction and kept rolling. "Mighta stopped the bad guy from . . ." Then, thinking better of what he was about to say, switched to: "Coulda saved your life." Better, but not much.

"Do you really think someone actually tried to kill me?" Darcy asked, casting about for a more tolerable botched burglary or some such lesser event. Anything but attempted murder. *Her* attempted murder.

"If Janes' killer thinks you're an eyewitness," Joe Baines said, now back in official mode, "he doesn't want you callin' him out of a lineup— or pointin' at him from a witness stand. Could be simple as that."

At that point, Hank brought up a matter that had been on his mind all along. "There's something else we should ask, Darcy. Did you have a full set of kitchen knives for the wood-block holder on your counter?"

She was beginning to like the way Lieutenant Hankenson said her name, damn it. "Yes," she answered. "Why?"

"There's an empty slot—and we can't find the knife that fits it. It's the slot that has a depression for what looks like a small hilt at the base of the blade," Hank said. *So now we likely know the intended murder weapon,* he didn't say. And the fact that the vacant slot accommodated a lethal eight-inch blade was left out of the conversation, as well.

Darcy answered, "The utility knife fits that slot. The hilt on it is a signature feature of the brand," she offered like a true marketer. She started to say more when something else flashed in her mind. The detectives assumed Darcy's sudden silence was due to the realization of how near to death she may have come. That wasn't it. "Minneapolis Cutlery," she finally added in a quiet voice. The detectives looked at each other, then back at Darcy.

"So?" Joe asked before Hank posed a less-blunt response.

She raised her eyes to meet their stares. "Minneapolis Cutlery is a Williams/Bailey client—like Mother Svendsen's Soup. "Does that mean anything?"

*Chapter* **9**

# R E A S S E S S M E N T

**HE MAY HAVE** prevented a homicide, but did he really? The incident at the Austin home didn't sit right with Lieutenant Hankenson although everyone else seemed to think the attempt on her life was real. In any event, Ms. Austin's protection was called for. Still, were things as they seemed? Something niggled at him.

He had already checked out how the "eyewitness" insertion came about in the Channel Seven, 10:00 news, and it added to his unease on the matter. An e-mail message was at its source, arriving shortly before time of broadcast. The four other local television stations in the coverage area received the same message. Normally, any such information would be checked out before it was aired in a news report and, in a half-assed way, Channel Seven made an attempt at it.

From its heading it was apparent that the e-mail message originated from the desk of the public relations director at Williams/Bailey, giving it credence to begin with. But Channel Seven's after-hours follow-up call to Williams/ Bailey seeking confirmation was not answered. What to do?

Competition for ratings is fierce among Twin Cities TV news stations. And since Channel Seven broke the "parking ramp" story earlier that day, it had hyped its exclusive coverage of the event. Even though its competitors later covered the incident audibly, they were without visual, so Channel Seven maintained its lead. The station did not wish to relinquish that lead in any way. Getting topped as a result of not running the e-mail information, while the competition did, was more than it wanted to risk. The decision was made to include it—disregarding its own confirmation policy.

Arguably, Channel Seven would have been justified in running its "eyewitness" statement if the information it received was found to be legitimate, regardless of the incident it seemed to provoke. But, when it was learned that the e-mail was bogus, Channel Seven News was abashed and repentant. True, the information came from the desk of the Williams/Bailey public relations director, but it proved not to be composed or sent by that person. In fact, no one was on the premises at the hour it was issued that anyone at W/B knew of. That meant some unknown person had to gain access to the offices without being checked in or out by security—just as someone had the night of the Janes murder—to make use of the mailing station.

If the killer could do it once, the killer might well be able to do it again, Hank surmised, brazen though it was. Even so, the sender had to use the unlocking code of the submitting computer. How? A further check revealed that the I.T.'s file cabinet, where all codes for office computers were stored, was not secured. Nor was it usually locked in the informal realm of the Williams/Bailey offices. *Now we have a person familiar with the office layout and office habits*, Hank also reasoned.

The next question Hank asked himself was, *Why take the risk to do this in the first place?* Perhaps it was a test of sorts, or a stunt, or both. If it was a test, was it a test of him? It was a long shot perhaps, but he knew the killer may have guessed that the police lieutenant in charge of the investigation, having been shown on TV, might watch the Channel 7 *News at 10:00* that evening. *So, take it from there, Hank.* Next question: *Was it really an attempt on Darcy Austin's life?* Answer: Perhaps just the appearance of it. Only he couldn't be sure of that. Next question: *So what if it was a hoax and I had not shown up to prevent the faux murder—what would the perpetrator have done then?* Answer: Maybe nothing beyond what was done. The assumption would have been that the killer was spooked in some way, fleeing the scene with the stolen knife. To the killer, in such event, nothing was lost but the added drama. Next question: *Given I'm correct so far, could the stolen knife have an intended future role?* Hank pondered but didn't answer that one. Nor his next question: *Was the killer finished?*

Much of this was wild speculation on his part. But then again, this case was off to a bizarre start from the very beginning, giving him the feeling that things could get weirder yet. *Stay with it, Hank. Stay with it.*

*Chapter* **10**

# S P E C U L A T I O N

**"COULD IT BE**," Sergeant Joe Baines asked, "—murder by client product? Jesus, that's wild," he added, pulling up a chair in front of the
desk of Lieutenant Hank Hankenson. He had his ubiquitous cafeteria
swill with him.

The other cop settled behind his desk with fresh-brewed coffee.
"It's a stretch," Hank replied. "The perp could have done Janes that way
just because Mother Svendsen's Soup was there to be used—novel a
murder weapon as it is. Same with the missing knife, if we can even be
sure a murder was intended there. Might be our guy's a first-rank oppor-
tunist."

"Yeah, but wouldn't you bring your own weapon to a planned murder? Something else's a little weird. He comes into the Austin house
from the dining room, goes to the kitchen taking a chance on being seen
or heard, then goes back into the dining room where he sits waiting with
the knife he took. Kinda round about, ain't it?"

"Coulda figured using one of her knives was better than a weapon
that could be traced back to him some way," Hank countered.

The sergeant was undeterred. "He couldn't see the knife-block from the dining room. Had to go into the kitchen to spot it. I looked."

"Okay. He knows there are knives in a kitchen. But more to your point, no pun intended, there's also a particular knife with an eight-inch blade, perfect for the job, including its hilt. Mounted in a wood block, no less—no noisy kitchen drawer to slide open. Minneapolis Cutlery, at that. If he knows all this . . . we've got a connection." Hank didn't look all that sure of himself despite his assertion.

"So, where do we go from here, then?"

"If we consider a client-product connection exists, it narrows things a bit. We'll know better if somebody gets whacked with a box of Big Oaties breakfast cereal like I saw displayed at Williams/Bailey. Or the Austin knife shows up between someone's shoulder blades."

"How do you whack somebody with a box of Big Oaties?" Joe Baines quipped.

Hank couldn't resist the set up: "Who knows? But, if it happens, we could have the first serial killer, cereal killer, on our hands."

Sergeant Baines let the remark pass in a way that let Hank know it didn't, then said: "You think there's more of this shit to come? Like this guy's not done?"

"It worries me. Yeah."

"Well, if there's somethin' to it," Joe Baines said, "whoever broke into the Austin house is somebody pretty familiar with Williams/Bailey clients and knew that the Austin lady had a set of Minneapolis Cutlery on her counter. How many could that include for crissake?"

"At least fifty-seven employees, a few more at Fantasy and an assortment of spouses and friends for starters—not to mention the clients of the agency," Hank offered. "It does narrow it some if we go with that, though."

"Also someone familiar with the inside of her house? He got around pretty good in there, remember."

"Maybe so, but just casing the place could do it."

"Either way, seems the perp knew exactly where Austin lived, if it was the ten o'clock news set him off. Had to know where the Minneapolis Cutlery was located on the counter, too, if we're still hangin' with that assumption," the sergeant added.

*No less reason to think the whole thing was a set-up from the beginning,* Hank thought. "Okay, I'm going back to Ms. Austin," he said. "Find who's acquainted with the layout of her place. At least it's a start, although the perp would be pretty reckless to hand us a lead like that."

"Worth a shot. Anyway, it's nice duty."

"What?"

A grin: "Checking with the Austin babe."

No grin: "Screw you."

Joe Baines didn't bother to comment on the flush he caught and dropped it. "We can't take this client connection thing for granite."

"'Granted.'"

"Right. Probably just a handy way to get the job done, like you said." Joe Baines sipped the brown liquid from his cup, now room temperature, then: "We can't even be sure Ms. Austin didn't just toss out the friggin' knife with the garbage, not realizin' it."

"Happens," Hank shrugged.

"How's our Titanium Doll doin' by the way?" the sergeant asked.

"Our who?"

"Came up couple of times. It's the moniker for the lady in our protection. Guess your first impression was right—she can be steely. Coworkers like her but seems she don't let men there, or anywhere else, get up close and personal, if you follow my drift." A wry smile, another sip from Styrofoam.

*How can he drink that stuff?* "She was all smiles with you."

"Yeah, but she don't see me as chase'n after her, neither." He raised his eyes to his boss's. "First base? What I hear, men don't even get up to bat."

"Is there a message for me in there?" Hank asked with an eye roll. And not waiting for an answer: "Anyway, I think she's okay with what we've tried to do. At least she's not ranting about over-protectiveness anymore. Seems we're getting through to her."

Joe Baines worked his eyebrows. "*We're* getting through to her?"

DARCY AUSTIN MIGHT well have complained, given her previous attitude. Under Hank's direction, the police had taken long measures to assure her safety after the assault in her home. Officer Marge Kennedy of the Bloomington Police moved into the two-bedroom house with her and was accompanying her on the way to work and back. Fortunately, they got along just fine. Edina patrolled the area regularly and, for good measure, Sig Nadler, the take-no-shit cop from Minneapolis, took up temporary residence in a house across the street owned by a gay couple.

Darcy went along with the whole set-up, after some convincing. She even went so far as to install a suggested home-security system. If her phone line was cut again, an alarm would sound, and an electronic break-in signal would transmit to a monitoring station via satellite. It would not be so easy for someone to penetrate her address a second time around.

IT'S ONE THING to guard against an assault and another to remove the incentive for it. Here, too, there was due diligence. The press cooperated with the Bloomington Police on this score with repeating bulletins that Darcy Austin was not an eyewitness to the Janes murder. Still contrite, Channel Seven issued an apology as to its "eyewitness" blunder, as well.

Darcy Austin might not have realized it, but she had prompted metropolitan cooperation across community boundaries as never before.

"WE'LL BE THROUGH checking all the alibis in a couple of days," Joe Baines reported to his lieutenant. "It's taking awhile to wade through all the folks at Williams/Bailey. Then there's those we're checking out," he added. "One's a former executive VP at the agency—Frank Ramstead. Left a little over a year ago with bad blood between him and the partners—especially Edson Janes. The other guy's Roland Bennett, who split off with a couple of clients and started his own shop not long after Ramstead left. Been some law suits over it, and Bennett's not happy with what he claims is legal harassment. Janes was the point man on all that."

Hank listened attentively, taking in the additions to what Darcy Austin related to him in their first session at Williams/Bailey, then said: "Looks like we've got a goodly number of prospects to keep us busy for a while. Anything else before I give the chief an update?"

"The Janes family's taking it pretty hard. Got word from the lab guys—it's definitely drowning. The 'Soup to Die For,' all right. And it gets nastier."

"How so?" Hank said.

"Lab says the soup Janes inhaled wasn't enough to do him. So the killer added water to the mix. Took like two full bowls to finish him. Lungs even suffered second-degree burns from the hot soup. And here's a lovely part, if that ain't enough. His body went into reflexive spasms during the drowning process."

Hank already knew about the last part but listened as the sergeant went on. "Whoever pressed his face into that bowl was pretty damned spiteful—or just plain sadistic."

"Thanks, you've just spoiled lunch," Hank said, checking his watch. It was twenty-past noon.

Joe Baines feigned dejection. "Your turn to buy, too. How 'bout we just run over to Bosa's—tide us over. I'll pop for the donuts."

Hank rolled his eyes. "Great, take a squad why don't we? Help reinforce the department's image. Tell you what—we go to Wally's for a sandwich and its back to me buying. Just don't order soup with your roast beef. Okay?"

# Chapter 11

# R E L A T I O N S H I P S

**DARCY AUSTIN WAS** unsettled when Lieutenant Hankenson appeared in her mind out of the blue. She had grown to like him after their rocky introduction, but that was the extent of it. So why did he crop up in her consciousness like that?

Someday she might look at things differently, but she wasn't ready to get involved with him or anyone else just yet. She had a rising career to pursue, prized her independence, and there also remained a difficulty she struggled with when it came to men in general. In her experience, and perception, men fell into two major categories: those who were in awe of her and those who sought to own her—neither of which worked. The first group tended to be weak while the second category was controlling or, worse, wanted her as a trophy, whatever other feelings they might have for her. It was a two-part dilemma that she knew was over simplified, but that's the way she felt.

No one in the "awe" category ever moved past "Let's be friends"— she just wasn't interested. Three men had moved past go in the second group—one when she was in college, two others when in her early professional life. It was a self-imposed dearth since then.

DARCY AUSTIN WAS "Miss Just about Everything," while attending Eden Valley High School. She also did some teen modeling outside of normal school activities. As one would guess, she was much sought after by her male classmates. Even so, it was not until her senior year that Darcy Austin had a serious liaison.

Blouse undone, skirt askew, panties around her thighs, it looked as though young Darcy Austin was about to consummate her first sexual encounter, with the school's star running back no less. The young hunk, in the back seat of his father's Oldsmobile, had advanced to where others had not. He was Eden Valley's leading scorer, after all. But, with time running out, Ms. Austin re-gathered herself. This is as far as you go with me, she determined. And, taking matters in hand, pulled him down, on fourth and goal, in a manner of speaking.

Not until her sophomore year at Macalester College, in St. Paul, did Darcy Austin have a male relationship of consequence. He was a linebacker on the football team, a weight-man in track, and a stud in bed. And while their relationship soared in the beginning, its magic waned in short order with her.

First warning: It was important to her male companion that she accept the nomination she'd received for homecoming queen, when the Fighting Scotsmen were scheduled to be trounced, once again, by the formidable Johnnies of St. John's University near St. Cloud, Minnesota. It wasn't the foregone trampling of the Scotsmen that bothered Ms. Austin, but recollections of being exhibited, a ridiculous crown atop her head, on the field at Eden Valley High. Nor did she enjoy or appreciate the beauty-queen scene in itself, even though she continued to model as a means of defraying the confiscatory tuition of Macalester College. Nevertheless, relenting for his sake, she accepted the nomination and soon thereafter was waving to the stands from the obligatory convertible circling the field at halftime—the scoreboard at the north end of the field reading Scotsmen: zero, Visitors: thirty-seven. "Mr. Football" was losing on two fields of play that day.

It didn't end there, but it soon ended. Mr. Football began dictating what Darcy Austin was to wear to parties as well as how she was to behave—like she was some kind of auburn-haired Barbie at his command. The relationship didn't span the school year. Nor did she engage in another courtship while attending the hallowed halls of Macalester—seekers be damned.

Darcy Austin had two dalliances upon matriculating into the "real world." She thought she may have found Mr. Right in the first of these. He was sensitive, caring, allowed her to do her own thing, was handsome and well groomed. But, before long, she realized that her thing was always his thing. She was making the decisions right on down to where they dined, the movies they saw, and what television programs they watched—even determining the time and tempo of romance. And when he wanted her to pick out his clothing for him—a total switch from Mr. Football—she realized Mr. Right was wrong. They parted friends, as is said.

The second stewardship was a fellow advertising practitioner. He was cool. They shared a lot in common, and their relationship blossomed until an old bug-a-boo recurred. It was the trophy-on-the-arm bit exacerbated by frequent visits to trendy nightspots around Minneapolis which enamored him and bored her. They were a thing in the modish warehouse district, which he loved, she detested. Then came the closer.

At the big deal annual Minnesota Ad Club advertising awards ceremony, Mr. Cool played the pre-banquet crowd ad-nausea, forsaking his date to fend for herself. The last card might have been played in the relationship if it hadn't been already. His earlier insistence on accompanying her to Marshall Field's Oval Room to select her gown for this evening had done that. And so the fate of Mr. Cool was pre-ordained with the headstrong Ms. Austin.

The following years proved chaste contentment for Darcy Austin, whose focus on a flourishing career also salved an independent bent. The Titanium Doll was actualized. Ask any man who did his best.

**IT WASN'T THAT** Darcy was without travails at Williams/Bailey, even before a murder dropped into her lap. Men she could handle. Women were sometimes more problematical.

She aroused competitive envy with some others of her sex. Fine. She was gorgeous with a drop-dead body plus smarts and talent to go along. It came with the territory. Williams/Bailey management, regarding her as a rising star in the organization, boosted the envy factor. Being private to where she was considered aloof, in some quarters, didn't help either.

Men who weren't threatened or intimidated by her, on the other hand, found her somewhere between fascinating to alluring. Despite her standoffishness, she was still sought after by eligible suitors, and some who were not. Even so, she didn't date much and those she did date didn't advance very far that anyone knew of.

Nonetheless, Darcy Austin was popular and well respected by the majority of her associates. Not a bad resume, all things considered. Yet there remained major difficulties for her at the office, manifested in two women she was assigned to work with.

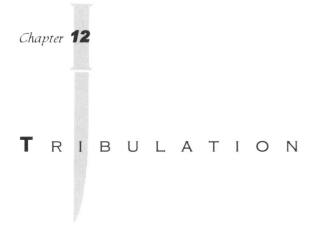

*Chapter* **12**

# T R I B U L A T I O N

**ERICA CARLSON WAS** an art-director at Williams/Bailey while Darcy represented the account service/marketing side of the business. Friction routinely existed between these two factions in advertising firms to some degree, but it was more than that.

Sweatshirt and jeans were usual garb for Erica Carlson. Only for client presentations did she demur to anything more formal. She had a decent shape, but it wasn't obvious under her normal wraps. Her straight, medium-blonde hair was cropped short and she seldom wore makeup of any sort. She was pretty but didn't seem to want anyone in on it.

By contrast, Darcy's auburn tresses had a natural wave and draped over her shoulders when not done up in a "business" bun. Even her casual wear was dressy by comparison to Erica Carlson's normal attire. When Darcy did dress up, her ensembles were impeccable and appropriate to the business or social occasion at hand.

These externals were only indicative of their internal contrasts. Erica was volatile and impulsive. Darcy was deliberate and reflective. Erica was vitriolic, insurgent and pushy. Darcy was diplomatic, thoughtful and consensus building.

While the mix didn't work with them personally, it did for the agency. The two women had complementary talents as far as agency management was concerned—Darcy providing a strategic approach to her work while Erica brought a balls-out, this-is-the-way-it-is, thrust to the table. And management recognized that both women could cut through "noise" and confusion from the perspective of their separate disciplines. That combination produced some outstanding work. As a result they were assigned together on several difficult projects, much to the chagrin of the two assignees.

Always smoldering, their relationship sometimes flared—business tensions building on personal ones. At the height of one of their debates, Erica Carlson tossed a utensil tray in Darcy's direction. It missed, but not by much. In another dispute Erica stormed out of the room in a pique, bumping Darcy aside as she did. "Creative temperament," others said, passing her behavior off as best they could.

Erica Carlson could get physical, as Darcy knew, and, as a brown-belt martial artist, she probably wouldn't mind taking her to the mat—or to the office carpet, if it allowed.

Not that Darcy was a physical slouch. Erica was still steamed over giving up a hit to her when pitching in a, "Creatives vs. Suits" company softball game—a triple at that.

And Darcy acquitted herself well on the Williams/Bailey volleyball team. Even with Erica Carlson climbing up her back half the time.

IT WAS ONLY a matter of time. In a late night session at the agency, things came to a head between them.

In the early part of the session the two women were getting along remarkably well, marketing strategy dovetailing with creative execution to the satisfaction of both. But then the glitch: Erica broached an alternative approach she wanted to present to the client in addition to the one they had fashioned. In fact, it came out, it was the execution she actually favored. Darcy, on the other hand, felt it was off strategy and shouldn't be presented at all.

The ensuing argument grew to the point where they were leaning over the table at each other. Darcy slammed her hands down on the tabletop making an emphatic point. Erica made a counterpoint by thudding the heels of her hands against the account woman's chest. Any lower and it might have been more than emphatic. The art director had crossed the line and Darcy pushed back.

Matters could have gotten completely out of hand but for Terry Barnhard, custodian at large, who just happened to walk into the station room at that moment, toolbox in tow. With that, the women broke off the encounter.

There was a lot of huffing and shuffling in the next moments, as papers and layouts were snatched up from the table. Arms full, the women pushed past the surprised custodian without a word to him or each other. *Guess they finished up for the night*, Terry Barnhard smiled to himself.

It was fortunate that Terry came along when he did, Darcy determined in a calmer frame of mind, driving home. Much as Erica Carlson had angered her, the agency was hardly the site to settle a dispute the way they were headed, if any place was. Maybe a gym—and perhaps it would come to that one day.

Darcy was taller and probably stronger of the two and she regularly worked out on the heavy bag in her basement to take out her frustrations—everything from body blows to high kicks that were not the greatest but getting better. She knew, if it ever came to a physical row, she would have to overcome Erica Carlson's martial artistry. And tonight she would have had to do it in a tight skirt and spiked heels while Erica was in her usual jeans and sneakers. That would have proved interesting, especially the high kicks. *Well, it didn't happen, and that was a good thing.* Nevertheless the basic travail remained. She still had to work with the woman.

IF ERICA CARLSON WASN'T enough to contend with, the other female nemesis in Darcy's world cropped into mind for no other reason but that she was still feeling sorry for herself. This antagonist came from an opposite direction but was just as big a pain in the ass. Jessie Campbell was the client from hell—*her* client from hell. Darcy didn't even have the option of standing up to this woman like she could with Erica Carlson.

When she got home, she was going to have a drink and forget about both bitches for what was left of her evening. Tomorrow would come soon enough.

SOMEHOW THE NEXT weeks passed with no more than low-key strife between Darcy Austin and Erica Carlson, once they stopped avoiding each other for a few days after their station-room conflict. There was no mention of that night by either of them—only knowing glances from Terry Barnhard from time to time acting as reminders. It wasn't exactly pacific between them, familiar patterns still in evidence. But Darcy had to wonder: was Erica Carlson as rancorous as before? Just maybe she wasn't.

**NO SUCH DOUBT** existed in Darcy's mind regarding Jessie Campbell's antics.

From the start of their relationship Jessie made it quite clear that she was the client, read boss, and Darcy was the account-service person, read server. To say that the relationship was strained as far as Darcy was concerned, was an understatement. Jessie knew Darcy resented her, seldom missing an opportunity to rankle the account manager all the more.

Darcy had asked Mason Williams to take her off the Gold'n Tender chicken business that Jessie presided over as its director of marketing. Be patient, give it more time, we'll give you more backup, see me in six months and we'll talk some more—was what she got back.

Behind this was the fact that Jessie Campbell made it clear to W/B management that she wanted Darcy Austin on her account. No fool, she knew Darcy was good at her work and Gold'n Tender benefited from her input. Besides, Jessie enjoyed lording it over Darcy, in her contentious way. The more Darcy's displeasure showed, the more the marketing director seemed to revel in the exploitation.

For the most part, Jessie Campbell was the flip side of Erica Carlson; their only apparent similarity being that they were both single-adult female contemporaries and chief antagonists of Darcy Austin.

Unlike Erica Carlson, Jessie Campbell was as glamorous as she was mean-spirited, and she was shameless in the way she lured attention to herself. In fact, Darcy came to the conclusion that the Gold'n Tender marketing directior was actually competing with her on that score. And Jessie Campbell could. She was striking, with long blond hair, a great shape and was always flawlessly dressed. The only area in which she gave anything away to Darcy was chest high, but not by much. It was a game, Darcy surmised: when more eyes turned Jessie's way than Darcy's, through her guile, Jessie won.

———————

**DARCY WAS ONLY** half listening as G'n T's production manager rambled on about how a new package zip-flap was about to revolutionize product sales, once the consumer wised up to how much it simplified life for her. In Darcy's mind, this group had been conducting the same meeting each week for two months now concerning inconsequential gibberish and redundancies of various sorts. *But what the hell, it's what the client wants, and it's billable time for the agency*, she reasoned. It was prevalent business practice, here and elsewhere, not about to change any time soon. And so the agency's account team and Gold'n Tender's marketing group—five from each side—were gathered in this inanity, once again.

Absorbed elsewhere, Darcy heard Jessie ask, in the recesses of her consciousness, "What do you think, Darcy?"

"Uh . . . about what?" Darcy responded, attempting to pull out of the lethargy Jessie Campbell pricked.

"Packaging—don't you think it's important?"

"Well, of course." More alert now. And wary. Jessie was building up to something.

Jessie had been sitting at Darcy's side, and now her voice moved behind Darcy as she pushed away from the table.

"It can make all the difference, set the product apart."

"Yes." *Where was Jessie going with this?*

"Focus attention. Gain interest. Are you paying attention, Darcy?"

Everyone else was. And Darcy became aware that all eyes in the room were now fixed to the rear of her. Jessie was speaking from a relocated position, but it was more than that. And when the account woman turned, she realized what it was. Ms. Campbell was sitting back in her chair, skirt, short to begin with, riding well above normality on her crossed legs. Packaging presentation.

Darcy tried to ignore Jessie's ornate blatancy, turning back to the table, even if few others did. "Haven't we been over that subject time and again, Jessie?"

Jessie Campbell was in command of the room, and loving it. "There's always a fresh way to view things, wouldn't you say?"

Oh my.

Jessie was working her game to the extreme and it proved too much for Darcy—a burn rushing through her. And then, against better prudence, Ms. Darcy Austin, professional account woman, hiked her skirt under the table and pushed back to where Jessie was posturing.

Now there was a whole lot of appendage on display. Maybe it wouldn't have been such a big deal if it weren't these two women in particular. Even the packaging guy was without words. *Mpls St Paul Magazine* could run one of its "Best of the Twin Cities" series and not gone any farther than this room for its material.

"Packaging's important, Jessie, but isn't it the product that really counts in the end?" Darcy posed, in her new pose. "You know, content, substance?

Jessie saw she was being challenged, in words and in deed. A little too successfully at that. Her fingers went to her hemline as if she was about to raise the ante.

She wouldn't dare, or would she? Darcy wondered. She didn't wait to find out. Having calmed somewhat, she returned to propriety and tucked her legs back under the table, ending her part of the joust. Mollified that she had won, Jessie yielded to decorum and rejoined the table, also. With that, and after a regrouping of the attendees, the session reverted to its normal tedium.

When the meeting broke up, some knowing smiles and glances were offered in Darcy's direction as its members departed. Maggie

Evans, Darcy's assistant AE, offered a furtive thumbs up and a wink. They understood.

The others now departed, Jessie sat staring at her account manager before breaking an awkward silence. "Well, that meeting wasn't so dull after all, was it Darc?"

"What?" Darcy questioned as if she had no idea to what Jessie was referring.

"Don't be coy. I perked things up and you joined in. Couldn't take being upstaged?"

Darcy replied with a whole lot of insincerity. "Why, Jessie, I don't know what you mean."

"Right. Well, I give you credit for showing some balls anyway," she said, surprising Darcy with a compliment of sorts, although it was hardly the best metaphor for the situation.

Darcy played the episode back in her mind, wincing internally. "So where do we go from here, Jessie?" she asked. "This can't continue, can it?"

"Why not, Darc? I won't hold that crack about content and substance against you."

*How gracious. Still the same bitch.* "I don't know," Darcy said. "Guess I was looking for some . . . movement."

"Tell you what, Hon—I'll think about it." Dropping the lid on her briefcase and snapping it closed, the client added, "Remember, I want that plan for Brenton Foods in northern Iowa. Thursday. Don't drop the ball on me." That said, Jessie Campbell strode out of the room with a militant gait. Their conversation, such that it was, was over.

Jessie Campbell, and Erica Carlson, were the pair from hell as far as Darcy Austin was concerned—her own personal hell.

*Chapter* **13**

# A S S E S S M E N T

FIVE DAYS AFTER the murder, things were already moving back toward normalcy at Williams/Bailey. At least they were in an operational sense, allowing for the absence of Edson Janes, whose funeral took place two days previous. The agency's clients forgave scheduling delays for the most part and even some missed deadlines. Although such amnesty was granted with an accompanying posture that suggested it had best not happen again. Clients were still clients.

Mother Svendsen's donated $50,000 to the Minnesota Food Shelf, a charity Edson Janes supported in life, and put up another $50,000 as a reward for information leading to the arrest and conviction of his murderer. Also, on the business side of things, Mother Svendsen's directed Williams/Bailey to eliminate the slogan "The Soup To Die For" from all future advertising, posthaste. No missed deadlines would be tolerated in this instance.

True normality at Williams/Bailey could not be expected to return for some time, however. Edson Janes' murder had to be solved in order to approach that anytime soon. And there remained the lingering conjecture

that a killer could be dwelling among staffers at the agency—not especially comforting.

The mending process would be speeded along, nonetheless, in that
advertising agencies tend to morph themselves through turnover greater
than in most other businesses, and could even be further speeded along
by purchase-merger activity prevalent in the industry. In a relatively
short time, few people at Williams/Bailey—if it still existed in name or
form—could regard the Janes murder as little more than a historical
footnote. The only constant on the advertising scene is change.

The news media was still speculating about the crime, but, for the
most part, it was not over hyping the situation. It was sensational
enough on its own merits. The Janes case had made it as a legitimate
"feed" as well, and Twin City newscasters enjoyed their play on the
national stage—some local analysts appearing on Larry King, the
O'Reilly Factor and even Oprah Winfrey.

With no arrests, the eyewitness tag was lifted from Darcy Austin
in absolution. She, along with everyone concerned for her safety, could
now relax on that score. Sig Nadler vacated his neighborhood stakeout
of sorts, and Marge Kennedy departed the Austin guestroom. Darcy, in
addition to regaining her privacy, felt the residual effect of Erica Carlson
and Jessie Campbell backing off at the office to some degree. There's a
plus side to everything.

NORMALITY WAS NOT the byword at Police headquarters in Bloomington, however, where its investigation, having uncovered no meaningful clues, seemed to be stymied. All that was known for certain was that
Edson Janes had been murdered at approximately 3:00 a.m.—a drown-

ing victim immersed face down in a bowl of soup he prepared for himself as evidenced by his fingerprints on the bowl itself and utensils.

It seemed Mayor Margaret Magneson, not the most composed person at times like these, was pestering Chief James Lott every hour of the day for an update on the affair, or so it seemed. To Hank's good fortune, Jim Lott, knowing his Crimes Against Persons Lieutenant had enough to contend with, without nuisance distractions from above, proved an effective bulwark for him. Lieutenant Hankenson's bad fortune was that he did indeed have enough to deal with—distractions or not.

None of the investigative team had come to the client-product-as-weapon scenario Hank and Joe Baines had previously entertained. Nor did the two detectives plan to bring the matter up for now. Hank decided they would let the team go about its business and see what it uncovered on its own. Besides, it was a still too much of a stretch in his mind. And even if valid, it merely pointed to inside work, as did everything else in the case with the exception of two former insiders. What other significance it might have, he and the sergeant had no idea.

"**WHAT WE GOT**, gang," Hank put to the group jammed into the department's crowded conference room for the initial check-point session of the investigative team.

Officer Jeff Ortendahl was first to respond. "I need to push on this Bennett guy some more," he said. "Didn't like Janes at all. Really pissed about the lawsuits Janes put to him. Cost him money he couldn't afford."

"Alibi?" Hank questioned.

"Home in bed, he says. Who isn't going to say that when the murder took place in the wee hours," Ortendahl replied. "Only way we break it, is his wife saying he wasn't there, and she's backing him solid. Either she changes her story or we place the guy at the scene some other way. But we've got motive here—Bennett Advertising's pretty shaky, with the legal suits and all."

"Okay, Jeff, stay with him. Anyone?" Hank asked.

"Dan and I are following the money," Marvin Johnson answered. "The three remaining partners probably got the most to gain financially. Same alibis—home in bed, wives vouching."

"I've pulled the financial reports," Dan Blacker added. "Mason Williams is gold plated and appears to have nothing to gain—his being the head guy and all. The other principals are pretty well off too. But who knows what greed can do? Or might even be personal."

Hank shrugged. "Question is, why would they want to destabilize the agency they own?'

"What about the Austin woman?" Jeff Ortendahl was back into it. "Couldn't she have reported the body after producing it? Happened before, hasn't it?"

"What's the motive?" Joe Baines cut in. "Maybe she wants to move up in the agency faster, but that's a reach. And she'd have to be pretty damn good to fake a break-in in her own home, and hit herself on the back of the head. There're footprints leading to and from the back of her house, and a cut phone line on top of that. Could be she had an accomplice but that's another leap. From all reports, she and Janes got along fine, besides." Finished, Joe glanced over at Hank. The glint in his eyes saying, How'm I doin'.

Hank stayed out of it.

"Just wonderin'," Jeff Ortendahl said, shutting down.

Marge Kennedy: "If she's the perp, she's sure fooled me. I've been living with her for a week now, and I'd bet she's clean."

"Anything on Frank Ramstead?" Hank then asked, glancing to his summary sheet—and moving the discussion off Darcy Austin.

"I've got him," Minneapolis Police Sergeant Dex Ames answered. "He's one of two guys here with a motive who wouldn't mind seeing M/B go in the tank. Janes fired him, and he had to take a job at another agency for half the money. Bumped into each other in a restaurant after, and got into a shouting match. Witnesses all over the place. Somethin' about the guy, too. He ain't no pacifist."

"Where's he say he was the night of the murder?" Joe Baines asked.

"Home in bed like everyone else. No way to verify it one way or the other. He lives alone," the Minneapolis cop answered.

"Okay Dex, stay with it." Hank said. Then to Officer Kennedy: "Marge, how's it going with the list of W/G employees?"

"Haven't turned up anything to get excited about," the short-time Winnetta Avenue resident replied. "Will keep going. Looking at clients and suppliers, too. Marvin and Dan are helping me on that."

"Got Fantasy on the docket?"

"You bet."

"Good." Then to Sergeant Nadler of the Minneapolis Police: "Sig, you're the utility infielder around here. Keep snooping around, unless there's something you got."

"Right. And no," Sig Nadler answered in his terse manner.

That about summed it up. Nothing. Not so much as a fingerprint that could be laid to the crime. Zip. Zero. Nada. Things were off to a great start.

# Chapter 14

## R E M I N I S C E N C E

**HANK WATCHED THE** room clear out and turned to his notes. He was just getting into it when he was aware of someone's presence. "What is it Sig?" Hank asked, looking up to the somber figure in the doorway and waving him back into the room.

Sig Nadler was smaller than Hank had supposed before meeting him, from his reputation as a hard-nosed brawler, but he could see he was tough as nails. And there was an intensity in his taut demeanor that warned he was not to be trifled with.

"I knew your brother, Lieutenant," the homicide cop said without any particular expression while pulling up a chair and settling himself.

"Oh?" Hank questioned, although he would have guessed that.

"Good man. Wanted you to know I thought so."

"Thanks. I thought so, too." Hank guessed Nadler was eight or ten years older than he was. That would make him a couple of years older than Brian. And although his brother was in narcotics, not homicide, it was likely the two cops would have known each other—Dex Ames was also around at the time, Hank knew.

"He had a gold pocket-watch didn't he?" Sig commented, as though it just now occurred to him. "Used to rock it back and forth on the end its chain—like when he was contemplating something. Had a golfer etched on its lid."

"Yeah, funny you remember that," Hank returned. "Won it in a tournament at Meadow Brook. He was a low handicapper."

Sig Nadler nodded. "Beat me by ten strokes last time we played."

Hank recalled a similar fate on the links with his big brother. Then, back to the watch, he said: "Carried it for good luck. Don't know what happened to it. Wasn't in his effects—I checked."

"Right. Well, like I said—just wanted to let you know." Sig Nadler shrugged. Then added: "Dex and I'll be going back to Minneapolis in a couple of days. Been assigned to the Rifleman."

"Hey. Congratulations," Hank said to the Minneapolis police sergeant. "The Rifleman's big-time stuff."

"Yeah, right. Way I see it, the chief and the mayor both think Dex and I'll strike out like everyone else put on this guy's ass. Works in their favor. Nothin' like a high-profile failure to wave to the press, next time they go after my hide."

"I don't think that's it. They're at the end of their rope and they know you guys are good. Gotta turn you loose in order to save their own asses."

"Maybe." Nadler said, getting up to leave. "Good luck finding your killer, Lieutenant."

THE RIFLEMAN WAS the moniker attached to an unknown assassin who operated in and around Minneapolis over the past several years, after first having made himself known on the St. Paul side of the Mississippi.

His victims were all high-profile personalities from the metropolitan area who skirted the law and had gotten away with it. Most had few indictments and none had a conviction. They evaded the law, but not the Rifleman. True to his sobriquet, a rifle was employed in the dispatch of each one of them—a different kind each time, specifically suited to the virulent occasion. His MO didn't stop there. The Rifleman had flair.

Perhaps the most spectacular of his lethal forays, since his initial St. Paul debut, took place on an afternoon in downtown Minneapolis. On that day, above the streets and skyways teaming with pedestrians, a bullet smashed through the tempered glass of a twenty-eighth floor office in the IDS Building and dismounted the head of one C. Norman Griffin, Esq. from where he was seated at his computer. When the Minneapolis police tracked the trajectory of what proved to be more of a small missile than a bullet in the normal sense, to its start point, they found the shooter's nest in a vacant office on the twenty-ninth floor of the Foshay Tower a block away. A Barrett M95 .50 caliber, bolt-action precision rifle was still in its firing position, mounted on a bipod and fitted with a 10x Swarovski scope. The business end of its MATCH grade, twenty-nine-inch barrel protruded through an open window of the 1928 skyscraper where the archaic option of an open window still existed. Four black-tipped, armor-piercing rounds remained in the rifle's five-round box magazine, the assemblage capable of striking a target a mile distant in the hands of a proficient shooter.

Once again, the Rifleman had left his signature. And when the serial number of the .50 caliber beast was traced, it led to its owner who had reported it stolen at an S.W.F.A. competition in Raton, New Mexico, three months before. Dead end.

The Foshay Tower was Minneapolis' original skyscraper and tallest building in Minnesota until 1972. Although it was now dwarfed by structures all around it, it offered a clear view to the IDS Tower—and, more to the point, a view into the victim's office. Through a high-power scope mounted on a long-distance target rifle, it was a piece of cake striking a target only a couple of hundred feet away. On the surface this would seem beneath the Rifleman's chosen level of accomplishment based on his previous performances, but for one factor. The shooter managed to locate his target behind the darkened reflective glass of the IDS that is impossible to see through from outside in daylight. The authorities still pondered that one.

THE RIFLEMAN DIDN'T miss. He hadn't yet, anyway. Six desultory shots over a nine-year period, found six dead—and, so far, not a clue as to the assassin's true identity. The area had lost a nefarious lawyer, a murderous gang leader, a racketeering money launderer, a bribe-extorting city council member, a predatory businessman and a long-corrupt state politician, as a result of his doings. A lot of people didn't think the Rifleman was all that bad for the community.

It was a while since his sixth, and last, hit. The citizenry wondered if he would strike again or if his handiwork was finished. The police wondered as well, betting on the former.

SERGEANT SIG NADLER'S visit provoked some thoughts in Hank's mind. Like his getting into police work in the first place—a visceral move he didn't fully understand even now. It wasn't his original intention. After receiving his MBA from the Carlson School of Business at the University of

Minnesota, he planned to take a job with a Twin Cities firm and settle into the normal life of a normal businessman like a normal person. It was his brother's death that turned him. Why, he wasn't yet sure.

Hank felt Brian Hankenson died because he was too close to where someone didn't want him. It was an execution, pure and simple. Somebody was lying in wait. Maybe that's what caused him to choose homicide, as well—seeking killers—even though he was doing so in a suburb where killers were in short supply. Was that it—avenging Brian's death in a roundabout way?

Hank's thoughts passed on to other aspects of his life. Here he was, edging toward mid-life crisis and never close to marriage. It wasn't for lack of female companionship—he had had his share of that. He was good-looking, had a full head of brown hair, and kept himself in shape. Women liked him, and he mixed with some pretty fancy company, which his brother's life insurance payout allowed him the luxury of doing. *Brian, I owe you*, he thought as that last bit came to mind.

Why was it he never met anyone he could get serious with? There were women, over the years, who were serious about him, and one particular relationship did burn hot for a time. But in the end the woman scared him with her career and social ambitions. He liked the finer things in life, but somehow she was too much—too driving a force. He broke things off, and they hadn't seen each other in more than a year.

Then Darcy Austin came into his mind, uninvited. The Titanium Doll. Here was a woman that did fascinate him and, his luck, she had to be made of metal. And how old, or young, was she? She must still be in her twenties—a decade or more between them. He'd have to look her age up on the Williams/Bailey personnel sheet. And what was it with her, he wondered? She didn't like men, but she didn't have any close women friends, either. *Wouldn't you know it would be someone like her,* he chided himself.

Hank tried to return to more immediate tasks in front of him. It didn't work. Just when he shook Darcy Austin from his thoughts, the Rifleman charged back in, along with reminders of his own early career. *Hankenson, you do have a way of getting involved in things you hadn't counted on.*

*Chapter* **15**

# I N V O L V E M E N T

**THE CENTER FOR** Criminal Justice and Law Enforcement beat the hell out of ROTC at the University of Minnesota when it came to arduous military-style training. DouglasHankenson could attest to that through personal experience. CCJLE was more like military boot camp, and young Hankenson was in the best physical condition of his life after graduation from that police academy. Plus, he was well programmed in the theoretical and simulated aspects of law enforcement and their associated hazards on the street. Now he was anxious to test his skills beyond the classroom, in the real world.

Love it or hate it, no one wants to take back the rigors he or she endured in the military, or the quasi-military training of police academies. It's degrading, humiliating, debasing, fatiguing, and abject—yet, in the end, gratifying and self-enhancing. Not everyone goes through it—nor can everyone who attempts it. And therein lies a deep pride of accomplishment of those who do. No one wants to give that back.

———————

AFTER COMPLETION OF his courses at CCJLE at the top of his class, Officer Douglas L. Hankenson applied and was accepted into the St. Paul Police Force, State of Minnesota, Badge 426.

He was on one of his first patrols, heading north on Snelling Avenue, passing through the Highland Village area when he picked up a radio bulletin on a domestic at 437 Sycamore, no more than four blocks from where he was cruising—Code 9, meaning violent.

He revved the Crown Vic, switched on his overhead lights, and pulled a hard right at the next intersection. "Lights *and* siren," the repeated words of one of his instructors at the academy cropped into his brain, prompting him to switch on his siren as well.

He sped down the eastbound residential side street covering the four blocks to Sycamore Avenue, and cranked left, narrowly missing a parked car on the far side of the street as he fishtailed through the turn. He traversed the rows of boulevard trees and neat stucco homes on forty-foot lots before slamming to a stop at 437 stenciled on the curb in white numerals.

Officer Hankenson threw open the door of his cruiser just as a scream came from inside the house. He called for backup, as was protocol, and banged his knee exiting the squad, which was not. Flexing his leg, which didn't help the hurt a whole lot, he debated what his next move should be. His training told him to wait for assistance while his instincts tugged at him to act now. But when he heard a gunshot from inside the house, followed by another scream, this one choked off, instinct trumped training. Protocol, along with the pain in his knee, were forgotten.

Unsnapping his service revolver from its holster, he charged up the cement steps coming off the public sidewalk and raced twenty feet to the entrance of the home. Without hesitating, he flung the screen door aside with his free hand and thrust his foot against the entrance door using the "take down" kick he was drilled in at the academy. The jam splintered, and the door burst open. Adrenaline coursing his body, and heedless of the twenty-to-one odds against surviving his next move, young Officer Hankenson, on his very first domestic, stepped inside the house.

FOR ALL HIS brazen recklessness, luck was with the rookie cop that day. Perhaps the utter boldness of his incursion did it, or the threat of his own raised revolver gave pause, or, more likely, just plain fate was working on his behalf. Whatever the reason, the stocky man in a worn T-shirt and faded jeans, black eyes fixed over the barrel of a nine-millimeter Ruger semiautomatic leveled at the officer framed in the doorway, did not pull the trigger.

The mouth of the Ruger nine looked cavernous from Officer Hankenson's perspective, but he had come this far and he wasn't about to flinch now. Not even crouching to present a smaller target as prescribed in lecture and text, he cradled his .38 Smith & Wesson revolver in a two-handed wide-set stance as if he were some sort of blue-clad Dirty Harry. Feel lucky, punk. Do ya?

For the moment, a standoff.

Officer Hankenson saw the woman face down on the floor, twisted into an awkward position with a dark stain expanding on the carpet from beneath her—the apparent victim of the shot he had heard at the curb. The man he faced held a whimpering adolescent girl in front of him, although he was too large and she too small to be an effective shield against a good pistol shot, which Officer Hankenson was. The man's daughter, Hankenson wondered? The prospect enraged the young policeman all the more. "Let the girl go, and drop the gun," He demanded, "or I'll blow your damn head off." Dramatic, though not exactly textbook procedure.

"Go to hell," the mouth below the black eyes replied.

"Do it now," Officer Hankenson persisted.

The backup squads arrived out front to a cacophony of sounds. Down winding sirens, screeching tires and slamming car doors may have been reassuring to Officer Hankenson, but to the shooter it meant his hand was forced. "Fuck you, cop," the man cried out and fired point blank at the uniform still standing in the doorway.

The bullet tore through Officer Hankenson's left shoulder, slamming him back against the splintered door jam, where he slid to the floor in a sitting position. With the shot, the young girl pulled free and stumbled to the carpet as she frantically tried to escape her captor. The shooter brought his gun after the girl, just as Officer Hankenson squeezed the trigger of his Smith & Wesson.

Backup rushed in. The girl, unhurt, crawled over to where Douglas Hankenson was sitting. He drew her in with his functional arm, the service revolver remaining in his functional hand.

Paramedics hovered over the woman on the floor. She was alive. The shooter, a stained hole in his grungy T-shirt where the .38-caliber bullet from Officer Hankenson's gun pierced his chest, was not—his black eyes open to the ceiling before a cop threw a jacket over his vacant stare.

The young girl was still clinging to the downed officer when a Para hustled over. Douglas Hankenson, lids heavy while hugging the girl with resolute determination, slipped toward unconsciousness with a smile of satisfaction on his face.

It could have done justice to the final scene of a movie.

---

**OFFICER HANKENSON CAUGHT** holy hell for his imprudent action. After which, he was awarded the Medal of Valor, the department's highest medal for gallantry beyond the call of duty, along with a Letter of Commendation, from the mayor of St. Paul, placed in his permanent service file. What other choice did the department have at the end of the day? Here was a dauntless hero, as far as the public was concerned, whose plaudits the *St. Paul Pioneer Press* played up in what it poetically termed, "The Shootout on Sycamore." In addition, there was the undying gratitude of a surviving mother and daughter—their heart-rendering recitals carried on Twin Cities television for the better part of a week without pause. The mother left little doubt that her estranged husband would have killed both her and her little girl if it were not for Officer Hankenson's bold intervention. "I love him," the daughter would add. "He's a nice man."

Six months later, Douglas Hankenson was promoted to corporal. As far back as records were kept, it was the shortest time that a rookie cop on the St. Paul Police Force ascended to that rank.

Yet, more notoriety was on the way . . .

**THE GOVERNOR OF** Minnesota was about to deliver a major speech on the steps of the State Capitol. He was heralding a new tax bill that had just passed both state houses and which he was about to sign into law. It was a bill he had pushed vigorously, reducing income tax rates by significant margins—even at the brackets of the so-called rich—in what was one of the highest-tax states in the nation. It was worth a hoopla assembly and the Republican governor was taking full advantage of the opportunity.

Political dignitaries of all stripes from across the state were gathered. So were business leaders who supported the bill, as was St. Paul officialdom, including members of the police force.

Sergeant Douglas Hankenson, hero of "The Shootout on Sycamore" three years prior, was there in full-dress uniform with his Medal of Valor—at the personal request of the governor. It would look good when the camera panned down the row of St. Paul's finest. All stops were out for this affair; all props were in.

Governor Benson approached the outside assembly from the Capitol Building's classic entrance, acknowledged the applause from the crowd with a two-handed wave, passed by the speakers' podium and, one by one, greeted the front row of notables awaiting his presentation on this beautiful June day. It could not have been grander.

Politics is a strange world in many ways, its denizens attacking each other at every opportunity on the civic stage, suddenly appearing as warm-hearted brethren in venues such as these. So it was, as Governor Benson passed down the row adjacent to the speaker's platform, shaking the hands of some of his most ardent foes with a huge smile on his face. The irony reached its zenith when the governor came to the man, front and center, who rose from his seat to take the governor's hand. The political differences between these two men were greater than the disparity in their height—the governor, at six-foot-three, looming over the shorter man by a good half foot as they greeted one another. Civility of the moment aside, it was no secret that these two men disdained each other, both personally and politically. But there it was for all to witness, bitter adversaries beaming as though they were lifelong friends. That is, until one of the men's head exploded.

**ARNOLD SVEN SPANO** led the opposition against the very bill being celebrated, just as he had most every other bill the governor ever favored. He was a career politician, spanning thirty-two years in office, having risen from the ranks of labor to become the most powerful man in the Minnesota Senate. And although he was corrupt as hell, even to the point of flaunting his excesses, his northern Minnesota district was solid. He would either retire of his own volition one day or die in office—the latter having now occurred.

**NO REPORT WAS** heard by the crowd—the firearm being too far distant, the breezes dispersing any peripheral sound that could otherwise have reached the "binocular seats" at the rear of the assembly. There was, however, the crack of broken sound barrier just after Arnold Spano's skull was penetrated, spreading much of his face over the stunned governor grasping the hand of the still-standing dead man before him.

Security whisked the blood- bone- and matter-stained governor from the stage—determined that the shooter would not get a second chance at their man, who appeared to be hit. With mental images of Ronald Reagan's near assassination from what seemed a superficial wound, they rushed the governor away. They need not have worried. While Senator Spano, for all intents, was nullity, Governor Benson suffered only a slight flesh wound from the blunted, spent projectile, creating as much a bruise as any penetration into the governor's stomach wall.

**GOVERNOR BENSON WAS** an outspoken reformer, his life threatened on several occasions by anonymous persons averse to diminishing the public trough in any manner, shape, or form. Many postulated it was only a matter of time before an actual attempt was made on the governor's life, given the shrillness of portent. The head of state was given a tight ring of security for this day's event. Yet there was one glaring shortcoming now apparent: the breadth of that ring. The shooter was well beyond its perimeter.

THE MAJESTIC ST. PAUL Cathedral towered from high on a hill directly facing the front entrance of the Minnesota Capitol. These stately buildings were two of the most commanding and celebrated structures in St. Paul, half-mile distant from each other, separated by the Capitol's elaborate mall, scattered monuments and a matrix of crossing roadways. Through the considerable early influence of Bishop John Ireland, the Cathedral commanded the higher ground of the two buildings, affording a clear line of sight to the Capitol along scenic Summit Avenue, which blended into John Ireland Boulevard. Not that it mattered all that much for the celebratory occasion at hand. But it sure made things easier for the shooter.

WHILE THE CROWD at the Capitol steps was not treated to the report of the rifle that was fired more than twenty-five hundred feet from where they were gathered, the junior priest in the quiet of the St. Paul Cathedral on Summit Avenue was—followed by clattering from above. Not sure just what the sounds were or how they originated, the priest searched about from under the huge atrium. Discerning nothing, but still curious, he stepped outside and circled the structure, coming upon a climber's rope descending the back of the building.

Before the priest determined his next move, a horde of vehicles appeared on the scene in a Technicolor of flashing lights, shrieking sirens and screeching brakes. Unimaginable only moments before, this site now bore full logic as a shooter's heaven for what transpired on the steps of the Capitol. So here it was that police and security arrived en mass— the befuddled priest, pointing to the rope as they charged up the embankment to where he stood.

A climb to the top of the cathedral dome, by a cop who was a former army ranger, revealed the shooter's perch. A rifle was propped against the railwork encircling the narrow walkway at the dome's apex. No need for an improvised shooter's rest up here—the railing provided a perfectly adequate forward mount for that purpose.

The weapon was a heavy-barreled, bolt-action M24 sniper rifle equipped with a 10-power scope. A single 7.62 x 51-mm round was expended from in its six-cartridge integral magazine. All that was missing from the scene was the person who squeezed the trigger.

AN OFFICIAL INVESTIGATION was hastened, a ready-list of Benson haters kicking it off.

In the hubbub of frantic activity, a lone voice questioned the direction the investigation was taking. It was that of Sergeant Douglas Hankenson, still amongst the high-ranking officialdom by default of the day's intended celebration. "I don't think the governor was the target," he dared to submit, for which he was immediately derided by all those within earshot of his words who didn't just dismiss him out of hand.

"And just who might the target have been?" chided a lieutenant of detectives.

"The guy without a face," Hankenson answered, more churlish than he intended, quickly adding, "Spano."

"C'mon, Hankenson," Chief Wilkins broke in, "that's bullshit."

It wasn't what Sergeant Hankenson wanted to hear from his chief but at least the boss was paying some attention to him. He stood his ground. "A good shooter doesn't miss up or down," he said, "even from that distance."

"What?" the lieutenant said. It wasn't really a question.

"If he misses its going to be to one side or the other," Hankenson continued. "That suggests Spano was his target all along."

"Aww, bullshit, Hankenson." It seemed it was the chief's favorite expletive. "Why Spano? He's been around forever and probably was going to croak on his own before long."

Sergeant Hankenson was more adamant than prudent: "Maybe Chief, but a good marksman knows the distance he has to carry and calculates his drop based on muzzle velocity. Even accounts for humidity and air temperature. I'd guess the shooter had his range pegged to a micro-meter."

"You're shittin' me," the lieutenant broke in. He was beginning to sound like the chief, with a different expletive.

Hankenson kept going. "He can't always predict what side breezes will do—only allow for them, best he can. So he can miss over long distances, side-to-side. Not up or down. And the governor stands a head taller than Spano—a clear target for a good shooter, if it was Governor Benson he was after. I think the shooter was waiting for Spano to stand up—knew he would when the governor came to him. Perfect."

The chief glanced over at his young sergeant who was beginning to make some sense to him. Not enough though, and the governor remained the focus, death threats overruling his sergeant's rationale. No way this investigation was going to change its course. What the hell, maybe the assassin was just a lousy shot. The chief didn't say anything, just looked away. This time, it was the lieutenant who offered, "Bullshit."

Others in the gathering who overheard Hankenson's assertions passed on comments which circulated on the street. They were not to the benefit of the young sergeant.

Two days later, a letter to the editor ran in the St. Paul *Pioneer Press*. It was the first time the public was to hear from its sender, though not the last:

> I've no quarrel with Governor Benson—I rather like the man, for a pol. Senator Arnold Spano is—was—another matter.
>
> I simply did what his district should have done years ago: remove him from office, albeit a bit more harshly than in the usual manner. But then, Pork, illicit favors, and jobbery held sway in the voting booth, I fear.
>
> I apologize for any discomfort the governor suffered. But with the Senator out of the way, he—and we—will soon recover from our wounds.
>
> Heed your sergeant, Chief Wilkins. It was a damn good shot.
>
> —The Rifleman

The letter raised a tumult in the Twin Cities metro. The *Star Tribune* reprinted the missive on its side of the river, TV news featured it, and it was the heated topic of talk-shows on which not all callers were unsympathetic to the Rifleman. Also, there was the moral aspect of the Rifleman's vigilantism, which editorialist and talk show hosts got off on. This thing had legs.

The discourse raised as many questions as it answered. Who was the Rifleman? Was the letter to the St. Paul paper a hoax? Did the Rifleman, assuming the letter was genuine, really intend to assassinate Senator Spano rather than the governor—or was he now diverting attention away from his true target? Other questions remained, as well: How did the Rifleman manage to go undetected at the Cathedral and escape so cleanly? Was he a madman, a master assassin, a crackpot, or all of the above? And, finally, would he strike another time?

Once again, Douglas Hankenson, as the sergeant referred to in the Rifleman's letter, was back in the news—his assertions about long-distance marksmanship confirmed by sharpshooters in the area who joined in on the discussions. In due course, it also came out that the sergeant, and the hero of "The Shootout on Sycamore" of a few years before, was one and the same person.

The City of Bloomington, Minnesota, was impressed. Sergeant Hankenson was tendered the position of detective on its force. And thus began Douglas L. Hankenson's nascent crimes-against-persons career with Minnesota's largest suburban community.

*Chapter* **16**

# PERSPECTIVE

**HE SAT ACROSS** the narrow table from the most gorgeous creature he'd ever seen. Hank Hankenson had been with this same woman before, but on those occasions she was either in casual attire to the extreme or residing in the antiseptic environs of a hospital room in a bleached-out patient's gown with a bandage on her head. The metamorphosis, if that's what it was, was stunning. Subtle makeup turned the woman's green eyes greener and full lips fuller. Auburn hair, no longer in a makeshift bun, framed a perfect face to perfection on its way to her shoulders. Her jewelry was exquisite, delicate—small-loop earrings and a matching gold chain at her neck, a single ring encircling the third finger of her right hand. She wore a black dress with a hemline short of her knees and a neckline that challenged Hank to keep his eyes where they belonged. He could only imagine where that hemline now rested under the table, which, of course, he did. What must she be wearing under that dress? Another image flashed in his mind. He had a creative imagination. *C'mon, Hank, get a grip.*

Or was it that he was just catching up to what was before him all along? Had he been trying to play the woman down in his mind before tonight? If so, any such pretensions were ended as of now. He'd known from the beginning that this was an attractive female—okay, even beautiful. But now anything short of ravishing didn't cut it. He needed a drink.

As if on cue, the swarthy waiter delivered the glass of Pinot Grigio and bottle of Heineken the couple had previously selected from da Afghan's beer and wine menu. The waiter had no attendant problem as to which beverage went where, while the couple perused the cryptic entrées of the dinner menu.

Hank had passed on Kincaid's for this occasion, one of his favorite spots. It was situated a little too close to what this event was ostensibly about, and may have proved uncomfortable for that reason alone. Also, it was a little too upscale and held a special-occasion ambience. He didn't want it to appear as though he had an ulterior motive. Besides, he liked da Afghan. The food was good and the casual setting was right for the session at hand. Yet, with all his careful forethought, he still wasn't prepared for the dazzling component across the table from him. Session? What session?

That they were together in a restaurant at all, amounted to happenstance. He'd first proposed getting together with her on the limp proposition of learning what he might about those people familiar with her home and its contents. Shortly after the checkpoint meeting in his office, he called her to say he could drop by her home in about an hour, and the rest unfolded. She asked if he'd eaten. He said no. She said she'd order in a pizza. He said he knew a restaurant she might like. She said fine. He said good—while thinking, great.

"What do you recommend," Darcy asked, fixing those emerald beams on him.

Fighting off the distraction of her gaze, Hank replied, "My usual's the Aushok, but we could do the Afgani Sampler for two if you like. Gotta tell you though, it's a ton of food."

"Sounds terrific. Let's do it." Darcy was one of those whose appetite never seemed to interfere with her dress size.

"Okay. Got to have the parsley salad with it," Hank said, signaling the waiter for their order and another hit on beverage. "You're in for a treat."

By the time their second round of drinks arrived Hank sensed the polite small talk was wearing thin. He wanted to talk to her about nothing in particular all night long, but thought he'd better get down to it. *You called this meeting*, he reminded himself.

"Darcy," he loved that name, "Can you tell me about the people at Williams/Bailey who've been to your home—familiar with it from inside?" He could have used the directive, "Tell me the people," but posed it in the friendlier form of a question. He was feeling mighty friendly right now.

She cocked her head. He liked that, too. "Not many, really. Women, mostly. My house isn't big enough for parties. And I don't entertain that much anyway. Let's see . . . Jason O'Connell has been by a few times . . ."

"Who's he?" Hank interrupted. He recognized the name from his data sheet but didn't know the relationship between them.

"An account exec. Reports to me on two of our clients. He's dropped work off at my place."

"Ever been in your kitchen?" Hank pressed. This whole thing was sounding sillier to him by the minute. Where was it going?

"Once maybe," she answered. "I think I gave him a cup of coffee while I looked over some things he brought me."

Once is enough, Hank mentally noted, not wishing to be so gauche as to produce a note pad unless he absolutely had to.

"Ed Janes came in. Strictly business," she added when his eyes widened a trifle. "Course you don't have to consider him, do you?" her look breaking away as she spoke the words.

Maybe someone he talked to, though, Hank considered. Although he realized that could have been anyone at the agency, and who knows who else? It was still going nowhere.

"Several women I work with have been over. Jessie Campbell," she said with veiled acrimony Hank picked up on. "She's my client at Gold'n Tender . . . never can wait for normal office hours." Pause. "My assistant, Maggie Evans. There's Donna King, another account manager like me. Lisa Marks, just a friend at the agency. And Andrea Shiff who works with Josh Williams at Fantasy. I think that's it."

"They've all been around the inside of your house?"

"Not much you can't see at a glance," she shrugged. "Pretty small."

"What's your connection with Andrea Shiff?"

"None, officially. She's Josh Williams' assistant at Fantasy Publications. Stops by at the office on occasion. Asks me questions on how I think Magenta should react, given a certain situation or other that she and Josh are wrestling with at the time. Supposedly they go for realism, and Josh thinks I depict his creation in some way. It's really weird stuff, but I kind of like Andrea."

From what Hank had learned, Ms. Austin matched up pretty well with the Magenta character as an independent loner. Andrea Shiff seemed a pretty astute lady. Or was Josh Williams the discerning one? At the same time he formed a mental picture of Darcy Austin in Magenta guise. His active imagination, again.

He gave a dismissive shrug. "Well, I don't expect we're looking for a woman. Assuming Jason O'Connell checks out, it doesn't seem likely it's any of your other visitors mentioned."

"I can't imagine it would be. And Jase can't be the one either," Darcy said. "He's a great kid with a pregnant wife at home."

"I'm sure you're right. Gotta do the drill, though," Hank offered in weak defense.

"Not that I think any of them are guilty, but why not a woman?" Darcy asked. "It doesn't take brute strength to hit someone over the head, does it?" It was like he was being sexist by not including a woman on his suspect list.

"Footprints," Hank said.

"What?"

"The footprints in your backyard. The ground was soft from all the rain we'd had, and there were some pretty well-defined impressions. Too big for a normal-size woman—so unless you tell me one of your female acquaintances is a giant . . ."

"Couldn't a woman put on oversized boots or something?" Darcy asked not yet ready to back away.

"Yeah, except the lab says the depth of the impressions calls for an 180-pounder or so, given soil saturation and ambient temperature that night. If it's a woman, we're back to pretty large." Then he paused, something occurring to him: "What made you say boots and not shoes, by the way?" He knew boots or heavy work shoes made the impressions outside her house but wondered how she arrived at that.

Darcy searched her mind, trying to conclude why she said what she did. Then: "The heavy steps . . ."

"Heavy steps?"

"I heard them—like hard-soled boots on the hardwood floor. Behind me."

"You never mentioned that."

"I didn't remember, until now . . . it just sort of came to me." Darcy said, followed by a deep swallow of her wine.

Their food arrived at the right moment for Darcy and the detective. They both needed a break about then. Unpleasant memories were being dredged up for her, and the investigation part of the evening had gone nowhere for him. The conversation turned to how the Minnesota Twins were doing and if they would get a new stadium after all the politicking was done. The Vikings, too. Important things like that.

LIEUTENANT HANKENSON DROVE Ms. Austin home in relative silence. He was no closer to anything than before. Darcy's house could have been invaded by someone other than an acquaintance familiar with the layout of her home and probably was. It was an easy place to case from the outside. The same questions remained that he discussed with Joe Baines at the office.

Still, if Minneapolis Cutlery was part of the intruder's plan, it did suggest someone who knew Darcy had a set of the knives in her home, and where to find it. And two Williams/Bailey client products were involved, if that was so. A coincidence? He didn't put much stock in coincidences.

DARCY SEEMED MORE settled than he, as they traced the sidewalk to her front door from the driveway. "I didn't know policemen could afford BMWs," she commented, having had it on her mind from the time he first picked her up in the Bimmer.

"Most BMW drivers can't, including me," he said smiling. "We just go into debt."

She'd also taken note of his expensive clothes. *Maybe he's on the take,* she considered. *Naa . . . not a Bloomington cop.*

Hank fidgeted as she unlocked the door and stepped inside to disarm her new alarm system, before returning to face him. "I'm really tired—got a full day ahead or I'd invite you in," she said. "Do you mind?"

Her statement was normally the kiss of death, but he believed her. He was exhausted too, and his next day didn't look like any reprieve, either. "No problem," he replied, feeling disappointment nevertheless.

"I haven't always acted like it," Darcy said, "but I do appreciate what you've tried to do for me through all this." Then lifting those gorgeous eyes to his added, "I really do, Hank."

It was the first time she called him Hank, and he felt a rush. *C'mon, Hank, you're acting like a school kid,* he reproached himself. More important, he wondered: *Am I breaking through, here?* "We're paid to serve," he finally offered. Not very clever.

"It's more than that . . ." her voice trailing off.

Was she giving him an opening . . . the Titanium Doll?

They stood looking at each other for a long moment. He wanted to draw her to him and kiss her but didn't know if she really wanted that, or would let him—the woman with no successful suitors that anyone knew of.

He held back. The moment passed. "Good night, Hank," she said in a soft voice, stepped back across the threshold and gently closed the door.

He wondered what the hell came over him? Damn. He'd never vacillated with a woman that way before. Why didn't he do what he felt like doing—the fear of rejection? Never bothered him until tonight.

But all was not lost, he consoled himself; she called him Hank not once but twice while he addled around. *Well, I guess that's progress, school-boy.*

He started the Bimmer, punched FM 99.5 FM, and began his drive home, to the salving strains of Felix Mendelssohn.

*Chapter* **17**

# P A T T E R N

**TEN DAYS AFTER** the Edson Janes murder, there was still no real headway in the case. The initial canvassing of Williams/Bailey employees produced nothing. Nor did the interrogation of clients, suppliers, and other persons with connections to the firm. The principal suspects in the minds of the investigating team, though not official, looked to be Frank Ramstead and Roland Bennett only because motive was established. There was a problem beyond that: lack of evidence.

Hank was at a loss. He'd seldom come across a murder with so little to run on, or even a hunch. Not that his experience with high-profile killings was extensive. Hell, it was nonexistent. But no clue at all? Maybe he was over his head—the thought occurred to him. Even so, he was the guy on the spot, and he had to deal with it. With Nadler and Ames gone, the only person he had around now with any seasoning in homicide was Joe Baines. He was a good man, but he had his limitations in these matters as well.

Much of the time it isn't astute police work that moves things from impasse but, rather, something dropping in out of the blue. Hank knew they needed a break of that kind if they were going to get anywhere on this case anytime soon. He could only hope such a thing would happen now. Just so it didn't involve another murder.

**"GOT THE HARDWARE?"** the man asked.

"Yeah. No way it can be traced, but you'll dump it in the Mississippi anyway," the second man answered.

"More obscure than that. Whacha got for me?"

"Thirty-eight Smithy—'bout as anonymous as it gets. Fitted with a can—case you run into trouble, unexpected like."

"I won't. The hammer?"

"A Winchester M70 carbine with a six and a half by twenty Leupold—more scope than you need. Short barrel's easy in tight quarters and still plenty good for the distance. Thirty-oh-six chamber."

"Good."

"Sure you want to go through with this one, pard?" He already knew the answer.

"Tired of being an accessory?" A question answered with a question.

"Just wonderin'. When haven't I been along for the full ride?"

"We know it's him. The gold pocket watch just nails it down. And it pisses me off even more."

"Me, too."

*Snick, snick.* The first man worked the action on the carbine like the expert he was.

The second man looked on, admiring the weapon. "How 'bout I get the Winnie back after you're done. It's a classic, made in '46. Shame to leave it at the scene."

"It's ballistic evidence if it's ever found in your possession."

"Not much chance of that. Really like to have it."

"Let me think about it."



**JOE BAINES HAD** his own thoughts. He agreed with Dex Ames' assessment while the Minneapolis cop was part of the team—Roland Bennett was the most likely suspect they had. But he put Frank Ramstead right up there. They each had motive, and their alibis weren't beyond reproach in his view.

Who the killer was, was one thing. How he managed to get in and out of Williams/Bailey, while getting past security, was another conundrum he grappled with. It took a key—or rather an activated card—to get into the offices after hours and the coding was changed with some frequency. That brought him to the idea of someone inside, helping out. If Bennett or Ramstead did the killing, an inside accomplice would almost have to be involved for either of them to gain access through the use of a card. And the killer needed to know that Edson Janes would be working late that night. Here again it suggested the help of an insider. It was either that or an insider was the killer and Bennett or Ramstead was the instigator, to his way of thinking. In any case, there still remained the problem of getting around security. Joe Baines wasn't an abstract thinker, and this exercise was giving him a headache. He swallowed two Anacins washed down with his cafeteria swill.



**IT TOOK AWHILE** before he was able to pick up his ringing desk handset and talk into it. He was still choking down the tablets that had turned to powder in his throat. Anacin worked best for him, but he wondered why the hell was it so hard to find the easy-to-swallow caplets instead of the round pills that would nettle a pachyderm. "Baines," he blurted into the phone as best he could, most of the second pill's remnants still lodged half way down his esophagus.

"Gotta cold, Sarge?" Detective Jeff Ortendahl asked.

"No, but CPR would help. What's up?"

"I'm in a warehouse building over in west Bloomington," Ortendahl said, his voice metallic and hollow over the cell phone.

"Yeah, I kin hear the echo."

"Joe, we got us a body here, and it's somebody we know from the Janes case."

"Holy shit. Who? How?"

"Well, a chicken leg's stuck in his throat, and I don't think he croaked on it by accident." No response. "You there, Sarge?"

"Just making sure I wasn't facing a like demise," Sergeant Baines rasped, clearing his throat again.

"What?"

"Never mind. How does he connect to the Janes case?" His larynx was doing better.

"You know that custodian guy we questioned at Williams/Bailey?

"Yeah."

"It's him. Name's Terrance R. Barnhard—readin' his ID, here."

"I remember. Works nights. You tell Hank yet?"

"Can't find him."

Joe Baines looked up. "Ah . . . that's because he's standing right here. What's that address you're at?"

*Chapter* **18**

# C O N N E C T I O N

**THERE IT WAS.** The open package of Gold'n Tender Chicken with its one missing item lodged deep in the throat of the dead man on the cement floor. Another lethal episode involving a product in the Williams/Bailey stable. Mrs. Svendsen's Soup, Minneapolis Cutlery and now Gold'n Tender Refrigerated Chicken.

And, this time, it couldn't be explained away as a "weapon of convenience." This time it was imported to the scene, the package displayed at the victim's side less anyone think he had choked to death on just any old chicken. It wasn't mealtime. Nor was the chicken cooked.

Hank pulled Tamara Hage away from the crime-scene investigators going about their meticulous work. The sight of the diminutive woman always astonished him. He was old enough to think medical examiners were supposed to look like Quincy from the TV series back then. She didn't look like she was from the cast of CSI, either.

"How long?" he asked.

"About two hours, from body cooling in relation to ambient temperature. Rigor's right for that, too," Tamara Hage answered in her tinny voice

made more so in the open surround of the building. Another incongruity—
Jack Klugman's Quincy sounded like 3M coarse-grain being put to hard
use. "It wasn't before 9:05 this morning, for sure," she added. "The building log shows someone was in here at that time, and everything was hunky-
dory. Not exactly high-tech stuff, that last part there."

Hank asked if the victim received a blow to the back of the head
before death? She squeaked in the affirmative as he expected she
might—the "squeak" as well as the "affirmative."

"The killer's having fun with us, Joe," Hank passed on to the col-
league at his side.

"Look's like our client thermon is provin' out," Joe Baines said. He
could have said "client theory," but he was trying to demonstrate the
breadth of his vocabulary.

"'Theorem,'" Hank returned. "Could be nothing more than a gim-
mick. Or maybe just the killer's signature—who knows—someone who
likes playing games. There's got to be more to it than that though."

"Well, his game ain't cribbage. That's for sure."

"The bigger question is, why do you die? Janes in the first place,
and now this guy? What's the connection?"

Before Joe could reply, Officer Marge Kennedy walked over with a
man in tow that she introduced as Brad Hoyt, owner of the warehouse
they were in. By way of introduction she explained that Brad Hoyt was
president and C.E.O. of Hoyt International, a developer of commercial
properties. Hank thought he remembered something about Hoyt being
mentioned as one of Bloomington's small business standouts, or some
such, in the Bloomington *Sun Current*.

"Pretty awful," Brad Hoyt said with a half-nod toward the body on
the floor, extending his hand to Hank, "something like this happening
in one of your own buildings."

"What do you know about him?" Hank asked, surprised at how young the casually dressed entrepreneur appeared.

"He works—did work, for us. Handyman stuff here and there. Moonlighted somewhere else."

"Yeah, we know," Joe Baines kicked in. "What was he doing here, today?"

"Electrical problem—breaker panel, I think. Not much maintenance in a space like this, but once in a while something needs fixing."

"Anybody else around here during the day?" Hank asked next.

"No. We use this building for miscellaneous storage. Nobody comes here unless they need something," Brad Hoyt explained. "Last winter I let a neighbor keep his Porsche and restored Mustang in here. Plenty of room, as you see."

"That how the body was discovered—somebody checking in for somethin'?" Joe Baines inquired.

"Right. Sam Dennison over there talking with one of your detectives," Brad Hoyt said, nodding to a man huddled fifteen feet to their left, Jeff Ortendahl taking copious notes.

"Thanks for coming over Brad, I know it's difficult," Hank said. Then asked: "You around if something else turns up we may want to ask about?"

"If I'm not in the immediate vicinity, I'll be somewhere in the five-state area for the next few days," Brad Hoyt replied. "I fly my own plane so I can always be back in a couple of hours if need be."

Hank perked up. "What do you fly?" He liked mechanical things.

"A Piper Saratoga and a Malibu. Had a problem with icing on the Saratoga once, that's when I got the Malibu. Got an order in for a prop-jet. It means more flight instruction, but it'll save me time in the end—the jet's a lot faster and has greater range. Can get me to Florida non-stop, where I've got some property."

Hank was listening with as much interest as Brad Hoyt was showing enthusiasm, talking about this. Here were two "toy" guys, and they knew it about each other by intuition. Joe Baines checked out. You wouldn't know there was a dead body a few feet away.

"I can take you up sometime if you like, Lieutenant," Brad Hoyt offered.

"Hank," Hank corrected. "Hey, I'd like that. Maybe after things settle down around here."

"Sure. Let me know." Brad Hoyt said, passing his business card to Hank. "That your Bimmer outside?" he asked, figuring he knew it was.

"The leasing company's letting me use it," Hank said.

"Great car. I had a 540. Got an SL600 out there now."

"Hey. I've always wanted to take one of those twelve-cylinder jobs for a spin."

"Be my guest."

"Take a rain check, on that, too," Hank said, filing away both of Brad Hoyt's offers in his mind. He liked this guy.


**"WHACHA THINK?" JOE** Baines asked his boss, back in the office.

"This one makes some sense to me, buddy boy," Hank answered.

"Wanna tell me?"

"Try this. Barnhard moonlighted crazy hours at Williams/Bailey. That we know. So, that night, he just happens to witness the Janes killing and recognizes the murderer. The killer wasn't aware of Barnhard, of course, or he would've offed him at the scene."

"I'm listenin'."

"Barnhard sets on blackmail. He tells the killer to bring the payoff to Hoyt's lonesome warehouse—a perfect spot, Barnhard thinks—where he's scheduled to be today, anyway. But Barnhard's not too sharp. He doesn't consider that it's also a perfect spot for a murder—his own."

"So, what you're sayin', the killer stuffs him with a Gold'n Tender thigh, leavin' his W/B signature for us."

"Like I said in the warehouse, Joe, the killer's having fun with us."

# Chapter 19

# T U R M O I L

**THE NEWS OF** the Barnhard murder was out soon enough, putting Williams/Bailey back in turmoil mode. Another employee was dead, if a minor one, and another of its clients' products was used as the dispatching devise. Both sides of this were distressing. Nor could one dismiss the prospect of someone else at Williams/Bailey being targeted next.

Other clients in the Williams/Bailey fold were getting antsy, as well. Could *their* products be used as murder weapons? If soup and chicken made it as terminating tools, what products could *not* be used for that purpose in the right, or wrong, hands of an innovative killer? Tuff-Wrap Plastic Trash Bags was especially concerned.

Knowing this had to be on their clients' minds made for another kind of anxiety at the agency. How many might bolt as a result? And there was the ultimate consideration: Could it result in the ruin of Williams/Bailey?

For now, there was no sign of client defection. Gold'n Tender matched the charitable contribution that Mother Svendsen's had posted, and put up a like reward leading to the arrest and conviction of the "perpetrator of these horrible crimes."

**PERHAPS THIS WAS** the end of it. The official position, and convention-al wisdom, was that the Barnhard killing and the Austin attempt were cover-ups for the Janes murder, and nothing more. Nevertheless, the agency and its clients remained nervous.

The media was going crazy. When had a case so bazaar hit the Twin Cities area, or anywhere else in the nation for that matter? The Rifleman assassinations, bad enough, didn't rival it. The second killing launched the case into a full-fledged national news story.

Hank was getting calls for TV appearances from across the coun-try, which he declined. "Too busy," was his standard dodge. Becoming a household face didn't appeal to him. Chief James Lott had no problem taking up much of the slack though, while Mayor Margaret Magneson pulled in the remainder. Both proclaimed they had the utmost confi-dence that the case would be solved in due course under Lieutenant Hankenson's competent direction. It was a public vote of confidence that took each of them off the hook by attributing all responsibility to Lieutenant Hankenson should he fail.

At least Hank could comfort himself in that they were keeping the newsies off his back.

**"DID YOU KNOW** him?" Lieutenant Hankenson inquired over the phone. Darcy Austin was becoming his eyes and ears inside Williams/Bailey.

While Mason Williams and the other two remaining principals of the agency, Jack Bailey and Martin Hatfield, were cooperative in their dealings with the police, he found that there was nothing like having someone in the trenches to turn up information that might prove critical down the road. In this instance, it was especially neat that his "mole" was who she was.

"Probably better than anyone at the agency, except maybe for Erica Carlson," Darcy said in answer to his question.

"How's that?"

"He worked at night, and Erica and I are regular night-timers around here. He came into the room where Erica and I were, ah, sorting things out about a month ago," she said, wondering why she brought up that incident in particular. "Saw him a couple of times since. Not sure about Erica."

"Anything else about him?"

"Not really. Quiet fellow, minded his own business. Not real bright, but nice. Good at what he did for us." She reflected a moment then said, "He seemed a little more distant after Ed Janes was killed, but lots of people were upset. No reason he shouldn't have been."

*Maybe something more was on his mind*, Hank didn't say.

Darcy went off in a different direction. "I can't believe Jessie Campbell, you know, my client at Gold'n Tender—she actually seems to be reveling in this. Instead of laying low like the Mrs. Svendsen's people, she's got us working up a promotion on chicken legs, if you can believe it. What're we supposed to call it, 'Thighs to Choke On'? It's insane."

*I guess every profession has its opportunists*, Hank reasoned, although this one was way out there. "Well, thanks for your help," he said, passing on her client travails. "Think of anything on Barnhard, I'd appreciate knowing." Then he added, after a pregnant pause: "Look, Darcy, things around here are still pretty hectic, but maybe we could slip out for lunch, or even dinner, one of these days. We just won't have chicken. Okay?"

"I'd like that," she said, surprising herself with the quickness of her response.

He didn't give her a chance to reconsider. "I'll call," and closed off.

Putting the phone down, Hank walked the hall to Joe Baines's office, catching him paging through a comic book. The sergeant started to duck the comic when he saw Hank coming, but it was too late for that.

"Picking up on your heavy reading I see," Hank said with a caught-ya grin on his face.

Giving up on any attempt to hide the comic book, Joe Baines tossed it out on his desk, face up. "It's *Magenta Comics*. Just doin' some research. Wanna take a look?"

Hank would rather have kept ribbing his associate but whisked the comic off the desktop and rifled through it. "Hey this Magenta babe's not bad," he commented along with a low whistle.

"Remind you of anybody?" Joe Baines said, waving his hand at the publication.

"Huh?" Hank looked up, uncertain, though he should not have been.

"Magenta. She look like anyone we both know?"

# Chapter 20

# C L O S U R E

**THE FIRST CLIENT** defection came on the following week. The RV division of Lakeland Boats and Recreational Vehicles announced it would leave Williams/Bailey from where, by the way, it had been assigned to Edson Janes' group at the agency. The other piece of news was that the division was moving to Bennett Advertising, where the embattled W/G expatriate and former Ed Janes rival, Roland Bennett, held forth. It wasn't the entire Lakeland account but it was a sizable portion of it. And the fact that Roland Bennett was the beneficiary of the move was of special interest to the Bloomington Police who held Bennett under unofficial suspicion in the Janes murder.

**IT COULD HAVE** been a coincidence of timing. It was no secret that Lakeland was not happy with Williams/Bailey for some time preceding Edson Janes' death, and Roland Bennett had worked on Lakeland in happier days while still employed at the agency. Things like this happen in the ad game. Yet, the business gain that dropped in Bennett's lap so shortly after Janes' death didn't look good from the conspiracy perspective.

Joe Baines was one of the speculators, and said to his boss, "Somethin' to it, you think?"

"If there is, I don't know what we do about it," Hank responded to his associate.

"But what's your take?"

"I don't know. Would you want things to unfold this way if you were Roland Bennett, under the eye of the police? Pretty blatant."

"Agreed, we don't have enough to bring 'em in with. But I'm stayin' close to the S.O.B. Whoever the killer is, he's been pretty blatant from the start, seems to me." There was no argument from Hank on that point.

DARCY LOOKED UP to Andrea Shiff standing in the doorway of her office. "Oh, hi, Andrea. C'mon in."

"Got a minute?" Andrea asked, pulling up one of the two chairs in front of Darcy's desk.

Andrea Shiff was a bit taller than Darcy, distributing more pounds over a larger frame. She wore nondescript clothing that was casual but still out of place at an agency like Williams/Bailey where even casual clothes bore designer labels. Her face was on the pale side, and her light brown hair was a near match to her complexion. She wore no makeup, which would have helped. Still, her features were pleasant enough and men noticed her abundant stature.

"Hectic as usual, but sure. What's up?" Darcy asked.

"Brace yourself." Then after hesitating: "Josh wants you for one of his episodes."

"Huh?"

"As Magenta."

"Just like that?" Darcy exclaimed. "Couldn't we have chatted about the weather or something before laying that on me?"

"Sorry. Had to get it out before I lost my nerve," Andrea offered, defensive.

Darcy knew what Andrea was proposing, and she didn't like it. "You're kidding. I can't do that. I won't do that. Tell Josh to do his recruiting at Deja Vu or Sheik's, not here. No, not me."

"I told him you'd respond this way, but he insisted I ask. He really wants you to do it."

Darcy was aware that Josh used live models for his comic books from time to time. Every one at the agency knew about it. He claimed it was how he got realism into his action depictions, although she always had a sneaking hunch there was more to it than just that. He had a special space built for his "combatants" to play out loosely scripted action scenes that he outlined in advance. The live-action choreographies were then recorded on video for when Josh did his final rendering. It was all pretty weird to Darcy, but it seemed to be affective for him. His stuff was pretty darn good, she'd heard.

"This is crazy." Darcy said. "Does Mason know about his son's lunatic request?"

"I think he does. You should talk to him."

"Oh, I will."

"Josh is right. You're perfect for Magenta, you know. I'd consider it."

"I already have," Darcy came back. "I'm going to Mason."

**"WHY NOT HUMOR** him?" Mason Williams said in his most consoling voice. "It's only for a bit. Then he'll move on. Take less than one week out of your time, he tells me."

Mason Williams had the look and manner of someone who'd be cast as the head of a advertising agency in a movie. Full head of gray-streaked hair, straight nose, and square jaw in combination with deft articulation and polished manner—packaged in a custom-tailored $2,000 suit. But as of right then, the eminent Mason Williams persona was not prevailing with the rankled Darcy Austin.

"Why me? There are a slew of women who would probably love doing it," she said with animation.

"He feels he needs you, Darcy—some titanic struggle with Samantha or somebody," Mason answered in defense of his son. "You know how Josh is . . . totally wrapped up in his characters."

It was apparent to Darcy that Josh had gone to his father before-hand to solicit his aid which, he no doubt guessed, would be needed in this instance. Mason was prepped and was applying the same persuasive powers that were instrumental in bringing many a client to Williams/Bailey. "I'll cover for you at the agency if you want to keep this quiet," the senior Williams continued. "Nobody around here needs to know you're even doing it if that's the way you want things. I'll say you're out of town on a new-business venture for me."

"I can't do it, Mason. I just can't."

"Why not? You've modeled before—it's not that much different, is it?"

"Parading around in a skimpy superheroine costume and wrestling with some woman on top of it? Not my idea of modeling."

"It's not real, it's choreographed—like a movie scene. Hollywood," Mason countered. Maybe that would do it.

"It's not a movie scene, and I'm not an actress, anyway." So much for the Hollywood ploy.

Mason Williams saw he wasn't getting anywhere and moved to Plan B. "Let me see," opening a file folder on his desk, examining it. "You're next review is five months away. How would you like it moved up to the end of the month?"

Darcy couldn't believe the transparency of his tack. "Are you buying me, Mason?" knowing he was.

"Not at all. You deserve it. This matter just called attention to an oversight on my part."

"Ah-huh." Darcy wasn't buying, but, at the same time, she also knew Mason ran a tight financial ship. He'd manipulate to the max, but he wouldn't short the agency by doling out money that was undeserved. Or would he?

"Actually, I've been thinking for some time that you're ready to move up a notch," he went on without heed to her "Ah-huh." "With our, ah, loss of personnel at the supervisory level, we need bolstering in the management area, and I'm confident you can provide some of it. The extra money is only fitting." He paused for effect, then dropped a big one: "With your promotion, we'll put Coquette Lingerie in your group." He was serving up one of the agency's plum accounts with its big budget, glamorous image and agreeable client.

*Higher management? Coquette?* Darcy twisted in her chair. "What about Garry Applequist?" she asked, trying not to show she was actually entertaining his proposal to her. "He's doing a great job, isn't he?"

"Sure. But Coquette needs more of a woman's touch. And we can use Garry's talents elsewhere."

"Lil Compton?" She asked next, referring to the AE on Coquette that worked under Garry Applequist.

"Lil's good, but she's still a little green—needs someone with your skills." Mason couldn't resist what he said next. It was delicate, but he thought it would help his cause by putting her on the defensive. "Ah, on the subject of lingerie . . . I'm reminded of a, shall we say, contest you and Jessie Campbell had in the office awhile back."

"You know about that?" Darcy exclaimed, feeling a blush burning into her cheeks.

"Please, Darc, everybody in the shop knew about it fifteen minutes after that meeting let out."

She should have guessed it would be so, but she had put the affair out of her mind as best she could and hoped that others in that session would pass it off as well. Pretty foolish. "Nothing like that will ever happen again," she said in a more subdued tone.

Mason saw how that shut her down some. *Good.* Then began his word messaging. "Darcy, Darcy. Don't worry about it. I know how contentious Jessie Campbell can be. I respect your spirit. I only brought it up because you might appreciate what I'm about to say all the more." The sage C.E.O. was about to play his final trump card.

"Oh?" Darcy was uncertain.

"As an associate management supervisor you'll need more freedom to operate in that capacity. That means less time spent dealing with our captious client. We'll assign a second AE on Gold'n Tender to handle grocer incentives and promotions. Can't have you bogged down with everyday affairs like that. Peter Gates will fill in there nicely, don't you think?"

*That would help.* Darcy saw where Mason was zeroing, and it held her attention.

"Plus, Jase O'Connell's ready to take on more responsibility. We'll move him to the AE spot. If that meets with your approval, of course."

It did.

Mason Williams sat back in his plush chair. "These moves should alleviate you of your everyday contacts with Ms. Campbell, I expect," he explained as though he needed to.

Darcy was overwhelmed. "You'll do all that?"

He had her, and he knew it. And he didn't even have to point out that someone who would hike her skirt up in a business meeting, should not be bothered by donning a perfectly good superheroine costume, skimpy or not. Of course, he would have phrased it with the utmost tact. He leaned forward and looked her in the eyes. "All of that. And I'll deal with Her Nibs—when she screams about it." Mason Williams rocked back again. "Now, Darcy," he said with a smile, "what are you going to do for me?"

"**Looks like it's** over," Sergeant Baines said as he entered his lieutenant's office with his palms held up, glancing toward heaven beyond the acoustic tile ceiling.

"No shit?" Hank Hankenson exclaimed from behind his desk, "What's happened?"

"Intercepted a call at the front desk from Edina. Bennett just committed suicide—how 'bout them apricots."

"Well I'll be damned," Hank rolled back his chair, not bothering to tender, "apples." "Any question it was suicide?"

"None. Even left a note," the sergeant replied. "Something like 'Don't know why, but I did it.'—that's the gist anyway."

"Where's the body now?"

"Still in his home at Indian Hills; his wife found 'im. Edina cops are waiting for us, seein' it connects to the Janes case."

**JOE BAINES WAS** close. The note read: "Two men dead—what have I done? God forgive me."

Roland Bennett's body was slumped over his desk, head turned to the side with an entry wound visible at his temple. One of his arms stretched toward the floor where his open hand hung over a nine-millimeter Beretta still lying on the carpet. The suicide note had water stains on it. His tears.

"When did it happen?" Hank asked his Edina equivalent.

Lieutenant John Almond answered, "His wife came home from exercising at Curves and found him like this—it was 9:12 a.m. when she called 911. She's upstairs under sedation. Pretty upset."

"Looks like a classic suicide, all right." Joe Baines concluded.

"Not much doubt there," the Edina policeman agreed. "You can see the powder burns, and I'm sure we'll find his prints on the gun. The guy was crying before he did it. Tear streaks on his face and blotches on the note. I'd say your Soup Murder just got a lid put on it."

"Looks that way," Hank acknowledged with a shrug. *Not funny*, he was thinking, *but maybe the truth. Maybe.*

*Chapter* **21**

# I N D U C T I O N

**DARCY DROVE NORTH** on 35W, wondering why she hadn't taken Highway 100 instead, with road construction compounding normal heavy traffic, then took the downtown exit onto Fifth Avenue South. On Fifth she passed through the fringes of the Minneapolis loop, coming to Washington Avenue where the old Milwaukee Road Railroad terminal had been rehabbed into a neat dining-shopping-entertainment complex after standing vacant as a major eyesore for umpteen years. There she turned left, heading north again, which seemed like it should be west to those not attuned to the offsetting bend in the city's downtown grid. A mile later she stashed her car at the curb, fed the two-hour meter and entered the Millhouse Building. Riding a lone elevator that jerked and bounced, she exited on the third-floor and walked down its long corridor. She stopped at a door marked Fantasy Publications and opened it.

"Thanks for coming," Andrea Shiff said, from where she was waiting in the anteroom on the other side of the door.

"Where's Josh and the rest of Fantasy?" Darcy asked, puzzled by the absence of other people.

"Oh. Josh and his minions are further down the hall—that's where we actually do the books," Andrea answered. "This is the anteroom for our video staging area. Dressing rooms over there," she said with a wave of her hand. "And the Pad Room's back around the corner. We have showers and a sauna in here. And there's a wardrobe and prop room, too. Pretty complete for our needs."

It was obvious to Darcy that this place took a little coin to build out. Comic books were not that lucrative as far as she knew, and this wasn't even the main office. *Mason must be a generous benefactor to his son's enterprise*, she thought. Then getting back to the immediate, she replied to Andrea: "The Pad Room?"

"That's where we do the enactments. It's a three-sided room, open in front with no ceiling. Had it built special."

"Yeah, I've heard about it. I wasn't sure what you called it."

"All the surfaces are padded so nobody gets damaged in the staging. Sometimes it's called the Bad Pad—a little humor there."

"Damaged? Bad Pad? I can't believe I'm hearing this," Darcy exclaimed.

"Well, damaged is a little strong, but it does prevent some inadvertent bumps and bruises," Andrea explained.

"Then why Bad Pad?"

Andrea ignored her, while lifting an object out of a clothing box on a nearby table. "Here it is." She smiled with pride, extending the deep-red garment to Darcy, "Tailored expressly for you—from the measurements you gave me."

Darcy looked the garment over with skepticism, if not alarm. "I'm supposed to wear that?" she gasped.

Andrea offered up a pair of matching underpants from the box, holding them out to Darcy with the thumb and forefinger of her other hand, a smile on her face. "Well, there's also these, now that you mention it."

"Oh, gee, that's a relief," Darcy responded. Darcy wore panties that scant, but they were out of view—not much of a certainty with the brief Magenta costume and its micro skirt.

"You can try it on in one of the dressing rooms over there," Andrea said, nodding across her shoulder in their direction. "We'll do the final nips and tucks when you come out. Then fit you with boots and gloves. I'm here to serve your every need."

"Well then, can you turn up the heat in here? I think I'm going to be chilly," Darcy said, as she accepted Andrea's offerings with resignation and headed toward the dressing room door with a "1" on it.

"Don't forget to take everything off before putting on the costume," Andrea called after her. "We want a good body fit, and Magenta doesn't wear a bra you know."

Darcy waved the garment from the dressing room door. "How *could* she wear one with this getup," she said before closing the dressing room door behind her, not knowing why she even bothered.

ANDREA LOOKED HER over with approval when Darcy reappeared in her stingy attire, circling the uneasy account woman. "Looks great. How does it feel?"

"A little loose in the waist."

"I see that. An easy tuck will do it."

"And kinda snug up here." Darcy held her hands at chest level.

"I thought I allowed enough, but guess not. What do you measure? Not cup size, there's no cup."

"So I've learned. Thirty-six, like I told you."

"That's what I worked to."

"Maybe just a little more, then," Darcy said, as though apologizing for her abundance.

"Umm-hmmm, right. Well, a little extension at the neck will take care of things."

*Does she have to say, things?* "And what about here, and here?" Darcy asked, traversing her hands from the halter's deep cleavage to its abbreviated sides.

"So some of you shows—it's supposed to. Don't worry, the essentials are covered," she said as if there were nothing to be concerned about. "You've probably worn evening gowns with as much exposure."

"That's different," Darcy said, looking down her front with unease. "Where's the mask? I think I need to hide my identity."

"We don't use a mask. It can hinder vision and Josh doesn't want a mask hiding facial expressions on his videos. He sketches in Magenta's mask when he draws, of course."

"Too bad. There goes anonymity." Pause. "What's this about expressions?"

Andrea ignored the question. "How's it overall?" she asked with a sweeping gesture of her hand toward Darcy's fittings.

"Just dandy. The top's skimpy, the skirt's dinky with a slit in it, and the underpants are tight as hell with hardly anything back here." Her hands were at her derriere as she finished her litany. "Otherwise it's fine," opening her hands at her sides in a concluding gesture of hopelessness.

"You'll get used to it. Looks great to me," Andrea smiled, lowering her head for closer inspection, making Darcy all the more uncomfortable standing there half naked. "Josh had me, well, enhance the other Magentas we've had. No need this time. You really are Magenta, you know."

"Thanks, I think."

Andrea continued to fidget with the costume as though perfecting a work of art, which struck Darcy as ludicrous. "How'd you get into this insane business, anyway?" she asked.

"Used to be a nurse. Now I'm a nursemaid—to Josh. Kind of follows, doesn't it?" Andrea smiled.

"No."

"Anesthesiology was my area."

"You didn't like it?"

"Put me to sleep."

Darcy rolled her eyes. "Bad, Andrea, bad."

"Actually, I found the job about as soporific as the patients under the knife. Then I met Josh—in a bar, no less. He told me what he did, and I was fascinated."

"With Josh, or the profession?"

"Some of both, got to admit. Anyway I'm here—reasonably happy and making more money besides."

Darcy wanted to utter something like, "To each his own," but thought it too clichéd. "Happy and more money is good," she said, instead. Not much better.

After a final admiring glance at her tweaking, Andrea turned away from Darcy and spread open a large file of layout sheets on a nearby table. "Here're storyboard roughs you can take with you and look over if you like," she said.

*I guess we're done doing clothes,* Darcy said to herself "Can I put a robe on, or something?" she asked, folding her arms across her chest.

"Oh sure, sorry. There's a robe over here in the other dressing room," Andrea said, hustling to retrieve it.

Darcy looked over the storyboards. "Good grief, looks like two women mud wrestling," she exclaimed, donning the fetched terry cloth and tightening it around her waist.

"Magenta's battling Vixen in this board, and she's having her rubber match with Sadanna in the other one. Magenta and Sadanna have fought twice before this—neither battle was conclusive. That's you there," she said pointing to the storyboard depictions of Magenta in action.

"Good to I see I win in both of these," Darcy said with some sarcasm. "How close do we stick to the so-called script?" She almost feared asking. "Seems like it would be kind of hard to control, just looking it over. And do I like that?"

"We try to adhere to the boards, but to tell you the truth, they're more of a guide than anything. But that's okay, some of Josh's best stuff comes when things sorta just happen."

"Like maybe a real fight breaking out—*that* sorta just happen?"

Andrea played things down. "Sometimes there's a little over zealousness—but we step in quick if any thing serious starts," she said, moving around the basic question. "Other than that, Josh wants it to be pretty free form. In any event, his magic pen takes over in the end—the Night Vigilante always comes out on top, on paper. It's attitude and moves he's most interested in. That's why he videotapes everything, so he can capture it.

*And not just for the drafting board*, Darcy suspicioned to herself. "He's crazy. And what's this about Magenta always comes out on top, on paper?"

Andrea shrugged. "You know what I mean."

Darcy didn't, but she went on. "Who are these women I'm supposed to frolic with in your Bad Room?"

"A girl named Holly Hartley will do Vixen. She's done small theater around town and stints at Solid Gold—you know, those fake girlfights they have on stage there. She knows her way around this sort of thing. Caren Dalton is lined up for Sadanna. Never done this before—she's an attorney downtown. You'll be one battle up on her, after Vixen."

Darcy was incredulous. "Where do you find these women, anyway? They can't all be under the thumb of Mason Williams."

"It's kinda like show business," Andrea explained. "Some women think it's exciting. They put it on their resumés, brag it up to their friends. Or they can stay anonymous if they want. We never publicize the participants. They're on their own in that respect—can go away quietly if they like."

"Gee, something for everyone."

"Sort of. And we do pay them. Give them copies of the videos, if they want. Never had a turndown there. Maybe it's to show their boyfriends, I don't know."

"Oh, my." Darcy said shaking her head. Then, "When do we do it?"

"Next month. So you'll have plenty of time to prepare. We'll do Vixen on the seventeenth and Sadanna a week later on the twenty-fourth. Then you're done."

"All this preparation for two lousy days."

"We only do it a couple times a year. In order to keep things fresh for Josh, and for—"

"I know. Realism."

Andrea paused for a long moment, then confided, "You're in good shape an' all, Darcy, but use the time to get ready, okay? Choreographed or not, you just could get tested a little in there," nodding in the direction of the unseen Pad Room. "Nothing serious, but you won't want to be embarrassed by a rash of spontaneity, would you? Just a caution."

"No, I wouldn't like that at all." *Caution or warning*—she wondered.

"Let's finish that costume," Andrea said. "Then, Josh would like to see you for a minute before you go."

"Yeah, after changing out of this thing," she answered. *I'd like to say a few words to him, too*, which she kept to herself.

*Chapter* **22**

# Enlightenment

**DEPARTING THE ANNEX**, Darcy followed the hallway farther down to a more opulent plaque reading, Fantasy Publications. She entered the lobby and stood facing an unoccupied reception desk. The back wall of the lobby was foreshortened at one end, which appeared to provide an opening to an area beyond. In the absence of a live person to direct her, she passed through the opening, finding her way into a large workspace on the other side of the wall. This was the real Fantasy Publications.

The setting was not atypical of an advertising agency's creative department. Eight offices lined the perimeter of the opening, three along each side with two more at the far end having the only windows in the place. In one of the end offices, she could make out Josh Williams at his drawing board some fifty feet distant. An office along the wall to her right was larger than the others and disordered with file folders, loose magazines, papers, and layout roughs. It appeared to be both a conference room and giant "junk drawer" for the firm. People working at large-screen Mac computers occupied four of the other offices. Another side office was unoccupied but looked lived in. Freestanding, in the center of the bullpen area, was an oversize copy machine capable of large-size document replications in four-color. And tucked into one corner of the bullpen was an ever-present coffee stand with sink, countertop microwave, and small refrigerator, which no functioning organization could do without.

Glancing about, Darcy's attention was drawn to a display on the opposite side of the wall of the reception area she had just passed by. And, since nobody seemed to notice her presence as yet, she turned to examine the display out of curiosity before heading for Josh's office.

The center of the display was dominated by a large illustration of Magenta in a heroic pose—wide, long-legged stance, clenched fists on her hips, and a skyward tilt of her head like she was staring into the beyond. On either side of her were Fantasy's other two comic book heroes, Sterling and Cobalt.

STERLING WAS FANTASY'S male superhero in tights. He was a noble hero with great strength and skill but an Achilles' heel. Or better put—an Achilles' jaw. Bad guys landing a punch had done him in on occasion. Cobalt, on the other hand, was a costumed antihero who didn't like people very much—bad or good. He was most often on the side of right, although the authorities were never quite sure of that. His dour demeanor didn't help his image but, nevertheless, he was one tough hombre. Once, in a crossover issue, he and Sterling clashed, and Sterling got clobbered by him. In other of Fantasy's crossover issues, Cobalt rescued Magenta once, and Magenta bailed Sterling out of a tight spot in another episode. Cobalt, it seemed, didn't need any help from his stable mates.

---

**DARCY READ FROM** a reproduction in the display taken from the conclusion of a particular *Magenta* episode: An observer asks a cop on the street, "That was her, wasn't it—the Night Vigilante? Where does she disappear to, anyway?" The cop answers, "We don't ask and don't care—we just stand back and admire her like everyone else." So was it with Magenta's readers.

All this was foreign lore to Darcy, as she continued to browse.

Below the large depictions of the three Fantasy stars was an array of cover reproductions under the heading, "The Golden Age of Comic Books." Darcy recognized Superman, Batman, Captain America, Captain Marvel, and Wonder Woman—superheroes familiar to the uninitiated such as she. And while unaware that many of the covers she was observing represented prized collector issues, they did shed light on other aspects of comic book history that she found interesting.

There was Superman, hoisting a car overhead, on the cover of *Action Comics*, which she had never heard of, instead of a cover entitled *Superman*, as she would have thought. Batman swung from a rope, over a city scape at night. Gotham, she supposed, from the Batman movie she'd seen. But here he was on a cover entitled *Detective Comics*. And he was without Robin. Wonder Woman, far different from her present-day configuration, snapped a chain binding her wrists on the cover of *Sensation Comics*. Captain Marvel whizzed through the air in *Whiz Comics*. And Sheena, Queen of the Jungle, tossed a spear at a charging lion on the cover of *Jumbo Comics*—all comic book titles she was previously unaware of.

Her attention drifted next to superheroes she didn't recognize. The Spectre displayed on *Fun Comics*; the Blue Beetle on *Fox Comics*; the Shield on *Pep Comics*; Blackhawk on *Military Comics*; and Human Torch and Sub-Mariner on *Marvel Comics*. Bulletman and Bulletgirl, Aquaman, Hawkman, and Green Lantern had their own comic book titles, and the Flash and Hawkman, were featured in *Flash Comics.*

Female superheroes were arranged below Magenta's large portrait. Black Cat, Lady Luck, Blonde Phantom, Supergirl, Mary Marvel, and the jungle queens: Sheena, Lorna, Tigress, and Ruhla. One superheroine, Phantom Lady, was shown on three separate cover reproductions, and Darcy wondered why she was so prominent. Then she caught it—the relevance. Phantom Lady was brunet, donned a blue costume sans gloves, boots, or mask, but other similarities were there. Lush flowing hair, familiar costume design, voluptuous body, provocative demeanor and that "attitude." "So that's, the derivation," she said under her breath. *Josh, you devil— retro look and all.*

Mounted in the lower corner of the display, Darcy noticed a framed inscription entitled: The War against Comic Books, which she went about reading:

> Dr. Fredrick Wertham, an anti-comic book crusader, published his book, *Seduction of the Innocent*, in 1954. He charged that comic books corrupted youth and debased culture. His book caught the attention of "civic minded" organizations, which prompted an investigation by the U.S. Senate Subcomittee on Juvenile Delinquency headed by Chairman Estes Kefauver.
>
> In response to the perceived threat of censure, major comic book publishers banded together and created the Comics Code Authority, adopting what it called, "the most stringent code in existence for any communications media."
>
> Thus began the decline in the Golden Age of Comic Books, as efforts to comply with the self-imposed code diminished

popular titles—most new titles in compliance with the Code, also failing. The comic book falloff was drastic.

In 1956, revisions of some popular superheroes revived the culture and led to the "Silver Age of Comic Books," that included such new titles as the Amazing Spiderman, Fantastic Four, the Hulk, Thor, X-Men, and Vampirella.

While Dr. Wertham's accusations and the suppressing Comics Code Authority had brought about a serious decline in comic books, within a few years, titles were once again flourishing in a free marketplace. In the final analysis, the comic book furor proved to be much ado about nothing. Today, Dr. Wertham's most hated title, *Phantom Lady*, is on every comic book collector's "most wanted" list—particularly #17, "The Bondage issue"—that he singled out for special reproach in his book.

Filled with more comic book erudition than she knew existed, and after a studied glance back at *Phantom Lady* #17, Darcy crossed the bullpen area to Josh Williams' location at the windowed end of the space. He was still concentrating on his work and hadn't noticed her approach. "Knock, knock," she said outside his open door.

"Hey, Darc, c'mon in," Josh said, looking up from his board where, Darcy could see, he was doing pencil figures on a pre-paneled layout sheet. Josh jumped up, extended his hand, and pointed Darcy to a steel-rimmed leather sling chair. "Sorry the receptionist wasn't here to show you in. Out doing errands."

"No problem. Gave me time to look around," Darcy said, fitting herself into the embracing chair. "Even learned some things about comic books."

"Crazy business," he nodded. "But I love it."

Josh Williams was in his early thirties. He wore a pullover knit jersey, jeans that had been around awhile, and sandals strapped to his feet—the "uniform," more or less, of his culture. Tall and well built, he was a good-looking man once Darcy got past his unkempt blond hair and near-invisible "stash" and chin whiskers. On scrutiny, Darcy thought he resembled his own comic-book character Sterling. She had to wonder: *If artists draw in their own image, as it's said, and as seemed to be the case here, how was it Josh did Magenta and other women so well?*

His physical appearance and stature would have made his father proud, were he to follow the senior Williams' path at the agency—with commensurate grooming, of course.

"Thriving enterprise you've got here," Darcy said, shifting her bottom in the snug leather sling. "You do all the pencils for Fantasy?"

"All the action figures, anyway. What we call a background penciller fills in the rest of the panels. When that's done, it all goes to the inker for, well . . . inking."

"Does the inker do the lettering, too?" Darcy asked, interested in the process.

"No, that's done on a Mac. But a Mac colorist gets it even before that. All that used to be done by hand—but no more. Big savings in time, fuss, and money."

"I can imagine. Computers changed the ad world, too," Darcy commented. Then added: "Do you write the dialog?"

"I do all the concepting, but no. Andrea writes the dialog for Magenta, under the pseudonym of Gregory Roche. Can't have it be known a woman is writing a book for late teens and young men, ya know."

"Hey, not fair."

"Sorry. Another writer does Sterling and Cobalt. Ted Baxter."

"Like Mary Tyler Moore's Ted Baxter?"

"Same name, anyhow. Mary's Ted Baxter died a few years back."

"I guess I knew that. I thought Andrea was your business manager."

"That too—and special assistant. Important woman around here."

"How about production and traffic?"

"Our production manager doubles on traffic. Traffic's not as big for us as it is at the agency."

"Neat. Anyway, you wanted to see me," Darcy said.

"To thank you, and say how glad I am you're doing this."

"Your father can be very persuasive," she said. "And rewarding, when it serves his purpose. He's got me believing I deserve a promotion."

"That's Dad," he said with a knowing smile. "But you know Darcy? I've always thought you were the perfect Magenta. Just afraid to ask, I guess."

"Hmm."

"How'd the fitting go, by the way?"

"Andrea's doing a few nits. And you were right to be afraid to ask. This thing's ludicrous, Josh."

"Not so much as it seems. Three years ago my stuff was boring the shit out of what readers I had. Circulation was in the toilet. When your core readers are in their late teens and middle twenties, it's hard to get by with stock biff-bam crap—and that's what I was putting out. Till I hit on this idea. It's made all the difference. Lots of comics have fooled around with live models, but we take it all the way to live action. Got three cameras going for different perspectives. It's done it for me. Circulation's ten times what it used to be."

"Just women models?" she challenged, still not buying it all.

"Taped a few episodes with men, but the payoff isn't as big. Basically that's biff-bam stuff with a twist or two. It's where I got the idea for Sterling's glass jaw, though. Too bad about the guy that got flattened in the Pad Room that time.

"Flattened? Oh, fine. What am I letting myself in for?"

Josh Williams ignored her and went on with his spiel. "Magenta doesn't have serious fights with men. She just bops them over the head with something or gains some advantage through smarts."

"Like dropping a safe on a poor sap?"

"That's the idea, but more subtle, I hope. Can't have her rolling around on the turf with goons—not believable when she wins that way. Other females, it's different. Our readers want Magenta to be strong, but also vulnerable. She always wins but not easily."

"More sensual that way, isn't it?" It was a rhetorical question, and before he could respond, Darcy added, "Are those the videos from your Bad Pad or whatever it's called?" She was gesturing to the rows of cassettes on his office shelves.

"Uh, yeah. Among others," he replied. "Why?"

"Rather handy. You don't peek at them now and again after you're through working with them, do you?" She asked it as though she already knew the answer, which she suspected she did.

"Clever girl, Darcy. I won't bullshit you. They can have their prurient side."

"'Woman,'" Darcy corrected. Then flat out: "Tell you what. I want my videos done on non-reproducible cassettes and turned over to me when you're finished using them for your sordid stories. Or, so help me, Josh, I'm not going through with this. Your father be damned. And I'm not bullshitting you, either."

Josh knew she wasn't. "All right Darcy," he said after some hesitation. "You got it."

# Chapter 23

# E U P H O R I A

EVERYONE WAS SATISFIED that the demise of Roland Bennett put an end to the Soup Case. Under suspicion all along, the evidence against him was substantial, and now it was punctuated by his suicide and the note he left behind.

He had motive. He detested Edson Janes. Their feud led to Bennett's leaving Williams/Bailey. And Janes' legal harassment kept him off balance with his upstart enterprise.

The police assumed that Bennett knew how to gain access to the offices of Williams/Bailey during off-hours, having worked there for so many years beforehand, and how to circumvent security measures in the building.

Circumstantial evidence mounted. Not only was Bennett aware of Edson Janes' late-night work habits, he knew Janes had been behaving true to form on the night of the murder. The marketing director of Lakeland had told him that Janes was putting together a last-ditch counter proposal to keep the Lakeland business from moving to Bennett's shop, and Janes was working around the clock to perfect his presentation. Bennett could have confirmed what he had to know about Janes' comings and goings from any number of people at Williams/Bailey without raising suspicion.

Also, he could have made the attack on Darcy Austin after the news broadcast that implicated her as an eyewitness to the murder. Living in Edina, not far from the Austin home, he'd be able to arrive on the scene between the times of the broadcast and the assault. He was a large man as well, befitting of the footprints left at the scene, although the footwear that made the impressions had not been found.

Bennett was now thought to have murdered Terrance Barnhard when the custodian, revealing himself to Bennett as witness to the murder, tried to blackmail him. The police were able to corroborate the blackmail scheme from phone records listing a number of calls from Barnhard's apartment to Bennett's home and office. Barnhard was not smart about covering his tracks, the police came to know.

Bennett had full knowledge of Williams/Bailey clients as well. Using client products to dispatch his victims would serve as vindictive irony for a man who harbored hateful feelings toward the firm that had pushed him out.

Finally, his suicide note carried the message that his killing spree proved too much for him in the end. And the fact that he was mired in debt could have also contributed to his suicidal state of mind.

MAYOR MAGNESON WAS delighted with her administration's conduct in the affair; Chief Lott was even more delighted with his department's performance; and the press was ecstatic with the dramatic closure they could milk for days on end. As for Lieutenant Hankenson, he was relieved it was over—sort of.

While matters in the case seemed to fit into place, two things still nagged at him. How exactly did Bennett beat the security system in the building? And would he likely know about the Minneapolis Cutlery in Darcy's home if it were in his plan to call attention to that particular knife, as he suspected it was? But, where was the knife? It wasn't found in Bennett's home or office. He resigned himself to the fact that he might never learn the answers. Unless something were to surface.

On the other hand, Joe Baines was elated. "I told you Dex Ames had a nose like a Bloodhound. He suspected Bennett from the beginning."

"That's Sig Nadler's nose you were telling me about," Hank came back.

"Well, Dex is the same breed."

"And you said 'Doberman.' 'Nose like a Doberman.'"

"A dog's a dog."

"Tell that to K9. They'll sic Cujo on your ass. He's no Pomeranian."

"Hey, I'm happy as an oyster. You should be, too. It's over. We got our man."

"He gave himself up—in a manner of speaking. And it's 'clam.'"

"You had the blackmail part figured out. Be happy with that. You're a hero. Case closed, uh . . . tight as a drum. How's that?"

"Fine."

"He must have known we were breathing down his neck," Joe Baines said.

"We weren't that close to nailing him," Hank reminded. "Besides, I got a feeling there's more here than we're seeing."

"Yeah? Like what?"

"Not sure, chum—not sure at all. Let's forget it for now and go have a bowl of soup at Byerly's," Hank said, checking his watch.

"Why didn't I think of that? We can have their chicken and wild rice soup—even enjoy it now."

"Yeah. Well, let's just watch each other's back while we're slurping it down. Okay?"

**A COLLECTIVE SIGH** of relief passed through Williams/Bailey. It was over at last. No more back-of-the-mind thoughts of a murderer lurking in the agency's midst. And the impending threat of client departures was also gone—no small thing.

Mother Svendsen's and Gold'n Tender were even off the hook on reward money, since no citizen was responsible for "arrest and conviction." That meant money wasn't going to come out of ad budgets, which corporations were wont to do when dealing with expenses that cropped up out of the blue. Morale at the agency was sky high for that reason alone.

**MASON WILLIAMS STOOD** by his promise. Darcy was named Associate Management Supervisor reporting to Martin Hatfield, who had taken over the lion's share of Edson Janes' duties at the agency. Thus raised a notch in the firm, she was out of Jessie Campbell's day-to-day sights. Her handsome increase in salary seemed almost inconsequential compared to that. Almost.

Darcy knew she still had to fulfill her part of the bargain with Mason Williams, and she had no intention of reneging. She was enjoying her new position too much. Nor did she feel guilty about her promotion. She deserved her new status on merit when she analyzed it, even though she never expected all the side bennies she got out of the deal. Like less of Jessie Campbell. Although most everyone at the shop was forthcoming with their sincere congratulations, she also knew there was bound to be resentment among some. It's just the way things go.

Marty Hatfield, her new boss, was an amiable sort, more open and pleasant than the sometimes dour Edson Janes. She admired Hatfield's professional competence, as she had Janes' before. He, in turn, was pleased to have Darcy as his chief associate. He would need her assistance in filling the void left by the departed senior executive.

Mason Williams expected the new alignment to work out to the agency's advantage. And to this extent he had snookered Ms. Austin. He planned to promote her to her new position and grant her relief from Jessie Campbell even if the Magenta issue had not come up. But why not satisfy that matter at the same time? He was a sly fox who knew how to finesse things in his agency.

JESSIE CAMPBELL WAS all over Jason O'Connell now that he had taken Darcy's place as her principal contact at the agency—accepting the change in her agency team with only minimal howls of protest. She still demanded brilliant execution in the same insane amounts of time she allotted for such things, but Jason O'Connell didn't seem to mind her mandates as much as Darcy had. He was young, eager to make his mark, and the marketing director played to that. There was another reason Jessie Campbell was placated. Instead of the bullying tactics she used on Darcy, she was able to exercise her feminine wiles when she needed Jason to jump through hoops, which mollified her and didn't disturb him—not in a negative sense, anyway. Then too, Mason Williams had provided her with a second AE in the promotional arena to pound on in a more traditional sense. She had it both ways.

While Darcy was elated about her situation at the agency, she didn't look forward to what she felt she must do next. Nor could she put off doing it.

*Chapter* **24**

# P R E L U D E

**THE ART DIRECTOR** lifted her eyes from her drawing board, almost successful in hiding her surprise at who she saw at her office door.

"Got a minute?" Darcy Austin inquired, working hard to disguise her discomfort. "I'd like to ask you something."

"Sure, why not," Erica Carlson responded with a half smile, pushing back from her work.

Darcy took a seat opposite her, and sat silent for a time, like she didn't know how to start. Which she did not.

"I've never known you to be reticent before, Darc . . . that and the fact that you're here tells me you've got a big problem," Erica Carlson quipped.

"You could say that," Darcy responded, breaking her silence. "And I do need your help."

"Well how about that." The art director tilted back in her swivel chair and clasped her hands behind her head. "This isn't a professional call is it?"

"No, not in the sense you mean."

"What then?"

"I'd like you to work with me. You know . . . on the mat."

"You're kidding. Why? So you'll be better prepared the next time we get into it in the office?" The art director threw up her hands. And before Darcy responded, she added in another tone altogether: "Congratulations on your promotion, by the way. You deserve it. Whatever our differences, I always thought you were good at what you do." Erica Carlson may have been a bitch but she was a forthcoming bitch.

Darcy didn't know which of those statements to address first, then decided on the second. "Thanks, Erica. I especially appreciate that coming from you." And, she did.

The art director shook off the comment with a toss of her head and returned to Darcy's initial request. "Wanna let me know why the mat?"

"I'd like to keep this quiet. Okay?

"And that is . . . ?"

"I'm going to do this thing for Josh and—"

"Don't tell me," Erica Carlson leaped in, "you're going to do one of his Magenta gigs." *Is that how she got her promotion?* Erica wondered. *Oh, well, she really did deserve it.*

"I'm afraid so."

"I'll be damned." *Why not, she's perfect for it.* "And you want me to help you so you don't get bounced on your fanny. Right?"

"Well, ah . . ." *Might as well face up to it.* "Yeah, that's about it."

The art director was silent for a time, looking down at her lap and tapping her fingers on her board. She questioned if she really wanted to help this woman who antagonized her so much in the past, despite giving Darcy credit for having the guts to come to her for a favor like this. Another consideration came to mind: she wouldn't mind kicking a little ass here.

Erica Carlson returned her eyes to the uncomfortable woman waiting for her response. "When do you want to start?" she asked.

**WITH THE DEMANDS** of the Soup Case off his back, Hank had the time to choose dinner over lunch before he punched the numbers on his remote handset.

"Congratulations," Darcy Austin extended, recognizing her caller's voice.

"And to you," he said, "I'm told you've moved up in the world."

"How did you know? It was just announced two days ago, and you've been a stranger longer than that."

"We cops keep close tabs in our jurisdiction. Watch your speed in Bloomington, by the way. I don't want to have to bring you in."

"Already had the treatment, remember? I suspect there'd of been a bare light bulb hanging from the ceiling of a dingy room if it were at your place instead of mine."

"I could've blown cigarette smoke in your face. I didn't do that did I?"

"We have a smoke-free office."

"Hey, I protect women. You tell me a man ogles you, I'll do a Terry on 'im and slap 'im with a ninety-dollar citation."

"Bloomington doesn't have an anti-ogling ordinance—that's Minneapolis."

"What Minneapolis does is good enough for me. I also bust little kids for spilling cones and dropping candy wrappers in Moir Park."

"Ridiculous law."

"Littering?"

"No, anti-ogling. What's a Terry, by the way."

"Police talk. It's a *pat down* on TV. I didn't do that to you either."

"Oh, I'm so grateful. Do you Terry women often?"

"We have woman cops for that. Don't want NOW after us. But you remind me, it's a woman I'm calling about."

"And who might she be?"

"That advertising lady with reddish hair. Want to know if she'd have dinner—like Friday night."

"I'll check."

"I'll hold."

Suitable pause.

"Says she'd like that."

"Seven sharp?"

"Says she'll be ready."

*Chapter* **25**

# Z E N I T H

**HE LIKED TO** think of Kincaid's as "Great Gatsby modern," the framed prints on the walls of the restaurant remindful of scenes from the St. Paul author's classic, set against tasteful contemporary architecture.

In this setting, Lieutenant Douglas L. Hankenson lifted his shallow glass of Talisker single-malt Scotch, no ice, to Ms. Darcy M. Austin's stemmed martini glass of blue-hued Bombay Sapphire gin and Tribuno, no ice.

"Congratulations, officially," he toasted.

"You too, officially," she returned.

Hank took a sip from his glass, put it down with pronouncement and looked up at the chimera across the table from him. "No intimate male friends, never been engaged. What have you got to say for yourself, young lady?"

"And you? You're a lot older than me, and what have you accomplished in that arena."

"Couldn't find anyone that would have me—and don't give me that back."

"Okay, you're not a lot older. Just older. "

"Not what I meant."

"I'm the Titanium Doll, didn't you know? No man wants that."

"Nice try lady, but I still don't buy it."

"What, the titanium part?"

"No, the man part."

"Oh, so I *am* the Titanium Doll?"

More like something molded at the hand of God, Hank thought but said, instead: "Golf clubs are titanium. Not a whole lot of resemblance I can see."

"Oh, gee, thanks a lot," she said, but her smile let him off the hook. "You probably know more about me from your snoops than I do about you."

"Snoops?" he asked with feigned indignation.

"Investigators, then."

"Much better. My snoops are professionals."

"We have snoops at our place, too—only they're called market researchers." Darcy then asked, "What got you into police work in the first place, Lieutenant?"

"My older brother, I think."

Darcy caught the tone variant. "Did I touch on something, Hank? I'm sorry."

"Don't be. He was a Minneapolis narc cop who got killed. That's all."

"And you followed in his footsteps? Tell me to stop if you don't want me prying into personal matters that might be hurtful to you."

Hank didn't shake her off. "Something like that. I'm not sure I really know myself. One day I was a high-tailed U of M grad with two sheepskins, headed for the business world like a normal person. Then Brian was killed, and here I am." He reflected a moment before adding,

"Don't know that I'd get accepted on the force, today—especially in a suburban location like Bloomington. But that's another story."

"Oh? Tell me."

"Sure you want to know, it might offend your feminine sensitivities?"

"I'll brace myself."

"Acceptance boards don't smile kindly on male WASPs these days." he said. "Hankenson is hardly Anglo-Saxon, but it doesn't matter—even in Minnesota, where Scandinavians are supposed to reign supreme. I'm afraid white males of any European derivation are getting to be an endangered species on police rosters."

"I'm used to thinking of women as workplace victims," Darcy responded.

"I'm sure they are in certain cases."

"Thankfully, it's not the case in advertising," Darcy said. "Women were accepted in the business before the feminist movement ever got started."

"This is getting way too serious," Hank grinned. "We're supposed to be having fun. You know about Ole and Lena?"

"Am I a Minnesotan? Is the Pope Catholic? Does a bear do what bears do in the woods? Of course, I know about Ole and Lena," Darcy smiled.

"Well how's this, then. Lena dropped dead at home, speaking of somber, and Ole called the Bloomington coroner's office."

"Oh, no," Darcy fawned, "How dreadful."

Hank slipped into a bad dialect:

"Ya, an' Ole asks the coroner, 'Kin yoo git 'er at da hoose, hare?'

"'Where do you live?' the coroner wanted to know.

"'Too foorty-too Eucalyptus,' Ole sez.

"'Can you tell me how to spell that,' the coroner asks?

"After a long pause, Ole finally sez, 'How bout I drag 'er doon to Oak Street 'n' yoo pick 'er up dar?'"

Darcy rolled her eyes and stifled a laugh. "I think it's time to order."

"Have you looked at the menu?" he asked.

"Not food, another martini," she said.

Forty minutes later Hank had done away with his ten-ounce, medium, but still pink, prime rib. Darcy had Atlantic salmon with Cajun sauce and did a pretty good job in almost finishing it. They shared a custard crème brûlée for dessert—Hank yielding on the "world's smallest chocolate sundae" he'd deliberated over but decided against. Sharing a crème brûlée was more romantic he concluded. Good move.

**DARCY DIDN'T DISMISS** him at the door this night, inviting him in for an after-dinner drink instead. It was an offer he had no intention of refusing.

Hank sat waiting on the davenport—a sofa or couch, really—davenport being a colloquialism for that form of furniture which originated in Davenport, Iowa. It was a Midwestern thing. Anyway, he sat on it waiting for her to return from the kitchen, which she did, carrying two cordial glasses of Corvoisier. Handing one over, she settled down next to him on the davenport/sofa/couch, and for the second time that night they touched their glasses together.

They each took a sip of the cordial nectar and, this time, Hank didn't wait for the moment to pass. He leaned his face to her, she didn't move away, and their lips touched in a gentle kiss.

"Would you mind putting your glass down," Darcy whispered, her lips brushing his as she pronounced the words. He did, she did, and they kissed again. Magic.

As their embrace held, Hank's hand went to Darcy's breast, lingering there for precious moments, without protest. There was no turning back now. He dropped his hand to her hemline, which had already worked well up her thighs on its own, and raised it still higher.

Suddenly, Darcy pushed away. "That's enough, Hank." She stood, adjusted her skirt and left the room.

Breathing hard, Hank gulped his Corvoisier, wondering what the hell happened to magic?

JUST ABOUT THE time Hank was catching his breath he lost it again. Reappearing from the hallway was yet another transformation of this woman. It was she, but she was now . . . Magenta.

The personae struck a pose in her deep-red costume then did a slow twirl for him. "Like my outfit?" she asked with a tease in her voice. Not waiting for an answer, she did another turn, a little faster this time, and the tiny skirt flared, revealing color-matched panties. Hank could see there was no bra to this ensemble, matching or otherwise.

Hank rose from the couch and walked over to where she stood, as best he could manage his physiology of the moment. He was ready to play his role.

Pulling her to him as if to entrap her—hell, he did entrap her—he glowered. "I've got you in my clutches, Night Vigilante." It was his best miscreant voice.

She struggled, a little—very little. "Oh, you're so strong. I'm powerless against you."

He reached down and scooped her legs up from under her, cradling her in his arms. "Prepare to meet your fate, woman," he said, carrying her down the hall from where she emerged.

"But I'm a superheroine," she protested, legs scissoring from her knees as they passed into the bedroom. "You can't do this to me."

He only grinned evilly and lowered her onto the bed.

"Oh, what will you do to me?" she asked, a fearful tone in her voice.

"I'm going to unmask you," he avowed.

"B-but, I'm not wearing a mask," she stammered, looking up at him.

"I'm thinking a little more broadly," he said, leering down at her.


**JUST AS HE** had not seen anyone so beautiful as the woman on the bed, he had never observed as perfect a female form as the one before him now.

Hank did not tarry long. He was loath to rush things like this, but he was having a tough time holding back his genealogy. Fortunately, "Magenta" was not requiring as much time as he feared she might. As it turned out, his timing was exemplary.

And so it happened that a first kiss lead to this consummate finality. Though there was pent-up demand involved in the equation.


**I'D OFFER YOU** a cigarette," Hank said lying beside Darcy, "but in Bloomington, tobacco is considered a controlled substance, and I'm without."

"Oh my. Then whatever shall will we do to pass the rest of the night?" she replied in a way that sent a shiver through him, despite his present depletion.

"Give me some time. I might come up with something."

"You can always see how the Titanium Doll measures up to Magenta," she offered in the way of a suggestion.

"Now there's a thought. Let me ponder that awhile."

"Just awhile," she responded.

*And then we'll tend to Darcy Austin, professional ad woman, if I'm still alive.*

HANK ROSE TO the challenge. After ravishing the Titanium Doll, he managed to conclude his evening with the formidable advertising woman's personate.

More than the sexual encounters of his life, he knew he had also ventured into serious emotional territory for the first time in his earthly tenure.

HANK AWOKE TO the unmistakable aroma of bacon and eggs as it wafted down the short hall from the kitchen. Disoriented at first, remembrances of the night before came into focus, stirring his groin.

He threw his legs over the side of the bed and sat up. Glancing around the small bedroom, he looked for his clothes on the floor where he had discarded them in haste last night, but found them arranged on a chair. His holstered Glock was set aside on a dressing table.

Tossed more casually on another chair was the Magenta costume worn by Darcy Austin for a brief time. Alongside the costume was the dinner dress and lingerie she had abandoned before that.

It wasn't a dream, he was happy to assure himself—yet, in another sense, it was.

Pulling on enough clothes to be presentable, he walked down the hall, making a needed stop along the way, then strolled into the kitchen. "I'm sorry," he mocked, as Darcy Austin turned from the cook-top to face him, spatula in hand. "Which of the women I was with last night might you be?"

Darcy was clothed in a white cotton robe. Her hair disheveled, her lipstick non-existent, no mascara of any kind, and barefoot, besides. She looked wonderful.

Darcy beamed back at him. "Why, I'm Ms. D. Margaret Austin, demure homemaker," she cooed—at least it sounded like a coo to Hank. "Sleep well?"

"I think I lost consciousness." He moved closer and kissed her. She held the spatula away to accommodate him. The pull back of her arm also allowed him to slip his hand inside the open cleavage of her robe unchallenged, cupping her bare breast and feeling the cool definition of her nipple in his palm. He wondered what else she wasn't wearing under that robe, and felt himself getting hard.

"Uh-ah," she said, stepping back after granting him his allotted moment, "it's after breakfast for any of that, Lieutenant. First, you need your sustenance."

He gave her a long, dejected look, but didn't argue the point. Instead he said, "You want to tell me about that Magenta stunt you pulled last night?"

"Didn't I tell you. I'm going to be Magenta."

"Hey, I'm trying to get to the bottom of things, here."

"Seems to me you accomplished that pretty well last night."

"Okay, okay. What gives?"

"Sorta got talked into, ah, a modeling stint—by Williams and son. I thought you might like to see how my ensemble looked."

"Oh, I did."

He wanted to hear more, but she closed off the topic by pushing a plate at him.

"Here's your eggs and bacon," she said. "I'll explain it all later. Hope you like over easy."

He seated himself before the breakfast offering. "I hope these eggs work their magic, or I may have to reserve your old hospital room at Fairview."

"I'm sure you'll survive," she chortled, placing her plate on the table across from him. "But we better eat if you've got anything else in mind. I've got an appointment in a couple of hours."

"Uh-oh," Hank said, looking at his watch. "How fast can you eat?"

# Chapter 26

# C O N T E M P L A T I O N

**HANK DIDN'T PUT** as much time in on his running these days as when he had a fling at marathons and 10Ks several years back. He placed seventeenth in his age group in the Twin Cities Marathon and twelfth in Grandma's up along the North Shore from Two Harbors into Duluth. He also earned silver and bronze metals from the Kaiser Roll 10K, held in Bloomington each year, attracting runners and wheelchair participants from all over the nation. Even had a turn at the Boston Marathon. He hadn't planned on becoming a long-distance runner. It started with attempting to lower his cholesterol, which it accomplished. A couple of miles at a time grew into longer stints and finally the marathons. Now his running was less fervent and pretty much confined to a six-mile trek from his town home on College View Road down to and around Normandale Lake and back. Still, it kept his fatty acids at an acceptable level.

He decided to forgo his run this Saturday. He was just too damned weary and pressed for time on top of it. But golf? That was another matter. He needed to stay sharp, after all.

**"HI, DON, I'LL** take an extra-large one," he said to the attendant on duty at Hyland.

"Hey, Hank. Haven't seen you since you became a hero," Don replied, pushing an extra large bucket of balls across the counter and charging him for a small one.

"Thanks, and thanks. What did Andy Warhol say about everyone having their fifteen minutes of fame—deserved or not?"

"I'm still waiting for mine," he returned. "Think you're shorting yourself there." Then turning away to other chores, "Hit 'em straight, kid."

**PLINK. THE FORGED** titanium head of the Mizuno driver rocketed the yellow projectile on a rising trajectory before bouncing down just ahead of the 200-yard marker, rolling past it. Golfers hit up hill at the Hyland range, and if the ball carried that far on the upward slope with range balls, it was roughly equivalent to 230 yards or more on the golf course, using Titlests, or the like. Not bad.

*Plink.* Another ball arched toward the same marker, this time with a slight drift to the right even though it traveled farther up the hill. A power fade. Still okay, but fades of any kind made Douglas Hankenson apprehensive.

He found himself thinking. Some things still stirred in the Soup Case as far as he was concerned. He held little doubt that Roland Bennett was implicated in the Williams/Bailey murders—that much seemed certain. But was there more to it than that? All the evidence pointed to Bennett, even if it was only circumstantial. He had motive, means, knowledge, and was being blackmailed. And his suicide note seemed to seal it. Yet, some things still worked at him.

*Plink.* Straighter, but not as far. Shit. Then there was the Williams/Bailey client aspect. Using client products as murder weapons really shook things up from a business standpoint at the agency—which could be construed as a way for Bennett to vent his bitterness toward his former employer.

*Plink.* Another fade—this one worse. *Damn.* Even so, there were still loose ends in his mind—at least relating to the first killing. How did the killer get into Williams/Bailey so readily without being detected? Not once, but twice, when considering the ersatz e-mail sent out to the media. Okay, the security wasn't that tough to defeat. The killer could have known the security man's habits on making rounds away from his desk, slipping by undetected to the card-activated elevator. And he could have used a stolen access card to the elevator, gaining entrance to Williams/Bailey—a card that never got reported as missing. But if he had an access card, it wasn't found in his possessions after his death.

Bennett did know that Janes was doing one of his all-nighters that evening without the need of an inside informant, but he may have had one anyway. And that could be the reason an access card was never reported as missing or stolen.

He'd also have to get back out of the Normandale complex without being spotted by security or seen by anyone else for that matter. Still possible, but the long shots were getting longer. No matter how he looked at it, things just didn't play out clean for him. Yet, everyone seemed satisfied that Bennett acted alone. Why shouldn't he be, as well? Or was it that they wanted it to be so, more than good sense and hard evidence would otherwise affirm? Lee Harvey Oswald acted alone, too. Sure he did.

His conclusion: There likely was an accomplice. His remaining questions: If so, how important was the accomplice's role in the matter?

And most important: Would the assumed collaborator now fade away forever, or was there something more in store?

*Plink.* A stronger fade yet. *What the hell?*

"Don't cup your wrists on the back swing, and keep that right shoulder from coming around on the downswing," Don instructed as he passed by collecting empty buckets from adjacent stalls.

"Right," Hank nodded.

*Plink.* The yellow range ball carried straight over the two-hundred-yard marker on the fly and continued on up hill, rolling slightly to the left in a controlled draw. Much better. *Can't overlook the details*, he commented to himself, tucking the blue driver back into his bag.

*Chapter* **27**

# P R E P A R A T I O N

**ABOUT THE SAME** time as Hank was driving golf balls, Darcy was driving her SUV to the town once professing to be the raspberry capitol of the world. That moniker had faded from when the community was still a stand-alone rural community west of the Twin Cities. It had also gained statewide fame as home to Bebe Shoppe, Minnesota's first Miss America, crowned in 1949. Originally settled by Czechoslovakians, there are still a few reminders of a more distant past, with street names like Smetans Road and Bren Street, plus a few remaining truck farms tucked into the rolling hills of the area. Once known as Little Bohemia, the politicians named it Hopkins. And Hopkins is now a second-tier western suburb of Minneapolis. As for raspberries, they are imported from Chile, farmland in Hopkins yielding to more profitable housing developments.

Having reached the still quaint main street of the downtown area, Darcy found a space at the curb, near her destination, where she parked the 4-Runner. Clamoring up the stairs of the two-story, red brick building, equipment bag slung over her shoulder, she came to an expansive open room that took up the great majority of the second floor. A huge plastic-covered mat stretched from wall to wall.

"No shoes on the mat, Babe. Take 'em off at the door," Erica Carlson ordered, looking up from her stretching routine in the center of the room. She was dressed in a white gi with a brown belt tied at her waist. "Changing room's back there," she gestured with a wave of her arm.

Darcy entered the makeshift women's room and changed into her sweats. Perhaps sweats were not de rigueur in these environs, but they'd have to do for this first session.

Erica looked Darcy over with a critical eye when she reappeared from the dressing area. "We've got to get you a gi if we're going to do this right—but okay, for now. Take a few laps around the room to warm up. I'll take you through some stretching exercises after that. Then we'll start."

Darcy did as she was told, came back for some arduous testing of her joints, and the major part of the session was soon to begin.

"Do you know anything about freestyle sparring?" Erica Carlson questioned her student. "Work out at all?"

"Not in the martial arts sense. But I do work out. Got a heavy bag in my basement," Darcy answered.

"Do any kicking?"

"Some. Good conditioner."

"Wanna try one on me?" Erica asked. "Don't hold back. You won't hurt me."

"You sure? I hit the bag pretty hard."

"Give it a shot," Erica challenged, patting her left rib cage with the palm of her hand. "Right here."

*Okay you asked for it.* Darcy was only too happy to have at her erstwhile adversary this way. She drew her left arm back as she leaned away from Erica. Then, pivoting on her left foot, swept her right leg at its mid-section target.

Erica seemed almost languid as Darcy's kick swung forward. Then at the last moment, she leaned away from the thrust, caught Darcy's leg under her arm—while twisting her body to absorb the force—and stabbed her lead leg behind Darcy's supporting ankle.

For what seemed an interminable length of time, Darcy was airborne. Then came a sound and feeling she would soon become familiar with during these sessions. *Whump*. She was flat on her back. With that, Erica Carlson stepped over Darcy's prostrate form and feigned a thrust of her foot to Darcy's solar plexus. It was the "kill."

"We've got a lot to learn," she said to the stunned woman on the mat. "Want to take a shot with your fist next?"

Shaking off the thumping she had just taken, Darcy attempted what Erica asked, with equal lack of attainment. This time she was taken over Erica's shoulder before crashing to the mat—pinned there by the knee of her instructor.

"Well, now we know, don't we Darc," Erica Carlson grinned. "Ready to settle down to a few fundamentals?"

"Ohhh." So much for any size or strength advantage.



It wasn't a problem for him on this busy Saturday at Ochsner's Sporting Goods Store on the Bloomington strip. Examining one of the .22-caliber rifles he had asked to see, he removed three bullets from his pocket, sans cartridges, and ran them down the barrel of the rifle with a fold-out cleaning rod he had brought with him. The setting was bustling and unsupervised. No one paid him heed.

———

AT HIS HOME workbench, the three .22-caliber bullets with the rifling marks etched into them at Ochsner's, were inserted into plastic accelerators mimicking a 30-06 round. Next he affixed each of the encapsulating accelerators to a 30-06 powder cartridge, completing the sabots for the use he intended.

He then prepared five more hand-load sabots in the same way, but using virgin .22-caliber bullets that were without rifling marks. They would serve as a test. He was a careful man.

The basement firing range stretched the length of the fifty-two-foot foundation of his ranch-style home and, from there, extended farther into an eight-foot excavation beyond the original footings of the building. The extenuation housed targets and bullet-absorbing sandbags at its abutment. A wood door closed it off when not in use. All in all, there were sixty feet to play with—short for a rifle range, ideal for a pistol range, and good enough for his purposes generally—this instance being no exception.

He pulled the noise-suppressers over his ears and settled into a classic sitting position with his elbows resting on the knees of his crossed legs. He brought the twenty-inch, short-barrel Winchester M70 up level, sighted through its Lupold scope, let out a half breath, held it and squeezed off the first test round. *Blam.* The noise would have been egregious in the confines of the cement-walled depression, but the protectors he wore rendered the report to a muted *thunk* in his ears. Sound-deadening mats placed over the basement windows kept any escaping sound to within a few feet of the exterior of the building. They also served as a sight barrier to any curious passersby.

From where he sat, the perforation on the target looked to be three-quarters of an inch low left of the bullseye. He made a minor adjustment on the scope, brought the rifle up and fired again, hitting the bull dead center. Three more shots followed in close sequence, encircling the bull exactly as he intended. He did not want one bullet to strike and damage the other. The shot group was perfect—as he would have expected from this range.

THIS PREPARATION WAS unlike his last undertaking where, in a secluded preserve outside of Northfield, some thirty miles south of the Twin Cities metro, he readied a Barrett M95, long-range target rifle of a much larger bore than the M70.

When zeroing the Barrett, he found that the side knobs on the fitted Swarovski scope—for up/down adjustment—needed more calibration than the knobs on top for side-to-side alignment. He expected that. The .50-caliber M95 had been pre-calibrated for a 5,000-foot shooting range, allowing for considerable drop. But soon the obliteration of metal cans 200 feet down line told him the rifle was readied for the sixty-seven yards a hand-held Bushnell laser-beam range finder had previously measured out for him. That was the distance from the northwest corner of the Foshay Tower, where he planned to position himself, to the southeast corner of the IDS Tower, repository of his target.

His remaining concern after that was side wind on the day of execution. Although it would take a significant gust to affect a .50-caliber bullet with a muzzle velocity of 2,800 feet per second over so short a span, he would be watchful of air currents, knowing that the venturi-effect brought on by surrounding tall buildings could amplify air disturbance.

Earlier, he had placed a hold on empty space in the Foshay Tower, using a fictitious name and firm. That enabled him to obtain a key to the space, which was sent to a P.O. Box registered under the same pseudonym, at his request. The key also gave him access to the stairwells in the building so he could get the M95 up to his "office" piece by piece without drawing undue attention to odd-looking packages in an elevator full of people.

The reflective glass skin of the IDS posed another obstacle for him to overcome. So he paid a visit to C. Norman Griffin's office, on the pretense of an official police call, putting a few questions to the scurrilous attorney. It could have been fanned as police harassment by liberal hand-wringing editorial writers always ready to protect the guilty, had the barrister wanted to make an issue of it, but he was not prone to drawing unnecessary attention to himself. The caller was counting on that.

While there, he studied the layout of C. Norman's office, making a mental note of where the lawyer was seated in relation to his southeast office window when working at his computer. One third up the window and four inches right of center would do it, by his best estimate. He was good at spatial relationships. Yet, he wanted to shorten the odds still further if he could. There was a reputation to uphold.

He got his opportunity when the attorney took a phone call, which led to an animated discussion distracting from the visiting police detective. Left on his own for the moment, the visitor rose from his chair, walked to the southwest window and stood as if admiring the view while waiting out the phone conversation behind him.

In so doing, he positioned his body between C. Norman Griffin's computer chair and the window in the neighboring Foshay Tower from where a strip of reflective tape mirrored rays from the afternoon sun. His body blocked his next move, should the attorney be observing him, although he saw by the reflection in the glass that the barrister's eyes were fixed on his desk at the moment. *Great.* He scratched a spot on the window with a diamond-tip tool drawn from his pocket. It wasn't enough of a scrape to attract the casual eye, but it changed the refraction properties of the glass to where a high-power scope would detect it from across the way.

There was one remaining artifice to put in place, then he was done. Returning from the window, he surreptitiously tucked a device under C. Norman's computer desk—its adhesive back fixing it in place. Now, he'd be able to tell just when the attorney was working at his keyboard—a final need-to-know.

He still wasn't sure. Not one hundred and ten percent sure, the way he wanted to be. That called for a night check, when the lights were on in the IDS and he could see his target seated at his computer from the Foshay, telling him everything was in order. Okay, he cheated.

With all this, he was prepared for a first round miss, nonetheless. He had a straight sight line to the window, could see his positioning mark on the glass and commanded a powerful weapon with the right load for the task. Still, he couldn't be certain his target would be precisely where he was supposed to be when he fired. He would be certain on the second shot, though, after the tempered glass shattered and he was given a clear view of the room before his target could react in any meaningful way.

THE BLAST FROM the monster muzzle blended into the street noise below. He worked the slick bolt action, shoving a second round into the chamber of the target rifle as the IDS window pulverized. The rechambering wasn't necessary. In the fraction of a second after the trigger was squeezed, the Swarovski Optik made it clear that there would be no open casket at the Honorable C. Norman Griffin Memorial Service. That would require the upper half of one's skull to be a plausible option.

The whole operation could have been accomplished more easily at night, of course, when his target would have been in full view from his shooter's perch. And C. Gordon was often in his offices after dark, as was known. It would have been a turkey shoot. But where was the challenge in that?

**HE PUT THE** Winchester M70 carbine aside and crossed the basement to the target area. There was a slight odor from the expended rounds, but otherwise there was no trace of the plastic accelerators from the sabots he had just fired off. He anticipated their total disintegration, but he wanted to make certain of it.

He dug the bullets out of the compacted sand, examining them for rifling marks from the carbine. He couldn't detect any. Bringing the bullets over to his workbench, he examined them, one at a time, under a scope. Still no sign of rifling marks.

Everything was set for the sabot shoot. The accelerators would evaporate into thin air with every shot he fired, and the imbedded .22 caliber bullets would bear the rifling marks of an unfired, unsold rifle in a sporting goods shop on the Bloomington strip. *Let 'em try and trace that.*

His partner would now have the collector's weapon he wanted, free and clear—after its purpose was served.

All things were good to go, in the police vernacular, including the site he had chosen for the deed. The Rifleman needed only to schedule the date and time for the execution, at his pleasure.

*Chapter* **28**

# F U R T H E R A N C E

**AT 11:00 A.M.** Saturday, Hank turned off county highway 1, onto the Flying Cloud parking lot adjacent to the Executive Terminal. Exiting the Bimmer, he was halfway between his car and the terminal when Brad Hoyt popped open the door of the main entrance and leaned out. "Got your clubs in the car?" he shouted from fifty feet away.

"Always," Hank returned. "But I thought we were going for a plane ride."

"We are. It's at the other end that we break out the clubs, okay?" Brad Hoyt smiled.

"Don't take off without me," Hank hollered over his shoulder, heading back to the BMW.

**THEY WERE STRAPPED** in, idling on the tarmac, the Piper Saratoga II TC throbbing through its warm up. Brad Hoyt was punching buttons, checking instruments, and talking to the Flight Briefer about conditions in terms Hank could only half follow as he listened in through his headset. With the small mike attached to the headset, he could have asked what it all meant but decided to keep quiet until they were clear of the runway—the pilot looked too busy to deal with interruptions just yet. Before long, most of his questions got answered without his having to ask. "We'll be flying at eight-thousand feet," Brad Hoyt said over his mike for Hank's benefit. "Cruise at 175 knots." More official intervention, then: "I program it in, the plane does the rest."

"Neat," Hank responded, not knowing what else to say without looking stupid. Then he added, with a trace of trepidation: "How's the weather where we're heading? And where are we heading, by the way?"

"Weather looks good," Brad Hoyt said, "Wait'll we get up, and I'll fill you in on the rest."

The Saratoga taxied to the end of the runway, and its operator ran up the RPMs until the airframe shook. The plane's brakes strained against the pulling force of the prop. Then, satisfied the engine wasn't going to give out any time soon, the pilot released the brake, and the Saratoga leaped ahead like a sprinter out of the blocks.

They sped down the runway picking up speed at a rate that surprised Hank. He expected the plane to use most of the length of the runway, as he guessed an airliner might, but, no more than a quarter of the way along its measure, the Saratoga sprang into the air like a jackrabbit chased by a fox. Only this "rabbit" had wings.

"We're heading to Detroit Lakes," Brad Hoyt announced as the plane continued its climb. "My dad's retired with nothing else to do, so he buys this nine holer up there with a lot of adjacent land and builds it into an eighteen-hole championship course. Forest Hills. Named it after the street he lives on so he wouldn't forget it. Thought you might like to do a round when we get there."

"Good thinking," Hank replied. "How long before we arrive?"

"About an hour. Nice day for a flight and golf, too."

"I like it. Where's Forest Hills in the metro area?"

"Bloomington. Actually, it's Forest Hills Circle. Can't be far from where you cops hang out. It's off Poplar Bridge Road, cul de sac on a hill."

"I think I know it now. Must not get many police calls from there, otherwise I'd be more familiar with it."

"No, not since my brothers and I left the nest, anyway. Mostly old farts there now."

"Where you living?"

"Lake Harriet. I don't like getting there, or leaving there—pretty congested. But I love being there." Like any local, Hank was familiar with the chain of lakes in Minneapolis. Lake Harriet was the one with the most expensive homes clustered around it. He could only speculate on the taxes that came with the territory.

They reached altitude, the GPS cluster deploying distance to go, bearing, air speed, arrival time, and a visual display of the plane on a course for Detroit Lakes. Some other information was displayed there, too, but Hank couldn't make anything of it. "Did JFK, Jr., have all these instruments at his disposal?" he asked, remembering that Brad Hoyt had told him that a Saratoga was the plane flown by Kennedy the night he crashed into the sea near Hyannis.

"No. Some of this stuff wasn't even available at that time. Technology keeps on rolling."

"He wasn't instrument qualified anyway, was he?"

"No, again. But one little button he did have could have saved him and his passengers."

"How so?"

"He was disoriented for sure; that's easy to happen over water at night—especially in haze without reference points. Can't tell up from down, much less where the horizon is. Got to believe your instruments telling you you're about to stall, or that you're going down."

"Can't you feel the plane diving, or climbing?"

"No you can't, strange as that sounds. But before he got into serious trouble—upside down and nosing in—Kennedy was probably confused about where he was." The pilot paused to point to an innocuous button on the plane's panel. "All he had to do is push this button and the plane would have homed in on the Hyannis Airport beacon and made a low pass over it, automatically. He would of seen the lights of the landing field, then been able to turn around and land pretty as you please."

"Simple as that?"

"Yeah. My guess, he waited too long. Then probably didn't believe his instruments saying he was headed in. I'd guess he was doing absolutely nothing when he hit the water.

"I'll be damned."

"Had something like that happen to me last summer—going to Florida to check out some property."

"Do I want to hear about it before we land?" Hank was back to trepidation.

"Sure you do. Flew into zero visibility, and the wings iced up on me."

"In this plane?"

"Yeah, it's why I bought the Malibu—it's got deicers."

Hank wondered why they weren't flying in that plane but didn't ask.

Brad Hoyt continued. "I didn't know I was icing up because I couldn't see my wings in all that shit. My first clue was when the controls got heavy. I panicked and manually banked to turn back while I was reprogramming the GPS. Took my eyes off the altitude indicator for five seconds, and when I looked back it was telling me I'd flipped over. My air speed indicator was shooting up, meaning I was going down. I thought, 'My God, I just killed myself.'"

All this was making Hank anxious. He checked the wings. No ice. The sky was clear. *But clear-air turbulence occurs in clear air, doesn't it? Why not ice?*

"Went back to my training," the pilot kept on. "Turned the engine off, gave it full flaps trying to cut air speed. I was near redline, where the airframe starts to go, but the plane slowed just enough. I put the yoke in my lap and the nose started to come up. I just prayed the wings would stay on."

"I assume they did."

"Yup. I restarted the engine, and got the hell out of there."

"Where'd you go?"

"Back home. I lost interest in Florida."

Hank was never so appreciative of a calm sunny day. And he was happy to learn that a spin of the GPS knob gave the nearest emergency landing facility and runway, which, Brad Hoyt told him, were sprinkled all over the state.

They passed the Alexandria checkpoint, just twenty-three miles from Detroit Lakes. This was fun, he told himself, even though he was still a little nervous. Maybe someday he'd challenge himself on that score. Right now he'd think about the round of golf he was going to play at Forest Hills.

THE NEXT WEEK passed without incident.

Having survived his flight back from Detroit Lakes, Hank was busy catching up with a more normal life: stacked up police work, running every other morning, and a round at nearby Dwan Golf Club.

Darcy Austin was inundated with her new responsibilities at the agency and was working out almost every weeknight, plus spending Saturday afternoon's with Erica Carlson in Hopkins—the latter regimen tougher than the former.

She and Hank hadn't seen each other since that consummating night and morning at her home. It was not where either one wanted to leave things. By the following Monday morning, Hank couldn't stand it any longer, busy or not. He picked up the phone and punched in Darcy's personal number at Williams/Bailey.

"Darcy Austin," she answered.

*Caught her.* "What, no preceding title or anything?"

"Good to hear your voice, stranger. I wasn't sure you were still a resident in these parts."

*The phone works both ways,* he thought but didn't say, although he knew he was probably the most guilty party given social mores, feminism notwithstanding. "I'm still in residence, and I miss you a lot. How's that?"

"Much better. Tell you what. How 'bout lunch?" her voice all smiley.

*So much for social mores.* "Like today lunch?"

"That's what I meant."

"Well, yeah . . . I can make that. We can go over to—"

"Your place," she cut in.

"My place?"

"Do we have a bad connection? I'll pick up a pizza at Poppa John's on my way over. Quarter to twelve. Okay?"

"Sure, great. You know how to get to my place?

"Just across from Normandale College on College View, right?" And without waiting for an answer: "What's your unit number?"

"Six thirty-three," he stammered, wondering why he was all tingly inside.

*Chapter* **29**

# V I S I T A T I O N

**IT WAS 11:44** when the door chime sounded. "Pizza," Darcy said with a big smile when Hank swung the door open. She stepped inside with a nylon insulator over her shoulder, emblazoned with a Papa John logo. As she sauntered by, she turned her face up to him and kissed him smack on the lips, heading for the kitchen without losing stride. "Very special delivery," she added as if she had to.

Hank stood there with a befuddled look on his face. "Don't look like any pizza delivery person ever came here before," he stated.

She ignored him. "How do you like the special wrap? She asked, zipping the insulator open. "Talked 'em out of it. Got any pop?"

*I'll bet you didn't have to twist any arms to get it,* Hank thought, reaching in the refrigerator for a couple Classic Cokes.

"It's their vegetarian special," she said, dropping two steaming slabs onto one of the plates she had pulled down from the cupboard. "Good for runners."

*How do women know where to find things in a strange kitchen?* "Uh huh. I miss my pepperoni, though," Hank grumbled, although it didn't show as he dove into the fare on his plate.

"Arrested anyone lately?" she asked before biting off a hunk of pizza trailing a length of near-molten cheese.

"Got to maintain a certain level of police activity out there. Let the citizenry know their taxes are going for something—even if it's to police harassment. You?"

"Extra responsibility isn't what it's cracked up to be. Also, been wrestling with some campaign issues for Minnesota Tourism." She didn't mention wrestling with Erica Carlson. "Looking for something fresh."

"How 'bout potholes?"

"Potholes?"

"Sure. California has mudslides, Florida has sinkholes, and Arizona has heaving pavement. All that's sissy stuff compared to the death-defying potholes we get around here in the spring." Swallow. "Ask any cop who's had to rescue a motorist out of them come spring thaw."

"You're a great help."

"Then there's chunk kicking."

"Chunk kicking?"

"You know, kicking those globs of icy slush hanging under your fenders in March—they splat real good when you kick 'em and they plop onto the street. Is that fun or what?"

"Somehow I don't think the Tourism Board will go for it."

Hank considered for a moment. "Then give 'em J.V. Schanken."

"J.V. who?"

"Schanken, You never heard of J.V. Schanken? What kind of Minnesotan are you?"

"No, I haven't, but you're going to tell me. This anything like Ole and Lena?"

"Absolutely not. J.V.'s for real—officially, anyway."

Another bite. Another trail of cheese. "Go on."

"Well, J.V. Schanken holds the record for the biggest northern pike ever caught in Minnesota. And you know how Minnesotans love their fish stories."

"Is this one?"

"No one knows for sure. It was back in the twenties, up around Ely, I think. Weighed forty-some pounds." Bite. Chew. "In those days you just called your catch in, and it was accepted as gospel. No questions asked."

"That's when people were still honest, wasn't it?"

"Maybe so, but when a curious journalist tried to check that record out recently, he couldn't find anything to verify the catch. Nothing in the local newspaper, although some other big fish were reported that same year. It turned out no one by the name of J.V. Schanken ever lived in Minnesota, either."

"Maybe he was from Illinois."

"Could be. Could also be the biggest fish story ever told, around here."

"How do you know this stuff, anyway?"

"I just do. Hey, let me tell you about some of the fish I've caught."

"Spare me."

"I snagged this muskie up on Mille Lacs. Had to toss the anchor out when it started dragging the boat—"

"Another time, Hank, please. But you raise a point, I must admit."

"Oh?"

"We could build a campaign around little-known stories in Minnesota. Just got to be intriguing enough—connected to a site people can visit. I'll take that thought back with me."

"See. You thought you were just having lunch with a dumb cop. Cookie for dessert? Chocolate chip."

"No, I didn't, and, no, I don't. But you can show me the rest of your place before I go."

That tingle again. "Sure. Follow me," *Be cool, man*.

**THERE WASN'T MUCH** more to see on the main level. Usual format: eating area, living room, small room Hank used as an office, and a powder room. He wasn't much of a tour director. It went something like:

"Here's this."

"That's nice."

"Here's that."

"That's nice, too."

"That's about it down here."

"Umm, okay."

"Wanna see upstairs?" Hank gingerly asked next.

"Lead the way. I'll follow," Darcy said, smiling at him. "I don't like men behind me on the stairs." That was true in most cases, the stares on the stairs were pronounced and inevitable. But, this day, guarding her fanny from close inspection was not the issue. She had a different motive in mind.

Granting her wish, Hank climbed the stairs, she behind.

**ON THE ASCENT,** Darcy unbuttoned her silk blouse, slipped it off, and dropped it over the railing. At the top landing she let her skirt tumble down her legs to the floor. On the way down the hallway, she kicked off her pumps.

Hank steered into his bedroom still leading the single-file procession. Then, stopped by his bed, with nowhere else to go, he turned around. He was about to say something frivolous like, "It's humble, but I like it," only the words never got out of his mouth—even though it was open.

Darcy Austin stood in the bedroom entry, one arm extended up the side of the doorway, the other on her hip canted toward the opposite side of the frame.

The view rivaled any Victoria's Secret presentation Hank had ever seen. Hell, it beat it. Her bra, cut low to begin with, plunged deep between her breasts. Her panties curved high at her hips in a graceful arc. And a garter belt held nylons high up her thighs. The entire ensemble, such as it amounted to, was black on black.

Hank took a step back and dropped down on the edge of the bed—riveted to the vision before him.

Breaking from her pose, Darcy's started toward him, bringing her hands to the center of her bra and unclasping it. Then, with a toss of her shoulders and an attendant shake of her torso, the frail garment traced down her arms onto the carpet behind her—her bare breasts moving in response to her body as she continued advancing on him.

Which bestowal was most erotic Hank would later ponder—under more composure than he owned at that moment—the pose, the shake, or the walk? The images would turn over in his mind many times henceforth without a conclusion. And that was just fine.

He stared; she spoke: "If you slide over, I'll remove my hose," she said.

He had responded to her, though not with words, until that moment. "As long as I don't have to get up."

She smiled. "I wouldn't want you to hurt yourself. Just scooch over there, kind of easy like."

Hank obliged, and Darcy sat down beside him, stripping one raised leg at a time. She slipped out of her garter belt, with a wriggle of her hips, and cast it aside, standing up in front of him again.

Starting her panties down over her hips, she paused. "I have a meeting at three, is that time enough for you?" Teasing, though she was, she was also handing him control.

"I'll try real hard."

"Oh, I like the sound of that," she said, restarting her panties on their downward course. Naked, she stepped close to where he could touch her. "Ready?"

"You're still wearing a watch and earings," he said, running his hands from her hips up to her breasts, nesting them in his palms.

"My, how observant of you. But they won't get in the way," she said. "Anything else?"

"We'll have to hurry," He answered. "We've only got two hours."

"I'm sure you'll manage the time carefully," Darcy purred back.



SHE DIDN'T LONG remain standing. Nor was it long before Darcy Austin, ad woman, and Douglas Hankenson, police detective, reached a rare, protracted state of being.



"WHAT TIME IS it?" Darcy breathed, upon her return to planet Earth.

Hank twisted his wrist out from under her. "One-thirty." As much a gasp as a pronouncement.

"We've got another hour," she said, looking up at him with an expression he'd come to know.

"I need twenty minutes of that," he stated flat out.

"For what?" she demanded.

"R and R, you sadist."

"I'll give you fifteen," she convalesced.

**TEN SECONDS OF** "R and R" had passed when Darcy asked: "What's that round scar on your shoulder?" suspecting she already knew what it was from.

Hank hesitated, then replied, "A badge I acquired as a rookie cop."

"It looks like . . . is it a bullet wound?"

"Yeah."

"You could have been killed."

"Should have been. I was stupid."

"Oh, God. How did it happen?"

"Like I said, I was dumb . . . a rookie in St. Paul."

"Tell me about it."

"Some guy was threatening to kill his family. I walked in, that's all."

"He shot you?"

"Yeah."

"You shot him?"

"That too."

"What happened to him?"

"He died. First and only man I ever shot."

"I'm sorry," Darcy said, seeing his unease. But she needed to know more. "When did it happen?"

"I don't know . . . fifteen years ago."

Darcy thought for a long moment. "I was in high school fifteen years ago." Another long pause. "I remember something . . . St. Paul . . . Oh, Lord—the 'Shootout on Sycamore'. You're him?"

Hank didn't answer, but his expression gave Darcy her answer. She stared at him awhile, then said: "You rescued that woman and her little girl, and you rushed to my rescue. You haven't changed, have you?" Tears welled in her eyes as she spoke.

He searched for something to say but couldn't come up with better than, "Sometimes fools rush in . . ."

Darcy put an end to his disquiet. "Come here, fool."

R and R was over.

**LIEUTENANT HANKENSON WAS** grateful for his training as a long-distance runner. He'd finish this test of endurance if it killed him—with the disconcerting knowledge that the original Marathoner did drop dead, according to legend, after covering the twenty-six-mile, three-hundred-yard distance from Marathon to Athens to proclaim the defeat of Persia. *Here lies Douglas L. Hankenson, who, like the original Marathoner, gave his life in the completion of his charge.*

Foreboding aside, Douglas L. Hankenson persevered, abiding the ravishment of his partner to a dead-heat finish. Of course, there were worse tests in life he fully appreciated.

In the afterglow, Darcy lay with her hands open to the ceiling, her thighs open to the compliant body above her. "Don't move," she whispered.

"I can't," the compliant body replied.

*Chapter* **30**

# D I S C O U R S E

**DARCY SAT THROUGH** her three o'clock managers' meeting with detachment, her mind still back at unit 633. She hoped no one noticed. The meeting was mostly about how the agency needed to cut back on expenses due to the loss of the Lakeland RV account that was not coming back into the fold after Roland Bennett's demise, having already moved to another shop. And how they would have to work hard to replace the business—the usual stuff after a billings tumble. There were some other things in there too, but they passed her by unheeded.

The meeting broke off after the obligatory rhetoric. Relieved it was over, Darcy started to leave when one of the other female managers approached her on the way out of the room. "You okay?" the attendee asked.

"I'm fine." Darcy answered. "Why?"

"Thought you looked kinda flushed in there. Sure you're all right?"

---

**WHEN DARCY GOT** back to her office she punched in the extension number of Andrew Heiam, creative group head and art director on the Minnesota Tourism account.

Funny how everyone seems to answer the phone differently, Darcy mulled, while waiting for a pickup. Some use their first names, some their last, some others use both of their names, and still others say, hello. *How come no one just says, "Hi,"* she wondered as the phone continued to ring?

"Hi," Andy Heiam blurted into the handset.

*Well, I'll be damned.* "Hi, back, Andy," not having to identify herself. "How you coming on Tourism?"

"Hey, Darc. Sorry about the heavy breathing. I was down the hall when I heard the phone ring."

"You don't have to apologize. Obscene callers make calls; they don't get them. Got anything on Tourism?"

"Nothing I'm happy with."

"Ever hear of a fisherman named Schanken?"

"Who?"

"Look, I've got something I'd like to toss your way. You open in the morning?"

"Lemme see. Yeah, nine-thirty's good?"

"Good with me, too. I'll come down to your office. Maybe nothing, but I'd like to see what you think."

"Want me to fetch Nan for this, too?"

"Sure, let's get her perspective. This shouldn't take long."

"Uh, you okay, Darc?"

"I'm fine. Why?"

"I dunno. You sound different."

———

*WHUMP*. **THAT FAMILIAR** sound again. Darcy was flat on her back, arms and legs splayed on the mat in a torpid display. "C'mon Darcy, get with it," Erica challenged, standing over her. "I'm killing you tonight."

Darcy opened her eyes and looked up at her tormentor. "I had a long lunch," she only half lied, with a commiserate groan.

"Well you didn't overeat, or you'd be puking by now," Erica said, kneeling down beside her. Then a suspicion popped into Erica's mind, "What did you do today?"

"None of your business," Darcy said, propping herself on her elbows.

Erica wasn't deterred, and Darcy's evasive manner lead her to a conclusion. "You had sex, didn't you. I can tell just looking at you," she asserted. "A nooner."

"Still none of your business," Darcy said, giving herself away completely.

Erica pressed: "Okay, who's the guy?"

Darcy didn't answer, but Erica was on it. "It's that Bloomington cop, isn't it?" she yowled, satisfied she got it right by Darcy's flush. "The guy who looks more FBI than local gendarme? I shoulda guessed it before."

Darcy couldn't hide, and she gave up trying. "Resisting an officer is a major offense," she said with an I-give-up shrug, surprising herself at how good it felt to get it out in the open.

"So's shamelessly bribing an officer of the law with your body— ever think of that? He read you your rights, yet?" A big grin.

"I wasn't paying attention to what he was saying." *Whoops, I really didn't mean to say that, did I?*

"No—just to what he was doing." Followed by: "What happened to the Titanium Doll we've all grown to know? Meltdown?"

Given her opening, Erica wasn't about to let things drop, tossing in a few more taunts to Darcy's chagrin. Darcy relented, and soon they were chortling like teenagers rehashing a hot date.

"Tell you what, Babe," the art director said, sufficed with her jibes for the time being. "Let's hang it up, here—you're not worth stink tonight, anyway. Get dressed, and I'll buy you a beer—you know, kind of celebrate your, ah, amour."

"You're kidding."

"I am not. We'll hit it hard, tomorrow night. Assuming you have a normal lunch like the rest of us."

Darcy surprised herself for the second time that night with her response. "Erica . . . why do I feel like this is the start of a beautiful friendship?"

"Gee. With a lower voice and a higher hairline, you could do Humphrey Bogart in the tarmac fog."

"Maybe I'm a little foggy right now. I never thought I'd be saying those words to you."

"I never expected to hear them from you, either."

"Is there a gin joint in Hopkins? We could go there," Darcy Austin said.

"Maybe you should buy the beer," Erica Carlson said.

THE NINE-THIRTY became a two-thirty. Nan Cisco had a copy deadline in the morning. Andy Heiam was open after two o'clock, and Darcy canceled an afternoon session to accommodate them both. That was how it worked in the ad game.

"So, what ya got, Darc?" Andy Heiam asked, poised over his elbows on the desk.

"Maybe nothing. But a thought," she answered, seated opposite him.

"Fire away."

"How 'bout we look into some weird things in Minnesota that could build tourism if presented right?"

"Weird things?" Nan Cisco raised a brow from her perch against a side wall of the office. "Like what? This is Minnesota. Land of milquetoast, millfoil, and honey."

"Sounds nuts, but there could be something to it," the art director said to the copywriter. Then to Darcy: "I sent Carrie to the library this morning—try and find somethin' on this Schanken character you mentioned on the phone yesterday. I spelled it wrong, but Carrie's a diligent intern. Came up with the guy."

"And does he hold the record for the largest northern caught in Minnesota?" Darcy asked.

"I thought you knew about that," the art director said.

"Just checking the legitimacy of my source," Darcy replied. "Could be jerking my chain."

Andy Heiam said, "He holds the record all right—it's the questions surrounding it that makes things weird—and interesting."

Darcy said, "That's what I heard." *How could I have questioned it?*

Nan Cisco's eyes were moving back and forth between Darcy Austin and Andy Heiam as though she were watching a table tennis match played across a desk. "Are you people gonna tell me what you're talking about, here?" she finally broke in.

"Here's what I got," Andy Heiam said. "This guy supposedly catches a forty-five pound, twelve-ounce northern in 1929—up on Basswood Lake."

"Supposedly?" the copywriter questioned.

"Well, other than this guy calling in his catch by phone, there's no confirmation he actually caught the damn fish. Even if it was Schanken who called. Can't even be sure of that."

"I thought you had to have an official weigh in—that sort of thing," Nan Cisco said.

"Not back then, I guess," Darcy inserted.

"Right." Andy Heiam, again. "It's not that Basswood Lake can't produce northerns in the forty-pound category, but this catch smells a little fishy."

"Oh, spare me the puns," his creative partner groaned. "Just tell the story, okay?"

"Sorry, couldn't resist. Anyway, when a newspaper reporter tried to check the whole thing out a few years ago, there was no record of a Schanken ever born or died in Minnesota according to state records."

"Maybe he was from Illinois," Nan Cisco said.

"Exactly what I said when I first heard about it," Darcy inserted.

"Could be," Andy Heiam continued, "but where J.V. Schanken came from, if he did exist, is only part of the story."

"I'm waiting," Nan Cisco said.

"Well, for one thing The *Ely Miner* never mentioned the catch," he said.

"So what?"

"Well, it reported other big catches in the area that summer—like a twenty-two and a-half pound lake trout landed by Sigurd Olson—the naturalist guy who lived up there. How come our monster fish didn't get squat in the paper when his did?"

"That is kinda weird," Nan Cisco conceded.

"Weird's what we want," Darcy said.

"Maybe a line like, 'Minnesota's record fish story,'" Andy Heiam offered.

Nan Cisco blanched for effect. "I'll write the copy—you just stick to drawing pictures." But she admitted to herself that it wasn't a bad start.

"Okay, why don't we work on that one? Could be fun," Darcy said. "Carrie come up with anything else at the library?" she asked the art director.

He rifled through assorted sheets of paper in front of him, then settled on an item. "How's this for weird? The source of the Mississippi wasn't discovered for 200 years after the river was first discovered in the 1620s, if you can believe it."

"No kidding?" Darcy was surprised.

"Don't you just follow the river upstream till you get there?" Nan Cisco questioned.

"Wait'll you hear." Andy Heiam was relishing the moment, commanding the room, notes in hand. "Every attempt to go up the river ran afoul of difficult rapids, harsh conditions and wrong turns into beaucoup tributaries," he read. "Then Father Louis Hennepin set out in canoes to find the source after becoming the first white man to lay eyes on St. Anthony falls right here in Minneapolis. Of course, it wasn't called Minneapolis way back then."

"Finding the falls shouldn't of been hard," the copywriter interjected. "All he had to do was follow the arrows off Hennepin Avenue." She grinned all over the place.

Andy Heiam came back with: "Arrows? Hell, he didn't even see the Indians." Big grin, back. "Not till he got further up the river, anyway."

Darcy Austin and Nan Cisco looked at the ceiling in unison.

Andy Heiam continued his tale, unabashed. "He did soon enough, though—see Indians, that is. And probably some arrows, too. But, these arrows weren't directional," he said to another roll of eyes from his captive audience.

"When the good father's excursion started out to find the river's source, the Sioux captured him at the first bend. They let him go later, but by that time he'd lost his enthusiasm for any further canoing."

"So who did find it?" Nan Cisco demanded.

"I thought you'd never ask." Andy Heiam smiled, before going on. "Well, in 1832, a writer—you should like that, Nan—by the name of Henry Schoolcraft found it with his faithful Indian guide, Yellow Hair. And he named the source Itasca."

"Yellow Hair did?" his creative associate asked.

"No, moron. Schoolcraft. Why did he name it Itasca, you may now ask."

"Because it's the Indian word for 'here's where it starts'?" Darcy offered without a clue.

"Sounds like an Indian word. But nooo, beaver breath," he replied.

"C'mon Andy," Nan Cisco pleaded, "the suspense is killing us. Isn't it Darcy?"

Darcy nodded exaggerated agreement. "Okay, Andy, let us know before we get any older."

Unabated, Andy continued at his own pace. "Schoolcraft took two Latin words and put them together, *veritas*, meaning true, and *caput* meaning head. True head, get it?

"I wouldn't touch that with a ten-foot keyboard," Nan said.

"Oh I'm sure you'll think of a good way to present it," Darcy said. "I like the story."

"So do I," Andy Heiam said.

"I give up," Nan Cisco said.

Darcy was almost afraid to ask, but did. "What else you got in your collection of goodies, Andy?"

"Couple more possibilities, but here's the one I really like."

Darcy again: "Go ahead, I suppose."

"Everybody knows about the North Shore, right?" he began.

Nan Cisco's sarcasm: "You mean the one up there on Lake Superior?"

Andy Heiam's puck: "The very same."

Darcy Austin's curiosity: "Scenic, but where's the weird?"

"Ever hear of the Devil's Kettle just past Grand Marais?" he asked them both.

"No," both of them replied in overlapping voices.

"You'll love this," he said. "There's this Brule River that flows into Lake Superior. Only, just before it gets to the big lake it goes over a sixty-foot vertical falls."

"So it's dramatic—I'm still waiting for weird," Darcy said.

"You want weird? Here it comes," he said, looking smug with what he was about to offer. "At the top of the falls, a bedrock knob splits the river in two. Half of it spills into a basin pool that flows into Superior normal like." Then he paused, as if to build suspense.

"And the other half?" Nan Cisco asked.

He threw up his arms in a grand gesture. "Nobody knows. That's what's weird."

"You mean it just disappears?" Darcy questioned.

Andy Heiam shrugged. "Well, yeah. It drops into a lava cauldron and is never seen again."

"How do they know it doesn't come up in Lake Superior somewhere?" Nan Cisco asked.

"They've searched—tried everything to find where it goes. No luck. That's why they call it the Devil's Kettle," he said. "End of story."

"I still can't believe they can't trace it," Nan Cisco said.

Andy Heiam looked down at the paper in front of him and picked up his spiel. "Geologists say there aren't the right kind of volcanic rocks or tube formations up there to carry the water away. And no one's found debris in the lake that an underground river might produce. No pooling points or backwaters in the area, either. They've even dumped ping pong balls into the cauldron and poured red die into it. Nothing shows up anywhere they can find."

"Wow. A good place to dispose of a murder victim," Nan Cisco said.

"Don't say murder victim around Williams/Bailey," Darcy Austin said.

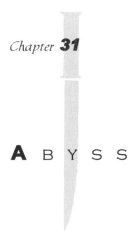

*Chapter* **31**

# A B Y S S

**CODA WAS ONE** of Magenta's most diabolical foes in the comic book pages of Fantasy Publications. A costumed "hit woman," she dispatched her victims out of pleasure as much as purpose. Unlike Magenta's other adversaries, Coda didn't challenge the heroine in direct conflict, playing a game of wits with her, instead. As a result, Magenta was forced to extract herself from devilish entrapments the villainess masterminded—narrowly escaping death each time. Episode #27, "Cavern of Doom," was just such an adventure.

Part One. Chase:

**MAGENTA PASSED BENEATH** the overhead banner identifying the entry to the Cave of the Winds, more remindful of a deserted mineshaft than a welcoming summertime tourist attraction, in its "closed for the season" bleakness. The gate at the entrance was ajar, its huge lock broken away. It was all too easy, the signs along the way on this chase and now the opened door to the Cave of the Winds.

A scalloped dialog balloon over the crime fighter revealed her thoughts: *Coda is up to her tricks—careful Magenta.*

Despite inner warnings, the Night Vigilante pressed on. The hit woman, who just claimed her latest victim, had to be stopped before more lives were surrendered.

Magenta's footfalls echoed as she scurried along the dimly lit corridor leading into the depths of the cave. Even the passageway's lighting was aglow for her.

Another scalloped balloon: *How convenient.*

Magenta came to a second opened barricade—this one at the spur leading to the Cavern of Doom—one more expedient along the trail. Taking the spur, she approached the cathedral-like space with its featured "bottomless" abyss.

And there was Coda—hands on hips, a hulking structure at her side. She had made her stand.

The balloon over Magenta: *At last we meet face-to-face, Coda.*

The balloon over Coda: *So be it, Maggie.*

Throwing caution aside, Magenta charged her foe. She should have known better. Crossing the expanse, the heroine tripped an unseen wire, releasing a net from the darkness above.

The weighted net engulfed the Night Vigilante, slamming her to the ground. And before she could free herself, Coda thrust a knee into her back, jerked her head back by the hair, and cupped a saturated pad over her face.

---

Part Two. Decree of Death:

**MAGENTA'S EYES FLUTTERED** opened. How long she had been unconscious, she didn't know.

A boom-like shaft loomed above her from which a cord snaked down from its foremost point to where it bound her wrists above her head. She strained against her bondage without success. Her strength was depleted, and she was woozy for the effort—a chloroform hangover.

Coda smiled down nastily at Magenta. The balloon over her head read: *Pleasant dream? I surely hope so because your worst nightmare is about to begin.*

Magenta diverted her eyes from Coda and traced the overhead boom to its platform. The apparatus was much like a medieval derrick.

Coda asked: *Like my charming device? Had it crafted especially for this occasion.*

Magenta didn't respond.

*It has a certain charm. Don't you agree?*

Magenta didn't appear as though she did.

*In just a bit, I'll show you how it operates.*

Magenta didn't appear anxious to know.

*Untie me Coda. Let's have it out woman to woman.*

Coda looked pensive. First balloon: *I don't know, Maggie, I'd probably just beat you silly—you in your present state and all.* Second balloon: *Besides, I've got something more exciting in store— you'll see . . .*

With that, Coda cranked a large spindle on the wooden contrivance, reeling in the rope attached to Magenta, lifting her off the cavern floor by her wrists.

Her quarry strung up to her satisfaction, Coda locked the spindle in place and released a lever allowing the machine to rumble toward the gaping abyss.

Magenta's stoic heroism had its limits, revealed in words and expression. *W-what are you doing with me?*

*Thrill ride, Hon.*

The boom thrust Magenta out over the edge of the precipice before Coda braked the contrivance, its foreword wheels at the edge of the crevasse.

Coda observed the heroine twisting over the black cavity. *Perfect,* Coda's balloon said. *Ohhh,* Magenta's balloon said.

Coda admired her handiwork. Balloon one: *A front-end loader woulda been easier.* Balloon two: *But that just doesn't do it for me. You?*

Magenta didn't reply.

*Now the real fun begins.* Coda fiddled with her machine. *When I activate this timing device over here, it begins releasing your tether in nice little increments.*

Next panel, first balloon: *The first three releases are just for fun.* Second balloon: *That's if it doesn't let go all at once.* Third balloon: *But the fifth—well . . . I'm afraid you're at the end of your rope, Hon.*

*You won't get away with this, Coda.* Magenta didn't appear all that confident of her statement.

*Oh, but I will—like starting right now.* Coda activated the timing device. *Guess that's it, Babe. Ta-ta.*

Turning to leave, Coda spoke over her shoulder. *You've got fifteen minutes before you discover whether the Cavern of Doom is really bottomless, Hon—just so you know.*

Left alone, Magenta twisted in space, the timing devise ticking off her remaining moments of life.

Part Three. Race Against Time:
**THE CLERK POKED** into the office of Deputy Chief of Police, Marko Cash, holding out an envelope.

First balloon: *For you, Chief.* Second balloon: *Delivery guy said you're s'posed to open it right away.*

Marko Cash extended a hand for the package, still staring down at the paperwork on his desk. *What's so blamed important?*

*Beats me, boss.* The clerk slapped the envelope in Marko's open palm, and tuned on his heels.

Marko Cash removed a parchment from inside the envelope.

A close-up panel showed a free-hand drawing depicting the Cave of the Winds with its gate ajar. Hand-scrawled words below the sketch read:

> *Chief Cash—*
> *Magenta will meet her doom 45 minutes from now.*
> *Providing, of course, this message reaches you at 2:00*
> *p.m. as I instructed*
> > *Save her if you can,*
> > *Coda*

Marko Cash knew that the Cave of the Winds was a perfect play-ground for Coda's treachery. The cave was a huge labyrinth, but the word "doom" narrowed it down to one particular spot. It was classic Coda.

Even making good time, it was still a good thirty-minute drive to the cave and at least another five minutes in a footrace to the Cavern of Doom, assuming the gates were left open.

His watch showed it was 2:05. Already five minutes lost.

He rushed to his car, and sped from Lake City, heading for his destination. The AMG C32 designation on the trunk of his car, and the three-pointed star, was for the car-heads among Fantasy readers.

Soon under way, Marko's speedometer showed 130.

He punched in the automatic dial on his hands-free cell phone and called for backup.

The speedometer now showed 155. *Coda didn't figure on 349 blown horses*, the scalloped balloon over Marko's head, revealed.

Part Four. At the Brink:

MAGENTA HAD ALREADY passed through three fearful releases, the device ceding a free fall followed by a jolting stop each time. It was enough to terrorize and pain, yet not enough to bring serious injury. Coda's diabolical mind would not want the Night Vigilante numbed to what lay in store for her.

As the fourth release approached, music began to emanate from the innards of the mechanism suspending her. The musical bars filling the panel were those of Christopher Rouse's "The Infernal Machine," from *Phantasmata*. Not that the readers of *Magenta Comics* were expected to recognize them as such.

Marko Cash dashed across the cavern floor, the resounding music calling the way to the dim chamber.

Magenta saw him rushing toward her. *The rope, Marko— catch the rope on the machine.*

Marko Cash saw the large spindle on the derrick begin to turn and hurled himself onto the structure just as it released the rope. Magenta was on her final plunge to the innards of the earth.

*Eeeeeeeee . . .*

Marko Cash made a one-handed grab, clutching the rope as it left its spindle, then clamping his other hand over it while being dragged and pummeled across the bulwark of the machine.

When his upper body jammed against the cross-members at the base of the boom, he came to a jolting stop. Battered and bruised, the policeman held fast, halting Magenta's drop to oblivion as the classical strains played out.

Part Five. Reprieve:

**NEITHER HE NOR** Magenta spoke as the rescue team moved the ungainly derrick back from its precipice.

Magenta knew she was alive only because Coda couldn't resist playing one of her diabolical games—in this instance, informing Marko Cash of the situation at the right moment to make things exciting. Naturally, Coda stacked the deck in her favor, as always. She planned to have Marko Cash arrive in time to witness the final plunge—not to prevent it. *Close. But you lost the game, Coda.*

Magenta's knees buckled under her when rescuers lowered her to the ground, and they cradled her down the rest of the way.

She smiled up to Marko, who was still straddling the machine above her, rope in hand. First balloon: *Thank you, Marko.* Second balloon: *But you've got to get a faster car.*

The cover of Magenta #27 depicted the Night Vigilante suspended over the Cavern of Doom, lashed wrists above her head—scant costume stressed to the essential limits of tolerance.

The crusading Dr. Wertham might well have turned in his grave.

# Chapter 32

# A T O N E M E N T

**JACK BAILEY WAS** a difficult, complex person. With a bulldog expression and in-your-face demeanor, he was a contrast to the smooth, diplomatic co-founder partner of Williams/Bailey. And while Mason Williams kept a consistent persona about him, Jack Bailey did not. He was charming and articulate in new-business presentations, stubborn and high-minded with clients, and caustically intimidating with employees. Despite the coarse side of the one partner, Messrs. Williams and Bailey made an effective duo with their offsetting skills. Nevertheless, they held one fault in common that limited the full potential of the agency, given its collected talent. They both were controlling individuals, requiring all work and process to pass through their hands.

Jack Bailey's office was also in total contrast to the fastidious Mason Williams' enclave at the other end of the building, which was intended to project an air of sophistication. Jack Bailey's office, the largest space in the shop, had all manner of things strewn about in haphazard fashion. Layout sheets, reference books, magazines, torn out newspaper articles and assorted props from previous television commercial "shoots" littered his desk, conference table and eclectic furnishings. Disparate wall hangings depicted assorted renditions of a brassy lifestyle that included a counterculture past juxtapositioned with black tie advertising awards ceremonies of more recent years.

Much of the agency's success was attributed to Jack Bailey. His creative talent was renowned. The numerous trophies and plaques on display at Williams/Bailey shouted national and international repute to clients, client prospects, and outside visitors to the agency.

Truth known, Jack Bailey was not the creative thinker he was given credit for being—not from a strict standpoint. Rather, he was quick to pick up on the breakthrough advertising of the few firms across the nation that produced truly original work and set new advertising trends. Jack Bailey was an excellent practitioner from there forward, and a tenacious executor of his work.

Not that it mattered all that much, with today's global network of instant communications, but there was a flat-out "creative" advertising firm residing in the Twin Cities from which Jack Bailey could draw inspiration and otherwise attempt to emulate. Fallon Wordwide had been named Agency of the Year twice within a decade by *Advertising Age*, the industry's trade bible, and yet again by the Clio Awards Group—a feat never attained by another advertising agency.

While Fallon fell short of Williams/Bailey in communications targeting, from the Edson Janes perspective, it didn't impede Fallon's phenomenal growth from that of an upstart group of a few years back to becoming a multi-office international agency of renown. This only intensified Jack Bailey's attempt to draft his twin-town neighbor. The creative freedom that was allowed in Fallon's shop escaped him, however.

———

THE "CREATIVES" IN an ad agency are the copywriters and art directors, Jack Bailey being of the latter discipline. The account people, who interface with clients, initiate projects and are responsible for the overall planning and budgeting of client campaigns, are called "suits." The media, production and traffic personnel in agencies, as secondary players, don't rate identifying nomenclature of this sort.

Darcy Austin was a suit, although in today's more casual business environment, suits don't usually wear suits unless they're involved in a major presentation to a client or client prospect—in which case the creatives present also wear suits. There once was a day when everyone wore suits all the time.

On this particular day, the suit was wearing a pair of Eddie Bauer jeans and a sweater while the creative was draped in Hugo Boss finery, attendant with dress shirt and tie, as Jack Bailey sorted through the layouts of the Minnesota Tourism campaign that Darcy Austin had brought to him, earlier in the day. He was not in a good mood.

"We thought this was a fresh approach instead of the usual 'Come visit' stuff," the suit said, in an attempt to fill the silent void beyond the rustle of Graphics 360 translucent marker paper.

Darcy would rather that Andy Heiam had done this, but he was off on a photo shoot, and time was short, what with the delays recent events had caused at the agency. So here she was in the office of the alter namesake and creative director of Williams/Bailey.

"Hmm," Jack Bailey said.

*At least he made a sound.* "I was really surprised it took two hundred years to find the source of the Mississippi River," Darcy offered, conversationally.

No reply.

*Keep trying, Darcy.* "And the Devil's Kettle—I'd like to see that myself."

"Not even close."

"Devil's Kettle?"

"Six pounds—all I ever got."

"I'm sorry?"

"The fish. Forty-five friggin' pounds according to this."

"Forty-five pounds, twelve ounces," Darcy filled in, relieved the creative director was conversing in some manner and anxious to display her newly acquired knowledge on the subject.

"I'll think about it."

"The fish?"

"The campaign."

Now she was back to concerned. Deadlines were looming. "Ah . . . when will you—"

"I'll take these to the lake this weekend. See me on Monday." Jack Bailey had a lake home in Nisswa, near Brainerd, Minnesota, in the heart of what was known as Lake Country.

"Sure. Fine. I'll tell Andy. Did you see the ad on Paul Bunyan and his blue ox up by Brainerd?" she asked as she got up to leave—knowing he had.

"I wish I hadn't."

*Never give up.* "The one on the world's largest ball of twine, in Darwin?" she dared persist.

His glare told her he had.

Jack Bailey was already working his gas pen on another project as Darcy wound her way past assorted paraphernalia in an attempt to leave. "Have a good weekend," she said upon reaching the door.

Jack Bailey grunted, not looking up.

*So much for conversing.*

# Chapter 33

# L A K E S I D E

HIS LAKE PLACE was a house, not a cabin, a log home, actually—although Twin Citians referred to any structure on a lake outside the metropolitan area as a cabin. It was located on Lower Cullen Lake Beautiful seventeen miles north of Brainerd adjacent to the quaint town of Nisswa. Jack Bailey could afford shoreline on the more expensive Gull Lake, which connected to Lower Cullen by a channel but chose not to locate there. Gull was bigger, rounder, more developed and more celebrated. But he preferred Cullen's rustic withdrawal. Also, he took pleasure in being unlike his more conventional acquaintances, who would embrace a spot on Gull in a heartbeat if they had the choice and the wherewithal. None of this was on his mind, however, as he dwelled over the Minnesota Tourism sketches and notes spread out on his game table serving as a desk.

There was no disputing that the creative director of Williams/Bailey was assiduous. And no question he was dedicated to the agency's creative standing in the advertising community. It was Sunday night, when he could be relaxing on his lakeside deck under the stars on a fresh Minnesota evening, instead of pouring over the campaign that was occupying him.

THE ALL-TERRAIN VEHICLE made its way down the Paul Bunyan recreational trail stretching 100 miles, Bemidji on its north and Brainerd on its south. The ATV's triple headlights illuminated the asphalt path as it ran parallel to Highway 361, southbound. It was an angular, broad-shouldered machine resembling a miniature version of a military humvee as much as an ATV. Its driver wore a heavy jacket and gloves, inappropriate for a late summer evening in lake country, along with kneepads and a modular helmet with its darkened face shield in place.

The hunkered ATV slowed to a crawl, turned left off the trail and crossed a long-abandoned railroad bed. There it turned left again, proceeding along Wilderness Drive bordered by trees on the left and secluded dwellings on the right that rimmed the southwest shore of Lower Cullen Lake Beautiful.

JACK BAILEY PUT aside the ad layouts that worked for him. "Schanken," "Kettle," and "Schoolcraft," were deemed okay for print ads—with his modifications, of course. "Bunyan," "Prairie Chicken," "Runestone," and "Twine," were out. Maybe, as sequential cuts in a TV commercial—even including that ridiculous Darwin ball of twine—they could have merit, though. He'd think on that.

THE ATV FOUND its way down the off drive, fifty feet from the lake home's double-door front entry. Lights off. The engine of the machine emitted a low gurgling sound. It seemed to hunker there like a hard-shelled beast observing its quarry against the sky and water backdrop, calculating its moment of attack.

JACK BAILEY EXAMINED the "Bunyan" ad one more time, his thoughts going to the concluding scene of the movie *Fargo,* when Margie the cop and her murdering captive each caught sight of the looming Paul Bunyan statue as they passed it by in her patrol car. Margie seemed to view the huge statue as the embodiment of gallantry, while the evildoer, who likely knew nothing of Minnesota lore, accepted the sculpture as a brooding assassin, ax in hand. To the creative director, it was the defining moment of a classic film.

Absorbed in contemplation, Jack Bailey wasn't aware of the closing sound outside until the thunderous clamor jarred his consciousness.

The ATV climbed the stairs with the dexterity of a charging animal, crashed through the white-pine doors of the lake home, and jolted to an abrupt halt in the space Jack Bailey occupied.

He sprang from his chair, facing machine and rider, splinters of pine cast about. "What the hell is this?" he shrieked. "Who are you?"

"Your executioner," the rider of the growling machine answered in a voice surreal behind the face shield.

The creative director stared in disbelief as the rider hinged the dark shield up over the crest of the helmet and leered back at him with a grin not cordial. "You," Jack Bailey cried out.

"Surprised?"

"Why are you here?"

"Didn't I tell you?"

The rider twisted the throttle, and the ATV lunged forward with 700 cc's of snarling might, four tires clawing at the hard wood floor.

Before the creative director could so much as raise his hands, the flat snout of the machine surged into his body, driving him into a wall with crushing force.


**THE RIDER CUT** the throttle and set the machine's brake.

The upper half of what was once Jack Bailey splayed over the hood of the ATV in grotesque fashion, his spine severed at the waist. The rear quarters of his body were imbedded in the splintered paneling, dished-out plasterboard and fractured timber supports. The rest of him was somewhere beneath the snout of the machine.

Reaching over the windshield from the driver's seat, the rider lifted the dead man's head by its thin hair, and examined the victim's face—its expression distorted, eyes unseeing, drooping mouth spilling blood and spittle. Satisfied, the killer released the head, letting it thud to the cowl without reverence.

The rider shut down the idling motor and dismounted. Then, removing helmet and jacket, placed them on the seat of the ATV just behind the emblem displayed on the side of the machine's cowl.

Moving to the kitchen, the killer snatched a ring of keys from the counter, with a gloved hand. "You don't mind if I borrow your SUV now, do you Jack? No need to answer if it's okay." Pause. "Fine then. See you at the funeral."

Exiting through the front entry that no longer supported doors, the killer punched the remote key for the black Navigator parked outside, climbed in and drove into the placid Minnesota night.

*Chapter* **34**

# P O S T - M O R T E M

ON MONDAY MORNING, Darcy called Jack Bailey's office as he had ordered her to do. No answer. She went to the coffee station, loaded up with fresh-brewed Dunn Brothers, took the stairs down to the creative floor, being careful not to spill her brimming cup, and walked over to the creative director's office. No sign of life, and the lights in his office were off. Unusual for the early-arriving agency partner. Maybe he had a morning meeting outside the office, Darcy speculated. He didn't mention it, but then Jack Bailey was not the most communicative person in the shop. She'd check later.

Thirty minutes later, Darcy got a call from Mason Williams. "You seen Jack this morning?" he asked.

"No," she replied, "I was by his office earlier. He wasn't in."

"Yeah. Jack said he'd be meeting with you on Tourism when he took off on Friday. That's why I called when I couldn't locate him."

"Sorry, Mason. Can't help."

"Well, that's Jack—hard to keep tabs on. Thanks anyway."

Darcy put the phone down. *If he doesn't show up before noon, Andy will be back and I won't have to deal with the Supreme Being, alone.* That was of some comfort to her.

After lunch, Darcy checked again. Andy Heiam was in, but Jack Bailey still wasn't. She called Mason Williams, who said he tried Bailey's lake place, his Eden Prairie home, and his cell phone. "He's probably in route from Nisswa," Mason said. "You know how he is about turning his cell phone off." Darcy didn't, but she accepted the explanation and went down to Andy Heiam's office to update him on where things stood on Tourism.

**THE VOICE ON** the phone introduced itself as Jens Olson, Sheriff of Crow Wing County, and went on to say, "Understand you're the one in charge of that Soup Case down there."

"*Was*, I'm happy to say," Lieutenant Douglas Hankenson answered, "What can I do for you, Sheriff."

"Sorry, but I think that's '*is*,'" Sheriff Olson came back.

Hank sat up straighter in his chair. "Explain please."

"We found this guy up here. His ID says he's with that advertising agency where the Soup Murder took place. John R. Bailey—name's on the door of the place, by his business card."

"You found him? Where?" Hank didn't like what he was hearing.

"He's dead, Lieutenant, busted in half by an ATV—right in his own place. That's where I'm at now."

"Jesus," Hank exclaimed. "No accident?" knowing it wasn't.

"Someone drove this thing through the front doors on the fly an' pinned 'im to the wall. Then left in Bailey's SUV. We found it in Pequot Lakes up 371—keys 'n' all.

"Jesus," Hank said again.

"Somethin' else," Olson went on. "This perp's a cool one."

"How so?"

"There's a jacket and a helmet on the seat of the ATV. Stacked up real nice."

"Meaning . . . ?"

"Don't know, for sure, but from where I'm standing I read North Star on the machine, North Star on the jacket, and North Star on the helmet. Seems like I'm supposed to notice that."

"I'm afraid you are," Hank said, the Williams/Bailey client list still fresh in his mind. "How do I get there, Sheriff?"

"Got a note pad? It's about two and a half hours from the Cities. A little more from Bloomington, I expect."

"I'll be there in two. Go ahead."

"Okay. Just don't get a ticket, Lieutenant."

**HANK AND JOE** Baines arrived, on Hank's schedule, without running afoul of the highway patrol or any locals along the way. The only delay being a missed turn onto Wilderness Road.

At the scene, it was obvious to Hank that the ATV had climbed the stairs outside, came through the front doors and crushed Jack Bailey into the wall, just as the sheriff had said.

Hank lifted Jack Bailey's head with a latex-gloved hand, exposing his face. "It's Bailey, all right. Met with him several times in connection with the murders down there."

"He's in the Bailey cabin, with identification in his wallet, but you never know for sure 'til someone makes a positive on 'im," Sheriff Olson said. "Couldn't find any neighbors around that knew him. Some are back in the Cities." Pause. "I'll have someone contact next of kin. He married?"

"Yeah," Hank replied. "From what we got, he and his wife led pretty independent lives. That's why it's not surprising you found him up here alone. Kids are gone from the nest."

"She'll have to be checked out," the sheriff said.

"We'll take care of that, Sheriff," Joe Baines responded.

"I'm afraid we've got our game-playing friend back with us," Hank added. "And I don't expect that's a housewife."

"Sure," Sheriff Olson nodded. "And it's Jens."

"Okay, Jens. I'm Hank. And this is Joe," motioning to the sergeant, still unnerved from his one-hour and fifty-four-minute ride from Bloomington to where he was now standing.

"Like it better that way. We're not too formal around here," Jens Olson said as if that wasn't apparent from his open jacket, plaid Pendelton shirt, well-worn jeans, and a belt buckle that displayed more metal than his badge, made all the more prominent by his extended belly.

"We just look formal," Hank said from inside his Oxxford suit from Hubert White, Minneapolis, graciously including Joe Baines in his remark. Then he was back to the murder. "What brought you to the site, Jens?"

"Jogger from down the way, passed by on Wilderness Road this morning. Don't have many of those around here," he commented under his breath. "Happened to see the front doors busted open. Came down the drive to investigate and found this." Jens Olson gestured to the machine and corpse. "Lights still on an' all. He was pretty shook."

"I don't wonder," Hank said.

"Looks like it's your Soup Killer, all right." the sheriff said, then added, "I thought he was dead."

"So did we," Hank shrugged, not mentioning the doubts he harbored about that all along. "Could be a copy cat, but I doubt it up here. Bears all the marks, besides. The killer went out of the way to be sure we knew he used a Williams/Bailey client product as the murder weapon—lining up North Star logos like that. Only thing missing from the pattern is a bash on the back of the vic's head. But that wasn't an expedient this time around."

"Fits with me," Jens Olson said. "So what was the suicide all about, down there?"

"I suspect Bennett was involved in the other murders but wasn't the main guy."

"Well, your main guy's long gone from here, I'd venture," the sheriff said. "Probably had a car stashed at Pequot Lakes where we found the Navigator, 'bout twenty miles up on 371."

"What time did it happen?" Hank asked

"Crime people think he was killed sometime around ten-thirty, best estimate. No witnesses to verify anything. Here or in Pequot. He musta been working on all these sheets of paper with drawings on 'em, over there on the table," Jens Olson said, motioning to his right, "before gettin' stuck with this thing," motioning to his left.

"Yeah, layout sheets," Hank filled in with jargon he had picked up of late. "Got 'em photographed? I'd like to have copies—along with everything else you got."

"Yep—I'll have it all messengered down to you." Then Jens Olson pointed to the center of the room and added, "Skid marks over here indicate the machine braked hard, probably coming to a stop, then started up again—real fast like."

"Sizing up its prey before the final leap," Joe Baines inserted. "No prints, I gather."

"None but Bailey's, and the usual assortment that won't tell us anything. I'd wager the ATV's clean."

Joe Baines looked to Hank: "I'll call the department—let 'em know we still got a case on our hands."

"Okay," Hank said. "While you're doing that, I'll call Mason Williams. I'm afraid he's got big trouble besides the loss of a managing partner." *And then I'll call Darcy*, he didn't say.

**THIRTY MINUTES LATER,** the three men were standing in the driveway—the distressful calls out of the way, the Brainerd crime-scene team finishing up inside.

They fell just short of kicking in the dirt like Minnesota men are prone to do when gathered in a circle this way. Hank would have messed up his Alden New Englands, but he almost felt like doing it anyway. It's in the blood.

"Beautiful day, too," Jens said, shaking his head.

"You have someone named Margie working with you?" Hank asked, with a wry smile.

"Who?" Jens asked. Then catching Hank's drift: "Hey . . . here's where we're supposed to be looking up an' say'n, 'looks like snow.' Right?"

"What happened to 'beautiful day?'" Hank asked in return.

"This is Minnesota. Don't like the weather, wait ten minutes," Jens said, a grin spreading across his broad face.

"Will someone tell me what you guys are talking about?" Joe Baines asked.

"Hop in, Joe," Hank said, opening the door of the BMW to his associate. "I'll explain on the way back."

"Do that," Joe Baines answered, "Nice and slow like—the way you're gonna drive. Right?

"Right."

LIEUTENANT HANKENSON AND Sergeant Joe Baines talked through more than scenes from *Fargo* by the time they arrived back at Bloomington Police Headquarters in near-legal time, appreciated by the latter.

"All hell's gonna break loose when the media gets hold of this," Joe Baines was saying to Hank.

"Can't be helped, pal. Keep your head down and let the chief and mayor deal with the newsies."

"Wanna press on Frank Ramstead, now?"

"He's on the menu. Hell, he's the only thing on the menu."

Joe Baines knew his boss well. "But what?"

"But we came up with zip last time. I'd like to dig deeper before we take an overt pass at him."

"Dex Ames didn't like him from the beginning."

"Well, let's see if his sixth sense is as good as you say. Have Dan check him for paper trails—military records, if any, job reviews, credit bureau, banking relationships, citations—anything else he can dig up. Maybe we can subpoena his bank records if we get something going here. Send Marge Kennedy out on a personal search. Check with his neighbors, acquaintances, and all that. She's good at discreet, and we need discreet."

"Check with Ms. Austin, maybe?"

"I'll handle that. Gotta be some bennies with this job."

*Chapter* **35**

# O B L I G A T I O N

WILLIAMS/BAILEY WAS an internal disaster. The Jack Bailey murder produced an atmosphere close to panic, and the ship began to leak. There were six fear-induced employee resignations on Tuesday—two more on Wednesday. And, after Jack Bailey's funeral on Thursday, Tuff-Wrap Plastic Trash Bags announced it was leaving the shop. There was no way they were going to risk having the next murder victim found with a Tuff-Wrap bag cinched over his or her head. The wonder in their camp was that Tuff-Wrap wasn't already the means to one of the murders. Its management had had enough.

Things calmed down a little after these events, but no one was sure when the next calamity might occur—either on the murder side of the issue or the desertion side.

Mason Williams was distraught. He'd lost his founding partner, his agency was in jeopardy, and everyone knew he had to be concerned about his own safety as well. Still he persevered. He was at the office every day, mingled with the staff and attempted to rally his people as best he could. Nor did he wait long to restructure the creative department in order to fill the void left by Jack Bailey and assure the agency's clients that positive action was being taken to sustain a high level of creativity on their behalf. He knew Jack Bailey's creative talent and drive would be missed. But he was also aware that his partner was controlling to a fault. He expected the shop's creative staff, released from its short leash, to flourish in new ways. He did not see the same personal failing on his end of the business. In his mind, he simply ran a tight ship.

**"HOLDING UP?" HANK** questioned over the phone.

"Yeah, but it's rough around here," Darcy answered. "How are you doing?"

"If it isn't the chief, it's the mayor, and the press is all over us. But I'll make it, public servant, that I am."

"Thanks for sending over copies of the tourism layouts from Jack's cabin. We had some other roughs around, but not as comprehensive. Saved us a step getting back up to speed." Darcy felt guilty discussing a business expedient under the circumstances and deviated somewhat. "Wayne Mitch has taken over Jack's role in the agency. He's already approved some of the stuff—yours included."

"Mine?"

"Your guys: Schanken and Schoolcraft."

"Does that mean I'm an ad person?"

"Well . . . I wouldn't quit police work just yet."

"Right. Speaking of police work, we've got surveillance on Mason Williams and Martin Hatfield," Hank said, turning to more serious matters. "We're going to add Wayne Mitch to the list, too, now that he's been named creative director."

"Marty Hatfield's my new boss, by the way."

"So I've heard. Look Darcy, we think we know why you were targeted, and that's past. But if you want us to—"

"No way," Darcy interrupted.

"You're sure? Might make you feel better to have someone around," Hank offered.

"When I want to feel better, I'll come over to your place."

"Well, in that case, I hope you're a little apprehensive right now."

"Actually, I am, but can't get away. Tonight though?"

"Your place or mine?"

"It's my turn. Eight okay?"

"Just started my timer."

"Okay. Gotta run."

"One question first."

"Shoot. Or is that not a good word to use these days."

"Nobody's been shot yet."

"Bennett was."

"He shot himself. That doesn't count." And without a break, Hank added: "How well did you know Frank Ramstead?"

"You suspect him?"

"Gotta start someplace."

"Just a little. He left shortly after I got here," Darcy said. "I'll fill you in on what little else I know about him tonight, but you might want to talk to Kevin Holbrook. He's at Carmady Baxter, an agency downtown. Ramstead and Holbrook were pretty good buds when they were here. Used to go on hunting trips together. They made kind of an odd couple."

"Hey, I think I know the guy. Took some of the same classes at the U, if it's that Kevin Holbrook. Friendly guy, talks a lot, sandy hair?"

"Sounds like him."

"So he wound up in the ad game. I'll be damned. Thanks for the tip."

"You're welcome. Don't forget tonight, in all your excitement."

"Oh yeah, that."

**THE FOLLOWING WEEK,** Hank had a lunch date set up with Kevin Holbrook at Nick & Tony's, and Darcy had a video date at Fantasy Publications.

**"I'M JUST A** Bloomington bumpkin," Hank Hankenson was saying, "what do hip ad types order for lunch in the big city?"

"It doesn't matter what you eat so long as you have a martini, olives preferred." Kevin Holbrook replied, "Just eat the biscuits they serve."

"Too much like donuts. What's the soup like, here?"

"I thought you'd want to avoid soup, from what I read."

"I forgot. Maybe I *should* have a martini."

"Someone at W/G sic you on me, Douglas?"

"Hey, Kev, just wanted to talk about old times. Ski-U-Mah, Goldie Gopher, and all that."

"Uh-huh." Pause. "I was pretty close with him a few years back,"

"Who we talkin' about . . . Goldie Gopher?"

Kevin Holbrook ignored him. "We used to hunt together."

"For gophers?"

"Think I'll have that martini now." He waved his hand in the air. "Waitress."

"Nobody drinks at lunch anymore, do they?"

"On this occasion they do."

"Actually I don't want—"

"Yes, you do." Turning to the waitress as she ambled over, he said: "Make 'em gin and dry. Traditional condiments." He held up two fingers.

Then, back to Hank: "Things sorta fell apart for Frank after he left Williams/Bailey."

At least Hank knew it wasn't the Goldie Gopher mascot Kevin was talking about now.

"He was a hard friend to begin with, but after getting ousted from W/B, his career backed up on him, and he got bitter on top of it. He was gonna be with Fallon some day, not Rumsey, where he ended up. His wife thought so, too. She left him when that didn't pan out."

Hank knew about Fallon. He'd never heard of Rumsey.

Their drinks arrived. "That was quick," Hank said. "They must appreciate you around here."

Kevin Holbrook let the remark pass, holding up one of the clear glasses with two large olives in it. "To the bygone days of the three-martini lunch. Didn't you have better things to do, Jimmy Carter?"

Hank lifted his glass in return salute. "Actually, the three-martini lunch was long gone before Jimmy made a big deal out of it. But that's politics. Was he bitter enough to kill?"

"Jimmy Carter?" Kevin took a big swallow.

"That's my routine. Answer the question."

Kevin paused for a moment, then: "I really can't say no to that, God help me."

"There's something to be said for what a good martini can get out of a person," Hank replied, rolling his glass in his hand. "Wanna tell me more?"

**DARCY WAS ILL** at ease. She had a right to be uncomfortable standing around in her skimpy Magenta costume with, she imagined, Josh Williams and Andrea Shiff looking her over every moment they weren't preoccupied with the Pad Room lights and video setup.

"Holly will be out in a minute," Andrea said. "She likes to primp."

"What for?" Darcy asked. "She's just gonna get mussed up right away, isn't she?"

"That's the way she is," Andrea shrugged.

Josh Williams offered a faint smile.

Holly Hartley made a grand entrance from the dressing room, wearing a yellow "Vixen" costume that was every bit as brief as Darcy's Magenta outfit. The difference was, she seemed to revel in the exposure. The yellow costume complemented her blond hair, done just so, as did the bright red lip gloss she wore. The micro skirt made her long legs appear all the longer, and Darcy could see, true to form, a bra was not part of her attire either.

"You met before?" Andrea Shiff said, knowing they had.

"Briefly," Darcy replied. "On the way in."

"Yeah, sure," Holly Hartley said with disinterest.

"Okay, you both know the basic plan. Whenever you're ready. Don't worry about perfection or anything like that. Just go with the flow."

"Yeah, sure," Holly Hartley said again.

*Not exactly Miss Congeniality*, Darcy thought. "Shall we, Holly?" she said out loud, nodding to the Pad Room and trying to be nice.

Josh Williams stared and waited.

Not a whole lot occurred in the first moments. The two danced around each other, coming together from time to time, bouncing off the padded walls as they jousted about. Boring. Their antics were loosely following the script all right, and there were a couple of babes out there being recorded, but nothing inspirational was forthcoming to Fantasy's benefit.

Josh brought a hand across his chest as a third-base coach might and, with that, Holly Hartley got aggressive. She grabbed Darcy by the hair, pulled her forward and brought a knee up into her midsection, doubling her over. With another yank of her hair, Darcy pitched forward and fell to her knees. She fought to catch her breath and tried to get up, but a forearm from the blonde spilled her onto her back.

Holly dropped down on top of Darcy, pinning her arms back, and for a moment it looked as though the "fight" might be over. But Darcy twisted away before her combatant gained complete control of her. That would have been horrible.

Darcy got back to her hands and knees only to be seized by the hair again and, this time, pulled backwards. She sprawled on the mat de novo, legs in the air. Still, Darcy managed to roll over and scramble to her feet before her pursuer could pounce on her again, not suffering any more damage to body or psyche.

Frustrated that Darcy escaped her, the blonde charged, grabbed Darcy by the arm, and spun her into a padded wall. Darcy knew she was in trouble. What would Erica do?

When her opponent came at her this time, Darcy planted her forward foot, twisted to one side, and brought her opposite knee up to waist level—

her opponent's waist level. And before the fast-closing woman could react, a lashing foreleg caught her in full charge, right in her mid-section.

Erica would have been proud. "Ooof," The breath rushed out of Holly Hartley as she doubled over Darcy's leg and collapsed to her knees. Now Darcy grabbed Holly by *her* hair, messing it up in the process. She yanked the blonde to her feet and brought a knee up into her gut. Holly's breath defected again, and with another "Ooof," she dropped back down to the mat.

This time Darcy really messed up her opponent's hair, jerking the blonde's head from side to side, eliciting little shrieks from her as she did.

The fight was out of "Vixen." Darcy put her on her back, straddled her and, in a final act, gripped her hair at the sides of her head and pressed it to the mat. Hard.

"Give it up, Blondie." Darcy demanded. Now *she* wasn't being very friendly.

"I give, I give," Holly cried out.

"Okay, that's it," Andrea Shiff said, moving onto the mat. Then, reaching the combatants, she said, "Great job, girls."

"Yeah, sure," Darcy grunted, stealing Holly Hartley's earlier phrase. With that, she stood up and strode out of the Pad Room without looking at Andrea.

"Ooohh." Holly Hartley groaned, not going anywhere at the moment. She didn't look at Andrea, either. Her eyes were closed tight.

"You set me up," Darcy said as she stalked past Josh Williams who appeared lost in thought, seated in his director's chair.

JOSH WILLIAMS HAD what he wanted. The following month Magenta #32 would reach the comic book stands featuring the "Hair-pulling Fight" between Vixen and the Night Vigilante. It was another boffo release for Fantasy Publications.

THIS TIME THE interrogation of Frank Ramstead was a lot harsher than before. Bloomington Police found that he had gone through two stormy marriages, and an unusual number of banking relationships. Adding to this, Kevin Holbrook had not had nice things to say in Ramstead's defense, portraying him as a person capable of extreme violence when riled.

Investigators were not able to subpoena his military records, nor gain access to his banking records. Nevertheless, it was learned that the discharge dates on his business resumé fell short of a normal military tour of duty, and his current finances were in shambles. On top of that, he couldn't verify his whereabouts on the night Jack Bailey was killed. With no back-up witness to corroborate he was at home, his alibi was hollow.

None of these matters incriminated him, in and of themselves, although they made investigators mighty suspicious.

Even so, Lieutenant Hankenson was still not convinced of his guilt. Frank Ramstead remained outspoken and vitriolic about Janes, Williams/Bailey, and now even Jack Bailey. *Would a guilty man do that*, he put to himself? Hank sensed there was something Ramstead wasn't saying. *Might he be covering for someone else, even at his own expense? And, if so, who? And why?* The more he probed, the more convinced Hank became that there was more to the story—even though his questioning got him nowhere.

With no smoking gun, Frank Ramstead was released, although he was instructed not to leave the state and all those other things suspects are warned about.

"He's a tough one," Joe Baines said to his boss after the interrogation was over.

"He knows more than he's telling us, Joe," Hank replied.

"Yeah. He didn't tell us he did it."

"Somethin' else going on here, pal."

"Sometimes I think you've got a nose like a Doberman," Joe Baines said. "You could be right."

No doubts existed in some other quarters, however. Frank Ramstead was tried in the press and found guilty.

DESPITE ALL THE negative disruption at the agency, Darcy Austin was more upbeat than her compatriots, at the moment. She was telling Erica Carlson about her Pad Room encounter with some verve.

"I thought you hated the whole idea," Erica interrupted.

"I think it's crazy, and obnoxious on top of it. That woman came at me like there was no scripting to this thing at all. Grabbed me by the hair—kneed me in the gut."

"So, wha'd' ya do?"

"I clobbered her."

"Way ta go. Our little sessions help, you think?"

"Hugely. I gave her a foreleg sidekick." Darcy omitted how she almost didn't make it that far. "The rest was a piece of cake."

"Sounds like a real fight broke out."

"I'll say. I think I was set up."

"Hmm. When's your next go?"

"Two weeks. They moved it back because of Jack Bailey's death."

"Considerate of them. How come your first event went off as scheduled?"

"Deadline. Had to get published and needed material—so they claimed."

"Gotta keep our priorities straight, after all."

Darcy turned tentative when she posed the question that had been in her thoughts: "Erica, if you wouldn't mind . . . could we continue our workouts for a little while longer?"

Much to Darcy's relief, Erica didn't hesitate. "Why not? You think the next babe will come at you like this one did?"

"I don't expect so. I said something to Josh, and Andrea knows I was teed off. That Vixen babe used to be a girlfighter at Solid Gold—likes to rough it up, I guess. But I'd still like to be ready in any event. Somethin' nutty about that place."

"Okay. We can work on that high leg sweep of yours," Erica advised.



**HANK WAS IN** his office when he got the call at 8:32 a.m. He was informed that Frank Ramstead had been shot outside his home, just a half hour before. He was dead.

# Chapter 36

# C H A R A D E

IT FIT THE pattern. Citizen commits high profile crime, evades prosecution and comes to Jesus, or more likely Satan, via the Rifleman.

Frank Ramstead stepped out on his front stoop to pick up his morning paper and was struck in the forehead with a thirty-oh-six that took out his anterior head. The bullet was recovered, along with a large portion of his skull and assorted brain matter, in the foyer, behind where his body fell.

From the trajectory of the bullet, the shooter was positioned on the opposite side of the street. He was assumed to have fired from a car as there was no "shooters rest," spent cartridge, or smoking rifle—all things the Rifleman had always left in evidence before.

With the hubbub over the Soup Killer, the Rifleman had fallen into the background where he may have preferred to be for the time being. But now he was back big time. At least it appeared so.

"Looks like we get to put a lid on it all over again," Sergeant Joe Baines said. "This is getting monotonous."

"Minacious is more like it," Lieutenant Douglas Hankenson returned.

"Huh?"

"Never mind. I'm going out to the course."

"There's reports to make out."

"Sergeants do paperwork. Lieutenants play golf."

THINGS QUIETED DOWN at Williams/Bailey yet another time. Darcy Austin concentrated on the Minnesota Tourism campaign, with only Lieutenant Hankenson and her upcoming final session at Fantasy to distract her. The former she didn't mind. The latter she did.

Darcy didn't know that the week before she was scheduled to revisit Fantasy Publications, she would read about her previous exploits at the Pad Room. "Hey, Darcy," Andrea Shiff said from Darcy's office doorway. "You're a smash," she added, tossing a copy of *Magenta Comics* onto the account woman's desk.

"That was fast," Darcy said. "How did you do it so quick?"

"We had a lot of things in place already, and just needed to fill in with the part you and Holly played out. And this copy isn't from the final run that will go to distributors. It's what we call a pre-pub, or file copy." Pause. "You did a great job, by the way. Thanks."

Darcy ignored her last comment and picked up the comic book, paging through it. *That Josh really can draw.* Doing a quick scan of the panels, she got to the "fight scene" toward the end of the book and slowed down to study it. "That arrogant blonde's doing more damage to me in here than she actually did," Darcy said, more of a complaint than a comment—and ignored the fact that Holly had almost taken her out early in the fracas.

"Got to make things larger than life," Andrea said. "Besides, that's Magenta and Vixen, not you and Holly."

"You said I *am* Magenta."

"Just keep going, you'll get back at her. Magenta always triumphs."

"Was there that much hair pulling?" Darcy cringed. "Looks like a cat fight."

"Poetic license." *And, it was a cat fight if ever I saw one.* "It's gonna be a big issue."

"Do I get a percentage?"

Andrea just smiled.

Darcy thought she might bring the comic book along to show Hank that night. It was kind of sexy. For sure she'd show it to Erica in the morning.

"I'M TELLING YOU so you can keep looking around kind of quiet like, if you want," the recognized voice on the other end of the phone said. "But it wasn't the Rifleman who did Ramstead."

"How can you be sure?" Hank asked, even though he suspected his caller was speaking the truth, if not certain of it."

"You kidding?" the voice said. "Sitting in a car waiting for the guy to step out for the morning paper scratchin' his balls? Not the way the Rifleman does things."

"Oh?"

"The Rifleman woulda taken Ramstead out from the top of the Washburn water tower with the likes of a Heckler & Koch at 500 meters. Then left everything behind to show how clever he was."

Hank knew his caller was right but said, "You know a lot about the guy."

"I'm supposed to nail him, remember. Gotta get in his mind."

"Seems like you've done that pretty well. But thanks for the heads up—I think."

"Play it the way you want, Lieutenant. But play it. Your killer's still out there."

"You think Ramstead got it because he knew something the Soup Killer didn't want him to spill? No pun intended."

"There's hope for you suburban cops, yet," Sig Nadler said with a smile in his voice, then hung up.

**"OKAY, THE RIFLEMAN** didn't whack Ramstead. Where do we go from here?" Joe Baines asked.

Douglas Hankenson answered: "As far as the public and the press are concerned, we can let it stay with the Rifleman for now; let 'em conclude that Ramstead was the perp in the Soup Case. Like Bennet, I'm guessing he was involved some way, but not how people think."

"Wonderful. And what do we really do?"

"Like Columbo. We act like we're taken in and hope the killer gets overconfident and makes a mistake. Or we just get lucky." In fact, Hank didn't think the killer expected to fool him for long; there was too much transparency involved. Instead, he felt it was part of the killer's overall game plan. He still wasn't sure where all this was heading, but why not play along? What choice did he have?

"If those don't happen, and somebody else gets snuffed at Williams/Bailey—what then?" Joe Baines questioned.

"Then I look like Inspector Clouseau," Hank quipped. "We'll keep security on Williams, Hatfield, and Mitch," he added more seriously. "Call it routine, while we're wrapping things up. That'll cover our asses to some extent if another attempt is made on a W/B principal. Meantime, while everyone's looking the other way, we do our damnedest to crack this thing once and for all—or, like I said, we just get lucky."

"No way you think it might have been Ramstead, and the Rifleman did him?" his associate questioned one last time.

"Can't buy it," Hank answered. "A more likely scenario is that the Soup Killer plans to strike again, and the Rifleman ploy is to get everyone to relax in order to make his next move easier. I'm betting he also wanted Ramstead silenced because we were grilling him, and he knew too much for comfort. It's killing two birds with one stone."

"Forget Columbo. You're bloody Sherlock Holmes," Joe Baines said.

**AS WITH MOST** investigations going nowhere, getting lucky is what often turns the corner—Sherlock Holmes and Columbo notwithstanding.

*Chapter* **37**

# A R M A G E D D O N

**THEY MET IN** the common area of the dressing room, having just stepped out from the more intimate private rooms to either side. Both women were in costume.

Caren Dalton's long, black hair matched her ebony "Sadanna" costume, falling down her shoulders to her back. Her milky white skin offered stunning contrast to both. Darcy noticed that Ms. Dalton was close to thirty-six on top, as opposed to her own "thirty-six plus a little bit more."

She was as tall as Darcy, strikingly beautiful, and looked to be in excellent shape. A workout babe. Were that her demeanor was as polished.

"How's Lieutenant Hankenson these days?" Caren Dalton asked, sizing up Darcy in her Magenta garb, as she was being studied in return. Ms. Austin would be desirable between the sheets, she saw. *Hank still can pick 'em.*

"You know him?" Darcy was surprised. Hank hadn't mentioned her.

"Very well—long before you came on the scene. We were, ah, dating."

"I see him from time to time. How did you know?"

"Read about your involvement with that Soup Case. Put the rest together. Not hard to figure out."

"Oh?"

"I suppose you're climbing into bed with him. If I know Hank, he's been in your pants by now."

Things were cool before. Now it was glare ice.

"Like that's any of your business."

She ignored Darcy's pique. "Does he still have that old staying power?"

"Why do you ask? Was he a little much for you back then?"

It did not promise cajolery in the Pad Room . . .

**"FAMILIAR WITH THE** story boards?" Andrea Shiff asked "Magenta" and "Sadanna" when they strode up to the Pad Room, both appearing stern and resolute. "This is supposed be the climatic struggle between archrivals, you know. Don't be timid, but be careful. We don't want anybody hurt."

"Let's just get started," Darcy Austin answered.

"Can't wait," Caren Dalton said.

They were glaring at each other.

Josh Williams smiled from his director's chair.

"Well, I guess you know what we're after," Andrea concluded. "Let's do it then."

There was no preliminary feeling-out period this time—nor did the storyboard "script" hold any meaning. The two women went at each other from the beginning—startling Andrea Shiff, and even Josh Williams, with the suddenness of their outburst.

They bumped, tossed, grabbed and held—upright, on their knees and tumbling on the mat. The intensity was fierce, and although it was apparent both women knew how to wage a disciplined fight, that soon went by the wayside.

Their costumes were not crafted for the mayhem taking place. Darcy's halter loosened, then let go. Caren's tighter fitting top held on a bit longer before also failing. It wasn't that unusual for a breast to be exposed in the Pad Room now and then, but nothing this overt had ever happened before.

Each of the women seized the advantage for a time—though never for long, and then not by much, as the conflict continued. Whatever else was seized, whether by happenstance or purpose, was another matter.

Andrea Shiff watched in astonishment, never having witnessed anything like this. She considered stopping the fray before a serious injury occurred. She put her note pad aside and started to rise from her chair, when Josh Williams extended an arm and motioned her back, while continuing to stare straight ahead.

Soon the combatants wore down—the pace they set had reduced them to groping, pawing and clinching. Finally, clutched together, they tumbled to the mat where the tussle soon subsided. Darcy was on her back, arms falling away, unable to continue the struggle. Caren Dalton was face down across Darcy's body. She made one last effort—though she hardly had the strength—to straighten herself on top of Darcy in a demonstration of triumph, but was denied her goal. Andrea Shiff gripped her by the shoulders and pulled her to Darcy's side. From there, fatigue won out, her body falling still. The battle was over.

"That's enough girls, it's finished," Andrea Shiff proclaimed as if that wasn't obvious. Then added: "You both okay?" That was obvious, too—neither was.

The brunette stared back at her questioner through half closed eyes. Darcy's eyes were closed completely. They both were silent and neither woman attempted to cover her breasts, rising and falling on heavy breath. What remained of Darcy's costume cleaved low on her hips. Caren Dalton's outfit hadn't fared a whole lot better in the carnage. But, for the moment, at least, factors of modesty held little sway with the depleted combatants.

ANDREA SHIFF RETRIEVED robes from the dressing rooms. Caren Dalton clutched the welcome terry cloth to her body while Andrea Shiff draped the other garment around Darcy. "Okay now, Darcy?" she asked. A nod. "Caren?" Another nod.

"What's going on between you two?" she questioned. No answer. "I've never seen anything like it. Sure you're both all right?" Two heads nodded, again.

Then Caren Dalton said her first words since the conflict began. "I whipped your ass," she said under her breath, in Darcy's direction.

Darcy didn't answer back.

Josh Williams sat in his chair throughout the whole affair, not uttering a word. A plot was forming in his mind. Then, again, were he to stand, it might prove embarrassing.

THE FOLLOWING MONTH, Magenta #39 was released, the bulk of its sixty-four pages devoted to the momentous third confrontation between the Night Vigilante, and Sadanna, the Dark Terror, Queen of the Bad Girls.

Readers expected this third battle between Good Girl and Bad Girl to be conclusive. Even so, they didn't anticipate what was portrayed.

Surprise number one: No obstructions or obscuring shadows got in the way as costumes yielded to the stresses of conflict. Readers were soon witnessing an honest to gosh topless girlfight.

Surprise number two: The bad girl gained the initiative in the struggle, then took full charge of the Night Vigilante.

Surprise number three: No outside influences reversed the tide for Magenta, as her fans had come to expect whenever she fell into troubled situations in the past.

Surprise number four: The Night Vigilante was displayed across a double-page spread in the aftermath of battle—on her back, one knee drawn up, arms at her sides, eyes closed, lips parted. It was a stunning portrayal, yet there was more— or less . . .

The fallen heroine wore gloves, boots, mask, and *nothing more*. Sadanna loomed over the fallen heroine in a provocative stance—the most critical article of Magenta's clothing dangling from her hand like a trophy of her triumph.

The issue, entitled *Magenta Defeated*—soon to be dubbed *Magenta Denuded* on the street—disappeared from the shelves as readers and collectors snatched them up, prompting a second pressrun. Fantasy Publications, breaking new ground, hit it bigger than ever.

# M A R K

**ALL THE PIECES** were in place. He had done his homework and now he was ready. It would be the last day on Earth for Miles Claymore Borton, ostensibly legitimate businessman, surreptitious dealer.

He parked the inconspicuous Celebrity at the curb. Other cars were stowed along this darkened residential street of the prestigious Kenwood neighborhood in Minneapolis—there was no reason his vehicle would draw attention. Turning off the car's lights, he reached over the front seat and hoisted two packages from the rear compartment of the sedan. He checked their contents using a small pen light in the darkness. Satisfied he had what he needed, he made certain the internal lights of the car were switched off before opening the driver's side door, exiting with the black nylon sack and elongated case he had just inspected.

From his location, which he had diagramed earlier, he had a two-way choice of positioning himself for what he was about to do. The easiest was to scale the two-story home, where he could fix on his mark from a stable vantagepoint. The occupant of the house was an old man, hard of hearing, who retired every night after the ten o'clock TV news. The old man would never know he was there even after the carbine was fired. He had already tested the "disturbance factor" and found it satisfactorily low for this purpose. Scaling the home was no problem. He had scaled a cathedral before this.

His alternative was to climb an elm tree in the front corner of the old man's lot. He felt a little foolish about climbing a tree like a kid but dismissed it. *What the hell*, he told himself, *deer hunters do it*. Besides, this was different—at least to him. He'd never done it that way before.

The stately tree was set back on the lot and surrounded by shrubbery. That gave him cover as he strapped on the climbing spikes like a Signal Corpsman about to string overhead wire in a combat zone. Do they still do that? he wondered, what with all the modern ways of mobile radio communications? He'd lost touch since the pre-high-tech days he spent in the military.

He looked up at the giant elm before beginning his ascent. It had a huge, majestic crown, its leaves just hinting to turn with the approaching fall season. Rows of elm trees lined the street, survivors of the plague of Dutch Elm Disease that swept across the northern tier of the nation from the east coast, some twenty-five years before. The disease had cut a swath from Maine to St. Paul, Minnesota, all but exterminating the great trees. But Minneapolis was where its westward march was halted. The devastation was significant, but so was the community effort to counter it. Infected trees were painted with red circles around their trunks, marking them for destruction. They were then cut down and disposed of in order to keep the Dutch elm beetle from advancing. City workers trenched around uninfected elms to prevent the disease from spreading through interconnected root systems. Special injections were given healthy trees, not unlike inoculating humans against influenza.

Many of the majestic elms lining Minneapolis boulevards were lost to the battle, and casualties still occur today. But the major war against the invading beetle was won. So now he had his elm tree to climb.

THE BORTON HOME was two houses down the block, across the street. When he parked, he could tell the house was occupied. And from where he planned to place himself, he would be able to see into the screen porch where he knew Borton liked to watch the evening news on TV and browse the *Wall Street Journal* on comfortable evenings like this. Tonight both of them would be taking advantage of this mild evening before the onset of brisker Minnesota nights ahead—each doing his thing.

He pulled on climbing gloves to aid his grip on the elm and save his hands from the roughness of its bark. The unregistered pistol rested secure in his shoulder holster. He didn't expect he'd need it, but one never knew. The Winchester M70 carbine was slung across his back with a carrying strap. He'd practiced this sort of thing before, and he soon disappeared into the huge canopy without incident.

*Borton is a fool*, the shooter observed from his perch on the elm's sturdy limbs. Ensconced in his sanctuary, Miles Borton felt secure behind a spiked steel fence, two German shepherds roaming the yard, and a state-of-the-art electronic alarm system wrapping the premises like a security blanket. Yet, Borton was now in the cross hairs of an instrument of death. So much for safeguards—yes, he was a fool.

A head shot was ideal for a .22-caliber sabot. It would penetrate the skull while not retaining the energy to exit. Instead, it would ricochet inside the cranium, scrambling brain matter like the yoke of an egg.

All conditions were favorable for the shooter. The site path was clear of branches on a breezeless evening, the range was short, the scoped rifle was more than adequate, and the target faced toward the shooter with only a nylon screen separating them. Those factors, in the grasp of an expert marksman, left little chance for the intended victim to survive the night. Correction: it left none at all.

*Pop.* It wasn't a loud noise, absorbed in part by the vegetative surroundings. He saw the dot between Miles Borton's eyes through the scope, before the dealer's face slumped forward, the man otherwise still seated in his favorite porch chair looking as comfortable as before. A second shot? He knew it wasn't necessary, but why not? *Pop.* He had a bird's eye view of slight movement as the small bullet punched through the top of the man's skull, setting upon its internal rampage.

He lowered the carbine, looked around and listened for any commotion around him. Nothing. Not even Borton's dogs looked disturbed, even though they perked up with each pop of the Model 70. *Good,* he thought. *I won't have to kill them.* He liked dogs.

A moment later, he slithered down from his roost to the ground. He was prepared to abandon the car if he had to. It couldn't be traced to him, and he could melt into the neighborhood labyrinth of shrubs and trees, making his escape on foot if need be. It wasn't necessary. He unfastened his climbing spikes, wiped them clean, and left them on the ground at the base of the elm tree, along with the other climbing gear stowed in the backpack. They would provide useless clues except for how the deed was accomplished, and who accomplished it—his signature, sans the rifle itself.

He just hoped the spikes hadn't caused entry wounds for those damned beetles. This would be the first time the Rifleman didn't leave the death weapon behind, and there would be some speculation about that. But he had promised the weapon to his associate, and that was just the way it was. It was also the first time he had used more than one bullet to dispatch his victim. More speculation, perhaps.

He packed the Model 70 in its carry-case, returned to the car and drove away without further incident. Not even a late-evening jogger to work around.

Satisfied no one was following him after a few "make-sure" maneuvers, he turned in the direction of his home. He had planned to ditch the car that evening, but now he saw no immediate need to do it. Come morning he'd be called to the Rifleman's latest hit, and he wanted to appear fresh.

It occurred to him, that he would be able to call attention to any wounds that the tree may have suffered from the climbing spikes when doing his investigation. Then the Minneapolis Park Board could be notified to do any necessary mendiing. No way he wanted to be responsible for the death of an elm tree.

*Chapter* **39**

# C O N S T E R N A T I O N

**"THIS IS CAREN,"** the voice on the phone said.

It had been some time since they last talked, but the timbre was just as Hank remembered. "Caren," he replied, a little startled by her reemergence. "It's been awhile. What's the occasion?"

"Been thinking about you lately and just wanted to touch base. Does there have to be an occasion?"

*Yes, there does.* Hank knew Caren Dalton better than that. "Nice of you. How's lawyering these days?" not wanting to press the occasion issue.

"Busy, busy," she answered. "Always people wanting to sue somebody."

"So I hear—and lawyers ready to abide."

"You got it. And you? You're a media star," she said, providing at least a partial answer to her own question.

"Like they say, everyone has his fleeting moments."

"As I remember, you've had a couple of those moments before now."

"I guess. Too bad this last one didn't end on a more positive note."

"Just because your man got whacked by the Rifleman before you nabbed him?

"Something like that."

"Still the modest one. Why not enjoy your celebrity? The press loves you. You're a hero. Make the talk show circuit and play the clever cop while you're hot."

Hank didn't respond.

"Hank?"

"Yeah."

"Oh, good. You're still there. Thought I lost you for a moment," Caren said, lacking sincerity in her tone on purpose. "What are you up to these days?" she quickly added, more upbeat.

"I thought you followed all the celebrity news," Hank answered with more sarcasm than he intended.

Caren wasn't put off. "Not the public stuff. I mean, what's going on in your sub rosa life—the stuff the press doesn't know about?" Pause. "By the way, I did hear about that advertising girl you've been running around with. You're a hot number by all accounts."

"We're friends."

"If you say so. I met her the other day, incidentally. Not bad— you've still got an eye."

She caught Hank off guard with, "met her the other day." "Darcy?" he questioned, knowing full well who.

"That's her. We kind of bumped into each other, but that's another story." Then: "Let's have lunch."

Another off-guarder. "Well . . . things are a little tight about now," Hank stammered.

"Same here," she replied. "How's the week after next?" Downtown, at Aquavit. Thursday. Eleven-forty-five. Say yes. My treat."

She wasn't giving him any wiggle room, as was her way, well remembered. The red flags were waving, but he relented. "All right . . . I think I can make that."

"Think?"

"Barring a terrorist attack on the Megamall or some such, I'll be there," he said, apprehensive as to what he was letting himself in for with this woman.

"Okay, but any excuse for not showing up better appear on the front page of the *Strib*, or you're in trouble with me, buster."

*And I wouldn't want that*, he didn't say. "Aquavit's in the IDS, Right?"

"Crystal Court level, Hon. Don't be late."

Hank rattled the handset back into its cradle. *Why do I have a bad feeling about this?*


**DARCY WASN'T LOOKING** near as spirited in Erica's office after her latest Magenta encounter.

"You're done with that comic book gig. Hang up your mask and be happy," Erica said trying to snap her out of her dour mood. "You wanted it over with, didn't you?"

"I don't like the way it ended," Darcy said in a low voice.

Now Erica was beginning to get it. "She didn't beat the crap out of you, did she?"

"Let's say we pretty much beat the crap out of each other."

"Oh? Magenta's supposed to win, isn't she?"

"The script was out the window as soon as we started. Worse than last time. I think that's what Josh wanted all along."

"You telling me you were set up a second time?"

"Yeah, what's more, I think my so-called adversary was fed a few tidbits to rile things up between us. I suspect she was the one selected because she could do that."

"To what end?"

"Look, the hair-pulling fight in *Magenta Comics* came directly from my skirmish with that Solid Gold babe. It had nothing to do with any script I ever saw, and I'm not so sure that that hair-pulling bit wasn't the plan all along."

"You think these scuffles were prompted along certain lines?"

"Yeah. It was like Goldilocks got a signal from Josh, then bam . . ."

"She went for your locks."

"Along with the rest of me."

"So what's gonna be in the next issue, you think?"

"I don't know. I don't even want to think about it."

"And why not?"

"What is this, *Twenty Questions*?

"Yeah. I'll let you know when the game's over."

"Josh can shove his next issue for all I care. Like you said, I'm done with it."

"But you're not happy. What's bothering you?"

Darcy hesitated before answering, and Erica picked up on it. "I thought you said there was no winner, here."

*Perceptive girl, Erica.* "Technically, no."

"Technically?"

Another pause, then: "I'm afraid she beat a little more crap out of me than I beat out of her. Leave it at that." Darcy didn't mention the part about coming out of her costume. Enough was enough.

"Okay. You met up with Ms. Hard Ass. So?

"Well, I was wondering . . ."

"You want to keep going with our night sessions?" It was Erica's final question.

"Like never before," came Darcy's final answer.

"Okay. We'll work on some basics, maybe a little Brazilian jujitsu while we're at it."

"Brazilian jujitsu?"

"On the ground stuff. She ever get on top of you on the mat? It's good for that."

"When do we start?" Darcy answered with a question of her own.

DELAYED AT THE office, their workout was much later than normal this time around. And little by little, those still left in the studio finished up and departed, leaving Erica and Darcy as the lone participants on the huge mat. This was of no particular concern. Erica could lock up with when she and Darcy left the premises—not an unusual situation in the "last one out turn off the lights" custom of the studio.

Perhaps it was due to the lateness of the session or the fact that they were left alone, or both, but the women eased off their normal regimen, soon resorting to playful tussling. Before long, it was more like a pajama pillow fight than a disciplined martial arts fray. Stretching the loose analogy further, their outfits could be said to resemble pajamas.

At the height of their frolic, an innocent brush brought about a reflexive retort, which escalated into further license. It was play, then it wasn't—the frolicsome liaison spilling into territory unknown to either of them before their tit-for-tat imbroglio this night.

As quickly as it began, it was over—Darcy pushing away. "I think our workout is over, Erica," she admonished without a trace of her recent giddiness.

"Uh-yeah. Sorry, Darc." Erica was apologetic if not timorous.

"My fault, too," Darcy offered. She hadn't started things in motion, but she couldn't absolve herself of her own participation.

"Sure it was." Erica took a deep breath. "Still friends?"

Darcy shrugged, paused for a moment, then said with a smile: "You might even say, bosom buddies." Another shrug. "What the hell—things just happen, sometimes."

Erica smiled back at her companion, relieved. "Okay, buddy. What say we quit this place and go find that gin joint of yours?"

*Chapter* **40**

# D I S C L O S U R E

**THINGS REMAINED QUIET** on the W/B front after the death of Frank Ramstad. Perhaps, it was thought, his assassination ended the killings that had plagued the agency for so long. Or, perhaps, wishful thinking was at work.

**DARCY WAS STILL** a little dreamy. She and Hank had had dinner the night before, in a set-aside room at La Dolce Vita where it was quieter and more appropriate to the occasion than the main dinning area. It was her birthday, and Hank was making a big deal out of it, saying she was still young enough to celebrate, not commiserate. Darcy didn't know if she agreed. She was thirty-one for God's sake.

It started nice and romantic-like with a champagne toast to "life ahead" and all that. But, into their food—amatory romance gave way to more primal stirrings. Eating soon became hurried—sloppy, in fact. Without a moment's thought as to dessert, Hank waved for the check, scrawled on its face and stuffed it into the accompanying plastic enclosure. From there, the pair pushed through the line waiting to be seated, and out the door. The question for them in the parking lot was: which was closest, his place or hers? His place won in agitated debate, so that's where the BMW sprinted. And that led to why Darcy was still a little dreamy today.

Jessie Campbell talked in her rapid staccato while Jason O'Connell took copious notes from a visitor's chair in front of her desk. Darcy sat back in an adjacent chair, listening hardly at all. It was a nothing meeting, and Darcy wondered why Jessie even called it.

When Jessie Campbell concluded the meeting's ostensible agenda, she excused Jason but asked Darcy to stay behind. So Darcy nestled down, while the eager account exec packed up his gear to head back to the agency and write his client contact report—on just what, Darcy wasn't sure.

Jessie Campbell followed Jason O'Connell to the office door, clicking it shut when he left. Reseating herself, she started off on a subject having to do with a new product line on which, she said, she wanted to bring Darcy up to speed. Again, it was prattle, and pretty soon Darcy's eyes glazed over, and her thoughts drifted away again, hoping Jessie wouldn't notice. Then somewhere in her semi-attentiveness the word "affair" cropped up. Darcy jolted out of her torpor. Women were attuned to words like that. "I'm sorry, Jessie, I thought you were on diced chicken livers."

"I was, but now I'm not. Dammit, Darcy, pay attention. What's wrong with you today?"

"Sorry. Long night."

"Long hours, again? Talk to Mason about your workload—I need your attentiveness during the day."

"Just a little worn. Sorry," she said. *Wasn't the job*, she didn't say.

"This isn't easy for me—I'm trying to tell you something not about chicken for a change, and I'd appreciate your listening. I'd rather be talking chicken instead of this, God knows."

"Uh, I thought you said something about an affair. Did I hear right?"

"My affair. That's what I'm trying to tell you about."

"What?" Darcy was wide-awake now.

"Look, Darcy, I'm scared."

"Scared? Are you pregnant?" Darcy asked, feeling more compassion for the woman than she expected she could.

"No. Nothing like that."

"What then?"

"I was with Frank Ramstead," Jessie answered, looking down at her desk. "Right up to the time he was . . ."

"Killed?" Darcy inserted in Jessie Campbell's pause.

"Yes."

"Oh, no. Do the police know about any of this?"

"No. At least I don't think so." Jessie said, looking unsettled. "They would have questioned me if they knew. Wouldn't they?"

"Shouldn't you come forward then? If they find out on their own, it won't look good."

"I know, but I can't bring myself to do it. It's not just the notoriety that'll come from it, even though, God knows, it'll be all over the papers and on TV news. I'd be under public suspicion for collaboration in a murder. Not only that, if the Rifleman thinks I was at the scene and might have seen him, I could even be in danger from him.

*Leave it to Jessie to put notoriety ahead of police suspicion and personal danger.* "Are you sure you want to tell me about this, Jessie? And were you at the scene?"

"Yes, I do. And, yes, I was."

Darcy was shocked by this disclosure. "But what if I go to the police, like I should? Why are you telling me this?"

"Because I trust you with my life, damn it. Happy now?"

It was a tougher confession for Jessie Campbell to make than the one that could mean jail, Darcy knew, and she didn't know what to say. Speechless was more to the point.

Jessie Campbell didn't seem to notice Darcy's reaction and continued her litany. "I was about to fix breakfast in the kitchen when Frank went to the front door, and I heard . . ." She didn't finish her sentence, nor did she have to. Then: "When I went to investigate, there was Frank, on his back with blood all over the foyer. I could see he was dead—I almost stepped on part of his skull that was blown away. It was hideous. I panicked and ran out the back door."

"The police didn't find any of your things in the house?"

"No. Everything I had with me I was wearing. It was an impromptu night—I didn't even have a toothbrush."

"What about your car?"

"He drove that night. We were cautious about parking my car around his place—even hidden in his garage."

"How did you get home?"

"Walked. My house is only five blocks from his."

"Nobody saw you together—then or before?" Darcy realized she sounded like a cop conducting an interrogation, and thoughts of that first day with a certain police lieutenant in her office passed through her mind.

"Nobody I know of. Like I said, we were discreet." Jessie Campbell answered.

"Jessie, I don't like this at all. I appreciate your trust in me, but you're putting me in the position of withholding evidence. Do you know that?"

"I'm appointing you as my acting counsel. It's client privilege."

"C'mon, Jessie, I'm not an attorney."

"Yeah. My real attorney wants me to turn myself in, too. But I'm coming to you before I decide to do anything."

"But why, for heaven's sake?"

"I want you to go to that cop friend of yours and tell him I've got information I think he'd like to have. In return, I want him to keep me shielded as long he can—hopefully, until this thing is cleared up and the killer is caught. That way, when it comes out about Frank and me—and, of course, it will—it won't be so sensational, and I won't be tried for murder in the press. It might even look like I helped solve the case."

*Vintage Jessie, always a plan, no matter how convoluted.* "But what if he puts you under arrest? It's public record then. Everything's out in the open."

"Maybe he won't arrest me when he hears what I have to say. I'll take my chances on that. He seems like a reasonable guy."

"He is."

"You're prejudiced."

"Then, I guess you have to judge for yourself."

"I have. Set it up, Darcy. Please."

It was the first time Darcy heard the word "please" pass Jessie Campbell's lips.


**LIEUTENANT DOUGLAS HANKENSON**, Darcy Austin and Jessie Campbell gathered in the living room of Jessie's south Minneapolis home.

Jessie Campbell set the venue and requested that Darcy be present.

Before they began, Hank asked Jessie if she was sure she wanted Darcy there.

"No offense, but I want her here to keep you honest, Lieutenant."

"I'm not offended," he said, "but it is one more person you're let-ting in on what you have to say. I trust Darcy to keep confidentiality, but it's your call."

"I trust her, too." Jessie said. "Can we get started?"

Darcy felt herself tear up at Jessie's reply. They may never be friends, but Jessie's advocacy got to her.

Hank explained that he couldn't guarantee Jessie anything, but that he appreciated her coming forward, even under these unorthodox circumstances.

"Cut the crap, Lieutenant," Jessie said. "I'm not doing my civic duty. I'm trying to save my ass."

This was more like the woman Darcy knew. "Jessie," she warned.

"That's okay," Hank said. "I'd just as soon get right to it, myself—just need to make things clear from the start. Go ahead, it's your show, Jessie."

Jessie Campbell was silent for a moment, deciding where to begin. Then: "I think the Rifleman has an accomplice," she stated flat out.

"How's that?" Hank asked, wondering where this would lead since he didn't believe the Rifleman had anything to do with the Frank Ramstead killing.

"I'll go back to the beginning. I don't know how much you know about Frank and Roland Bennett, but they were friends and became closer after they left Williams/Bailey."

Hank nodded. "I knew they stayed in touch with one another, yes."

"Well, Frank and Roland confided about some personal things," Jessie went on. "Frank even told Roland about his affair with me, which I didn't like. You know about my affair, Lieutenant?"

"Darcy told me that much. Go on."

"Frank said Roland would keep quiet about it," she continued. "He told me he knew Roland was having an affair himself—and being a married man, Roland wouldn't want that to come out in retaliation. That was Frank's insurance in the matter."

"What does this have to do with the murder?" Hank asked.

"Murders." Jessie corrected in the plural. "I think Roland Bennett was killed, too."

Hank suspected that as well, but it wasn't the official call, and he was surprised to hear it come from her. "What makes you think Bennett's death wasn't suicide?"

"Because, for one thing, I knew he was scared shitless that he might be killed."

"By who?" Hank asked.

"His mistress," Jessie said. "He was terrified of her."

"What?" Darcy couldn't help saying.

"How does that tie to the Rifleman?" Hank asked behind Darcy's exclamation.

"He killed Frank didn't he? Not that Frank was any kind of trademark target for the Rifleman—like a big-shot crook and all—I think he was killed because the Rifleman thought Frank knew too much from confiding with Roland Bennett."

"Confiding about what?" Hank asked, puzzled as to where she was heading.

"I think the Rifleman and Bennett's mistress were involved in the Williams/Bailey murders," Jessie Campbell asserted.

"Frank told you that?" Hank questioned, trying to reconcile Jessie's allegations.

"No, but he implied it," Jessie said

The room fell silent. Darcy's stare went from Jessie to Hank who was sitting back with a distant look on his face.

*Chapter* **41**

# R E G R O U P I N G

**LEAVING THE SESSION** at the Campbell homestead, Hank knew he had some heavy thinking to do. Deciding the office held too many distractions, he headed to his townhouse complex, instead. At home, he turned off his cell phone, brewed himself a cup of green tea and settled into his favorite chair. Later, after his deliberations, he'd pour himself a single malt Scotch.

He'd been an idiot, he thought, for not putting the pieces together earlier. Bloomington would simply have to produce more murders to get him on top of his game as a homicide dick; that's all there was to it.

Jessie Campbell's assertions were convoluted and flawed, but she triggered things that he should have picked up on before now.

He'd assumed, once it was known Terry Barnhard was blackmailing the killer, that the handyman was witness to the Janes murder, even though Barnhard claimed he did not work that night at Williams/Bailey. There was nothing to disprove his claim either, since there was no record of his arriving or leaving by security, and no one at Williams/Bailey reported seeing him earlier that day. Yet, when blackmail showed up on the "screen," he and everyone else took it for granted Terry Barnhard was on the premises that night and saw the murder take place.

Hank sipped his tea, burning his tongue. *Damn.* One of the questions all along was how the killer, whether it was Roland Bennett or an accomplice, got in and out of the building without being detected—twice, if you considered the e-mail news release fiasco. Though it was doable under the right circumstances, it just seemed improbable.

And then there was Barnhard. Could he have pulled that off, too? He was a klutz. Again, an improbability.

Hank weighed an alternate scenario. Barnhard was *not* on the premises and never saw the murder take place. With that assumption, how did Barnhard know the right person to blackmail? Only one way: the night security guard told him, Hank concluded. And that meant the security guard knew all along who the stealth visitor was in the Williams/Bailey offices that night—in fact, allowed the visitor to enter "undetected." In that scenario, the guard wasn't derelict in his duties that night, he was complicit in murder. It made sense because Barnhard and the security guard had to know each other pretty well, what with Barnhard signing in and out so often in his comings and goings at night. What was his name? He'd look it up when he got back to the office. He had some mean questions to put to him. Could the murderer actually be the security guard? Hank dismissed it. The killer he was seeking was far too clever for that to be so—recalling the interrogation of the man after the Janes murder. He, like Barnhard, was not too bright.

But why would he get involved at all? Money? No suggestion he had any at the time of questioning. A woman? That made more sense. Jessie Campbell's suspicions fit into this equation. She hadn't nailed it as far as Hank was concerned, but she hit on the proposition that a woman was involved. If so, that would explain a lot. That could mean the security system wasn't defeated; it was *seduced*. "Ahh," he took a deep breath and said out loud: "The scent of a woman." *A clever, diabolical, game-playing woman*. If a woman, what woman? Jessie Campbell? He didn't think so. He'd check fingerprints to corroborate her story about an affair with Frank Ramstead. Hers should be all over the inside of Ramstead's house, bedroom included, if she was straight with him on that account. It wouldn't necessarily absolve her, but it would help her overall credibility. And, she did come forward when she didn't have to. More than anything, though, he couldn't think of Jessie Campbell as less than obvious about the kinds of games she played, nor in her conduct, generally. Not so with the game-playing killer that led him on this chase so far. Not so in the least.

He couldn't yet reconcile the masculine pointers left behind—the large, deep footprints, the "heavy step" Darcy heard behind her when she was attacked, the descending blow to the back of the head of the standing Terry Barnhard. The macho aggression exhibited by the killer was not woman-like at all. But then, maybe that was intended to throw him off. In football they call it a misdirection play.

With all that, and that was a helluva lot, he hadn't settled on a motive for the killings. It was time to turn his attention to that leg of the three-legged stool of means, motive, and opportunity that comprised the criminal act. At first he had assumed the motive was personal revenge. Then he shifted toward the possibility the killer wanted to destroy Williams/Bailey—a variant of the revenge motive. But now, it seemed beyond even that—beyond any rational motive. But what? The pure pleasure of killing? Perhaps.

His brain stretched to the max, Hank got up from his chair and headed for the kitchen. It was time for that single malt Scotch.

*Chapter* **42**

# A F F I R M A T I O N

**HANK WAS IN** his office the next day when the call came.

"Lieutenant Dan Mittendorf," the voice on the phone said. "Robbinsdale."

Robbinsdale was a first-tier suburb to the west of Minneapolis. It was another community that lost much of its independent identity to metropolitan expansion. Hank remembered delivering telephone books in Robbinsdale when he and his brother were kids. Back when Northwestern Bell hired youngsters for that task every year.

"Hey, Mitt," Lieutenant Douglas Hankenson responded. "Why so formal?"

"Sorry, Hank. Didn't know if you'd remember me."

"How could I forget? Convention in St. Paul. In the bar, you told me how you almost got your ass shot off in 'Nam. I, on the other hand, was able to thrill you with my harrowing R.O.T.C. exploits at the U."

"Been a while since then. I've been laboring in obscurity while you've been basking in the celebrity spotlight. 'Cop of the Year' stuff."

"A passing thing. They'll roast me tomorrow."

"No way. The press loves you. Goes back to that Sycamore Shootout."

"Not you, too?"

"What?"

"Never mind. What's up, Mitt?"

"Nothing much. Oldest kid's starting at ASU down in Tempe this fall. Wife's goin' back to school, too. Out your way. Normandale College."

"Uh, Dan, you didn't call after these many years to share your family chronicles with me."

"Sorry, got a little carried away—pending tuition and that sort of thing."

"I feel for you."

Lieutenant Mittendorf settled down to business. "Wanted to let you in on a vic we found last night. Stabbed to death."

"Didn't see it in the paper," Hank said.

"Too late for the *Strib*'s early edition. Dog barked till a neighbor called. We found him at five this morning.

Hank couldn't resist. "The dog?"

Dan Mittendorf picked up from there. "Damned mongrel liked to take my leg off—not real friendly after what happened with his owner."

"Lemme guess. You're calling because you think I'm big on mutts."

"What I hear it, your big on pedigree."

"Okay, wise ass. Let's get back to the mongrel's owner."

"Four neat thrusts through the heart, any which would of been fatal, plus one through the left eye socket for good measure—and pleasure—be my guess.

"Pleasure?"

"Just a feeling I get. Deliberate assassination, anyhow. No break-in. Nothin's missin'. The killer was obviously invited in. Then they hopped into bed together."

"A woman?"

"Yeah. He wasn't with another man if that's what you mean."

"Can you be sure?"

"Hair samples on the mattress. Female all the way. Even a pubic hair. She musta been straddling him at the time. Looks like he was having an orgasm when she stuck the knife in him—fresh sperm on the sheets. Now that's a real climax."

"Okay. But I'm still wondering why you're telling me about this."

"The guy's name is Julian Bellows. Mean anything to you?"

Hank had just looked up the name when he got to the office that morning. "You suddenly got my interest, pal."

"Thought I might. He was the security guard at Normandale Towers—"

"On duty the night of the Soup Murder," Hank said, finishing the sentence for his Robbinsdale counterpart. "I wanted to bring him in for more questioning. Couldn't locate his whereabouts this morning."

"He's only lived where he got killed for a short time," Dan Mittendorf said. "Rented the place under another name, which seems strange." Pause. "What'd you turn up on him back then—anything?"

"Zip. Claimed he didn't hear or see anything suspicious that night. Said he musta been making his rounds at the wrong time. No reason to doubt him. Background check was clean except for a few minors."

"Why'd he leave there?"

"Got fired. Building management felt he should've been more diligent. More likely they wanted to demonstrate to tenants that they were taking steps to tighten security by dismissing the guy."

"Did you suspect any complicity on his part?"

"Like I said, no reason to. We knew the killer could of steered around security—the system's not foolproof. No motive, and with a clean record . . ." Hank stopped in mid-sentence, then asked, "Do you have the murder knife, Mitt?"

"No trace of it."

"What can you tell about it from the medical exam?"

"Hold on. Got the report right here. Let's see . . . narrow blade, eight inches long, five-eighths-inch top edge to cutting edge, upward curve at the tip, not razor sharp, but sharp enough. So say the stab wounds."

"In other words, a common kitchen knife."

"Precisely. Except for one thing," Dan Mittendorf said.

Hank said. "It had a hilt."

"Yeah, marks on the body where the blade was stopped by it. All the thrusts went right down to it. How'd you know?"

"A stab in the dark."

"Very good, Hank. But somehow I don't think that's it."

"Not a knife from Bellows' kitchen?"

"Doesn't look that way. There's a set of knives stashed in a drawer. One fits that blade description, but it's not the weapon."

"You know that for certain?"

"Unless the killer took time to scrub it clean and place it back in the drawer. Besides, no hilt on any knife here."

"That's because it's not Minneapolis Cutlery."

"Huh?"

"Never mind. What color was the hair you found?"

"Light brown, almost blonde. Fits a lot of women."

"Eliminates the freckle-faced Irish lass next door to me."

"And that cute Asian chic two units down from the Bellows place."

"Can you get DNA from the hair?"

"Doesn't look like there's any roots. So doubt we can to pull that fingerprint without sending it out for mitochondrial testing—that'll take awhile. Lab here can do a few tricks, though—get us a pretty good match if we can find a person to match to."

"Prints?"

"Nothing I'm hopeful about, but we'll see."

Silence for a moment, then Hank said, "Wanna ask me again about complicity?"

"Did I stir up the soup?"

"Let's say you whet my appetite. Look, Mitt, can you keep the specifics on that knife between two old-time conventioneers for now?"

"No reason I have to know it was more than just an ordinary knife that happens to be the missing murder weapon."

"Appreciate it."

"What's with that knife, anyway?"

"The newsies are going to make connections between Bellows' murder and the Soup Killings simply because he was the guard on duty at Normandale Tower. But there'll be nowhere to go with it. The Soup Killer's supposed to be dead.

"It never got out that a knife disappeared from the Austin house the night the assault was made on her—one that matches up with the one you just told me was used on Bellows."

"No shit? Makes the connection a lot stronger."

"Yeah, that's for you and me to know. If it gets out that it was Minneapolis Cutlery used on Bellows, another one of Williams/Bailey's clients, it's going to connect up with the Soup Killer's MO. The press'll go nuts. The killer let me know what she wants me to know. That's enough for now. I don't need the media crawling all over the place and hanging on my back."

"You knew the Soup Killer was still alive and well? And female?"

"Suspected as much."

"You'll keep me informed from your end?"

"You'll know what I know as soon as I know it. You may gain star-dom when this gets cleaned up, Mitt."

"Could be in the shitter if it doesn't. Meanwhile, the murder weapon is just a knife that's missing from the scene—that's all I know," Dan Mittendorf said.

HANK WAS IN the BMW the next day when his car phone chirped. It was Lieutenant Mittendorf chasing him down. "Got more for you, Hank," Mittendorf said. "Coulda told you some of this before, but I wanted the full report first, with complete lab work."

"Okay, let me have it."

"Not much of consequence from what you already know. We can't get DNA from the hair we found without a mitochondrial test. As I sus-pected—no roots. There's a touch of chemicals, though, and some other characteristics in the strands that the lab picked up—could help in a match to a live person."

"What about prints?"

"Only female prints we found belong to the cleaning lady and a neighbor who says she's a sometimes visitor. We checked them both out, and they look clean. Our hit lady was careful covering her tracks."

"Doesn't surprise me." Then Hank asked: "Did Bellows have any money? Or spend any, recently? Just wondering."

"No to both of your questions."

"Thanks, Mitt. Send me the report?"

"You bet. Sorry there isn't more to it."

"It helps confirm some things in my mind. "First it's soup to die for, now its sex to die for. I guess that's some progress."

"Hey, that's good. You ought to be in advertising," Dan Mittendorf said.

"Someone else told me to forget it."

"Hear back from you sooner than later, I hope. Can't hold the lid on this forever, Hank. The chief's gonna be pissed as it is."

"Neither can I—and join the club."

*Chapter* **43**

C O G I T A T I O N

**HANK SAT ALONE** in his office, attempting to piece together what he knew about the Soup Case after his conversations with Dan Mittendorf. His door was closed and all his phone calls were redirected to the front desk. He left instructions with Grace Anderson out front that he was not to be disturbed under penalty of dismissal. His usual hollow threat. Thus ensconced, he began his deliberations.

The track marks of the knife used to kill Bellows confirmed that his murder was connected to the Soup Case. And the way it was done, the killer was now letting him know she was a she, if he hadn't already figured that out. Now there could be no lingering doubts.

The killer would have expected that the Robbinsdale police would notify him if they were at all alert. And that he'd eventually match Bellows' wounds with the missing Austin knife. Leaving that knife at the scene would have made it too easy. He could almost hear her saying, "Figure it out, smart guy. I'm not going to write you a letter." And then, "You won't have to publicly reveal the linkage when you do figure it out." She was letting him stay on the hunt, devoid of communal and departmental pressure. Was this a thoughtful killer, or what?

Hank moved on to Roland Bennett. Jessie Campbell said he had a mistress he was terrified of. Why? He then surmised: if his mistress was the killer, which she most certainly was, and Bennett was exhibiting remorse or getting unstable due to his complicity, even if unintended complicity—that would be reason enough for a diabolical conspirator to do away with him without batting an eye.

Next up for his consideration was Frank Ramstead. Ramstead had the same distaste for Williams/Bailey as did Bennett, and the two were close. Still, Hank's gut instinct was that Ramstead wasn't directly involved in the murders. But did he know something about them? It was a good bet that he did, from what Jessie Campbell told him. Was the grilling Ramstead was getting from the police making the killer nervous? Another good bet.

This killer liked game playing, but why try to pass off Ramstead's killing on the Rifleman, he put to himself? Then he saw it. The killer planted transparency in the imitative act so he could decipher it for what it really was. Back to fun and games. How was the killer to know he'd get a call that would make it even easier for him to figure out? Or did she anticipate that as well? He also had to consider that the Rifleman ruse was another way the killer was letting him operate under the public's radar, so to speak.

But what wasn't he getting? How did it all tie together? Was the link between victims and killer stronger than it appeared? What key element was still missing? Tough questions, yet something more definitive would take shape in his brain if he just thought it through. Sure it would.

Another thing bothered him. The killer revealed she was female. She didn't have to do that—it narrowed the search. She could have killed Bellows like she did the others and no one would have been the wiser as to her sex. Why do it? And why now? She couldn't have known he was already onto Bellows' involvement, could she? Was she drawing to a climatic endgame? It scared him. *Get her soon, Hank. Get her soon.*

*Chapter* **44**

# S H E A R I N G

**"LOOK DARCY," HANK** was saying over the phone, seated in his office. "I don't want to get everyone upset over there, but I'd like to check this out. It's all I've got for now."

He had already confided to Darcy that he felt the Soup Killer was a woman and that she had been right to say early on that it didn't have to be a man. He thought that might soften her for what he was requesting now. It was unusual, even bizarre, but why not eliminate as many women as possible, with what he had to work with, while still on the hunt? That was his reasoning anyway. It was only a little hair. What harm could it do?

He found out soon enough; Darcy *was* upset. "You want me to be the sheep herder for this hare-brained scheme of yours?" Hare-brained relates to rabbits, not hair—but the connection was made, nonetheless.

"How many women are there with light brown hair at Williams/Bailey? Can't be that bad."

"It's not the number, it's the imposition."

"Well I can't sneak up on them and snip their tresses. It's strictly voluntary—can't force anyone to do this without a formal charge, and that's not in the cards."

"And if anyone refuses, she's under suspicion of murder. Right?"

"Not at all. I'm trying to eliminate women from contention, not incriminate them."

"Doesn't look that way."

"C'mon, Darc. I'll call and smooth things over with Mason. I know it's a shot in the dark, but, frankly, I've got nothing else to go on. Mason should be happy to get his people exonerated."

"I don't think Mason's going to look at it that way. Besides, people around here are beginning to think the killings are over. This'll just stir things up again."

"Just say there's some inkling that the Soup Killer could have had an accomplice, and we want to match some hair samples as a routine measure. That's all."

"That's all?"

"Yeah. See how easy?"

"Oh, now that you explained it, I feel much better."

DARCY WAS RIGHT. Mason Williams didn't like it when Hank broached the idea to him. But when Hank confided to Mason that he suspected the Soup Killer was still out there, he decided to go along if the women were given free choice in the matter—no coercion or pressuring. And he wanted to keep it as low profile as possible for obvious reasons. He also let it be known that he was granting this favor only out of respect for the way Hank had handled the murder investigation at Williams/Bailey up to this point. But he warned Hank not to expect a repeat of this sort of thing—he stopped short of using the word, harassment—in his shop. Hank was duly grateful.

Given her marching orders, Darcy solicited seven volunteers, took a sample from the hairbrush of a woman who was on assignment and thought she wouldn't mind, passed on two nervous dissenters, and was unable to contact one other person who was vacationing on the Eastern Seaboard—all by mid afternoon. This accounted for the entire light-brown hair female contingent at Williams/Bailey.

It proceeded much better than Darcy had anticipated. There was more of a spirit of cooperation than any grousing about invasion of privacy she rather expected, while escorting her former live-in bodyguard, Marge Kennedy, from office to office. As the designated shear person, Marge Kennedy made a point of thanking each person for her cooperation and finished her rounds without arousing ill feelings among those sheared. Williams/Bailey suffered not so much as a stir for the experience. All was well. For now . . .

# Chapter 45

# R E V E L A T I O N

**TROUBLING QUESTIONS WERE** still roiling in Hank's mind when he strode into Aquavit at 11:46 the next day, finding Caren Dalton nested at a corner table right where she said she'd be. She looked up from her copy of *Barrister Magazine*. "I ordered you a martini," she said, without a hello.

"On duty," he said, pulling out a chair, and sliding it under him: "I'll have to pass."

"Pretend you're working undercover; heading off a terrorist attack like you mentioned on the phone. Got to live like 'em to find 'em, you know."

"Terrorists don't drink."

"Don't kid yourself. When preparing to blow themselves up for Allah, they do."

"Yeah, well maybe. Gin?"

"I don't know what they drink. Fermented fig juice, or something."

"Not them. My martini."

"You get an aquavit mart, here. What else? This is the Aquavit restaurant."

"That stuff's poison. Only whacked-out Norwegians can drink it."

"You'll love it with vermouth."

"Do I get an olive, or will it come with a pine nut?"

"Olive. I remembered to specify that for you."

Their drinks arrived in the same formulae except hers had a twist.

Ten minutes later the waitress came back for their lunch order—her pad to her chest, pencil poised. Caren ordered a salad.

"I'll just have the half sandwich," Hank said to the waitress. "Roast beef."

"No soup?" the waitress asked with widened blue eyes. "It comes with that."

"Forget the soup. Bring me one of your appetizers instead, if that won't upset the chef."

"What appetizer would you like, sir?" The waitress smiled and looked cute.

"Norwegian herring—you've gotta have that around here."

"Ja, sure," the waitress offered in her best Scandinavian parody, tossing her blonde head pertly to one side.

"Oof-da," Hank said, watching the waitress hustle off to do his bidding. Then turning back to Caren Dalton, he added: "By yiminy, I think I like this place."

"You just like the waitress' ass. The décor's too sterile for you, and you're gonna complain the food's too chic when it gets here."

"Even a roast beef sandwich? Why are we here?"

"I like it."

"Any other reason?"

"Unlike a lot of places, it's quiet enough for civilized conversing."

"Now we're getting to it. So what's on your civilized, conversing mind?" Hank took a sip of his drink and winced.

"Your girlfriend for starters, now that you ask."

"Oh?"

Caren took a deep breath, and Hank knew something was coming. "You know, in the old days before political correctness, how two men would duke it out over a woman? And the winner got the prize."

"A Kewpie doll?"

"No, a real doll."

"Forgive my presumptive nature, but I get the idea you're coming to a point, here."

"Nothing gets by you. What a detective."

"Yeah well, I'm kind of happy with the girlfriend you say I have. Can we get back to terrorists or some other more agreeable subject?"

"No—"

"Hear about the terrorist instructing a human-bomb class—his body strapped with explosives?"

"Hank—"

"'Pay attention,' the instructor says, 'I'm only going to do this once.'"

"Hank. For heavens sake."

"Get it? He was going to blow himself—"

"I get it. Okay? Can we return to the subject here?"

"Does this place have a take-out option? I think I remember a meeting I've got to attend."

"Well, maybe this will hold you in your seat for a while," Caren Dalton said, tossing a comic book on the table that she had been holding hostage between the pages of *Barrister*.

"What's this?" Hank asked.

"A proof copy of the next *Magenta Comics*. It'll be out in a couple of weeks."

"Really, Caren, I thought you were into heavier fare."

"Well, I'm into this fare. So's your girlfriend."

"Sorry, not following."

"Remember when I told you over the phone that I bumped into her?

"Ms. Austin? So?"

"So this." Caren flipped the book open to where it was marked with a Post-it note. "I'm the one standing here. She's the one on the ground with no clothes on."

What he was hearing and seeing caught Hank off guard. "You two acted this out?"

"Not exactly, we fought it out fair and square. I won, as you can plainly see."

"Like this?" Hank said, staring at the spread with Sadanna, topless, standing over Magenta, naked.

"Close enough."

Hank couldn't entirely dismiss what Caren was telling him. He knew that Darcy was participating in what she called "modeling" sessions for Josh Williams. Hell, he'd even seen the Magenta costume on her—as well as off. She didn't say much about either session but seemed to be up after the first one. Then mumbled something about being glad it was over, after the second. He sensed she wasn't happy, and he hadn't pursued it with her. Was he now looking at why?

"It's bizarre," Hank exclaimed. "How did you . . . ?"

"Get involved? Simple. Our firm does legal work for Fantasy Publications. Josh Williams saw me in the office a few times, liked the way I looked and asked me if I'd do a gig for him."

"And you just went along with it?" Hank was still incredulous.

"What the hell. I'm in good shape—work out every day. Never fought another woman before and thought, why not? There are women boxers, you know. And wrestlers, too. I thought it might be kind of exciting. Then when he told me the woman I'd go up against was your sweetie, how could I refuse?"

"Go up against?" Hank broke in. "I thought this stuff was supposed to be choreographed."

"Window dressing for your girl. Josh told me I could free lance as much as I wanted. Said that's how he got fresh ideas for his stories."

"He told you all that going in?"

"Yeah. And he got what he wanted. Pretty sexy, too—way it came out."

"And unfair, don't you think?"

"The blind-siding part? Hey, I pushed all her buttons beforehand. Your Ms. Austin wanted to tear my head off by the time we got into that stupid Pad Room. I didn't exactly sneak up on her."

Hank pushed back in his chair. "Uh, Caren, what's your point in telling me this?"

She leaned her face over the table. "I won the fight. Aren't you impressed?"

"No."

"What do I have to do, go two-out-of-three falls with her?" Caren questioned. "Not that there'd be any need for a rubber match."

The food arrived and the conversation stopped. Hank tried to duck the comic book, but the waitress caught a glimpse of it in his hand. "Oh, Magenta," she said. "Way cool. My boyfriend reads every issue. Did you see her battle Vixen last month?" She brought her hand to her hair and gave it a tug.

"No," Hank said, already eyeing the herring with suspicion.

"Yes," Caren said. "But wait'll you see the next issue. Magenta gets her pants beaten off."

"Can we just eat?" Hank directed at Caren.

"Oh, wow." The waitress said, wide-eyed once more. "By who? Bet it's Sadanna."

"By me," Caren said.

"Huh?" The waitress looked puzzled.

"You were right the first time," Caren abjured. "Sadanna whips her butt."

"Oh, wow," the waitress exclaimed again.

"You already said that," Hank muttered to the waitress.

The waitress ignored Hank and said to Caren: "How do you know that, if it's not out yet?"

"I was there," Caren answered.

"Huh?" More puzzelment.

"Check Shinder's news stand down the block in a couple of weeks," Caren said. "You'll see all there *is* to see."

"Cool," the waitress bubbled.

"Now we're back to cool," Hank grumbled under his breath.

Caren kept going. "Sadanna actually rips Magenta's costume clear—"

"This conversation ends right now, or I'm joining the people at the next table." Hank interrupted, followed by a deep swallow of his aquavit martini—poison or not.

# Chapter 46

# R E V E R B E R A T I O N

HANK WAS STARING at the bedroom ceiling—wondering if he should bring the subject up. He'd like to get Darcy's version of the affair with Caren Dalton, but he was wary of broaching it.

Something was wrong. She was still good with him in bed, but she was bothered, he could tell. Was it him? Or did it have to do with what Caren Dalton told him about.

Truth known, it was both. Darcy was a little miffed that Hank hadn't told her anything about his past relationship with Caren Dalton. And she still hadn't gotten over the battle she had with her, and the way it came out.

Hank turned his head, observing Darcy on the bed next to him. She was lovely lying there, the sheet at her waist her only covering. He was about to speak, but decided this was not the time. Something else came up and it wasn't lingual. The subject of Magenta vs. Sadanna would have to wait for more immediate matters.

**"DID YOU SEE** Jamie Kay's column in the paper?" Darcy asked over the phone. She didn't sound happy.

"No," Hank answered, surprised at her sharp tone. Just moments before, he arrived in his office from Darcy's home, and everything was placid when he left. "Haven't seen the paper yet and don't usually read her, anyway," he answered in reference to the notorious Minneapolis gossip columnist.

"Then let me read you her lead tidbit," which she did without pause:

"Lt. Hank Hankenson, fab burb cop of Soup Murder and Sycamore Shootout fame, cozied with Caren Dalton, barrister beauty, at Aquavit yesterday. They sizzled once upon. . . . Now again? Buzz is, ad woman Darcy Austin, the lieutenant's sumptuous accessory of late, and the legal-lass tussled over him. Two gorgeous babes fighting over you? Every guy's fantasy. Does the restaurant scene indicate the winner, Hank?"

Darcy was upset before reading the account aloud; now she was livid. "Sumptuous accessory?" she screamed at him.

"Whoa, Darcy, I didn't say that. Blame the writer, not me."

"I'll blame you," she kept on. "How come you never mentioned Ms. Sizzle to me before?"

"That was a long time ago. Sizzle is just Jamie Kay's hyperbole, anyway."

"And the cozy scene at Aquavit? You didn't mention that either."

"C'mon, Darcy, it was nothing like that. She practically insisted I have lunch with her. Outside of that, I haven't seen her in over a year. Haven't even talked to her."

"But you were lovers. Admit it."

"A long time ago, like I said."

"But you never told me about her."

"Darcy?"

"What?" Her voice was still strained.

"I love you."

Silence.

"Darcy, I love you," Hank repeated.

Continued silence. Then, more subdued: "You never said that to me before."

"Yeah—I just knew it before. From the beginning. Just took awhile for me to admit it to myself."

Silence again.

"Darcy?" Hank was apprehensive.

After a seeming eternity, she replied. "I'm crying. Okay?" Another pause, then, in a low voice: "Me too, Hank. Guess you could tell by the school-girl tantrum, just now."

Hank let out a breath. "I think we've got something to commemorate," he said with relief. "Dinner tonight?"

"Yes. I'd like that. One thing, though."

"Uh, sure." *Oh-oh.*

"Why did she insist on seeing you?"

He thought he'd better answer straight out. "To show me a comic book."

Darcy had her own proof of Magenta #39 and understood what he was telling her. "It wasn't as bad as that, Hank. Not that awful."

"Doesn't matter, Darcy. She lost as far as I'm concerned."

*Chapter* **47**

# P R O F I L E

**THERE WAS NO** question in Hank's mind that Caren Dalton set up the Jamie Kay bit—just the thing a gossip columnist would eat up. And he was sure Josh Williams turned Caren Dalton loose against Darcy without warning her. They made a pair—Josh and Caren.

Sincere or not, it was apparent Caren Dalton made a play for him as well. And, in the process, attempted to humiliate Darcy in his eyes and embarrass her publicly in the paper. Caren was as cunning, ruthless and purposeful as always—and just as beautiful, he had to admit. All the qualifications of a fine trial lawyer.

Cunning, ruthless, purposeful—the words stuck with him and led him to a profile forming in his mind. No, it wouldn't take a man's strength to dispatch the murder victims the way it was done, but athletic prowess would certainly help—along with ruthless, cunning, purposeful.

THE DETECTIVE SERGEANT burst into Hank's office, breaking his train of thought—only a little, as it turned out. "Jeff Ortendahl's report from last night says someone was prowling around outside the Wayne Mitch household," Joe Baines declared.

"Oh-oh. Nobody caught, I take it," Hank replied.

"A shadow chase. Never got close."

Hank knew there was more to come, by the wait'll-you-hear expression on his associate's face. He just had to play along in order to extract it. "Okay, how do you know the shadow nobody got close to didn't belong to a neighbor's pet llama that got loose?"

"Guy next door to Mitch is some kinda agronist—leaves his sprinkler on a lot."

"That's 'agronomist.' So, he's got a green yard. Where we going?"

"Footprints."

*Now we're getting to it.* "Human ones, I take it."

"Yup. Ground was real soggy—got some good ones."

"And . . ."

"They match the one's we got outside the Austin place. Looks like putting surveillance out there paid off. Didn't get the collar, but maybe stopped him from another W/B murder. "

Hank sat back in his chair. Stopped *him?* Another misdirection play. This perp could make it as an offensive coordinator for the Minnesota Vikings. *But, I'm on to you, Babe.*

*Chapter* **48**

# I N T E R C E P T

**"HOW WE GONNA** handle this one, Boss?" Sergeant Joe Baines questioned, gesturing to the report they had just gone over on Lieutenant Douglas Hankenson's desk.

Hank was pensive. "I don't know. I'm dubious."

"About what?"

"About the conclusion."

Joe Baines was not so reticent. "There it is. Her hair. Jesus, what else do we need to bring 'er in?"

"For questioning. Yeah. But a formal charge? Not ready for that."

"And when might you be, pray tell?"

"Maybe after questioning," Hank relented. "But, it won't be my decision once the chief gets back tomorrow and sees this report—not unless we turn something up in the meantime."

"Pick her up tonight?"

"We better."

HANK POSITIONED THE BMW so that Joe Baines and he could watch the Subaru Impreza in the Normandale Towers parking ramp. He figured this was as discreet a way to handle the situation as any, under the circumstances. It sure as hell beat striding into Williams/Bailey and hauling her off in full view of the staff. It was just after 7:00 p.m. now. There was still a smattering of cars in the ramp although, for the most part, it was quiet and devoid of traffic—a much better setting for an intercept of this nature.

A few minutes later, the detectives spotted two women coming down the ramp together. Hank hadn't noticed Darcy's truck in this isle, which he now realized must be further down the corridor. *Shit.* He would have to deal with both of them at the same time.

When the women came closer, he and Joe Baines climbed out of the BMW and approached them on foot.

Darcy looked puzzled when she saw the two policemen. "Hank, Joe; what are you doing here?"

"Sorry about this, Darcy," Hank answered. "But we need to bring Ms. Carlson in for some questions."

Erica looked stunned, not finding her voice for a moment. No such problem with Darcy—she looked directly at Hank and said, "You set me up. You asked if we'd be working out tonight. You took advantage of me."

"It seemed better than barging into Williams/Bailey," Hank said in a weak attempt to offer an acceptable explanation. He had thought of letting Darcy know about this before hand but thought she might feel compelled to tell Erica Carlson about it. He wanted a clean intercept.

"You want to question me?" Erica Carlson said. "Why?"

Hank said, "Your hair samples, Erica. I'm afraid they match those found at the Bellows murder scene."

Bellows' stabbing death was covered extensively in the media. There was no need for Hank to explain the incident he was referring to.

"What?" Erica exclaimed.

"It can't be," Darcy said right behind her.

"But I was out on location the day you took samples at the office," Erica said. "How could you . . . ?" She stopped short of completion, turning to Darcy with a questioning expression on her face.

Looking miffed, Darcy said: "I'm sorry, Erica. I took some strands from your hairbrush at the office. You were going to be out all day. I didn't think you'd mind. "I'm sorry," she said again. "I should never have done it without your permission. But I didn't think—"

Erica cut her off. "Forget it, Darcy. You couldn't know it would lead to this."

Joe Baines said, "If you'll come in with us, Ms. Carlson, we can keep this as quiet as possible. It's the best way, believe me." He was trying to play good cop. Hank had a lock on the counter role at the moment, whether he liked it or not.

Erica raised her face to the two men. "Do I have a choice?" she asked.

"You're not under arrest, if that's what you mean," the sergeant answered.

"Do I need a lawyer?"

"You haven't been charged," Hank said. "But that's up to you. You can make a call when we get to headquarters, if you like."

"I won't need to. My counselor's right here beside me," she said, nodding to her companion.

"Hey, Erica. I'm no lawyer," Darcy protested, wondering why it was that two people inside of a week wanted to appoint her in that role.

"You'll do fine for now. I want you with me," Erica Carlson said.

"But . . ."

The art director waved off Darcy's nascent protest, gathered herself and said, "Let's go, officers. I haven't ridden in a new BMW."

*Chapter* **49**

# I N T E R R O G A T I O N

**IT WAS ONLY** a short throw to the Bloomington Police Station from the Normandale Tower ramp. It just seemed like a long trip. Joe Baines tried to ease the tension with a few banal offerings, without success. Darcy wasn't talking to Hank, and Hank thought better than to try and calm any waters just yet. He was in deep trouble with her and he knew it. So much for discreet intervention.

The tension in the interrogation room wasn't much better, but at least words were now being exchanged around a table. It may have resembled a suburban version of *NYPD Blue*, but even at that it was an improvement over the car ride over. And there was coffee.

The questioning began.

Erica said she had no idea how her hair could have been found at the Bellows murder scene. And no, she didn't suspect anyone pilfering strands of her hair. Yes, she knew Julian Bellows. No, she wasn't a personal friend of his—not even a congenial acquaintance. Yes, she often worked late when he was on duty—signing in and out at the security desk. No, she hadn't seen him since building management fired him.

A question of her own was: "If Darcy was able to get hair samples of mine from my office, why couldn't someone else have done it just as easily?"

It was a valid question Hank couldn't pass off.

With Erica Carlson's statements, backed up by Darcy at her side like a guard dog, the interrogation was getting sidetracked. Her hair could have been planted at the scene, taken off of a brush in her home or at the office. But that aside, some hair wasn't as easily obtainable, nor otherwise explained away. It was indelicate. It hadn't been brought up, to this point. But Hank had to broach it now.

He lowered his voice and said. "There was a pubic hair found on the bed where Bellows died, Erica."

She was wary. "So?"

"Correlation tests suggest that's yours, too." He answered. "Of course, we'd have to make a direct comparison to make absolutely sure . . ."

Erica had put up a brave front before now, but this hit her hard. Her world was caving in on her, and she began to crumble, eyes filling up.

Darcy jumped in. "That's enough, Hank. Can't you see what this is doing to her?"

Hank could, but didn't respond.

Erica dropped her face to the table, her hands clenched above her head. "Damn, damn, damn," she sobbed, pounding the table with the side of her fist, jostling coffee mugs with each blow. Darcy shifted closer, putting a consoling arm over her. Joe Baines dabbed at splashed coffee with paper napkins. Hank just watched.

When Erica's outburst dissolved to sobs, Hank said to her, "Why did you pound the table like that?"

"Why?" Darcy shouted. "Because of you."

Hank looked past Darcy as best he could and spoke to Erica again. "You used your left fist. Why?"

Erica raised her head from the table and peered at him through moist eyes, puzzled. "I'm left-handed," she offered, not knowing why he asked.

"Oh?" Hank questioned again. "You signed in with your right hand tonight. And, as I recall, your credenza at Williams/Bailey is on the right side of your drawing board." Lieutenant Hankenson was an observant S.O.B. "Want to explain?"

"It's a long story."

*And it's a long night ahead*, Hank didn't say out loud. He pondered for a while, tapping his fingers on the table, then got up from his chair and walked over to a dartboard hanging on the far wall of the interrogation room, under a hand-lettered sign reading, "When all else fails." He removed four darts that were stuck in the target at desultory angles, and stepped off ten paces. From there he turned and said: "Erica, I want you to come over here and toss these darts at the target—two with your right hand, two more with your left. Okay?"

Erica sniffed and nodded, even if she was still a little blurry-eyed.

Darcy tossed a verbal dart. "This is insane, Hank. What do you hope to prove?"

Joe Baines sat watching, knowing his boss, pretty damn good in situations like these, was up to something. "Wait and see," Joe said to Darcy, not sure himself what he was going to see.

Erica Carlson blew her nose, separated herself from Darcy and walked over to where Hank was standing. "Give me the darts," she said. It was the old Erica.

"Left hand first," Hank said.

The dart snapped into the target ring outside of the bullseye.

"Nice toss," Hank commented. "Now the right hand."

The dart hit the target a little farther out from the bull and didn't look as good getting there."

"Not bad," Hank said. "Back to the left hand if you don't mind."

This one dug in even closer to the bullseye with a sharp crack.

Hank admired the toss "I'll take that one any time," he said.

The last throw, right handed again, was high-wide of the bull. Not bad, but still not as good as her left-handed tosses.

"You're not faking?" Hank asked.

"No," Erica answered, feeling better for the diversion.

"I didn't think so," Hank said. Then he turned to Darcy who had grown quiet through the dartboard proceedings. "Darcy? Any comment?"

Darcy answered, "She's right handed when she does layouts. But it's her left I have to watch out for on the mat." Then she asked: "Hank, where is this going?" She sounded calmer if no less concerned.

Hank didn't answer Darcy, turning back to Erica instead. "Now I think it's time to share that 'long story' with us, Erica."

ERICA CARLSON TOLD of her early tutelage. How her mother, a second grade teacher, insisted her left-handed daughter learn to write with her right hand. "The world is right-handed. Better to join it than fight it," she would say. And insisted: "You write properly by guiding your pen across the page with your right hand—not pushing it across the paper with your left hand." Erica also told how she was made to draw with her right hand, when she showed an early interest in art.

"So I joined the right-handed world in all things proper," Erica said. "But, still, my left hand is dominant in most other ways."

*You can bow to a pedant mother, but Mother Nature will have her sway,* Hank passed through his mind after Erica finished her tale. He was silent for a time, then said: "I'm not going to detain you any longer, Erica."

"You mean I'm free to go?" Erica stammered.

"I'll drive you both back to your cars," he answered, adding: "Erica, I want you to travel straight home from there. Someone from this office will call to see if you've reached home, and there'll be another call later on to check on you. When you get to the office in the morning, I want you to call in. Ask for Joe or me. If we're not available, identify yourself and someone will take your call, and call you back to make sure you're where you say you are. Keep us informed of your whereabouts. It's only for the next couple of days until we get this thing straightened out. All right?"

He got a nod in the affirmative.

He looked at Darcy and said, "I want you to stay close to Erica, Darcy. Keep confirming her whereabouts. Someone will always be on hand to take your calls." He didn't get any protest, but he added to both of them: "Sorry to put you through all this, but bear with me?"

Two heads nodded. Erica was so happy to be getting out of there she didn't ask the obvious, but Darcy did. "Why are you doing this, Hank? What's going on?"

"I don't think Erica has anything to worry about, but I have to take precautions—it's CYA time." Hank answered.

"But the dartboard. What was that about?"

"Erica would have used her left hand."

"Huh? What do you mean?"

"Bellows wasn't killed that way," Hank answered. "Let's just leave it there for now."

Joe Baines had figured out where Hank was going, although he would not have turned Erica Carlson loose, even so. Too much freedom—there were still some things to check out. To his way of thinking, Hank was sticking his neck out for her because he believed she was innocent—and what he believed, he usually acted on. But it was still risky from the perspective of the older cop. What if she bolted? Hank's "precautions" wouldn't stop her. And there he'd be—hung out to dry.

**HANK DROVE THE** two women to their cars and watched while each of them drove off. Then, deciding not to wait until morning, he called Lieutenant Dan Mittendorf at home, on his car phone. "Sorry to disturb your reverie, Mitt," he said when a groggy voice answered, "but I need to chase down a few things."

"That you, Hank?" Mittendorf croaked, trying his best to sound alert.

"You in bed already?" Hank said. "Who's protecting your burb?"

"Dozed off is all. Watching Hannity and Colmes. Colmes always puts me away. What's up?"

"Question: were all strands of hair you found at the Bellows scene checked out under the scope?"

"Damned if I know," he said, still shaking off cobwebs. "I'd have to check. There were several strands in one spot. My guess is the tests were taken from those. Can't guarantee all of them were, though. Why do you ask?"

"I think the hair was a plant."

"You shittin' me?"

"You have any doubt the Bellows' killer was right handed?"

"Not the least. All the stabs came straight down on the vic's left side. Accurate too. The one through the left eye socket was a clean strike," Dan Mittendorf said.

"Would be hard for a lefty to do that, from what you're saying."

"Would be tough to pull off. Hell, those stabs were accurate for a good right hander. Wanna give me the rest of what you got?" He was wide-awake now.

"Found a match to the hair. She's—"

"Hey. You've got a live one in custody?"

"Live one, yes. In custody, no."

"Jesus. Why not, if you know who she is?"

"She's left-handed. Besides, I trust her."

"Which of those things comes first?"

"She's not the one, Mitt. Why be so careful about fingerprints and leave your hair all over the place?"

"Still think you're hanging way out there, pal. First order of police business is to cover your ass, remember."

"I'll catch some flack, but I'm betting she doesn't run."

"Or commit another murder. It's your career."

"Well, assuming she doesn't do either or both, I think I can hold off the wolves for another forty-eight hours. Meantime, I'd like something from you."

"Sure. Go ahead."

"Ask your techies to do a close-up on all the hair fibers they collected. See if they can pick up any variances."

"You think they might've missed something?"

"Could be all those hair fibers are not the same, just look like it to the naked eye. I'd like you to make sure every hair is put under the scope. If it was a plant and the murderer was having sex with this guy, she might have left some of her own hair around there, no matter how careful she was."

"It's a long shot. They're going to piss and moan, but I'll have 'em check it out."

"Hurry friend. Like you said—it's my career."

*Chapter* **50**

# A C C O M M O D A T I O N

**HANK BRIEFED HIS** boss about the interrogation of Ms. Erica Carlson the night before, then dropped the bombshell.

"You what?" Chief James Lott yelled, surprising himself with his shrillness. "I went along with keeping a lid on things earlier, but you just turned her loose? What if she takes off?"

Lieutenant Hankenson hadn't felt so uncomfortable in front of his chief's desk in a long while, but he kept his cool. "She's already in the Williams/Bailey offices this morning," he offered in defense. "She called me when she got home last night, before she left home this morning and when she got to work. I had Darcy Austin confirm her whereabouts at the office, besides."

"That's not good enough, Hank. She could bolt at any moment, and the department would have its dick hanging out. You should have booked her, at least."

"Look, Chief, she's not our killer, and I don't want to publically embarrass her if not necessary. I'll take full responsibility for any foul-up."

"Be assured you'll get full credit in that event. I'm concerned about the department as much as you. Margaret will have my ass, too—no way the mayor's gonna take the fall if something goes bad here."

Hank questioned his own resolve more than he let on, but held firm. "Give me two days, Jim. I'll put a locator cuff on her, if you like. She'll agree to it. No way she runs with that on. If I don't come up with something definite in forty-eight hours, I'll bring her in. Okay?"

Chief Lott rocked back in his chair. "Even if all that hair shit comes out the way you hope, it doesn't prove she's clear. Somebody else could have been in that bed with Bellows another time. That and your left-handed theory gives her some wiggle room, but it's not conclusive."

"It's maybe the difference between bail and no bail, if it comes to an arrest. And, reasonable doubt if it ever gets to trial. Besides, if there are other strands around the murder scene, and we can get a link to someone else . . ."

"A hell of a long shot. You're probably going to have to book Carlson sooner or later. Why put it off?"

"Because I believe she's innocent, and I plan to find the real killer. That way there's no fuss—not for Erica Carlson, anyway."

Chief Lott came back in his seat. "In two days? What do you know that I don't?"

"Some things are coming together. Give me the forty-eight hours, Chief."

James Lott had witnessed it before—the uncanny sixth sense his Crimes Against Persons Lieutenant seemed to have, and that he often wished he possessed as a criminal investigator in his earlier career. The compassion too. What was it to Hank if Erica Carlson got booked? And he'd be protecting his own ass, by doing it.

It was against Chief Lott's better judgement, but he surprised himself with some compassion of his own. "Forget the cuff," he said at length. "A tail would be good, though. What the hell. It's only a couple of days."

Hank was more relieved than he showed. "Thanks, Jim. I knew I liked working here."

"Yeah, sure. You're crazy to do this, you know. And I'm even crazier for going along. Now get the fuck out of here before you've only got forty-seven hours."

# Chapter 51

# D I S C L O S U R E

**DARCY AUSTIN AND** Erica Carlson met at TGIF located in the shadow of the Radisson South tower. Neither had slept very well and they needed to talk things out. A restorative breakfast was called for—with lots of black coffee.

Erica began by bringing up Darcy's stridency of the night before. "Don't be hard on him. He didn't have to turn me loose like this. Probably shouldn't have, with what he's got to lose." Sip. "He's a good man, Darc. Don't blow it because of me."

"I know, I know," Darcy replied, taking a bite out of her crumpet. "He was just doing his job, but I felt betrayed, the way it happened—he used me. Besides, the whole damn thing is frustrating."

The art director stirred the oatmeal she wasn't eating. With her left hand. "You don't wonder how my hair got on the scene?" she asked.

"Sure I do. I just don't believe it got there on your body. Besides, I know how you use your hands and weren't faking those tosses. That just proved it."

"Astute guy. How many cops would have picked up on that left-hand bit?" Then: "No doubts before that?"

"Just puzzlement."

"Thanks. I'm puzzled too—Jesus, even a pubic hair. And I got to assume it's mine from what Hank said." Erica swirled her oatmeal again, now getting cold. "How did that happen?"

"Think someone followed you into the restroom or something?"

"Oh, wow, that'd be tough. I suppose if somebody trailed after me all day they might be able to accomplish it. Not likely though. And wouldn't I notice somebody tailing me like that?" A swallow, followed by: "When it comes to the hair from my head, it sounds like there were several strands on Bellows' bed. Not like one or two strands that just might of flecked out in the office someone could have picked up."

"Maybe from your hairbrush, the way I did." Darcy offered rather sheepishly.

Erica didn't blanch. "Could be, I suppose. But they'd have to risk being spotted doing it. And I usually take it with me when I leave work."

A sudden thought flashed into Darcy's mind. "The mat." It came out like someone shouting, "Eureka."

"Huh?"

"The mat." She said again. "You know. That late workout we had."

"We had a lot of them."

"Not like that one . . ."

Erica caught up to her. "Uh-oh."

"There had to be some of your hair left on the mat that night. I mussed it up pretty good."

"Yeah, I remember," Erica replied. Then she hesitated before saying, "Do you think that night could explain the . . . pubic hair? It's not like we, uh . . . Nobody's clothes came off."

*No they didn't*. But Darcy recalled their loosened outfits and the open belts from their martial arts tunics. She wondered how to say what was next on her mind, and the best she came up with was: "I visited the area, you know."

Erica twisted in her chair. "Yeah, I remember that, too."

Darcy wasn't comfortable with her next statement either. "Erica, you weren't wearing panties. It just might have done it."

Erica fidgeted more than before. "Okay, okay. But, if you're right, who could be lurking around like that? Spying on us? Picking up after us?"

"Someone who knows us and our itinerary pretty well, I'd say."

"That's pretty scary, Darcy."

Darcy nodded. "Something tells me we should watch each others backs till this gets settled. And something else . . ."

"What?"

Darcy didn't look happy. "I should tell Hank about that night."

"Careful, Darc," Erica cautioned. "Men have their egos, even if things didn't go all that far. Like I said, you don't want to mess things up with this guy."

"No, I don't." Darcy replied, paying the check the waitress dropped off. "But it helps your case. Besides, I don't like keeping secrets from him."

"You know something, Darcy?"

"What?"

"It was a nice visit."

They both flushed, got up from their unfinished breakfasts, and headed for the office.

**TRUE TO HER** agreement of the night before, Darcy called Hank and confirmed that Erica was in the office this morning. Then, bolstering her courage she said she wanted to talk to him. "Coffee, if you can get away?" she asked. "How's Lund's, around ten?"

"Sure. Wanted to talk to you, anyway," he responded.

**DRIVING OVER TO** meet Darcy, Hank's car phone chirped. "You hit on something, pal," Lieutenant Dan Mittendorf said at the other end of the connection.

"Tell me."

"For starters, there's a couple of strands that show a definite difference from the ones we checked, before. The chemicals in the hairs are different, too.

"Fantastic," Hank exclaimed. It was the second time he breathed a sigh of relief that morning. Only this one was bigger.

"Something else," Dan Mittendorf said. "I was going through Bellows' personal phone directory this morning and spotted the name Sarah Rosen. It was under C instead of R or S, which seemed odd. And then I recalled seeing that name in his checkbook register. So I went back to his register and there she was—forty bucks every other week. So I gave Ms. Rosen a buzz, and found out she cleaned for him. That's why she was under C."

"I get it. And . . . ?"

"Said he was the messiest guy she ever worked for, nastiest, too—"

"Mitt. The point?"

"Sorry. Get this. She put clean sheets on Bellows' bed the day of his murder. Said he was expecting someone that evening and wanted the place to sparkle. That means—"

"The non-matching hair strands weren't from sometime before—they got there that night."

"You got to stop finishing my sentences—but, yeah. Since Bellows was out all day, according to the cleaning lady, he didn't entertain a daytime lady friend before his nighttime dalliance, either."

"Mittendorf, you're fabulous."

"If you say so, but should've been more diligent in the first place," Lieutenant Mittendorf said. "You caught us short. To the naked eye all the hair strands looked the same, but that's no excuse. Should have checked them out. I owe you, bud." Pause. "We'll do a cross-check on the new strands we identified against the Williams/Bailey hair samples you sent over before."

"Okay, Mitt, but I don't think you'll find anything. And you don't owe me a thing," Hank added. "You paid off big time. Thanks for coming out of the blocks so fast."

"Sure. Know where to head next?"

"I think so."

"I bet you do."

THE MAIN REASON Hank wanted to get together with Darcy was to make sure things were okay with her after last night. But he tried to make it look as though he needed information from her and asked about W/B's vacationer whose hair hadn't been sampled as yet. "Just routine," he said. "Need it for closure." It was a ruse.

Mission accomplished, Hank could see she was okay with him as he listened with feigned interest to her brief on the still-absent employee. Another woman suspect was concerning him—and that's where his thoughts dwelled now.

When Darcy finished, Hank put his note pad away, and the conversation wandered until Darcy confronted the subject she had on her mind from the beginning. She had rehearsed how to say it several times, especially how the most "private" of items might have been planted at the murder scene. But she still stumbled through the actual recounting of it.

She finished her disclosure with: "I've never had inclinations of that sort, Hank, believe me. And I don't now. Neither does Erica. It just happened—what else can I say?"

If Hank was impassive while hearing her out, he was downright stoic at this point. He sipped his coffee, saying nothing.

"Hank. For heaven's sake, speak to me. Something. Anything."

He put his paper cup down and stared straight at her. She held her breath.

"Finish your coffee, Darcy," he said after a long moment. "I've got work to do at the office, and I'm sure you do, too."

Her throat caught, and her eyes welled up. She was losing him. She could feel it. She wanted to offer something more, but what?

Hank took a last sip, and raised his eyes back to hers. "You helped formulate some things for me this morning, Darcy. Thanks for that." Another painful pause. "On the murder, that is. Forget about the other part." Then his crooked smile creased his face. "I mean forget it completely."

Darcy couldn't believe her ears. "You're—you're not upset?"

"Why should I be? Like you said, things happen sometimes. So?"

Hank felt how painful it must have been for Darcy to tell him about that night. But she did it because she wanted to be honest with him, and to help Erica Carlson, as well. He never felt more respect for her than at that moment.

Darcy stared back at him. He really meant what he was saying. His crooked smile was sincere. Her eyes welled up again, then flowed over until she was bawling into a paper napkin with an antlered creature embossed on its surface. Hank rounded the table and pulled her up to him, where she buried her face in his shoulder.

Sobbing in a public place like that was not Darcy's way, attracting onlookers from surrounding tables in the process. Right then, though, she just didn't give a damn.

*Chapter* **52**

# V I D E O S

AFTER HER SESSION with Hank, Darcy was having a hard time concentrating on the workload on her desk. That and the events of the previous twenty-four hours proved too traumatic for her to settle down. She pushed aside the marketing plan for Coquette Lingerie, admonishing herself for passing up the opportunity to become more familiar with its intricacies. She also ignored two phone messages from Jessie Campbell. *Let Jase or Peter handle it.* She wasn't up to dealing with Jessie Campbell just then.

Still fidgety, she glanced around her office for something she could settle down to, when yet another thought occurred to her. The videos. With all that had happened in recent days, she'd forgotten to pick up the non-reproducible VCR's of her Pad Room forays that Josh Williams had promised to turn over to her when he was done using them. How many times had he ogled her near-naked body by now? The picture in her mind wasn't reasuring.

She picked up the phone and punched in the number listed on her agency phone/address sheet which included Fantasy personnel. Two rings later Josh Williams answered. "Josh, this is Darcy," she said evenly, trying not to show how pissed she still was at being set up for his depraved capers. "I forgot to get those videos from you. Can I swing by?"

"Oh, sure," Josh replied. He tried to sound upbeat, but disappointment in his voice betrayed him. "Not today, though. I've got to dash to the printers."

Sure, Darcy thought to herself. You can't just put them out for me to pick up? Or have them delivered? No matter. She didn't feel like making the trek today, anyway. Besides, something could happen to the videos, left out for pickup. Or so it could be claimed. Best she pick them up herself.

Josh Williams continued: "Got some panels to pump out in the morning. How 'bout stopping by after lunch? Around one-thirty—two?"

Darcy was checking her calendar as he spoke. There wasn't anything on it that couldn't be pushed one way or the other. "All right, Josh. I'll be down."

"Great, I'll have the videos ready," still pretending he was happy to give them up. "Be good to see you," which he didn't have to fake.


**JOSH WILLIAMS WAS** puzzled. It was only a couple of days since he last viewed the "Darcy/Magenta" videos he hoped Darcy had forgotten about, and he wouldn't have to surrender. Wishful thinking. Darcy's battle with Caren Dalton was the most erotic thing he had ever taped, and he didn't look forward to parting with that video in particular—not that her hair-pulling episode with Holly Hartley was all that far behind. It lacked the nudity, but anything Darcy Austin did was sexy as far as he was concerned.

But when he went to get Darcy's videos, he couldn't find either one where, he could have sworn, he'd put them on his office shelving. He felt a twinge of panic—Darcy would never believe him if he told her he couldn't locate them. He had to keep looking.

Josh Williams didn't have any luck in the annex either, but he did come across a couple of videos he didn't recognize while searching, each of them labeled in what appeared to be some kind of code. Curious, he brought them back to his office and plugged one of them into his VCR.

He stared at the TV screen in disbelief as the video played through to its finish. He ejected the first video and inserted the second. It was similar to the first one except there was a different male partner involved. What he had just witnessed, recorded in a familiar setting to him, was shocking enough in and of itself. But what was more, both of the men appearing in the videos were now dead. One by his own hand—according to the police—the other by an assassin. His hands were shaking. Was he nervous or scared? He wondered which. Glancing around the outer offices, everything seemed normal enough. People were going about their afternoon affairs—maybe with a little more hustle than usual, since they were preparing for their long weekend starting tomorrow. He had granted them Friday off as a reward, after they had put two books to bed under harried circumstances.

He could have used the respite himself, but he had to get a jump on the storyboard for the next Magenta issue. The deadline was already on top of him. And he'd also have to confront the topic of the videos he just viewed, forgetting for the moment he still hadn't found Darcy Austin's videos.

*Chapter* **53**

# A B D U C T I O N

**THE FOLLOWING MORNING,** Jessie Campbell was getting ready to leave for work. Contrary to out-of-school tales, she did not have chicken for breakfast, but then, she did have an egg. She dressed, touched up her hair and makeup and scurried about collecting the desultory notes she had worked on the previous evening. She was stuffing them into her briefcase when she heard a rap at her back door. Puzzled as to who it might be at this time of morning, she hustled to the door and, without thinking, swung it open. "You," she exclaimed, more puzzled than before. "What do you want?"

"To pay a little visit," the person responded. "Mind if I come in?"

Jessie Campbell did mind. "I'm just leaving for the office. Can we talk another time?"

"'Fraid not," the intruder said, stepping into the house, pushing her aside and reclosing the door.

Jessie Campbell didn't know what to make of the intrusion, but she knew she didn't like it. "Get out of here," she demanded. "I'm late for work, and I'm leaving right now." Then she gave a push of her own and a brief scuffle followed. She was no match for the intruder, however, who dragged her kicking and squealing into the living room and tossed her into an overstuffed chair.

Her anger turned to fright as the intruder loomed over her, holding her down by the shoulders until she stopped squirming. She started to say something but her voice cracked, and the intruder spoke first. "Now, Jessie, you're going to do what I say. I want you to call your secretary and tell her you don't feel well. She'll believe you because you won't sound well. Tell her you'll try and come in this afternoon. She'll believe that too, because you always show up. Right?"

"And if I won't?" Jessie managed to challenge.

"Then I fear you've already spoken your last words, as of right now," the intruder responded, brandishing a knife so close that Jessie could almost feel the chill of the steel on her face. It had an eight-inch blade with a small hilt at the base of its handle. Never had a kitchen knife appeared so lethal to Jessie Campbell. The intruder stepped back and reached into Jessie's open briefcase on a table, withdrew her cell phone from it and pitched it into her lap. "Use this. You won't have to get up."

Jessie didn't know where this was going, but she was fearful enough to do as she was told, poking the quick-connect keys to her secretary. The intruder was right. She didn't sound well speaking the words she was told to say.

"Nicely done," the intruder said, after the call was completed. "Now let's get to it. I understand you've been sharing your theories about Roland and Frank with the police of late. That so?"

"I . . . just some thoughts," Jessie answered. "Really, I don't know anything about their deaths. Honest."

"It doesn't matter now anyway. Take your clothes off," the intruder said.

"My clothes?" Jessie verged on panic. "Are . . . are you going to rape me?"

"What do you take me for, Jessie?" the intruder smiled back. "Just take them off. You can stop with your bra and pants. Do it seated right there, if you don't mind."

Jessie Campbell hesitated, but when she saw the threatening look in the eyes of the intruder, she decided not to argue. Fumbling at the buttons of her blouse she opened it, wriggled around, and managed to get it off where she sat. She folded it and laid it across the arm of her chair. Jessie Campbell was a neatnik, even now.

It was obvious her lacy bra was designed for its primary function only. That did not include upper-level concealment—especially from where the intruder stood over her. Jessie Campbell wavered at that point, and checked into the cold stare of the intruder once again before deciding she'd best proceed. She undid the waistband of her skirt and lifted her hips from the seat of the chair. Then scooted her skirt under her derriere and slipped it down her thighs to her ankles. From there, she kicked it off onto the carpet. Neatness was now forgotten.

Her panties matched her bra, scooping to a provocative triangle in front. It was a captivating display.

"Nice bod," her captor said, admiring the marketing director in her state of undress. "A touch more on top and you really could rival your account lady."

Jessie Campbell didn't like the word "touch" used in any way under these circumstances.

"Fetching undies," the intruder continued. "But no hose? You're a professional woman, Jessie Campbell."

"I-I was going to put that on when I got to the office," she replied, feeling foolish answering the question.

"What are they?" the intruder asked, waving a hand at Jessie Campbell's body.

"Huh?" Jessie was as confused as she was frightened.

"Your bra and pants. The brand."

"Oh. W-why, Coquette."

"Woulda been my guess," the intruder smirked. "Mason arrange a discount for you when you whined to him about Darcy Austin being moved out from under your thumb?"

Jessie didn't answer this time but looked guilty as charged.

"Good you're wearing it. I like my victims associated with Williams/Bailey clients. My signature, you might say. I brought Coquette along, just in case. But seeing you're already wearing it, you won't have to get naked before putting it on for me."

"You . . . you're the, the . . . *murderer*," Jessie stammered, backing as far down into the cushions of the chair as it allowed; as if that was going to help. She should have arrived at her conclusion before now, but denial had to play out first.

"You have me, I'm afraid."

"Are you going to kill me?" she screeched, fearing she already knew. Adding: "In my lingerie?" ridiculous as that sounded.

"No, no. Nothing so drastic as that, Jesse. But I am going to restrain you for a time," her captor said, producing a roll of silver-gray tape from a jacket pocket. "You and that chair are about to become one, Jess. But not to worry; duct tape will stick to your skin, but it really won't hurt much—if you stay still, that is. Otherwise you'll raise some nasty welts on that lovely skin of yours. So behave."

"What are you going to do to me then?" Jessie Campbell was pushing back in the chair again, her concern about rape, if not murder, resurfacing in her mind.

"Relax—I'm just going to leave you here," the intruder assured her. "That is, after I compose an e-mail—an SOS of sorts—for your office, and program it to send, umm, midafternoon. Something like: 'Help, I'm taped to a chair in my Coquette underwear.' Sound okay?"

Jessie Campbell didn't look as though it did.

"Well, I'll have to work on the composition."

While the proposed e-mail message wasn't to the liking of the marketing director, the alternatives she could think of were much worse. "You'll leave me here? But I know who you are," she blurted out before realizing she was presenting a problem to which there was a ready solution.

She needn't have worried. "Yeah, I thought of that," the intruder replied. "Guess you'll just have to tell your rescuers all about me when they arrive." Then: "Oh, by the way; need to go potty before we start with the duct tape—you'll be here awhile? I'll have to escort you to the bathroom, of course. But better to go now than in your panties and all over that nice chair."

There was a pregnant pause while Jessie Campbell weighed the indignities of going to the bathroom with her captor at her side, or having to go in her pants later. Her breakfast coffee was already making its workings known. "All right," Jessie relented in a soft voice, eyes cast at her bare feet. "Let me up, please." Never before did Ms. Jessie Campbell appear so humble.

*Chapter* **54**

# S E T U P

**ANDREA SHIFF WAS** on the other end when Darcy picked up on the first ring of her phone, having just returned to her office after a visit down the hall. "Hi, Darc. There's been a change in Josh's schedule, but he wanted to make sure you get those two videos you wanted. Can you make it this morning instead?"

It'd be a pain to reschedule her day again, but Darcy thought she could do it. "What time?" she asked.

"How's ten-thirty?"

Darcy checked her watch. That would give her a little more than an hour to rearrange things and get down town. "Short notice," Darcy said, a little put out. "Why the sudden rush?"

Andrea picked up the pique in Darcy's voice. "You never know with Josh," Andrea said. "But no more jockeying around, I promise. If Josh can't hand the videos over to you personally when you get here, I will. Guaranteed."

"Okay, Andrea, I'm holding you to that," Darcy said.

**HANK SAT AT** his desk, staring into what space his office allowed. He was now sure that he knew who the killer was, but he had to consider his next move. He also had the feeling there wasn't much time left before another shoe dropped, if murder qualified for such a mundane metaphor. Yet, he didn't have enough to invoke a search warrant from a judge. He'd have to come at it from a different angle: Darcy again. He placed a call to her office, but Maggie Evans picked up instead. "She isn't here," the cordial voice of Darcy's assistant related. "She told me she'd be back shortly before lunch, though. Can I leave a message, Lieutenant?" She knew his voice by now.

"Nothing special," Hank said. "Just tell her I called," He had Darcy's cell number but chose to wait rather than interrupt her wherever she was off to.

When he didn't hear back after a while, he called again. This time it was ten past noon and, after three rings, Hank was already resigning himself to Darcy's voice mail when a male came on. He was out of breath and chewing on something. "Darcy Austin's office," the voice said. "Jason O'Connell speaking."

"Jason, this is Hank Hankenson," he returned, glad to be talking to a live person instead of a machine. "Darcy around?"

"Haven't seen her since earlier this morning," Jason said. "Told me she was heading out to Fantasy to pick something up. I expected her back by now."

Hank didn't like the sound of that but put it aside. "Well, okay," he said. "Let her know I'd like to talk to her when she gets back, will you?"

"Sure thing. I'm anxious to talk to her, too. Some questions on Gold'n Tender need answering and Jessie's not around either. Usually one or the other is available. I don't think Jessie Campbell has missed a day since I've been at the agency, sick or not. Doesn't even like to take vacations."

"So where is she now?"

"Home sick, they tell me."

"Nothing serious, I hope." It was an idle statement.

"Man, that woman would have to be next to death not to show up for work. I should dispatch an ambulance to her home, but I'm enjoying my freedom from harassment too much."

After his conversation with Jason O'Connell, Hank punched in Fantasy's number to see if he could reach Darcy there, only to get a recording telling him no one was available. He waited a few minutes and tried again. Same result. Strange for a business, he thought, even for one on the flaky side like Fantasy.

He called Darcy's cell. No answer. Now he was getting frustrated, and a little troubled—his cop instincts kicking in.

He sat staring at his cradled phone, trying to decide what to do next when the words, "that woman would have to be close to death" popped into his mind. He pulled the center drawer of his desk open and pushed around in the clutter until he found the business card Jessie Campbell had given him when Darcy and he met at her home, two days prior—remembering it listed her home phone as well as her office number. He hesitated, feeling a little foolish, but went ahead and called her home number.

The phone rang several times, before the answering machine came on with its innocuous message. *Hate those damn things,* Hank said to himself, re-cradling his handset without leaving a message. He realized Jessie might not want to answer the phone if she wasn't feeling well but, on top of his other failures to connect with anyone, his sensors were now on full alert, even if for no hard reason he could point to.

He decided to call Jessie Campbell again, and left a message this time. Then he tried Fantasy again. Still the same recording.

His success rate improved with the next calls he made. The first one was to Minneapolis City Hall, where he asked for either police sergeant Sigurd Nadler or Dexter Ames. He got Dexter Ames. "Dex, this is Hank Hankenson," he said. "Remember me?"

"Hey, Lieutenant. Got that Soup Caper all wrapped up?"

"Not as well as I'd like, but making some headway, I think."

"You need me and Sig to come out to the big burb again? We could use a break from this hell hole."

"You're welcome around here anytime, but right now I need an assist from where you're at. Like right now."

"If I can help," Dex Ames said. "What's up?"

"You know about Fantasy Publications, right?"

"Sure, part of Williams/Bailey—Millhouse Building in the warehouse district. What about 'em?"

"Well I've been trying to reach there for a time, and all I get is the answering machine. Normally it wouldn't bother me so much but—"

"Want me and Sig to check it out? We were just gonna leave on another call, but we can swing by if you like. Practically in our backyard."

Hank knew that. "Great. How soon can you get there?"

"You are antsy. Ten minutes okay?"

"That's a lot faster than I can make it. It's probably nothing, but . . ."

"Time's wastin' Lieutenant. Get back to you."

Hank's next call reached the man down the hall. "Sergeant Baines," Sergeant Baines said.

"Joe, can you get someone over to Jessie Campbell's house? It's near where Frank Ramstead lived. I'll give you the address."

"Sure, what's up?" Joe Baines asked.

"Likely nothing. But let's check on her. She's supposed to be home sick and doesn't answer the phone."

"I don't answer the damn phone when I'm home sick either."

"Yeah, well, she's kind of different, from what I hear. Like I said. Probably wasted effort, but I'd like to make sure. You can call first. If she picks up, drop the whole matter."

"Okay, otherwise I'll go myself. Maybe take Marge Kennedy with me, so I don't look like some lecter ringing her doorbell."

"It's a 'lecher' you look like, but suit yourself. I'm checking things out at Fantasy. Something's bothering me there, too."

"That's why you're the 'loot,'" Joe Baines said and hung up.

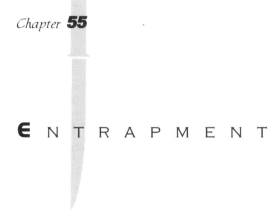

*Chapter* **55**

E N T R A P M E N T

**ON THE THIRD** floor of the Millhouse Building, Darcy passed by the Fantasy annex with its infamous—to her especially—Pad Room, reaching the reception area of Fantasy Publications farther down the hallway. It was 10:35, she was only five minutes late, which wasn't bad considering the traffic and road construction she contended with in downtown Minneapolis.

Entering the reception area, she found it empty, just like the last time she was there. With no one on duty in what Darcy thought may qualify as the least-attended reception desk in the Twin Cities, she rounded the reception wall into the bullpen behind it.

It was as she remembered, but now the space was deserted except for Josh Williams, who she could make out at his drawing board at the far end of the open area. No sign of Andrea. Darcy thought she might be in the Pad Room annex, or the ladies' room, for that matter.

She noted the commanding wall display once again, with "Magenta" looming above the lesser portrayals in the exhibit. It was unchanged as far as she could tell, although she wondered why it seemed all so ominous to her this time.

With no Andrea around, she headed for Josh Williams' office, even though he'd said he was under deadline pressure. She didn't want to disturb him if avoidable. In the ad game, she had developed a great appreciation for deadlines. Oh, well, it's only a pick up.

Her high heels set up an eerie echo in the empty bullpen as she crossed it. And halfway there, she thought she heard footfalls behind her. She turned, then relaxed. "Oh it's you, Andrea. You startled me." Andrea Shiff looked different, Darcy thought. Her hair was shorter and it was darker than her normal blondish hue. Her pale skin looked ghostly by contrast, or did Darcy just imagine it? Was there a resemblance to someone else . . . ?

Andrea returned a closed-mouth smile and stepped closer.

"Have you got the videos?" Darcy asked, feeling a sudden unease.

"You won't need them," Andrea said, coming closer yet.

Darcy turned her head back to Josh Williams' office. He was still there, but now she became aware that he hadn't moved one iota from the time she first saw him seated at his board.

"Josh can't help you, if that's what you're wondering. He's indisposed." Andrea said, still grinning in the same unpleasant way.

Darcy felt a tightening in the pit of her stomach. Something was wrong and all she could think about now was getting out of there. She tried to move around Andrea, but the bigger woman blocked her path.

"Okay, that's enough Andrea. Out of my way," Darcy demanded, with no result. Instead, Andrea grasped Darcy by the arm with one hand, while extracting a packet from her jeans with the other.

Darcy wanted no part of this. She pulled away, braced and brought her leg up into Andrea's rib cage, forcing the woman to fall back. The kick was well executed and would have been more damaging if not constrained by Darcy's skirt and heels, causing her to fall off balance as well.

Darcy kicked off her shoes and pulled her skirt up in order to deliver a more lethal kick, but Andrea was on her before she could—wrapping her in a bear hug that caved her back and lifted her feet off the floor. Swallowed in Andrea's vice-like embrace, Darcy still managed to thrust the heel of her palm under Andrea's jaw, clashing her teeth together. Andrea's hold on Darcy broke, and she dropped to one knee. Darcy might have attempted to finish Andrea at that point, but her only impulse was to escape. She ran to the reception room only to find the door to the hallway locked. Now she would have to turn and fight to the end. She spun around, finding Andrea Shiff right behind her.

**THE NEXT ENCOUNTER** didn't last long. Andrea swung an arm around Darcy's back, pulled her forward and thrust a pad into her face. Darcy's struggling grew weak, rapture overcoming will. Then she went limp in Andrea's arms.

**ANDREA DIDN'T EXPECT** to come across anyone in the hallway, what with Fantasy Publications being officially shut down for the day. Nonetheless, she checked to see that the corridor was clear before dragging Darcy's slack body back down the hall to the Pad Room annex. If she were to run into someone, it was no big deal. She would just kill him, her or them. Such measures did not become necessary, however. She reached the annex without incident, pulled her quarry inside and locked the door behind her.

Andrea Shiff knelt beside Darcy Austin on the carpeted floor of the anteroom—preparing for the next part of her game plan.

*Chapter* **56**

# D I S C O V E R Y

**HANK WAS RE-ENTERING** his office from a visit down the hall, when his phone rang. He moved around his desk and picked up the handset. By the ring, he could tell it was an outside call, so he answered with his formal, "Lieutenant Hankenson," salutation.

The voice on the other end was not so formal. "Ya know the missin' knife you were lookin' for, from the Austin woman's house?" Minneapolis Police Sergeant Dex Ames said.

"Yeah, sure," Hank replied, recognizing the caller's voice.

"I think we found it." Then nothing.

"Are you going to let me know where, Dex?"

Dex Ames was pausing for his version of dramatic affect. "We think it's the one buried in Josh Williams' chest."

"Holy shit. You in the Millhouse Building?"

"Here on floor three. Sig's with the paras right now. The doc just arrived."

"A doctor? Josh isn't dead?"

"No, but close. Knife nicked his heart."

Hank was almost afraid to ask the next question. "Find anyone else there?"

"Not a soul. What kind of a business is this? No people around."

"A weird one," Hank replied. In a sense he was relieved, but he still had the feeling all was not well concerning the missing Darcy Austin. And where was Andrea Shiff, and the rest of the staff?

"Looks like a scuffle took place around here but no indication Williams was involved in it." Dex said. "Looks like he was stabbed where he sat at his board. Nothing else disturbed in his office. And there's no blood anywhere outside of it, either."

A scuffle? Hank got a sinking sensation in his stomach, his hunch now moving toward a conclusion he didn't want to come to. "I'll be right down," he said.

"We'll keep a light on for ya," Dex said.

**NO SOONER HAD** Hank strapped himself into the BMW than his carphone chirped. It was Sergeant Joe Baines. "Hank, we got a situation over here—at the Campbell place."

Hank started the car, an uh-oh cropping up in his mind. "Tell me, Joe." He was on his way downtown no matter what Joe Baines had to say.

"Found Ms. Campbell strapped to a chair with duct tape wrapped around her. Damnedest thing I ever saw."

"What?" The BMW picked up speed on Old Shakopee Road, heading east toward I-35W. "Is she okay?"

"That depends on what you mean by okay. No wounds or anything, but she's pretty drugged up. Some sort of downers, be my guess. Pretty groggy. Keeps slurring something like 'endra' or 'Enron,' near as

I can make out, an' wavin' her hand in the direction of her computer. She get hurt in the stock market or somethin'? Anyway, the medical guys just got here. Looking her over now."

Hank said, "I think that's 'Andrea' she's trying to say, not 'Enron.'"

"Jesus. How do you know that?"

Hank reached the cloverleaf at Ninety-eighth and spiraled down the ramp to I-35W leading into downtown Minneapolis. "Listen, Joe," he said, not answering the question the sergeant put to him, "see what's on her computer desktop, will you? "

"Already doin' it. Good thing Marge came along. I'm helpless with those gadgets, and she's a whiz."

Hank passed under the I-494 bridge, avoiding a Buick poking along in the fast lane. "Good. Have Marge check Jessie's e-mail, too. See if anything came in or went out during the day, okay? Call me back if you find anything."

"Sure thing," Joe Baines said. Then: "Where are you, by the way."

"On 35W, heading for Fantasy Publications. Josh Williams has a knife in his chest—the one we were looking for, sounds like."

"My Gawd. How'd you hear?"

"Dex Ames called. I'll fill you in later."

"All right." Then, out of nowhere he said: "She was in her underwear."

"Come again? Who we talking about?"

"Jessie Campbell. Bra and panties is all she had on besides the duct tape."

"What the hell's that all about?" Silence for a moment, then: "Joe, check the brand of her lingerie, will you? See if you can do it without looking like a pervert—I'd be curious to know."

"Who sounds like the pervert here?" Joe Baines said and was off the line.

HANK SPED PAST the congested cross-town interchange and was close to Forty-sixth Street when his carphone sounded again. "You hit it, Sherlock," Joe Baines said. "An e-mail was set to go to Campbell's office at 2:30. It said to come rescue her before she goes all over her chair. Somethin' like that."

Now Hank realized that Jessie Campbell was alive only because the killer wanted her to contribute to her unfolding scheme. He glanced over to the digital display on his dash, the numerals illuminating 1:49 back to him. "If SEND was set for 2:30, we've got about a forty-minute jump on her."

"How do you figure—what are we say'n here?"

"Our gameplayer. Andrea Shiff," Hank said, slowing for the downtown Fifth Avenue exit.

"The right-hand lady to Josh Williams?"

"No lady, but she is the right-handed woman we've been looking for. Find the brand?"

"Oh yeah, the underwear—Coquette. I had Marge do the search for the label."

"It figures."

"Wouldn't you?"

"Not that, the brand."

"Care to explain?"

"Later. When Jessie Campbell comes around—should be just about 3:00, I'd guess—let me know what she has to say."

"Will do," Joe Baines said, clicking off.

———

**HANK PULLED UP** to the Millhouse Building four minutes later and left the BMW on the street. There were flashing lights all over the place with stop-and-go traffic moving by at a snail's pace. A crew of Minneapolis cops waved the passing vehicles by as best they could, but Minnesotans are world-class rubber-neckers in situations like these.

Hank disconnected the portable carphone handset from its cradle and tucked it into his inside coat pocket. He didn't want to miss a call from Joe Baines. When a cop came over to tell him to move on, he held up his badge and got a come-ahead sign, instead. He flashed his badge again at the two uniforms standing guard at the yellow-taped entry of the building, and they waved him passed. He decided to clip his badge to the outside of his coat the rest of the way, for expediency.

Another cop in the elevator motioned him in and pressed "3," figuring that's where he was headed. *I should have so many uniforms at a crime scene in Bloomington,* Hank thought, as they rumbled to the third floor of the building in the slow-moving elevator. When the door banged open at the third level, his thoughts returned to more worrisome matters, and his sinking feeling came back with a vengeance. Stepping into the corridor, yet another uniform escorted him to the Fantasy offices.

Minneapolis police sergeants Dexter Ames and Sigurd Nadler greeted him when he entered the bullpen area while the crime-scene crew, not paying him notice, continued about its meticulous chores. For a while there, he almost felt like a celebrity.

Josh Williams was gone, taken to Hennepin County Emergency before Hank arrived.

"Know anything more about what happened here," he asked the detectives.

"Like I said," Dex Ames responded. "Looks like a struggle took place in the space we're standing in. Some stuff knocked around, as you can see. At least one of them was a woman. Found a high-heal shoe sticking out from under that cabinet over there," he said gesturing in the direction of the find.

"Some stuff's in the reception area, too," Sig Nadler interjected. "It started here and ended up out there, from what we can tell," with a nod toward the reception room. "Probably the woman missing the shoe was trying to get out when she got caught out there and didn't make it."

Hank glanced at the shoe encased in a transparent plastic evidence bag. *Is it Darcy's?* he put to himself, then asked out loud: "How do you know she didn't make it out?"

Sig Nadler said. "For starters, we found a pad saturated with chloroform in the reception room. That probably ended the struggle right there. Then there's the matching shoe, and the rest of what appears to be the woman's clothing down the hall in another area, where there's a weird three-sided structure with strobes and a couple of mounted cameras."

"The Pad Room," Hank muttered in response to what the detective just told him.

"What?" both sergeants asked in unison.

"They video stuff there," Hank said, more interested in the women's clothing they just referred to than relating any further explanations on his part. "Can I see the clothes?" he added.

The sergeants led Hank back to the annex. The clothes were neatly folded on a table against a wall between two doors in the anteroom, where the Minneapolis cops had found them.

"Door on the right leads to dressing rooms," Sig Nadler explained without being asked. "One on the left's got costumes hanging in it, along with other weird shit."

"Prop room," Hank said, like a show-business aesthete, although the full extent of his knowledge derived from a tour of Normandale

Community College in Bloomington. There he was shown a room in the Theater Department such as Sig Nadler just described in not so aesthetic terms. "The Pad Room's that way I take it," Hank said, with a wave to the far end of the room.

"Yeah, just around the corner," Dex Ames said, picking up on the lieutenant's descriptive nomenclature.

Hank turned back to the folded clothes in front of him. The silk blouse and wool skirt he recognized as Darcy Austin's. The lingerie had to be hers as well. He knew what she favored.

He looked at the two sergeants waiting for a reaction from him. "They belong to Darcy Austin," he said. "We've got to assume the killer's got her."

"What's with the clothes?" Dex Ames questioned. "This perp some kind of a pervert or rapist on the side?" Then noting Hank's concerned expression, said, "Sorry Lieutenant."

"I don't think it's rape we have to worry about," Hank answered. "These clothes are here as part of a script—a tapestry of sorts. The shoe left in the bullpen, the chloroform pad in the reception area . . . these clothes. It's painting a picture for us. I know how she likes to do things."

"She?" Sig Nadler asked.

"A dyke?" Dex Ames asked, still not convinced about the rape scenario.

"She, but I doubt she's a dyke," Hank answered. "Andrea Shiff, Josh Williams' assistant, is our killer, and she knows I know it by now. She just doesn't care. In fact, wants me to know."

"You shittin' us?" Dex Ames questioned.

Hank picked up where he left off. "And, unless I miss my guess, we're gonna find more of her taunts around here telling us what's next on her agenda. It's a game she's playing—and it's with me."

"I'll be damned," Dex Ames said.

"Sorta like the Rifleman," Sig Nadler said.

*Chapter* **57**

# R I D D L E

HANK ASKED IF either of them noticed anything else that seemed out of place or unusual, getting two negatives in return. Next he asked to examine Andrea Shiff's office, and Dex Ames ushered him back to the main area and the space next to Josh Williams'. Sig Nadler broke off and returned to the crime-scene investigation now in cleanup mode.

Hank knew Andrea Shiff would toy with him. Give him enough to tease him along, but not enough to stop her from what she was up to. And, thus far, she'd been successful in doing just that.

"Anything you see?" Dex Ames inquired. He was watching Hank survey the small room filled with folders, files, and stacks of papers that the lieutenant was not bothering to sort through or read.

"Should be right in front of us," Hank said under his breath. "Just have to see it, even though we're looking right at it."

"Huh?" the perplexed detective said.

Hank had noted the comic book tossed among assorted items on Andrea Shiff's desk. It was the issue entitled, *Magenta and the Cavern of Doom*, the same one he caught Joe Baines reading and had examined himself. He knew the themes: entrapment, chloroform seduction, tip-off to the lover cop, and a death-plan plunge into oblivion. He didn't have to look through it. *Thanks, Andrea, now tell me more.*

Then Hank saw it, the sergeant noticing the lieutenant's fixation. "All the space around these offices," Hank said. "Nothing but illustrations of comic-book characters and comic-book reproductions stuck up on the walls. But not here," he added, waving a hand at three magazine ads pinned up on the wall above Andrea Shiff's desk.

Dex Ames didn't follow. "Some scenic ads? So what?"

"Location, location, location," Hank muttered.

Dex Ames was lost. But he suspected the burb cop he was learning to respect a great deal, was on to something.

The ads were from the new Minnesota Tourism campaign that Hank had inadvertently prompted and which Darcy shepherded through the agency. One was the J.V. Schanken "fish story." Another depicted Henry Schoolcraft's upriver passage to the source of the Mississippi. And the third featured the Devil's Kettle cauldron. Once again, it all connected back to Williams/Bailey—the theme was intact.

*Which one is it?* he asked himself. Basswood Lake, Itasca, or Magney State Park. His mind turned them over. *It's multiple choice.*

He considered the time element. This game was supposed to kick off with the pre-composed e-mail message scheduled to arrive at Jessie Campbell's workplace at 2:30, calling for her rescue. Jessie Campbell would then be identifying her assailant at about 3:00, allowing for the rescue to take place and her drugging to wear off enough to explain what happened. Her story would identify Andrea Shiff as the killer and point the way to Fantasy Publications and Josh Williams' stabbing. That would consume about another forty minutes or so. By the time Hank was supposed to be at the point he was now, it should have been somewhere around 4:30, by this reasoning. And, for any game to be worth playing—even with Andrea stacking the deck in her favor—the distance to her ultimate destination would have to figure into it in order to make things interesting.

He mentally ticked off the travel times to each location. Basswood Lake? Too far. Itasca? Too close. The Devil's Kettle? Yeah, just right. It was a Goldilocks scenario. Plus, the Devil's Kettle was the perfect allegory to the Cavern of Doom with its enigmatic drop to nothingness. It was the setting for Andrea Shiff's endgame.

He glanced at his wrist; it was 3:34. *How much of a lead would Andrea Shiff build in for herself?* Once again, she would not give him enough time to intercept her, yet enough so that he'd have to try—even if his odds were long. And if he was supposed to figure out her riddle by 4:30 earliest, as seemed to be the case, he'd now shaved something close to an hour off her schedule.

Andrea would be driving cautiously, Hank reasoned, so as to avoid being stopped for a traffic violation. Also, having to care for a hostage would slow her down some. She would have factored all that in, of course. And if his guess about Andrea's contrived lead time was accurate, she was planning on reaching Magney State Park somewhere between 5:00 and 6:00. She'd still have to get up to the Devil's Kettle from there. A lot of assumptions, but what else did he have to go on?

Hank reasoned Andrea Shiff probably knew he'd get this far—she'd left him a program of events along with a virtual road map. Nevertheless he was at a huge disadvantage. Even with the time advantage he'd gained, he didn't know how he could possibly get there before it was too late. She'd made sure of that. Still . . .

Hank turned to Dex Ames, who was still observing him with interest. "Dex, I think our girl's headed for a place called the Devil's Kettle. It's bout twenty miles past Grand Marias, up on the North Shore."

Dex Ames had to ask: "How do you know that?"

"You sound like a sergeant I work with," Hank said moving past the question. "Look, Dex, I've got to get out of here, but I need your help. Okay?"

Dex Ames felt Hank's urgency. "What ever you say, Lieutenant."

"Have your people get in touch with the Cook County Sheriff's office. I'm pretty sure that's in Grand Marais. Tell them to watch for two women heading up to the Devil's Kettle—that's a waterfall in Magney State Park. It's one of the ads here on the wall," he said with a point of his finger. "Pretty deserted up there this time of year, especially late in the day. Any cars in the parking area should be easy to check."

Dex Ames scratched notes on a pad all police officers keep like part of their anatomy, saying nothing, as Hank rattled off more instructions.

"If not two women, look for one woman with a large wrap or package of some kind." As he said it, he wondered how one woman could get another non-ambulatory woman over the 500 steps and steep trails that he'd read about in order to get up to the Devil's Kettle. He wasn't going to put it past Andrea Shiff to figure out a way, though. "Keep me posted on your progress, will you Dex?" He handed his card to the police sergeant. "I'll keep my cell on, wherever I go."

"One more thing," he said, snatching the Cavern of Doom comic book up from the desktop and showing it to the sergeant. "See the costumes these two women are wearing?" pointing to the illustrations of Magenta and Coda.

"Yeah. What about them?

"See if you can find something that looks like either one in that prop room down the hall. Then call me. Okay?"

"Sounds nuts, but you got it."

"Good." Hank, looked the sergeant straight in the eyes. "I can't explain everything right now, Dex, but believe me—what we do next is critical if we're going to save a woman's life."

"We're talking about Darcy Austin?" Dex Ames asked.

"Yes." That sinking feeling, again.

"Nice lady. I'll get things rolling on this end," Dex Ames said, picking up Andrea Shiff's office phone, placing a call to Minneapolis Police Headquarters.

Hank crossed the bullpen, punching in Bloomington Police Headquarters on his cell, and got the voice of Grace Anderson at the main desk. "Grace, will you go into my office and look up Brad Hoyt in my directory?" He held while she hustled.

He stared up at the wall display of superheroes with the huge Magenta figure seeming to stare back at him as he approached. *Why does it look so damned ominous?*

"Got the number right here," Grace Anderson said over the cell.

# Chapter 58

# O D Y S S E Y

**HANK WAS HEADING** south out of the downtown area when he got Hoyt International on the car phone. He was told that Brad Hoyt was somewhere in the metro area but not in the office. At least he wasn't in Florida, or Istanbul for that matter, for which Hank was thankful. Deferring to the importance of a police lieutenant's call, the woman on the phone volunteered a cell-phone number to call, which he did.

"Brad Hoyt," the voice said.

"Brad, this is Hank Hankenson, remember me?"

"Hey, Lieutenant, you looking for another golf outing? We don't have many days left around here till the snow flies, you know."

"Nothing I'd like better, but right now I've got another matter that needs attending?"

"Uh-oh, serious stuff?"

"Life and death, pal. I need your help."

"Sure. What can I do?"

"You got one of those planes operational?"

"Yeah, sure."

"How fast can you be ready to fly?"

"You're not kiddin' are you? Let's see, I can be at Flying Cloud in about fifteen minutes if need be. Where are you?"

"Just coming up on the Crosstown from Minneapolis. I can do about the same."

"Where we going?"

"File a fight plan for Tofte, okay?"

"Tofte—up on the North Shore?"

"Right. We're going a little farther than that, but at least I know there's an airport there. If you know of an airstrip at Grand Marais, you can file for that—but we're still going farther up."

"Not sure I like the sound of this—then again, maybe I do. I'll call ahead and get the Pilatus fueled up. We can be on our way before four-thirty, I'd guess."

"Pilatus? Where did that come from?"

"Switzerland. Took delivery last month—a turbo-prop jet. Sounds like you're in a hurry."

"You got it, pal. How fast can we get there?"

"An hour to Grand Marais, be my guess. Maybe a little quicker."

It was beyond anything Hank had hoped for. "Holy shit. How fast does that thing go?"

"Air speed's 310 miles per hour. We're talkin' twelve-hundred blown horsepower."

"Pilatus it is, Brad."

WHEN HANK SIGNED off, his message service told him he had a call from Dex Ames, which he returned with the press of a key.

"Got hold of Sheriff Johanson up at Grand Marais," Dex Ames said, in his familiar grumble. "He'll be on the lookout for our two missing women. Setting up a road check at Magney."

"Good. Anything else turn up?" Hank questioned.

"Couple of things. Checked out the cars parked around the Millhouse Building. Austin's SUV is in the lot across the street. Josh Williams' car is in the back lot to the building—one of those new Thunderbirds with the retro look. Andrea Shiff's '96 Camry is missing. She's registered with a Porsche Boxster, too, but that's in her garage at her home. Paid a visit to her residence."

"So she's probably driving a car that'll fit in anywhere she goes. What color is it?"

"Beige."

"Oh, great. I'd wager its got different plates by now."

Dex Ames concurred. "Probably," he said, before switching to another subject. "Checked out that prop room you asked me to. No trace of the costumes you mentioned. All kinds of other weird ones though."

"Uh-huh. Did you happen to come across a set of heavy boots while you were rummaging around in there, by any chance?"

"How in shit did you know that?" Dex Ames said, not hiding his surprise.

Hank skipped over the question, saying, "Hang on to 'em Dex. I think they're going to fit the footprints we found at the Austin home, and another place you haven't heard about yet. Fill you in later. Okay?"

"You amaze me, Lieutenant. We could use you on the Rifleman case."

"You don't really want me on that, now do you, Dex?"

*No, I don't.* "Good luck where you're headed, Lieutenant," Dex Ames said, dropping the Rifleman subject, and hung up.

**HANK GOT THROUGH** to Joe Baines, just after jogging onto County Road One heading west, and brought him up to date, including his planned flight to the Devil's Kettle. The sergeant was not conciliatory. "You crazy? Even if you're right about this nutty plan, and even if you spot somethin'—what're you gonna do about it up in the sky, for Christ's sake?"

"Maybe land," came the reply.

"You *have* gone bonkers. That Kettle place is up in the freakin' mountains—nothin' but trees, cliffs, and rocks. Where you gonna land?"

"Haven't figured that out, but I'm thinking."

"Oh, swell," Joe Baines said. "What am I gonna tell the chief?"

"So long for now, chum," Hank said, signing off.

Grim as the situation was, Hank was reminded of a favorite local radio talk-show host's banter about how a person sometimes has to "make a move" in traffic, to get anywhere. They were prophetic words to him now. He was about to "make a move," big time.

**ANDREA SHIFF USED** the freight elevator at the back of the building to get Darcy down to where the Camry was parked, without an intervening incident of any kind. Everything had worked to perfection so far, and they were now en route. A syringe of 2.5 milligrams of Versed assured that Darcy Austin would be quite manageable for the next several hours, spread across the back seat where Andrea had placed her, wrists bound for good measure. Andrea could monitor any untoward stirrings in her rear-view mirror, and from her driver's seat, she could issue supplemental dosages of the anesthesia through a tube extending to an I.V. needle implanted in her hostage's forearm, as needed. It was jerry-built but effective.

SOME THREE HOURS later, the Camry passed through the maze of crisscrossing highways at Duluth and reached Two Harbors, some thirty miles to the north-east along the north shore of Lake Superior on Minnesota 61. They had traveled two-thirds of the way to their destination without incident, 270-plus miles north of the Twin Cities.

Two Harbors was Andrea's first planned stop. There she switched the Camry with a black Tahoe that she had stashed in an isolated garage near an Erickson Service Station in the harbor area. The Camry had served its purpose to this point, but now they were in truck country. Besides, Andrea reasoned, the authorities were looking for a Camry by now.

While at the Two Harbors "rest stop," Andrea administered a final shot of Versed through the makeshift I.V. setup, before transferring her hostage to the Tahoe. She took care to go easy with the dosage this time. Darcy would have to be ambulatory, as well as compliant, when she brought the SUV to its final stop.

ANDREA LOOKED FORWARD to the grandeur still ahead: Gooseberry Falls, Split Rock Lighthouse, Lutsen Mountains, quaint Grand Marais, and, finally, Magney State Park with its glorious wonderment, the Devil's Kettle. And throughout the voyage, she would be treated to myriad panoramas of Superior, the lake like an ocean. The wonder of it put her in a talking mood. "We'll be there soon, Hon, how ya doin' back there?" she asked, glancing into the rearview mirror.

No response.

"I suppose you're wondering about our journey. Right?"

Still no reply.

"Don't feel like conversing? Well you just lie still and rest. I'll do the talking," and Andrea continued to do just that. "Let me explain some other things you might be wondering about as well." She paused, as if to gather her thoughts. "You see, there was this woman who saw Fantasy Publications as a stepping stone into the ad game, what with the man at Fantasy being the son of the boss at a really good agency. She figured she might ride into ad land with him one day soon, only to find out the laggard had no interest. Bummer."

Andrea moved around a slow moving driver, not waiting for one of the extra-lane passing zones spaced along 61's otherwise one-lane-each-way thoroughfare north of Two Harbors. It was impulsive and imprudent, moving well over the speed limit in order to accomplish it. She admonished herself—no way did she want to attract the Highway Patrol. She'd be more judicious the next time she came up on a road dawdler.

She continued her monologue. "The woman tried on her own, but there were no openings at Williams/Bailey, Edson Janes told her, as did other agencies around town. Gee, maybe she'd just have to create some, she thought."

They came to a passing zone, and the Tahoe sped past three vehicles, cheating the speed limit by a "safe" five miles an hour. "But no, that would be naughty of her. Instead she went to Roland Bennett who was running an agency of his own. He was wonderful. Promised her a job as soon as he had one available. In the meantime, he wanted to see how good she was in bed, so she showed him. She was damned good, and he was damned well pleased."

Andrea eyed a police cruiser going in the opposite direction, watching it pass out of sight in her rear view mirror with no sign of altering its course, before picking up where she left off. "In bed with him, she learned how much he hated Edson Janes. Janes not only stood in the way of a job for her at Williams/Bailey, his legal harassments against poor Roland were keeping her from a job opening up at Bennett Advertising, as well. Now if something were to happen to Mr. Janes . . . Then when Bennett told her he wished Edson Janes dead, things just fit into place. Neat, huh? She always wondered what it would be like to kill someone."

Darcy wasn't able to respond, but she did understand what Andrea was saying, much to her horror. She tensed against her bonds without success. She wouldn't be able to escape her abductor in her present condition, in any case, she realized. She'd have to be patient and wait for her opportunity.

Andrea proceeded with her monologue. "So our woman seduced the security guard at Normandale Tower, which was easy, and that gained her 'undetected' access into Williams/Bailey when Edson Janes was doing one of his all-nighters.

"She was just going to beat his brains out with a sap, but then she thought, 'Why not drown the bastard in his own soup?' when she saw him spooning it up in the agency kitchen. And so she did. Oh, the rapture, the power she felt—pressing his face into his fucking soup and watching him die. It was orgasmic. Just had to add a little water to finish the job." Then Andrea changed pace and subject: "You should see it, Darcy. The lake is just beautiful from here."

Darcy passed on the splendor of the moment.

Andrea went back to her narrative. "Okay, where was I? Oh, yeah. By now, Roland Bennett was sharing his mistress with his friend, Frank Ramstead. How nice of him. She didn't mind, though. Frank was younger and more virile. She even got him down to her 'fantasy room' where she fitted him with a superhero costume, while she dressed up in hers, before *doing* it. Neither of their costumes stayed on for very long as they engaged in mock battle right up to a big climax, in more ways than one. Poor Frank. He loved it but didn't know he was being recorded on video. Later, she coaxed Roland Bennett to her special room. He looked ridiculous in his Sterling garb—his belly and all—but turned out he relished playing the game, once he got into it. Oops, there I go with a pun. Well, he didn't know his sex act was on video, either. Ah, the wonders of modern electronics. One can't have enough insurance against what might crop up in the future, you know."

Darcy tried to speak but her lips refused to move with enough precision to form words. "What's that, Darcy? You say something? I suppose you want to know why they were killed, right? Well, when Roland Bennett learned from that idiot handyman blackmailer that Edson Janes was killed by his very own mistress, he went ballistic."

"And here I thought I was doing him a favor," Andrea said, dropping her third person pretext. "It wasn't good to have him out of control, like that. Even threatened to go to the police. A suicide seemed like a good solution—though not to him, of course. Bawled like a baby when I held that gun to his head and made him write a goodbye note. Then it was goodbye."

Andrea went quiet for a moment, admiring the scenery again before returning to her dissertation. "Later, when Frank Ramstead started figuring things out, he had to go, too—just a matter of when. First, there was a blackmailer to dispense with. Busy, busy, busy.

"Well, it seemed only fitting to use the same thematic as with Janes. Doing away with W/B folk with their client's wares is rather creative, don't you think? See—the agency should have hired me. So I chose Gold'n Tender chicken for Barnhard. He snacked a lot, seemed only appropriate. This was getting to be more and more fun." Andrea paused, looking into the rearview mirror. "You following this, Darc?

Not getting an answer, she proceeded with her dissertation. "You know, you really didn't escape your demise that night when your cop nearly drove through your picture window. Just wanted it to look that way, and to see how on the ball your detective friend was. Went to a lot of trouble setting that up. Glad he didn't disappoint, although he scared the shit out of me. Didn't expect him that fast. But if he hadn't charged to your rescue like Marko Cash, I'd have just bailed out like something spooked me—taking that cutlery piece with me, though—thought I could make use of that puppy down the line.

"Think I had your guy fooled for a while with those footprints in back of your house. Nothing like heavy boots plus a little ballast to add pounds in a hurry. Right from the ol' Fantasy prop room. And here, most people are trying to *lose* weight. Handy, that prop room. The boots were Big Foot's—one of Sterling's former antagonists.

"I had grander plans for you, Darcy. Just didn't know exactly what they'd be until that ad campaign you got going for the State." Pause. "I wonder if Marko Cash, er, Hank Hankenson can do nearly as well this time? Left him the clues. Oh, look, we're passing through Lutsen. Grand Marais's just ahead a few miles. Skied up here. Great golf, too."

Darcy had to face what she'd tried to deny up to now—Andrea Shiff was going to kill her when they reached their destination—and that had to be the Devil's Kettle from the scenes she was describing en route. Darcy strained at her bonds again, with the same empty result. But her mind was gradually beginning to clear. She became aware that she was dressed in sweat clothes, and she sensed she was wearing something underneath. But what? It didn't feel like her lingerie.

"That jerk-off handyman," Andrea began again. "Here I thought he musta seen me stuff Edson Janes. Turned out he wasn't even there that night. Learned about me from his security buddy, who I'd thought was at least smart enough not to expose himself as an accessory to murder—even to a trusted friend. Then he was stupid enough to tell me that he'd let Barnhard in on it."

She sighed. "It's not as though I was going to let Julian Bellows live forever, but let me tell you how stupid the man was. When he got worried after I whacked his friend Barnhard, I told him I only trusted him, not anyone else. And he believed me. Of course, if he hadn't, I'd have taken care of it then and there. At least his gullibility bought him some extra time on the planet."

Andrea snickered as a thought came to her, "I had fun implicating your close personal friend, Erica Carlson. Got the idea watching you two cavorting on the mat like a couple of Lesbos. I especially liked the pubic hair bit. You?"

Silence.

"Then there's good ol' Jack Bailey," Andrea rambled on. "I had a nice theme going, and he fit in perfectly. Never liked the man—arrogant and bullying beyond belief. And then I had him, right in the cross hairs of that North Star ATV. The look on his face, watching him die—that was way cool.

"Couldn't do Frank Ramstead like that—not a member of the W/B family. So I shot him with a thirty-oh-six. Figured everybody but a cop you and I both know would blame it on the Rifleman. He didn't contest it publicly, but I knew he knew better—wanted to wait me out, be my guess."

At that point, Darcy spoke her first words of the trip. Kind of. "Wadj boud Jesh?" she managed.

With some difficulty, Andrea deciphered what Darcy was trying to say. "Oh, Josh. Well he has his problems at present. The good news, Darc, is that your long-lost knife has turned up by now. The bad news? Well, a couple of things. One, Josh may never draw again because of where it was found and, two, you're not going to get it back—not in this lifetime."

Then, after contemplating, Andrea said, "I wanted Josh to find those videos of Roland, Frank, and me, once he discovered your Magenta videos were missing from his office and he had to go searching. I'd love to have seen the look on his face when he saw the likes of his superheroes exploiting his precious Pad Room the way we did. But then, who knows? If he doesn't die, perhaps it'll provide him with inspiration for some future adventures. He's a little sick, you know."

*And you're not?* Darcy intoned.

"Incidentally," Andrea added in footnote, "I hope you appreciated what I did for you in your scuffle with Caren Dalton in the Pad Room. She didn't have much left—you really battled her—but she was gonna try and take your pants down if I hadn't intervened—I mean for real. Josh had prompted her on a few things, you know. You can thank me for saving . . . well, your ass. Nice tits, though—both of you.

"None of this was lost on Josh, as you might have guessed when Magenta wound up naked in that next issue. He was really pissed at me for intervening—he wanted to see if it would happen for real.

"But, did you know? Josh almost didn't go with that episode—not all the way, anyhow. Might be too much for Magenta fans, he fretted—see their heroine, ending up butt-naked like that. And here it turned out to be his biggest issue ever. Will Magenta redeem herself in a future clash with the lascivious Sadanna? Who knows? Josh is hardly in a position to decide that right now and, I'm afraid, his surrogate heroine—that's you, Darcy—is about to meet another fate altogether."

*Chapter* **59**

# A R R I V A L

**ANDREA MADE OUT** the flashing lights ahead as the Tahoe approached Judge C.R. Magney State Park, prompting her to cut short her spiel. *He didn't disappoint*, she said to herself. *The clever S.O.B. called out the Marines. We'll just see what good it does him.*

She saw the barricades across the entrance to Magney Park on the left side of the highway as they came closer. The highway itself was still open, as she suspected it would be, even though patrol cars were parked on both sides of the road, light racks ablaze. Traffic was slowed in both directions, but the sheriff's department was not about to close the only thoroughfare tracking the north shore of Lake Superior, blocking traffic for miles in either direction. That, Andrea also expected. The Minnesota Highway Patrol, in its arrogance, just might have, and Andrea noted their cruisers were on the scene. But she anticipated that the Cook County Sheriff, more PR oriented than the State Troopers, would prevail if it came to a jurisdictional show-down. Andrea Shiff did not overlook matters like that.

Would they still be watching for a beige Camry, she wondered. Probably, but not exclusively. And if they were peeking into vehicles as they passed, looking for a dishwater blonde with longish hair, they'd be misled again. But then, she could see that their prime concern was to keep vehicles or pedestrians from entering Magney Park, as she passed by the barricade without incident.

Andrea Shiff never had intended to enter Magney at its entrance, sheriff deputies or not. Traveling two-tenth's of a mile farther up the highway, she turned into the Naniboujou Lodge parking area on her right, as she planned to do all along.

The lodge was built in 1928 as a playground of the northland, Babe Ruth, Jack Dempsey and Ring Lardner as its primary backers. Andrea often wondered why more tourists, especially Minnesotans, weren't aware of its existence, along with its wonderful shoreline along Lake Superior. Under present circumstances, however, that was just fine with her.

There were enough cars in the lot so the Tahoe could blend in, yet not so many people moving about to be a bother. Matter of fact, it was just about perfect. Andrea, glanced at her watch. It was 4:02—that was pretty much perfect, too. She stuck the Tahoe in a remote corner of the lot.

*Chapter* **60**

# A S C E N T

**HANK EXITED MINNESOTA** 101 at the Executive Aviation Building parking area at the Flying Cloud Airfield. It was 4:33. He parked next to a red Mercedes SL600. That led him to think Brad Hoyt had already arrived.

He entered the building and got a wave-on from the woman behind the desk. He could tell she expected him. Without breaking stride, he passed through the double doors onto the tarmac where one of the prettiest aircraft he had ever seen with a propeller on it graced the area some thirty feet away. With its silver-bullet nose, wings turned up at their tips, five porthole windows lining its fuselage and a stabilizer wing mounted high on its slant-back tail, it commanded the tarmac. Brad Hoyt was into his preflight walk-around when Hank came up. "Pretty impressive," Hank said. "This should get us there."

"It'll get us nonstop to the West Coast if you want," Brad Hoyt answered.

"No need, but nice to know. How fast to where we're going?" Hank asked again, as he had from his carphone.

Brad Hoyt pretended he hadn't heard the question before, although he had more precisely calculated its answer since the last time it was put to him. "Fifty-five minutes," he said. "You can climb in the plane while I finish up. Steps are on the other side."

Hank checked his watch as he passed around the front of the Pilatus, having guessed earlier that they might be ninety minutes in the air before reaching Magney State Park—this was a break. More time gained. Mounting the steps that reached down from the plane's fuselage to the tarmac, Hank entered the cabin of the Pilatus, model PC-12, executive-configuration aircraft. To his right were six leather passenger seats, accompanying tables and a door at the rear of the compartment labeled cargo bay. To his left was the cockpit with a gleaming instrument panel, rivaling that of a 747, in Hank's mind.

Stripping off his suit coat and tossing it over the lead passenger seat, he settled into the right-hand seat of the cockpit. No sooner had he strapped himself in and donned his headset, than Brad Hoyt settled in next to him and started the plane's engine. It wasn't anything like Hank remembered in the Piper Saratoga, as the turbo jet surged to life without a stutter, its four-bladed prop dissolving into translucence before his eyes. He fixed on the chrome exhausts on either side of the plane's cowl, appearing much like the tusks of a wild beast to him. Somehow, that gave him a good feeling at a bad time.

There was the familiar chatter with the Flying Cloud tower as the plane taxied onto a runway. He could tell it was running west by the position of the afternoon sun. Scanning the instrument panel, he located an analog indicator in the array of digital gauges and was assured of his sense of direction. The needle pointed west.

Brad Hoyt was making both a visual run of the instruments and carrying on a radio conversation with the tower. Somewhere in the verbiage, Hank heard "two-seven west" and correctly assumed that this was their runway for take off. The smooth running jet revved through its paces emitting a high-pitched whine, while imploring release from the oversized disk brakes that Hank just knew the Pilatus had to have.

Brad Hoyt communicated with the Flying Cloud tower one last time before turning the plane lose. The Pilatus raged down 2-7-West and nosed skyward long before Hank expected it could. No rabbit hop into the air with this baby. The climb was so steep he didn't know how the plane sustained it. Yet the craft continued to rise without the slightest protest, banking left as it did. Hank glanced again at the gauge he had become friendly with and watched it change from west to south to east to north, where it stayed. The Pilatus was passing over Minneapolis, dead on its course.

"We'll be cruising at 17,000 feet," Brad said. "Cabin's pressurized so you don't have to worry about oxygen." Pause. "Now, wanna tell me why you were so vague about an airport destination up there?"

"I did say Tofte," Hank replied.

"It's the way you said it. Along with that farther north shit you handed me. By the way, I made the flight plan for Grand Marais, that is further north."

"I wasn't sure there was an airfield there."

"Neither was I, until I checked. Now let's have the rest."

"Look, Brad, I'm not sure what we're going to find or do, I just need to get there. This may be a monumental debacle—"

The pilot broke in. "And waste of time and fuel?"

"That, too. But I gotta do this, Bradley," Hank said. Then dolefully offered: "I think I can get you equivalent gas mileage for a car, from the department."

"Gee, thanks."

"How long can this thing stay up?" Hank asked out of nowhere, changing the subject.

"About a normal workday, if need be."

"A lot longer than we'll need," Hank returned, further assured.

Reaching altitude, Brad Hoyt put the Pilatus on automatic pilot and pushed back in his seat. "The next forty-five minutes are all yours, pal. Want to start from the beginning? Take your time."

Hank passed the situation through his mind. One thing he knew for certain, Andrea Shiff did not count on this projectile with wings when leaving her markers for him to follow. That on top of the early start he'd gained, he would arrive on the scene before she expected he could and that was his little surprise for her. What he could make of that edge, he wasn't sure. It was the only thing he had going for him, though, and he would push it for all it was worth.

Then he began telling Brad Hoyt what they were doing in his airplane—as though he were sure himself.

ANDREA SHIFF GOT out of the Tahoe and stretched. All had gone well, and even the weather was cooperating. The sky was clear, and it was warm for early October in these parts, the ambient temperature on the dash of the Tahoe indicating seventy-three degrees on their arrival. Perfect for a hike, she mused, and set about her business.

She was dressed in sweats much like Darcy was wearing—both outfits of muted hues.

She retrieved an equipment bag from the rear of the truck, slipping her arms through the carry straps that positioned it on her back. It was shrouded in a dull-green sheath that hid its bright yellow color underneath—no problem for a seamstress of superhero costumes.

She then extracted her hostage from the back seat of the vehicle. Darcy, though wobbly, could negotiate on her feet. Andrea clasped Darcy's right wrist to her own left wrist using a set of handcuffs from Fantasy's prop room. Her captive didn't resist.

Locking the truck, Andrea glanced at her watch. It was 4:42—still on schedule. With a last look around to make sure they weren't being observed, she guided her unsteady hostage toward the highway they had just exited in the Tahoe.

The traffic on 61 was light, although the sheriff's barricade down the highway caused southbound vehicles to back up on occasion. Andrea and hostage waited among the trees on the lake side of the road for a suitable break in traffic. When it came, Andrea hustled across to the other side of the two-lane highway with considerable haste, considering the less functional ward she had in tow. Once across, they disappeared into the woods, treading the rugged terrain leading away from the lake.

PASSAGE WAS NOT as arduous as the thick forest would seem to indicate. And after a brief stretch, Andrea Shiff located the deer path she was seeking. It not only permitted easier transit, it aided her direction—meandering toward the main path that led up to the Devil's Kettle, as Andrea knew it did. Upon reaching that juncture, she'd be well above the police guarding the entrance to Magney Park and out of their view. She'd still need to be wary of guards that could be posted farther up the route, but she suspected that a scouting party would have already been to the falls. And once the route was cleared, it was not likely they would expect anyone to gain access to the Devil's

Kettle that far up from the base of entry—especially not someone hampered with a hostage.

There were always oversights of this sort, and Andrea Shiff had, so far, exploited them to her advantage. An innocent appearing drive by of the barricade; an on-foot approach through the woods, approaching from the north, not the south; and a pliant, ambulatory hostage who was not much of a burden at all—none of which would be in the constabulary mind set, she guessed. If there were deputies stationed above her, she would make sure she saw them before they saw her, then determine a way around them. If that were not possible, she would kill them. In this, she would have the advantage of another oversight: the deputies would not be expecting anyone to approach without their first having been alerted by their associates below.

Andrea would avoid the killings if she could. The silenced 9mm Smith & Wesson Hush Puppy pistol with an eight-round magazine that she carried was more than adequate for that purpose and would not alert the base camp below. But then she'd need to proceed at a faster pace— the victims might be missed in routine radio checks.

**WHEN THEY REACHED** the main path leading up the glacier-worn mountain, there was no indication of other humanity that Andrea could detect. They did encounter non-humans along the way though, including a defiant grouse that stood its ground without a sign of trepidation—not for the women nor for the bald eagle carving circles in the sky overhead.

All was going nicely, Andrea thought. Darcy, although lubberly and, at times, stumbling, was moving along better than Andrea anticipated she might. Nor was Darcy resisting her tether to any degree, more occupied with keeping her balance while stepping over exposed roots, ground undulations and scattered rocks on the trail. *That Versed's good stuff,* Andrea commented to herself, observing Darcy's compliant progression up the path.

Every so often, Andrea caught a glimpse of the Devil's Kettle and its adjacent falls through the trees, though they were still far ahead. Then, coming to a lookout bluff, she was able to view both falls in their entirety. The spill to the right could be traced from top to bottom in its fifty-foot tumble—its waters then flowing toward Lake Superior, well below Andrea's observation point. The falls on the left raged with more fury, plunging into a gaping lava-rock cauldron with no visible outlet. This geologic veneration, the apocalyptic Devil's Kettle, was her goal.

Beyond the look-out bluff, there was a precipitous decline before the trail turned back up again, climbing to a higher ascent. The drop was so steep it would be unmanageable for casual hikers were it not for 150 sturdy wooden steps built into the hillside as part of the Superior Hiking Trail Project, which meandered 200 miles, from Two Harbors to the Canadian border. The Superior Hiking Trail formed a ridgeline, rising and falling between 1,750 and 602 feet above sea level on its wilderness traverse of outcroppings, cliffs, lakes, rivers, and creeks. The Devil's Kettle was on one of its many connective spurs along the way.

Andrea and hostage descended the steps in relative civility. Then came the climb to higher altitudes and another flight of wooden stairs implanted in the rugged terrain, leading up the steepest part of the trek. The climb was exhausting, but the sturdy steps with safety railings and intermittent landings afforded resting points for Andrea and her beleaguered ward. *How high are we,* Andrea wondered when they finally reached the head of the stairway. *Fifteen-hundred feet? Seventeen-hundred?*

She looked back at the boundless lake. It was no time to dwell on the beauty of it, made more so by trees in the foreground already changing into their bright autumn hues, but she couldn't resist.

Viewing the vast waters that Native Americans celebrated in song and story as Gitche Gu'mee, she recalled the fabled Native American legend that Gitche Gu'mee never gave up its dead. White men would learn the truth of that tenant, in time. The lost crew of the *Edmund Fitzgerald* being a recent reminder.

Andrea Shiff would add a tenet of her own: the Devil's Kettle never gives up its victims.

*Chapter* **61**

# E N D G A M E

**THE TWO WOMEN** came off the forested trail, emerging onto the Brule River embankment above the twin falls. It had been a one-and-one-half-mile ascent from where they began at the highway.

The Brule flowed with surprising calm toward the crest of the falls where the headrock split it into two turbulent offshoots—one apparent, the other arcane.

The Brule was a shallow river at this time of year, no more than two feet deep on average, passing through a gauntlet of rocks scattered about its lava-based bed. Some of the rocks were visible under the clear, flowing waters, while others protruded above the surface. The scene was far more tranquil than in the spring of the year, when the river increased in depth several fold, becoming much more petulant, submerging all rocks in its path save the giant head rock at the precipice of the falls. In some years, after a heavy snow melt, the flow was so heavy that it washed out the highway bridge below, on its rush to the world's largest freshwater lake.

Over hundreds of thousands of preceding high-water seasons, many large rocks had been worn flat near the head of the falls. In the low ebb of autumn, these rocks provided a virtual walkway from the northwest shore of the Brule leading out to the spill of the Devil's Kettle falls, should anyone dare use them for such purpose. In that sense, the rocks could qualify as the "Devil's Walkway."

At its shallow stage, a person could wade across the Brule and never sink below their knees. This was not advisable, however, as losing one's footing could lead to being swept to the near-side falls and certain death on the rocks below, or carried to the far-side spill and dispatched to the bowels of the earth, as far as anyone knew.

Yet, with all this exposure to danger, there were no restraining barriers to protect the unwary or discourage the foolhardy. All this was just fine with Andrea Shiff, though, who was familiar with the situation from a previous visit.

**IN HER STILL-CLOUDED** mind, Darcy was aware of where she had been led, and why. She also realized there was little she could do given her present state. Resistance was useless. She could have dropped to the ground along the trail, becoming dead weight for Andrea to deal with, but she held little doubt that if Andrea was not able to bring her up the path, she would kill her then and there. If there was any chance for escape, it would be at the top of the climb, when the intoxicant in her veins was more dissipated. Her disappointment now was that she still could not trust her mental acuity or physical response. *Will I die?* she wondered. It was a question she would not have needed to ask, were she less confused of mind.

**ANDREA SHIFF CHECKED** her watch again. It showed 5:28. Still doing just fine. "I'm going to remove the handcuff from my wrist now, Darcy," she said. "I need both of my hands free, okay? But you don't, so this bracelet goes on your other wrist. Hold it out like a good girl."

Darcy allowed her other wrist to be shackled, still acquiescent.

"Don't try to run now, hon," Andrea said. "I'll only catch you, and I won't be nice about it when I do." Even so, Andrea was not going to tempt fate. She slipped her backpack off, zipped it open and withdrew a length of rope, which she secured around Darcy's waist and fastened the other end to the trunk of a small tree. "Now keep your hands away from those knots," Andrea warned. "I'll be watching."

Again, Darcy obeyed her abductor, feeling she would only fumble clumsily with her tether, trying to free herself, anyway. And the tie around her waist was knotted at the small of her back, making it all the more difficult. Even if she could get free, she knew it would be easy for Andrea to recapture her. So, she waited.

Andrea began removing equipment from her bag and assembling it. Timing was critical now. She would have to hustle, but she had rehearsed every move.

**HANK SQUIRMED IN** his seat as the Pilatus passed over Duluth Harbor, where he could see the ore boats departing and cargo ships arriving from ports all over the world, each making its last season voyage before the harbor would close to shipping for the winter months. Lake Superior seldom froze over due to its vastness, but the channels connecting to the other Great Lakes did, as did the harbor at Duluth where shallower waters formed Superior's arrowhead.

The digital readout on the plane's instrument panel recorded 5:32. They had been in the air only forty-seven minutes, but it seemed much longer to Hank, who was on the edge of his seat the whole time.

"How much longer to Magney Park?" he asked, as if he didn't already have a pretty good idea.

"No more than ten minutes," Brad Hoyt replied. "Got to do some maneuvering before we get there, remember."

Hank did. Brad Hoyt was going to maintain course to the Grand Marais airstrip and descend to 3,000 feet on approach. When below the radar screen at Grand Marais, he would veer away from the airstrip, while continuing to descend to 2,200 feet, and pick up Highway 61. From there he would follow the scenic North Shore Drive like a tourist in an SUV—only a little higher up.

Hank watched the altimeter as the Pilatus descended, then leveled off. As far as Brad Hoyt could tell from his route map, the terrain to the left of the plane, rising sharply from the road didn't reach more than 1,700 feet. So at 2,200 feet, they didn't have to worry about clipping treetops with the plane's left wingtip. At least while they stayed with the highway.

ANDREA SHIFF POSITIONED the tripod-mounted digital Canon XL-1S on the river embankment and framed it on the headrock that split the river into separate falls and turned the camcorder on. The establishing shot. She then panned right while zooming in for a tighter shot on the Devil's Kettle falls only—the head-rock moving off frame. That was important. Making sure the camcorder also pictured the flat rocks leading out in the river, she locked the lightweight Sakar tripod in place and shut the Cannon down.

Later, when she was ready to restart the camcorder, it would be by its remote feature.

Satisfied with her video composition, Andrea Shiff removed a Sony Ultra Slim Boom Box from her pack and placed it along side the camcorder. It was small but adequate. It didn't need to produce a lot of volume for what she intended. Next, she unfurled a 9mm low-stretch climbing rope and, mentally calculating the length she would need at mid-river between the two falls, secured one of its ends to a shoreline tree with a climber's clamp.

Stripping off her sweat suit, she pulled a Petzl C86 canyoning sit-harness up her bare legs, tucking it under the short skirt of the garment she had been wearing under her sweats, which bore a musical symbol on its bodice. Next, she wheedled the stainless steel attachment point of the harness through a slot at the waist of her garment.

Picking up another rope, this one of a thicker 12.5mm low-stretch variety, she carried it closer to the mouth of the falls at the shoreline and secured it to a tree with another clamp.

Returning to her equipment bag, she fastened a tool belt around her waist and fitted it with the instruments she would need.

Andrea glanced at her watch. The entire exercise had consumed less than six minutes—just as she had practiced in another venue. Now it was time to tend to her hostage.

Darcy was watching Andrea's every movement and, as her captor approached, she prepared to fight for her life.

She needn't have tried. When Andrea unshackled Darcy's wrists, her strength and reflexes were still weak and slow, and Andrea was quick and strong. Not that it would have mattered much anyway—Andrea came prepared in yet another way for any resistance Darcy might offer.

---

**DARCY FELT HER** mind clearing with the cold splash on her bare legs above her boots. She realized she was over water. Confused, she looked down. Her sweat suit was gone, exposing the Magenta costume she had been wearing beneath her sweats.

Andrea's arms encircled her waist from behind, half lifting, half dragging her toward the rushing sound that grew louder with every step. She was on her feet, somehow, sort of—tugged along the flat rocks leading out into the river, still disoriented from the chloroforming Andrea had dosed her with when she was on the embankment.

Darcy could feel the harness under her skirt and knew it had to be like the one she watched Andrea fit herself with, earlier. She could see it was clasped to a rope leading to a tree on the embankment. While she had no way of knowing, it provided a life line if she should tumble into the water before the prescribed time. Nor could she tell that Andrea had her own separate fastening, for another purpose.

**WHEN THEY REACHED** the final footrock before the falls, Andrea Shiff withdrew her right arm from around Darcy's waist, extracted an object from her tool belt and pointed it toward shore. A red light on the Cannon XL1S glowed to life, letting Andrea know her grand event was now being recorded. "Showtime," she shouted above the noise of the turbulence, tossing the wand over her shoulder and into the river. "Wide-awake now, Magenta," Andrea urged. "I want you to know it was Coda who bested you."

*Magenta? Coda? She is mad.*

Reaching to her belt again, Andrea brought a knife to Darcy's midsection. Darcy imagined the worst, but Andrea had other plans. The blade came up in a quick motion, severing the rope tied to Darcy's waist halter. There was no need for a safety line any longer, nor the knife. It followed the remote wand into the river.

While the Canon on shore recorded the two women out on the river, it did not reveal the climbing rope still connected to Andrea's caving halter. That item, by intent, was blocked from the camcorder by Darcy's body.

Darcy was still under her abductor's control even though the effects of chloroform, on top of the Versed, had dissipated to where she was aware that her death was imminent. She sensed that Andrea wanted her aware and wide-awake for that moment. She knew her captor's sadistic side all too well by now.

"C'mon, Magenta," Andrea coaxed, again. "Time to go."

It was the most difficult thing she had ever done, but clinging to every last moment remaining to her, Darcy suppressed a response to Andrea's prodding—plus her own fright.

Growing impatient, Andrea was tempted to hurl her quarry into the water. Still, she wanted more. She longed to see the terrified expression on Darcy's face as she swept to the mouth of the Devil's cauldron. It would be Coda's triumph over Magenta. Recorded on video for the world to see. Andrea decided to wait a few moments longer. It was only right that her victim be fully alert at the end. Only then could the camera catch the full impact of the event.

*Chapter* **62**

# C R E S T

AT FIRST IT was hardly noticeable over the thunder of the roiling waters, but the dissonant sound grew louder, and Andrea Shiff turned her head to where it seemed to be coming from. Looking up, she saw it.

The Pilatus loomed out of the low-level sun, a pitched wail preceding its silvery form—swooping down at her like a huge bird of prey.

*Well, I'll be damned*, Andrea said to herself. *He made it after all.* A broad grin spread across her face as she raised her right hand over her head and waved. "Hey, Marko," she cried as if she could be heard. "It's me, Coda." Then to Magenta: "Your detective's here, Babe. Now he'll see us both die." She knew he'd get there, eventually. The use of a civilian plane didn't particularly surprise her, but the swiftness of his arrival did. He firgured out how to do it. She really admired that.

ANDREA SHIFF HADN'T planned to die this day—only create the appearance of it. The camcorder was to show both she and Magenta spilling over the Devil's Kettle, while not revealing the escape she had arranged for herself. It was a scheme fraught with danger, but it was a risk she was willing to take. If it worked, she was free and clear of the law, thought to be dead. If it didn't: *C'est la vie.* She'd just learn what another realm was like.

But now her artifice was compromised. "Marko" was here, and he would see. *My perfect plan, and that smart sonofabitch thwarted it.* She shrugged it off. *Nobody lives forever*, she intoned as if it were of no consequence. Besides, her endgame was not a total loss in her mind. Darcy Austin and Magenta, the two most precious personae to Josh Williams were to disappear from the face of the earth forever—at the hands of one of his own villainous creations. It would all be recorded, too, if he lived to view it one day. How ironic, she thought. Josh loves his videos.

**WHEN THE SLEEK** aircraft shattered the air above her, the hand Andrea Shiff had waved now gripped the Smith & Wesson Hush Puppy.

**PING, PING. "JESUS,"** Brad Hoyt yelled. "What was that?"

"She's shooting at us," Hank replied as they passed overhead and sped out of range. "Turn this thing around and go back."

"She hit us, for crissake. You want to go back?"

"She's only got four shots left. I counted the muzzle flashes. Go back," Hank persisted, making an assumption about the feed on Andrea's weapon.

"Oh, that's okay then," the pilot said, twisting the yoke and banking the Pilatus into a tight turn. "And what's with the weird outfits? Dare I ask?"

"Coda and Magenta," Hank replied, like the pilot should know about such things. "Let's go. Tromp on it, or whatever you do."

Brad shook his head, but complied. *Tromp, it is.*

ABSORBED WITH THE plane making its turn out over Lake Superior, Andrea Shiff's grip loosened around Darcy's waist, providing what Darcy knew was her last chance to save herself.

She twisted away from Andrea, breaking free. Her leg swept up as she continued her turn. The move she had practiced many times before seemed like slow motion as the looping kick rose toward its target. Her captor reared back, bracing for the blow she saw coming.

Even though the kick lacked the impact Darcy strived for, it caught Andrea under the arm, driving her sideways. For a tense moment, Andrea teetered on the edge of the footrock. Then she lost her balance completely, splashing into the water. All further efforts were useless. She was swept down the river and over the crest of the Devil's Kettle falls. Andrea Shiff was gone.

Darcy's physical outburst took its toll in her weakened condition. Head reeling, balance failing, she, too, toppled over the edge of the footrock and into the rushing waters.

*Chapter* **63**

# T U M U L T

**THE FOOTROCK WHERE** Darcy fell obstructed the full force of the river's current, preventing it from sweeping her away as it had Andrea Shiff. Even so, eddies swirled around her, and she was slowly being drawn toward the brink of the spill.

As Darcy's pace toward the falls quickened, her knee struck a submerged branch wedged in the rock-laden riverbed. *Hope.*

As her upper body passed over the branch, she thrust her arm down, catching the limb where it bowed up from its lodging. Grasping it with all her might, she twisted her body and thrust her other arm under the span, locking it to her side, while keeping her head above the shallow waters. For a horrific moment, the bough gave ground, but then it held.

Darcy was almost afraid to breathe. But her drift to the unthinkable had ceased for the moment.

---

THE PILATUS COMPLETED its turn and streaked back toward the falls. As it approached, Hank could see commotion among the sheriff's deputies and the State Troopers in the Magney parking lot. They knew something was going on in the bluffs above them. A contingent was already starting up the Devil's Kettle trail, which Hank guessed would take fifteen to twenty minutes, rushing it. Too late to do any good.

When the plane closed on the falls, Hank was greeted with a terrifying sight. One woman was down in the water near the crest of the Devil's Kettle, the other was nowhere to be seen. He held his breath. Closer yet, he could tell by the color of her hair that the woman in the water was Darcy Austin. "Get us down," Hank shouted. "Now, now, now."

Brad Hoyt could hardly believe what Hank was asking him to do. "Are you crazy? Where?"

"In the river." Hank insisted. "It's shallow. Belly land it."

"Do you know what you're saying?" It was a rhetorical question. "The plane'll be trashed, and we'll probably both be killed in the process."

Hank was adamant. "Bring it down as close to the falls as you can."

"You're out of your mind," Brad yelled back, but the plane slowed on a descending path. "What if the river carries us back over the falls?" It was a valid question. Not rhetorical.

"Not deep enough and too many rocks for that," Hank said with authority, though it was only a guess on his part.

Brad suspected the reply was bogus as the plane skimmed the head rock of the twin falls, staying its course. "Hold on, we're gonna hit," he yelled.

Water and sparks flew every which way as the proud bird gnarled into the rock-filled stream, its fifty-three-foot wingspan clawing the embankments on either side, breaking off piecemeal before the plane ground to a stop. The plane slipped backwards in the current for an anxious moment, then stuttered to another halt.

"What the hell ya gonna do, now?" Brad Hoyt asked, bemoaning the sudden loss of his perfectly good four-million-dollar aircraft. At the same time, he was grateful they weren't plunging over the falls in a wing-torn aluminum capsule. Hank was grateful as well—for what the pilot had sacrificed on his behalf. But he didn't have time for thanks giving. "Open the door, Brad. I've got to get out of here."

Brad Hoyt anticipated him, his hand already on the release control, which to his surprise, operated perfectly. The door unfolded into the river with a splash, settling on the rock-strewn bed of the river. "There you are," he said. "Do what you gotta do."


HANK WAS OUT of the plane almost before the hatch came to a stop, plunging knee-deep into the shallow river. His tasseled loafers were not the best for this, but he left them on thinking his stocking feet might be worse yet. Pain wasn't the consideration, traction was. He trudged straight for the falls, losing his footing several times and nearly going down, before realizing how foolish he was being. Had he fallen, there was no guarantee he'd be able to regain his footing against the current.

Changing course, he headed for the embankment to his left. And, scrambling up on shore, he turned and ran toward the equipment he saw scattered ahead of him, paying scant attention to the classical music he now heard. Closing the distance, he spotted a rope fastened to a tree, leading into the river. He bent down and scooped it up as he passed, guiding it through his hand as he headed straight for the rocks in the river leading to the crest of the Devil's Kettle. Was he being foolhardy again?

*Chapter* **64**

# B E D E V I L E D

**THE ASCENSION ROPE** grab, model B17R, ratcheted up the climbing rope latched to its host's sit-harness. The webbed foot cord, designed for caving, provided the body lift. Incessant dousing and unrelenting deluge of the falls did not deter the climber. Nor did the peril of a death fall.

**HANK NEARLY SLIPPED** and fell as he scampered across the stepping stones but made it to the footrock nearest the crest of the falls. Darcy was in the water just out of his reach. "Hold on, Darcy, I'll get you," Hank shouted like he knew how he would. Which he did not.

"Hank, oh Hank—I can't hold on any longer," she said in a voice he could hardly interpret over the rushing water. She was numbed, fatigued and near the end of her endurance. Still, she felt a glimmer of hope at the sight of him, rope in hand.

"Just a few seconds more," he said. "Darcy Austin can do it, even if Magenta and Coda can't."

He hoped his words would buy a few extra moments. Her eyes fixed on him, and she almost managed a little half smile.

HANK COULD SEE the underwater limb Darcy was clinging to, and wondered how much longer she could—or, for that matter, how much longer the limb would stay in place. It scared the hell out of him.

His mind searched for options. Darcy was several feet away, almost equidistant to the surging crest of the falls. By laying face down and extending himself as far as he could, he guessed he might be able to reach her if she stretched a hand back to him. But even if they clasped hands he knew he could not pull her to safety against the current from a prone position.

He'd have to go into the water after her, although there was a strong chance he would not be able to keep his footing against the swifter current this close to the crest. Even if he did reach Darcy, what then? Could they both get back? He wasn't sure. He had the rope, but fastening it to her would be like tying down a tent in a hurricane. And getting back to the footrock to pull Darcy clear was another suicidal gamble. Still he'd attempt to tie the rope to Darcy until help arrived, even if he didn't make it back himself.

He started to step into the water when Darcy called out, "Stay there, Hank."

"No Darcy, I'm coming for you."

"There's another way," she insisted. "Pass the rope to me."

He could tell what she was calling for was not impossible, using the current in his favor—the same directional flow that carried Darcy to where she was in the river. But then what? How could she hold onto it, or tie it around her while still clinging to her mooring. Was she saying this just to save him? Or was there something he didn't know about?

"Hurry, Hank, do it," she pleaded again.

Hank hesitated but complied.

The feed went as hoped, the rope flowing to Darcy's position. When it reached her, she relied on the leverage of her arm tucked under the submerged limb to maintain her hold, and grasped the end of the cord with her free hand. Her fingers were numb and unresponsive, but she threaded the rope through the attachment loop on the harness belt she was fitted with and extended it out of the water back toward Hank.

Hank dropped down and stretched his body out over the rock as far as he could, took the rope from her, and scrambled back to his feet. He saw that she had attached the rope to herself in some way, but he couldn't be sure how secure it was. The thought of it not holding terrified him, but there was no other recourse.

Reeling the rope in, he felt the resistance of Darcy's body as the rope drew taught.


ANDREA SHIFF APPEARED like an apparition over the crest of the falls, moving in Darcy's direction. Just like Sherlock Holmes' nemisis, Professor Moriarity, who survived the plunge over Reicenbach Falls—Andrea Shiff didn't die after all. For a moment, she stared at Hank—the eyes of killer and pursuer locking together for the first time.

The rope Andrea mounted bore against the giant headrock of the falls, and Hank could see it would limit her ascent in Darcy's direction. But she could get close. Close enough, he thought, to reach Darcy's trailing legs in the water.

He was struck with a new danger. If Andrea locked onto Darcy he might not be able to pull the two of them against the current. Worse, Andrea might well be able to pull Darcy away from him—leverage, current, and gravity working in her favor. He would go into the water, too, if she won that tug-of-war—he would not let go of the rope at his end under any condition. He had to move Darcy away from her closing pursuer, and do it now.

**WRAPPING THE ROPE** around his hands to prevent slippage, Hank pulled hard, hoping against hope that Darcy's tie would hold. The climbing rope seemed to stretch, then Darcy nudged toward him—just as Andrea Shiff grasped her by the ankle.

**HANK BRACED HIMSELF**, setting his feet against the rear edge of the rock to gain as much purchase as he could. The spray let him know he was almost in the water with his back foot, giving him more to worry about.

He thought he heard a crashing noise behind him, but couldn't turn to see what it was, while struggling against the combined weight of the two women, the current, and Andrea Shiff's contentious pull in the opposite direction.

**"WATCH OUT, HANK,"** Brad Hoyt yelled from the shore. "The wing section."

The large wing fragment, severed from the downed Pilatus, had traveled over and around the riverbed rocks, picking up momentum as it traversed its obstacle course toward the Devil's Kettle. And now it was headed straight for Hank on its final  sprint to the falls.

Hank crouched down as the crumpled aluminum flashed into his peripheral vision. Whirling by within inches, it would have struck him but for the deflecting eddies of his rock platform, causing it to veer away at the last moment. Now the two women were in its path. Hank froze. If it struck them head on it would take them for certain; and unless he released the rope in his hands, it would claim him as well.

Darcy ducked her head under the water and leaned away from the charging structure as it pitched toward her.

Hank watched the jagged metal scour over Darcy, slashing her leg, then raking into Andrea Shiff before plunging over the Devil's Kettle crest and into the gaping lava cauldron below. It had not claimed any of them. Not yet.

*Chapter* **65**

# D E N O U E M E N T

**DAZED AND BLEEDING**, Andrea Shiff hadn't given up. She had lost her grip on Darcy, though not her resolve. She could see that her climbing rope was frayed but that mattered little to her. She planned to die anyway, now that her escape plan was thwarted. What did matter was bringing Magenta along with her. Her bearing rope need only hold a little longer. If Marko wanted to join them in the Devil's cauldron, that was his decision.

Andrea Shiff reached out for Darcy again—just as her bearing rope severed.

**HANK COULD HAVE** sworn the woman was grinning at him as she tossed over the Devil's Kettle falls in a plunge to nothingness. It was a vision he would not forget.

His hands were bleeding as he heaved on the rope. No longer did he have to contend with the added burden of Andrea Shiff, but, with all else he had been through, he was drained to the point of collapse. Then the pull got lighter. Brad Hoyt was on the rock beside him.

**THE RESCUE TEAM** Hank saw heading up the Devil's Kettle path—an eternity before—now tended to the survivors on the embankment. Hank lowered Darcy onto a blanket, while someone put a second blanket over her. A para treated the gash on her leg.

Her lips were a cast of blue, and her face was pale white, but Darcy looked up at Hank with eyes as green as ever and spoke to him. Her voice was so weak he couldn't hear what she said. He leaned in closer.

"What, Darcy?"

"Hank," she repeated.

"Yes?"

"Tell your friend he's got to get a faster airplane." Her eyes closed, a faint smile on her lips.

Hank wiped at his face with the side of his hand. He couldn't smile back just yet—even though he was likely the happiest man on God's green earth.

*Chapter* **66**

S H O W T I M E

IT WAS A a media circus. Here was a death-defying rescue, captured on video at the Devil's Kettle, with action that topped anything Hollywood could dream up. Even the name of the site screamed action, adventure, thrills, and chills. It was everything Andrea Shiff planned it to be. And but for a glitch at end of the "script," it was, as she might have put it, *perfect*. Not known to her now, of course, that glitch made it even more perfect—the villain dispatched for the grand finale. Happy ending.

All the boffo box-office ingredients were there: a beautiful heroine, a bold hero, a courageous co-rescuer, and a diabolical villain. To say nothing of the notorious Williams/Bailey killings that led up to the climax at the Devil's Kettle, nor the special allure of Fantasy Publications characters come-to-life in the adventure. If Magenta and Coda were not household names before, they were now.

Andrea's plan was to make it appear that she plunged over the falls to her death, taking her captive with her. Then, with climbing equipment, she would save herself, and no one would be the wiser. Who could have doubted the video she set up to record the whole thing?

But her plans were spoiled with the early arrival of Lieutenant Hankenson prompting Darcy's escape from her grasp. Later, after ascending the falls she had plunged over and coming after Darcy Austin, she entered the side frame of the video cam for the world to witness right up to her final demise.

The slim-line boom box placed alongside the Sony camcorder to provide musical background for the event was Andrea's final touch. Eijie Oue conducting the Minnesota Orchestra in Igor Stravinsky's *The Rites of Spring* may not have been in keeping with the season but, the movement, *The Sacrifice*, was right on point.

**ALTHOUGH THE TWO** protagonists in the affair were reluctant celebrities, they were pushed onto the national stage, regardless; Bloomington Community Relations was not about to lose advantage of Lieutenant Hank Hankenson, nor was the PR Department at Williams/Bailey going to let Ms. Darcy Austin off the hook.

**"IT'S YOUR SEGMENT,** Lieutenant," the Fox News personality submitted, "what say you?" Then, seeing his guest's reluctance, the "humble correspondent" tossed out uncharacteristic softball questions that would have put a CNN interviewer to shame.

**"PERHAPS I SHOULD** change my assessment of the greatest generation," the NBC anchor offered by way of introducing Hank Hankenson and Darcy Austin to his television audience.

**HOLLYWOOD AGENTS APPROACHED** Darcy Austin. So did *Playboy*, which recognized a qualified subject for its pictorials.


**"WILL YOU GO** to Hollywood?" asked the female anchor of a network morning news show.

"I like Minneapolis just fine," Darcy answered.


**"WILL YOU APPEAR** in *Playboy?"* a male TV interviewer asked, his eyes lowering to her chest.

"No," Darcy said, crossing her arms in front of her.

"Not even as Magenta?" he pushed. "That way you could wear a mask, you know."

Darcy stared back with those incredible emerald eyes of hers. "Is that anything like your wearing a wig?" she replied. Viewers fell in love, if they hadn't already.



**LIEUTENANT HANKENSON WAS** lauded both for his bravery and pursuit of the killer, as the story was told and retold in the national media. It was apparent that Andrea Shiff, master assassin, regarded him as her chief antagonist.



**BLOOMINGTON CHIEF OF** Police James Lott considered retirement after winding up his round of local interviews. Why not go out on top? He shared his thoughts with his lieutenant, and asked if he'd have an interest in the position. "A lot of politics," Hank replied. "I'd have to think about it."

**MARGARET MAGNESON ANNOUNCED** her bid for re-election as mayor of Bloomington. Nobody doubted she would win a third term.

**SERGEANT JOE BAINES** and Detective Marge Kennedy were featured in the suburban *Sun Current*. Each praised the other for the parts they had played in the case, focusing on their rescue of Ms. Jessie Campbell in her home. Marge Kennedy looked pretty, smiling in the accompanying photograph, while Joe Baines held his stomach in as well as could be expected.

**SERGEANTS SIGURD NADLER** and Dexter Ames appeared on local TV, flanking the Minneapolis mayor. At the photo-op ceremony in the atrium of the gothic city hall, the mayor awarded each of the detectives a Certificate of Merit. She even looked happy doing it, while pointing out the major role the Minneapolis Police Department played in the killer's downfall.

**WILLIAMS/BAILEY BECAME** a hot shop. After months of calamity and the erosion of its client base, the agency was now thriving. So were its clients. Mrs. Svendsen's Soup was featuring its new slogan, "The Soup To Live For." Gold'n Tender Chicken, North Star ATVs, and Minneapolis Cutlery were all enjoying spiked sales. Tuff Wrap Trash Bags, after its earlier choke, returned to the W/B fold.

MINNESOTA TOURISM BRACED for a banner year. The hotels along Lake Superior's north shore were booked months in advance. An offhand remark by Lieutenant Hankenson that he might play in the Annual Health Care Charity Tournament at Superior National Golf Course, locked up the entire month of October, a year hence.

IF DARCY AUSTIN was getting an inordinate amount of attention at the agency, it didn't seem to bother Mason Williams, even though he cherished attention focused on himself. He now included her on all new-business pitches as a featured player at Williams/ Bailey. Vanity was one thing, the bottom line was another. In further recognition of Ms. Austin's market value, Mason Williams awarded her the additional title of New Business Overseer, whatever that meant.

ERICA CARLSON AND Jessie Campbell each received their share of media attention—the former going along with it, the latter reveling in it. Ms. Carlson took every opportunity to tell of Lieutenant Hankenson's interrogation skills, commending his insight in absolving her, when the evidence seemed to implicate her.

The centerpiece of Ms. Campbell's interviews was the invasion of her home by Andrea Shiff, and how she was left bound and drugged as part of the killer's scheme. She didn't shy from describing how she was forced to strip to her underwear, and what she feared might be in store for her at that moment.

Titillation always picked up an audience, and Jessie Campbell was a good study.

**AT A WELL-ATTENDED** press conference and ceremony at Flying Cloud Airport, Pilatus Aircraft, Ltd., of Stans Switzerland, presented Brad Hoyt with a new Model PC-12, like the one he destroyed on the Brule River. He needed only to continue payments on his previous Pilatus aircraft, and assure the Swiss firm that he would not fly Lieutenant Hankenson on any more rescue missions. It seemed a fair exchange.

**REPRINTS OF FORMER** Magenta episodes were making Josh Williams rich and famous. Not one to overlook an opportunity, he reissued selected issues of *Magenta Comics* while convalescing at his home.

**JESSIE CAMPBELL WAS** in Darcy's office with the door closed.

"You can't go through with it, Jessie," Darcy said. "It's not professional."

"But I want to. It's your client, after all, you should want me to, too."

"Posing for Playboy's *Book of Lingerie?*"

"In Coquette Lingerie. That's the whole point of the feature. 'Lingerie to be discovered in'. And your client, I remind you, is excited about it. I'm just a prop as far as they're concerned." Apparently, Jessie Campbell didn't mind this kind of notoriety.

"You won't be wearing the lingerie for long. The way it goes, Coquette will be the prop, and you'll be the feature—on a two-page spread, I suspect."

"You used to model. What's so bad?"

"That's different. I didn't display myself."

"No? How about that jewelry ad I still see stashed about in offices around here? A necklace your only apparel."

"There were shadows. My face was turned away from the camera," Darcy excused, although the "stashed" element remained a torment to her.

"Not all of you was turned away."

"It's art. That ad won a Clio Award. Besides, it was back when I first got out of college."

"Not old enough to know better?"

"All right, Jessie. So what about Gold'n Tender management. Don't they care?"

Jessie Campbell sat back with a satisfied smile on her face. "They're fine with it," she said. "They think it'll sell more whole breasts."

It was a Minnesota moment.

# Chapter 67

# W I N D D O W N

**THE PROTAGONISTS AND** supporting cast having received their time in the limelight, the Andrea Shiff saga began to subside but for remnants of her legacy.

Hank was able to work at his desk for hours at a time without being bugged for an interview or appearance. He was enjoying the relative return to normality when there was a knock on his office door. Sergeant Sigurd Nadler of the Minneapolis Police was at the entrance. "Got a moment, Lieutenant?" he asked.

"Absolutely, Sig," Hank replied in earnest, "Come in. Close the door."

"Thanks," Sig said. "How're things now that all the hubbub's dying down?"

"Swimmingly. And you? I thought the mayor was gonna kiss you on TV the other night."

"The hug was bad enough. Good thing she didn't lay one on me, we'd both of puked," Sig Nadler said, looking like he'd just caught wind of something in ferment.

Hank switched the subject. "Thanks for coming through when I needed you, Sig. Dex, too. You guys make a good team." Motioning toward his credenza, he asked, "Like some coffee?"

"Yeah, I'm an addict. Black, thanks."

"So what brings you here?" Hank inquired, pouring into a porcelain mug from the Bunn carafe.

"You know that drug dealer in Kenwood that the Rifleman offed a few weeks back?"

"Sure. Did 'im with a twenty-two."

*So everyone thinks.* "Well, I was there the next morning after he got whacked."

"I expect you were."

"Found something on the little shit," Sig growled, then added in a more admiring tone, "Damn those were pretty shots. One through the forehead, one through the top of the head."

"I'm sure—he's a good shooter. What was it you found, Sig?"

The Minneapolis detective reached into his inside jacket and brought out a folded handkerchief, which he placed on Hank's desk, unfolding it with care. There was something reverent about his manner as he lifted its contents from the handkerchief by its chain. He held it out to Hank. "Thought you might like to have this."

Hank took the silver and gold pocket watch in his hand. There was no mistaking its etched golfer on the hinged lid of the watch. It was the artifact that once belonged to his brother. Hank remembered his conversation with Nadler, about how Brian used to twirl the watch by its chain. Hank was quiet for a long moment, then said: "You didn't have to bend any rules for this, did you, Sig?"

"No one claimed the personals. I'd say it's yours—bein' next of kin to its original owner on my say-so."

Hank raised his eyes to the sergeant. "Compliments of Sigurd Nadler?"

"Yeah—and the Rifleman, you might say. That watch helped him identify his mark, be my guess. He's a vigilante—don't expect he cares for cop killers a whole lot."

Hank nodded. "I thank you both, then." There was a pause as the two men studied each other. Then Hank said, "Haven't heard much from the Rifleman, lately. Anything new on that front?"

"Been quiet. 'Course, he coulda blown away some clown with a muzzleloader and it wouldn't of made the Variety section of the *Strib*, what with the play your Andrea Shiff was getting."

"Muzzleloader?"

"You never know," Nadler answered with a wry smile.

"Well, let's hope he doesn't show up with a blunderbust in Bloomington."

"The Mall'd be a perfect setting for him. But he'll stay clear. Knows there's a smart cop in Bloomington. Likes him, too, from that Letter to the Editor he sent to the *Pioneer Press* after that State Capitol hit." Another grin.

Hank acknowledged the compliment with a nod, and said: "Tell you what. Leave a warning note for him to that effect, will you?" Then it was Hank's turn for a wry smile. Also, he filed "muzzleloader" away in his mind, wondering if the Rifleman would be partial to a percussion-cap muzzleloader or a flintlock on some future sortie?

**HANK WAS SURE** he knew who the Rifleman was. The clues were there. And he guessed the Rifleman knew that he did. So what? Where was the proof? Still, he wondered if "the blue wall of silence" was holding him back from pursuing the matter more intently. No, it wasn't that, he concluded. And even though he liked the man, and owed him in each of his identities, Hank was still a cop. *You've got a pass for now, Rifleman. But be careful, pal. Be very careful.*

*Chapter* **68**

# A L L I A N C E

**THE TWO VISITORS** dropped in on the convalescing patient at his home. He held a long-term health care policy from the St. Paul Companies (the premiums were cheap at his age) so the callers were greeted at the door by a professional in-home caregiver.

The caregiver took a coat from one of the callers and a jacket from the other—signs that the Minnesota winter was soon to bite. That nicety accomplished, they were led to a bedroom where the convalescent was propped up in bed wearing pajamas and a rumpled bathrobe open at its front. He was reading *Hannibal*.

Josh Williams put his book aside and surveyed the two women standing at his bedside. One was coordinated head to foot—silk blouse, tailored skirt, hose, and heels. The other was displaying worn blue jeans, a sweatshirt with "Ruff Hewn" emblazoned on its front, and running shoes with an N on their sides. The refined Titanium Doll and the hard-ass art director, shoulder to shoulder.

"I still don't have my kitchen knife back," Darcy Austin smiled, "can you put in a word to the Minneapolis Police?"

"Can I do a storyboard for one of your upcoming sagas?" Erica Carlson followed with more earnestness.

He passed on both questions, though considering the second. "Look at you two," he said. "I thought you were big-time antagonists at Williams/Bailey—and here you are, practically holding hands."

"That was another life," retorted Darcy Austin.

"Before she discovered how adorable I am," added Erica Carlson.

"I can't get away from all this mutual admiration shit. I'm stuck here hearing it on TV every goddam day, in the aftermath of that fucking Soup Case. Give me a break."

"Hey, we love each other," Erica put in. "Haven't you heard about our furtive rendezvous in the Hopkins Do-Jo?"

"We've got a deep bond," Darcy said before thinking it through.

Josh Williams thought about that one for a moment, before saying: "I'm not *that* isolated from the world. People tell me things, you know."

"Can we change the subject?" Darcy asked, still chagrined over her previous remark.

"Sure," Josh Williams smiled. "Tell me," he continued, while trying to look serious, "anything exciting happen since I was stabbed nearly to death?"

Erica rolled her eyes. "Would you like to experience Darcy's front kick?" she asked back. "I'll bet she can bust your stitches right there in bed, smart ass."

"She'll have to pull that tight skirt up to do it," Josh Williams said with a sly grin. "Might be worth a few sutures."

"Can we talk about something else?" Darcy asked again. "I hear it might snow." No one paid her any attention.

Erica put to Josh Williams: "How's Magenta coming along, by the way?"

Darcy groaned.

"Great," Josh said to Erica. "The staff got the last episode out without me. I was afraid sales might drop off after Darcy, er, Magenta got her butt whipped last time out . . . uh sorry, Darc," he added, nodding her way. Then back to Erica: "But copies are flying off the shelves. Of course, your little stint up at Devil's Kettle helped," he addressed back to Darcy.

While giving Darcy a look out of the corners of her eyes, Erica said to Josh Williams, "You already had a mega-hit before the Devil's Kettle thing happened. Face it. Readers got off on seeing our heroine get her ass kicked like that—her bare ass at that."

Darcy flushed, then came in with, "We can talk about the way you set me up when you're well, Josh Williams. I don't like pummeling people when they're in a weakened state. No matter how much they deserve it."

"Uh-oh, she's getting riled. Stay down, Josh," Erica warned.

Darcy gave Erica a mock shove.

"Hey, Sterling got his lumps too, you know," Josh Williams offered in his defense. "Cobalt clobbered him."

"So what's that got to do with anything?" Darcy disputed.

"You don't know? Sterling is me," Josh Williams returned. "I'm hurt."

"Wanna let me in on this?" Erica asked, not steeped in Fantasy's character lore.

"You'll have to visit Josh's office, once he's on his feet," Darcy said. "I'm sure he'll be glad to give you a primer. Might even show you his sordid videos after hours."

**A THOUGHT CAME** to Josh Williams in the midst of the repartee: women who once despised each other coming together. He'd tuck that away—play with it, see where it led for a future story line. Later, though. For now, he'd just enjoy the banter.

*Chapter* **69**

# C R E A T I O N

**ALONE AFTER THE** departure of his guests, the creator turned to his work. Josh Williams knew that the popular bromide, fact follows fiction, is really the other way around—at least when it comes to storytelling. And he was a master of that application. He would twist and sensationalize things, but his modus operandi had always been fiction imitating life as he knew it to be.

He also loved picking up aspects in life, then embellishing them for a defined target audience. It occurred to him that perhaps he should try his hand at the advertising business. It was the same damn thing, when he thought about it. *Got the contacts, too,* he smiled to himself. Maybe in another year or so, he'd consider a move like that. After all, how many episodes of voluptuous women scampering about in skimpy outfits could a guy do, without becoming bored? *Hmmm.* He'd have to mull that one over. Maybe he could split his time between the two disciplines.

**HE TAPPED THE** keyboard of his G4 Mac PowerBook, ablaze in concept. The rest of *Hannibal* would be digested later.

Storyline sketch:

"Synergy."

Ingrid Carson, alias Lynx, calls on Sharon Noble, a.k.a. Magenta, at her home.

The two women know each other, having worked together on social events in one persona and crossed paths on the night streets in another guise. While essentially on the same side of the issues in both manifestations, their respective personalities are at odds with each other.

—I think I can help Magenta, Ingrid offers.

Sharon is indignant. —Magenta doesn't need help, she asserts. —And why do you want to? We've never been friendly.

Ingrid is direct. —Don't tell me Magenta is just fine after what Sadanna did to her. —Besides, I'm offering to assist because I can help myself at the same time. Not out of fondness. Okay?

Sharon is still miffed. —Magenta never lost a fight, until—

—Yeah, Ingrid inserts. —but you've had some close calls. And Sadanna took your pants—

Sharon cuts Ingrid off. —It was a hard fight. She lost some things, too. Can we move on?

—Magenta's a great fighter, but against a tough opponent who takes it to her, she gets in trouble, Ingrid explains. —I can teach you a few things.

—You'll teach *me* a few things?

Ingrid doesn't back down, issuing a challenge.

—Face me on the mat and I'll show you.


The women square off in Sharon Noble's state-of-the-art workout room, dressed in spandex shorts and sports-bras.

The encounter is brief. *Wham.* Sharon is on her back, Ingrid on top of her.

—I wasn't ready, Sharon excuses. —Let's go again.

The ensuing skirmish lasts longer, but Ingrid puts Sharon down again, and teases: —Wanna see me do your top?

—You wouldn't dare.

—Someone else might, if she gets Magenta down like this. Sadanna's set a precedent, you know. And not just your top . . .

—Okay, okay, Sharon breaks in. —You made your point.

Ingrid gets up and extends Sharon a hand, helping her to her feet. —I didn't think another woman could do that to me, Sharon says, —except maybe Sadanna.

—You've had some battles you could've just as well lost. Now, are you ready to hear me out?

—What's your proposition, Sharon asks?

—I coach you on defense—you help me on offense. We both benefit. What do you say?

Sharon doesn't have to think about it long, after what just happened. —All right. You're on, she answers.


Ingrid Carson soon becomes a frequent visitor to the Sharon Noble homestead. Not only do the women improve as fighters, but the former antagonists become close friends in the process. Very close friends.

As Magenta benefits from her workouts with Lynx, she prepares for another confrontation with her bad-girl nemesis. She wants retribution, needs vindication. —*Next time*, she vows, *you won't have it so easy with me, Sadanna. And there will be a next time Sadie—count on it.*

**JOSH WILLIAMS LEANED** back from his sitting position in bed, setting the PowerBook aside. Punching out preliminary scenarios like this was his way of setting up future issues. It let him get his arms around the story line and helped him to visualize the illustrations he would do when blending narrative with dialog. It also established a blueprint for his staff to work from.

In a few days he'd be back at his board. He knew he had a winner here. At this point in his career he had a sixth sense about such things. More important, it would lead to a later episode—another meeting between Magenta and Sadanna. That one promised to be the biggest ever.

He still had to determine just how that next battle would play out. Expectations would be high. It would come to him, he assured himself. It always did.

# Chapter 70

# C O N T I N U U M

**JOSH WILLIAMS GAVE** Darcy the key she had requested, and instructed her on how to disarm the night alarm system. She wouldn't say when or how she'd be accessing the site—just that he owed her the favor, and she wanted to use it one night. It was all pretty transparent to the discerning young Mr. Williams, though. And he didn't mind granting the request. Not one bit.

**THE WOMEN FACED** off in tight fitting athletic gear. Perhaps this attire would hold up better than the costumes they wore in their previous meeting. Perhaps.

"This time you won't have Andrea Shiff around to save your ass." Caren Dalton warned.

Darcy Austin wasn't intimidated. "Just watch yours, Hon."

"Oh, I will, Sweetie."

"Ready, then?

"It's all the way, Babe."

**WOULD FICTION FOLLOW** fact this time, or would it be the other way around? Josh Williams would have to determine that in the end. He had several considerations to weigh. But regardless of which way he'd eventually go, he'd make sure it was nothing short of sensational. He intended Magenta #42, *Return Engagement*, to be his most spectacular book yet.

Right now, however, he was more eager to see how the contest would unfold in actuality. For when the two antagonists entered his Pad Room, as he expected, they would activate the mounted camcorders prepositioned to record the event—telltale red lights masked so as not to give them away. An electronic signal would alert him at his home. Josh Williams, the clever rogue, had seen to it all.

He'd witness the event on a closed circuit, fifty-two-inch HDTV Hitachi monitor. He preferred to see it as it happened, should he be around when the signal sounded, but the affair would be preserved for him in its entirety in any event. Either way, 1,080 scan lines per inch would make it the next best thing to witnessing it in person. Plus, he'd have a video of the second battle between the two most gorgous women he knew of for his collection.

**EVERYTHING WORKED AS** cued. The event—viewed live, as he had hoped—was all he could have wished for and more—the voyeurism, as well as the climatic finish.

He'd be hard pressed to better what he just witnessed. Now it was a matter of scripting and illustrating it. Only, before composing *Magenta Comics*, he had to compose himself. He was a little untidy after the viewing.

HE WAS LOST in creative thought, the strains of Hector Berloiz's *Symphonie Fantastique, Opus 14,* flowing from his surround-sound system—Osmo Vänskä, conducting the Minnesota Orchestra. Josh Williams had become an aficionado of sorts. Beyond appreciation, he learned that classical music stimulated his mental clarity and imagination. So it seemed, anyway. Was there something to the "Mozart effect" that was said to raise one's intelligence for a time?

Just as the *Reveries-Passions* movement was concluding, a vision shattered his reverie, jolting him upright. What was it? A woman? A spirit? *Andrea's* spirit? The apparition was gone, but its image lingered disturbingly. His hand drew across his chest, fingers tracing his scar, through the fabric of his shirt. Real or imagined, he wasn't sure. The line between the two was thin where he lived.

Shaking off his start as best he could, he resettled himself in his chair. And staring into the late-day shadows of his surroundings, drifted back toward contemplation—his serenity gradually returning.

Which side of the thin line he now occupied was not certain—the final symphonic refrains, *Dream of the Witches' Sabbath,* the only measure of time, while his senses dwelled elsewhere. In that realm, his thoughts came back to Andrea, again.

He did not voice the words, conjuring them from his ephemeral state of mind: *Come out, come out, wherever you are.*